Ink Stains & Ill-Fated Lies

Also by Kellie Doherty

The Cicatrix Duology

Finding Hekate
Losing Hold

Broken Chronicles

Sunkissed Feathers and Severed Ties
Curling Vines and Crimson Trade

Ink Stains

&

Ill-Fated Lies

(The Broken Chronicles—Book 3)

Kellie Doherty

Desert Palm Press

Ink Stains & Ill-Fated Lies

(Broken Chronicles – Book 3

By Kellie Doherty

©2023Kellie Doherty

ISBN (trade) 9781954213517
ISBN (epub) 9781954213524

This is a work of fiction - names, characters, places, and incidents are the product of the author's imagination or are used fictitiously. Any resemblance to actual persons living or dead, businesses, events or locales is entirely coincidental. All rights reserved.

No part of this publication may be reproduced, distributed, or transmitted in any form or by any means, including photocopying, recording, or other electronic or mechanical methods, without the prior written permission of the publisher, except in the case of brief quotations embodied in critical reviews and certain other noncommercial uses permitted by copyright law.

For permission requests, write to the publisher at lee@desertpalmpress.com or "Attention: Permissions Coordinator," at

Desert Palm Press
1961 Main Street, Suite 220
Watsonville, California 95076
www.desertpalmpress.com

Editor: Raven's Eye
Cover Design: Rachel George Illustration

Printed in the United States of America
First Edition January 2023

Acknowledgements

This book was written during a pandemic which also happened to be one of the worst years of my life personally. There are so many creative and wonderful people who help publish a book, and I'm grateful for every single one of them. Without them, Adaris' story would've never even made it onto the page.

First, as always, I'd like to thank Lee and the entire Desert Palm Press team for believing in this story, in black sand beaches and glowing anklets, in ancient grimoires and searing sunlight. I'd like to give an immense thank you to the fabulous DPP editor—CK King—for looking at this story with fresh eyes and seeing the random plot holes I overlooked, and to the ever-amazing cover designer—Rachel George—who listened to my scattershot of ideas and created this stunning illustration. Thank you to everyone in DPP who touched this book and made the story better for it.

Second, I have to give the biggest thank you to my fabulous critique group—Tam, Louise, Brooke, and Molly. They were the first to read this story and upon ripping it apart, made it so much stronger. We've been meeting every week for many years, and I know I'm a much better writer because of their insightful comments. (Seriously, to all the fellow writers out there, get a critique group; it's awesome!)

Third, to my family and friends. 2022 has been a rollercoaster of the highest highs and the lowest lows, and through it all, my loved ones pushed me to keep being creative, to keep writing, to keep pursuing my dreams (this book included) and for that I am forever grateful. From mailing me tea when I was low to being a sounding board for my difficult characters to even coming up with the weapon Adaris uses, my family and friends have been amazing, and I will never stop thanking them for it.

Fourth, I have to give a shout-out to you—my readers! I wouldn't be able to do what I love—telling stories full of broken magic and disaster queer characters—if not for you. Your support means the world to me. Thanks so, so much.

Now, grab a cup of tea, maybe a few cookies, and enjoy the adventure!

Dedication

For all those who seek adventures out.

Chapter One

ADARIS KAVARI STOLE A glance at the sun peeking over the mountain top, heart lurching like a newborn thunderfawn at the sight. The valley wouldn't offer her protection for much longer. Grasslands spread around her. Only a few lush, green-topped trees dotted the area. She needed to find the hidden cave she was hunting for, but a group of Moon Knights walking the cracked cobblestone path that cut through this valley had distracted her. *Damn it all to the depths.* Anxiety clawed at her insides. The sun was rising steadily, and she refused to be caught in that blinding sunlight like some sunsick fool.

As a scribe, her quest was to find interesting stories. The right one would earn her a higher-ranking quill—the teal variety—and might help fix her reputation, too.

But she wouldn't be mauled by a suncreature for it. Or worse, eaten. The corrupted beasts would be waking up with the sun, and it wasn't safe to be in the open any longer. Not for a common scribe like her. Not for anyone, really.

Turning her cloak to the rising sun, Adaris faced the handsome knight she was questioning and dipped her white feather quill into the small pot of ink secured within her belt pouch.

The knight was still regaling her with his adventures. The story was...adequate thus far, but she couldn't deny the pull of a Moon Knight. They usually had the best stories, but this knight's tale of saving a traveling merchant caravan wasn't that compelling. Definitely not the story she was looking for. She snuck another glance at the tall mountain behind her, knowing the shadows she stood in wouldn't be dark for much longer. If this knight didn't say anything interesting soon, she'd have to leave. Find someplace to hide.

The knight shifted inside his armor, the metal clanking. "That's when we saw the suncreature."

Adaris snapped her attention back to him. Fear curled in her belly from the mention of the corrupted creatures who roamed this area. "What kind of creature was it? Perhaps a ground-breaker like a neades?"

"Not this time," the knight replied, regarding her with ink-black eyes. His dark lips lifted in a grin, apparently glad to have caught her attention once more. "The merchants were being attacked by a horde of bukavacs."

Bukavacs? Now that was interesting. The amphibian had a flat slimy body, six legs, and a wide mouth. With their long tails and equally long horns, bukavacs were not usually seen this far north. The pure-white suncreature with orange slime and crimson eyes was a corrupted version of the original creature. It lived by the coastal swamps, so it was odd that they pushed so far inland, away from their natural habitat. That sort of nugget of information was why Adaris always stopped for the Moon Knights, always listened to their stories, always went out of her way to hear about their adventures. They had the most thrilling tales.

"One moment please," she murmured, flipping through the pages in her book.

It could be connected. She stopped on the recent call for the scribes to gather stories about suncreatures and their sightings to refamiliarize herself with smaller details of the task. Ah yes, there was a Vagari, who could apparently corrupt natural beasts into suncreatures. The crafting was new and unheard of, but a woman named Misti Eildelmann had sworn it to be true, and the scrollkeepers believed her. Her testimony had caused a flurry of excitement. Misti's encounter had been a major keystone story, one that connected other stories to make a clearer tale. That one keystone story had sent all the wandering scribes out to uncover more...Adaris included. The stories seemed to be building on one another, building to something dangerous, possibly even war.

As she penned the knight's words, a lock of her long, crimson hair fell onto the page, smudging the ink. She tucked the hair behind her ear then lifted her gaze to the knight. "How many of them were there? Any females? Anyone slimed by one?" Perhaps the bukavacs were their next test subjects. If she could find a connection between this unusual sighting and that Vagari, it would earn her the teal quill for sure. Maybe even restore her violet quill that she lost a season ago. "Go into as much detail as you can."

The knight shifted. "Unfortunately, I didn't get a good look. My t'zil took care of them. I was on the other side of the caravan, ushering the merchants to safety."

Disappointment hit Adaris like a slap of saltwater, but she kept her features schooled, nodding as the knight told how he kept the merchants contained and protected. Being a wandering scribe, she had long ago learned that every story needed an engaged listener in order to respect the storyteller—no matter how dull the tale. Protecting people was admirable, of course, but Adaris needed more than a wailing caravan of merchants to be accepted into the next level of her career.

When the knight paused, Adaris jumped in. "It's quite commendable how you kept all those people safe, and I'll certainly record it in the history books. However, I would love to speak to someone about the bukavacs."

Adaris knew she didn't need to speak to just "someone," she needed to talk to the head guard of these knights. The person who actually fought the suncreatures, the t'zil. She also knew a white-quilled scribe wouldn't easily be granted an opportunity to speak to someone that far up the chain of Moon Knight command.

The knight cocked his head, waiting for her to finish.

She gave him her best smile. "I need to speak to your t'zil."

The knight eyed the thick, heavy book Adaris held, bound by dark hide with slips of colored paper sticking out at seemingly odd locations, each one the start of a new story. His gaze landed on the white feather quill in her hand, now dripping with black ink. "Are you a high enough color for that?"

A part of her deflated inside. So, he knew what the scribe quills signified. She flourished her quill—the lowest color a scribe could have, a beginner's quill—and stepped forward. "Of course. White quills are held in the highest regard, you know." The lie dripped off her tongue like honey, as though she had told it many times before—because she had.

But the knight tilted his head, narrowed his eyes. A ray of sunlight glinted off his helmet, and Adaris looked up. Something flew across the mottled purple-blue horizon, big even from this distance. A suncreature, probably, or a suncreature's first meal. *Don't lose your nerve.* She shrank from the piercing yellow orb into the shadows of her hood.

"The more stories you've woven together, the closer to the truth you've become." Realizing she was a little too close, Adaris stepped back a pace, giving the knight more breathing room. The stark lines she noticed around his eyes relaxed. Even in plate armor, the knight feared what she could do as a Divus, a Blood crafter. She kept her gaze steady, unwavering, and just like that, the knight nodded, caught in her lie.

"This way, then," he said.

The thrill of victory lifted Adaris' steps as she followed the knight down the cracked cobblestone path toward the rest of his group. The grasslands shimmered around them, dew lingering on the blades of red and pink common this side of the mountains. It had been a stroke of luck that she'd spotted this group of five. They'd been near the bottom of the valley when she'd been traveling mostly at the top. She had to run to even reach them, and her bad leg ached from the effort. Even as they strolled along the path to catch up with the others, her leg hummed with pain. Her gait rolled with the injury she'd carried with her from childhood.

"Hail," a lady knight called from further along the cobblestone path, her rough voice pulling Adaris' attention as the knight she'd been questioning caught up to the other four.

Adaris raised her hand, but the sun had crested the mountain, light spearing into the valley between the treetops high above them. She stopped. Her skin pricked. Thankfully, a few trees dotted this pathway. She tucked herself beside a large darkwood, the branches curling high above her, leaves bright green. The shadow it cast would be enough, for now.

The group of knights chatted for a few moments, then the lady knight ambled over. Stopping a few paces away, the knight wore full plate armor, though her helmet was currently tucked under her elbow. A half crescent moon was etched into the silvery chest plate marking her as t'zil, the ranking official of this group...though there existed another rank above hers still. Locks of light brown hair curled around one shoulder, and pale spots dotted her dark-brown nose and cheeks, flowing down her neck and disappearing beneath her clothes. The male knight's racial traits had been hidden by his armor, but Adaris recognized this knight as a Myceli Nemora, caretaker of fungus, mushrooms, and the like.

Are all the knights in this group so attractive? Adaris shook that thought away. The knight's storm-gray eyes were so much like Adaris' own it made her stare a moment too long before replying.

"Anoc'suna," she said, a standard word for greeting in the Nemora language, and the knight grinned. "I heard you stopped a horde of bukavac suncreatures? Could you spare a moment to tell me about that? I'd like to record it." She lifted her book and quill.

The knight's gaze swept over Adaris' black cloak and dark, scaled armor, thick pants tucked into even thicker boots. Her attention lingered on the numerous pouches around Adaris' waist and the curved tek, her only weapon, hanging at her back. Being a wandering scribe, she was used to it. She shifted her weight off her aching leg and waited, trying hard not to look at the ground, at the shadows that were rapidly getting too light for her comfort. Did this lady knight know of colored quills and what they signified?

Finally, the knight chuckled. "The fight was nothing much, I'm afraid. Or...nothing interesting enough for the books."

"I beg to differ," Adaris replied, giving her an easy wink. "A suncreature so far away from its natural territory is interesting in and of itself. Did anyone get injured? A firsthand account of the attack would be a story worth only the best history books. As are all suncreature sightings and killings."

It might even be a story worth a teal quill. Even if she'd had to lie to get it.

The knight pursed her lips, then launched into her tale. Adaris recorded the details. The bukavac suncreature horde came and tried to grapple some merchants into the river. A sword flick there, a crafted, shimmering cobalt shield here—it was almost too easy for the Moon Knights to take the horde down.

The bukavacs came from the ocean swamps and not the freshwater rivers, which meant this group of knights did, indeed, stumble upon something curious. Yet Adaris knew it wasn't the story that would connect to many others. The creatures had come from the small river, which could have easily led back to their home habitat. This story wouldn't help get her reputation back.

Still, Adaris listened. Raptly. Only her hand moved, the scratching noise fading to background as it always did when a knight told their tale. Their adventures always swept her away, and she went willingly each time.

Finally, the knight ended her story. She took a swig from her flask and grinned. "And that's that. Did you hear enough for the books?"

"I did. Thank you for such a detailed encounter." Adaris stepped back, favoring her left leg.

"You wrote down quite a lot. Qual over there said you listened intently to his story, too." The knight motioned to the first one Adaris had spoken to. He lifted his gauntleted hand in a wave.

Qual. Adaris noted his name—which she'd forgotten to get in the first place—and eyed the page. The thick parchment was covered in her messy script, stories ready to be taken to the Athenaeum of the Ancients to be cataloged and woven with the others. She lifted her gaze to the lady knight. "Can I have your name, for the history books?"

"Bleu Lista." The knight grinned, gesturing over to Qual. "And his last name is Pinde."

Adaris nodded and wrote that down, too, slightly surprised that the Nemora woman had a last name, as it wasn't part of their custom. Lista must be the Myceli offshoot the knight was from, so named for the fungi she could grow most easily.

Knight Lista's eyes crinkled at the sides. "Are you always this interested in a knight's story?"

"Yes," Adaris replied. "I actually wanted to become a knight when I was younger."

"Then why didn't you?" Knight Lista asked.

Adaris dipped her head for a moment. "My heart wanted adventure...but my leg said otherwise." Adaris tapped her thigh.

"Ah." Knight Lista nodded.

Silence stretched between them, as the valley slowly filled with sunlight. The dew burnt away. White creatures lifted above the valley, too far away for Adaris to see properly, but the flicker of crimson hinted of suncreature fire beneath their scales or feathers or fur. Adaris' heart clenched at that and at the sight of golden light slowly curling around her tree, stealing part of her shadows and pooling on the crimson and pink grassland.

"I should leave you to your adventures. Thank you for all you do in keeping us safe." Adaris tucked her book into her belt, slipping the feather quill next to it. She waved at the knights, then headed up the valley away from them. Away from the rising sun, too. She kept to the shadows of the trees the best she could, but she hoped they wouldn't notice.

"Scribe!" Knight Lista called from behind Adaris, who looked over her shoulder. The knight's body was nearly silhouetted in the oncoming light. "You should accept yourself as you are. Even someone with a lame leg could still have an adventure worth telling."

Adaris' stomach flipped. She had accepted her fate a long time ago, being a scribe instead of a warrior. A recorder of tales instead of a maker of one. Her leg wouldn't allow her to become any different, and she'd long ago made peace with her past.

She shook her head and smiled, then turned back to the ridge. The once blue-black sky had lightened completely to pinks and oranges, and the walk back up would take a while. Too long, actually. Her chest tightened, panic worming its way into her again. She'd have to rest—to hide—somewhere close by, or risk being eaten by the corrupted creatures walking with the day. Not to mention the sun goddess worshippers who so favored doing their destruction by daylight. She'd have to find the cave tomorrow night, when it was safer.

She picked up her pace, heading for a small thicket of trees nearby. A safe enough place to stop and sleep away the day. She ducked beneath the thick canopy of brown and green needles. Only once the sky was completely obscured did she allow herself to breathe easier. Stopping the knights hadn't been a waste of paper or ink like some of her other stories, but it certainly hadn't been the big break she'd been hoping for.

"How am I ever going to get a differently colored feather?" she muttered, pushing aside some low hanging branches. Her hand came away sticky with spicy-smelling sap.

Not by lying, a voice told her. *But it wouldn't be the first time.*

The lie she told to talk to Knight Lista felt like a burning seed in her belly. She wanted to fix her reputation as a scribe—one she only had herself to blame for tarnishing. She pressed a hand through her long crimson hair, then twisted one lock with her finger in thought. A lie had banished her back to the white quill, and yet she still twisted words to be more in her favor. She had to get a better story, had to repair her reputation. And more than that, she had to get the coin that came with the promotion as well. Her brother needed it.

It was why she lied to the knight about the quill colors. Technically, only higher-ranking quills—violet and the coveted black—were able to speak to the higher-ranking officials, but how was someone supposed to gather the best stories if they were barred from questioning certain people? It had never made any sense to her. *How am I supposed to find a better story?*

Needing to rest, she lowered her pack, then sat cross-legged on the needle-strewn ground next to it. The air smelled thick of sap and grew warmer with each passing moment.

Under the safety of the trees and shadows, Adaris could ignore the sun rising even higher than before.

Perhaps she didn't need to speak to anyone to get a better story. The thought made her still. She had traveled to this valley in search of a hideout, after all. A sun goddess worshipper named Zephri had compiled a list of their hideouts in the mountain range he lived in. The Athenaeum of the Ancients had recently procured his books, and she had grabbed one the last time she'd been at that library. Stolen one, more like, but she had every intention to give it back when she was done. *What was his nickname for the hideout cave?*

She pulled out the thin black book—Zephri's book—and pored through its pages. There. A starlight cavern, that was his name for it. Packing the book away, she rose and went to the edge of the thicket, scanning the valley once more. Though she had missed the cave when heading down to catch the knights, she spotted it from her new vantage point, an opening where the black stones had white speckles. *The starlight cavern.*

Adaris stared at it a moment longer, looking for signs of movement. She saw none. Her palms slickened at what she was considering. Heading into a sun goddess worshipper's hideout would be risky. Worshippers of the fiery sun goddess weren't known for their hospitality and kindness. Quite the opposite. They wouldn't like a scribe poking around their hideout. *I could be killed for it.*

But it might give exactly the kind of story Adaris needed—surely a hideout would have all kinds of information. Perhaps even research into the creation of the suncreatures. Whatever the intel, she knew she had to go inside the cavern. The story pulled her.

She couldn't risk heading into the sunshine, though. *Not now, with so many suncreatures circling overhead.* As soon as the sun dipped below the horizon, Adaris would breach that hideout and glean whatever she could from inside.

Chapter Two

AFTER SLEEPING THE DAYLIGHT away in the thicket, Adaris picked her way to the cavern. Blackness pressed in on her, and she welcomed it after the sunlight, but she couldn't see in the dark. The Vagari half of her bloodline didn't grant her that, even though it showed through in the curious twist at the tip of her ears. She dug into her pack. Pushing past wrapped bread and dried meats, she grabbed a daygem and whispered the activation word. The daygem brightened in response. Everyone knew the words but not many knew the source of them. Adaris knew. The activation word came from before the Great Rift. A long-forgotten tongue of the ancient elven race now used only sparingly.

She lifted her daygem higher, the pure-white light sphering around her and brightening the grass and dirt and stones. The closer she got to the cavern, the more rocks littered the ground. Stones jutted this way and that. Her boot caught on the edge of one, caught wrong. She slipped. Grabbing the cavern wall a moment too late, she fell. Pain blossomed on the inside of her arm, and she landed in an awkward kneeling position on the cave floor. Her daygem bounced away, further into the tunnel. *Depths!* Long, thin gashes oozed white blood on her forearm. Her kind bled easy, skin tearing at the slightest puncture.

Sighing, she pressed a hand to her chest and sank into her crafting. Warmth filled her like a shimmering ember. With her crafting, she knit the scratches on her forearm back together. A headache quickly started in her temple from that slight burst of crafting, but at least she'd healed herself. Others might have said it was a waste, using her crafting for such a small thing, but Divus could only heal small things on their own bodies, so Adaris did it often.

Which, to be honest, wasn't often at all.

After picking herself up, Adaris went to into the tunnel itself to retrieve her daygem. The book mentioned that the cavern tunnel would lead to the actual hideout, so Adaris followed it, letting the daygem brighten her way. As she walked deeper, her thoughts turned to her fellow scribes. One of her scribe friends had done a deep dive into researching the ancient languages, and he never failed to bring it up. As the daygem washed the tunnel in a white light, she could almost hear his quiet voice whispering about linguistic history. A Divus as well, she missed his easy company and the way his warm hands danced over her skin. Elias could make her forget everything she'd ever known, and quite easily, too, but as much as she longed for his touch, she couldn't stay with him. In order to get the best stories, scribes usually wandered alone.

"If only you could see where I am now, Elias," she whispered.

Adaris took in her surroundings and the tunnel stretching into darkness. It suddenly occurred to her that if someone were to enter the cave, there would be no place to hide. Skin prickling, she listened for any sound of movement.

After a few moments of silence, she put a spare cloth over the daygem, so it wouldn't give off as much light, and crept deeper into the tunnel. She walked for a long time and wondered if, perhaps, she'd been led astray, but then she reached a small, square room filled with crates, water barrels, and unlit candles. Her daygem's glow revealed a circular sun pattern carved into the stone floor. *Depths!* Ponuriah's symbol often adorned the clothing or skin of her worshippers, but Adaris had never seen it displayed with such boldness, etched into a floor where it couldn't be as easily hidden. This was definitely a hideout.

She swept the room, looking for anything interesting. Books, notes, artifacts, anything she could use for her story. Her daygem glinted off a small plate of crumbs and a water flask near a crate in the corner of the room. A thin book with a white cover and blank spine lay open, facedown, on the cave floor next to the crate. Adaris bristled—leaving the book that way would ruin the spine; the sunsick fools obviously didn't know how to take care of their property. Then she realized what that open book probably meant.

Someone has been here. Recently.

She glanced around, looking into the dim corners where someone could hide. Her nerves stretched thin. She'd read numerous books—hundreds of pages—about the sun goddess worshippers. In each recount, every meeting had been terrifying, and many ended in bloodshed. *They'll burn me alive if I'm caught here.*

Coming inside may have been a very bad idea.

But if she found any books and notes, artifacts belonging to them, explored more of this hideout even, she might be able to record a story that would repair some of her name. *I could lead the master scrollkeeper here and they'd know it wasn't a lie.* It couldn't be. Not this time. Not like the story she "recorded" about Mica Kia, chief stargazer of Celestial Abbey.

Desperate for the black quill and the coin it awarded her, Adaris had foolishly spun a tale about how Mica poisoned others to claw her way to the chief stargazer position. The story was too big to not be double-checked, and the master scrollkeeper caught her dead in it. Parts of it had been true—the name, the position, the fact that Mica went from being a dwarf star to a chief stargazer—but the biggest part—the how—had been made up. One juicy piece that Adaris had lied about to make the story bigger than it actually was. She had a violet quill back then, second only to the coveted black. That one lie had sent her all the way back to white.

This hideout could be her key to getting the teal feather quill—the next level up in her career—and she was determined to see it through. She took some notes about the contents of the room on a new page in her book. The scratching of her quill seemed to fill the whole rock room, bounding down the tunnel behind her, but she had to record everything. Then, she forged through the archway ahead of her into a connecting room.

A wooden desk covered with loose papers almost blocked her way inside. A tower of worn books rested on the chair behind it. Her gaze widened as she stepped inside and her daygem's light eased into the rest of the narrow room. Wooden bookshelves packed with tomes hugged each wall. Journals lay toppled on the stone floor. Bottles of ink and quills sat on each shelf. Paper stuck out at odd intervals in almost every tome as if someone had been writing in them or noted places to look for later. An odd scent permeated the space, something old and damp and burned.

She gasped. *A library.* As she scanned the spines, she noted that each was inscribed with handwritten lettering. *No official markings.* It seemed none of them had been bound by leatherworkers, bought by the presses, or distributed by the scribes. Her pulse skipped as fast as her thoughts. Drown it to the depths, she hadn't just found a hideout, she'd found their library!

Putting her pack and weapon down so she could move down the narrow aisle without snagging anything, Adaris pulled the books from the bookshelves one after the other, flipping open the covers and scanning the pages. She was a fast reader, but there were hundreds, if not thousands, of volumes. She could spend many nights in this haphazard library and not get to them all.

One entire journal talked about the brimming attack on Marion and the Athenaeum of the Ancients, then noted the city's defenses and how to circumvent them. Another spoke about how the sun goddess worshippers were seeking more goddess shards for their goddess's avatar before launching their true efforts into capturing the Groves.

More shards? Goddess shards were all but a myth, a legend the stories claimed existed but had yet to be discovered. Yet this spoke of finding more. Supposedly, the goddess sisters had split themselves asunder after a battle for dominance—most of Ponuriah's fiery shards creating the suncreatures, and the moon goddess Aluriah's icy shards doing who knows what. It was an ancient tale, ancient crafting. Adaris, who didn't even believe in the gods and goddesses of the world, didn't believe a word of it. A note scribbled in the margins mentioned how there should be a shard near this hideout, but they hadn't located it yet. Adaris gasped. Could the shards actually be real? Not as a part of a goddess, because that was ridiculous, but perhaps as a shard of power from the ancient times.

All of these journals and notebooks had something incriminating inside them. What other things might she find in this cave? She took a step toward a second archway leading to another room when a tingle in her spine stopped her. She'd been inside for a while, perhaps she should go back. Leave before the occupant returned. She gathered as many books as she could into her bag, stuffed some loose papers into her many pouches, and snuck back through the storage room, then down the tunnel toward the cavern entrance.

Early morning sunlight leaked into the cavern, forcing Adaris to blink a few times until her eyes adjusted. Keeping herself tucked into the shadows, she looked out into the valley. Crimson grasses rolled away from the foothills, blazing with the coming dawn. Her gaze snagged on a tall woman heading to the thicket of trees she'd hidden in earlier. Adaris watched the woman meander, unhindered by the soft light dappling over her oddly mottled, purple-green arms and glinting through her bright purple hair.

The woman stilled, and then turned toward the cavern. Adaris was sure of the shadows surrounding her, even when the Nemora woman seemingly locked her gaze onto Adaris'. *Surely she can't see me.* The Nemora's loose, tan tunic and pants flowed in the gentle breeze. Her violet eyes glinted. She waved.

Adaris didn't move.

The Nemora glanced sharply to her right, further down the valley, then back to Adaris. She pointed to the valley, then to Adaris and darted into the thicket. Hiding from something?

Adaris crouched deeper into the shadows. The woman was signaling something, but what?

A man in traveling clothes darted into view, heading up the valley, terror clearly painted on his face. The man gasped, sank to his knees, and toppled over, an ax embedded in the back of his head. Adaris froze at the sight.

A troupe of six people crested the hill behind him. Adaris tightened her hold on her pack straps, blood pulsing through her ears. She couldn't be discovered. Not with a stack of stolen books in her bag. She couldn't go outside either, not during the day and the attackers so close. The figures came closer—four men and two women decked out in traveling gear, long curved swords lashed to their sides, walking confidently in the sunshine like she would during the night. One of them pulled the ax out of the man's head with a sickly grin. Adaris caught a glimpse of the circular designs tattooed into their foreheads, sun markings meant to scare non-believers. *Sun goddess worshippers.* Without pausing to think of the consequences, she turned and ran.

Back through the tunnels, she limped as quickly as she could, past the storage area and into the library. The narrow room became oppressive, the overflowing stacks of books leaving no place to hide. Footfalls and laughter drifted down the tunnel she had just fled from. *Now what?* Adaris went into the next room and found a sleeping area, a few cots on the ground, more dishes, and unlit candles. A crate sat in the corner with a few dice on it and some coin. A body rotted nearby, emitting a familiar damp, old scent. Another body lay under it, burned so badly it was little more than a skeleton. Her muscles tightened, and she had to swallow a scream. No other archways, no other tunnels, nothing.

She was trapped.

They would find her and kill her like the poor souls in the corner.

Like the traveler outside.

The worshippers had reached the storage area, their loud and bantering voices echoing down the corridor. Her heart pounded like the frantic, caged bird she was. She had to leave. *I have to find a way out.*

The glow of her daygem cast a shadow, a narrow, awkwardly shaped fissure in the wall behind the crate. Did it go somewhere or was it just an alcove? It didn't matter, she was out of time. She had to hide.

Hearing the worshippers rustling some paper and books behind her in the adjacent room, she deactivated her daygem and slipped her tall, lithe frame into the fissure, dragging her bulging pack behind her. Rocks scraped her scaled armor, surely too loud as she pushed herself into the narrow space. Dust made her eyes water and filled her nose.

The crack was more than an alcove. Deeper and deeper she pushed, squeezing herself blindly inside until she was suddenly free. She stumbled and nearly fell out on the other side.

The voices were closer, and candlelight flickered through the gap from their sleeping area. A woman's voice, shrieking with glee, soon followed. Adaris flinched, inhaling shallowly and slowly so they wouldn't hear. Not wanting to be seen or heard, she shouldered her pack and felt her way deeper into her newfound area.

Following a rough tunnel with her fingertips, she kept her back to the hideout and hoped this cave system would eventually open up to the outside. Not that she wanted to be outside in the sunlight, but she certainly didn't want to be anywhere near the sunsick people behind her. Her bag thumped heavily on her back as she crept along. After a while, she no longer heard voices. No footsteps followed either. It seemed she'd had a stroke of good luck. She couldn't wait to pore through the books and record everything properly. It would be an amazing story to tell, perhaps even big enough to skip the teal quill and gain a violet. She activated her daygem once she was far enough away from the hideout and kept limping along.

But her hopes were dimming. The further she went, the staler the air grew. Colder, too. The tunnel seemed never-ending. Slowly her fears crept after her. How long had she been walking? What if this tunnel never opened up to the outside? What if she circled back to the hideout? What if she got lost? Her leg started to thrum with pain, the old wound coming back to haunt her.

Adaris had to rest. She pulled her bag onto her lap and leaned back against the cave wall. The stone drew heat from her. She shivered. After taking a swig of water, Adaris sighed.

"So this wasn't my best idea," she admitted out loud, voice hollow against the barren stone walls.

There were some smaller branches off this main tunnel, but she didn't want to get too lost and had kept to the largest one. Her only course of action would be to go back the way she came. Hopefully, the worshippers were gone or would be soon. It not, she'd have to sneak past them. Her gut clenched at the idea. A small beetle-like bug crawled on the tunnel wall across the way, catching her attention. Unless...

Adaris scooted closer to the bug. She did something she never would have done around other people. "Hello, little friend," she whispered.

The bug stopped crawling. It waved one of its four antennae in her direction as if feeling for her, sensing for her, then it scurried onto a nearby rock and looked at her. About as big as her pointer finger, the bug had beady eyes that shimmered in the daygem's glow, as did its segmented black shell. It waved its antenna again, very clearly saying hello.

Adaris chuckled.

Sometimes talking to animals didn't work, but her mother had instilled in her the majesty of the beasts and had reminded her again and again of her Vagari bloodline. So, every now and then, Adaris would speak to the creatures of this world. And every now and then, they'd listen. Unlike her mother or other full-blooded Vagari, she couldn't actually hold conversations with the beasts, and she couldn't draw strength from them, heal them, tame them, or command them.

Only sometimes she could talk to them and sometimes they'd understand.

Their father was a Divus and their mother was a Vagari but each child only got one true crafting ability. Adaris got their father's Blood crafting, and Rasa got their mother's Animal crafting. The amount of power ebbed and flowed in each person as well. *It flowed through my brother and ebbed in me.* She was grateful she could do this small thing, even if it was a fluke. As far as she knew, her brother couldn't do any Blood crafting at all.

The bug cleaned its antenna, so Adaris asked, "Can you show me something? I would like to—"

She hadn't even finished when the insect darted off. Adaris quickly rose and followed. The black bug scurried along the rocky floor and disappeared into another fissure in the wall, this one tucked between two boulders. Adaris wouldn't have even noticed it without the insect. Dim crimson light filtered through this gap, like the room beyond was on fire. When she held her hand to it, no heat met her palm. Maybe the bug had been listening to her after all. This fissure was tighter than the first, though. She was uncertain she'd be able to fit through, and her bag would be another story. Pressing her face to the crack, she noticed something shimmering on the other side. Something crimson. Something curious.

She had to find out what. She tried to insert her pack in front of her, shifting the books and pouches and stuff around in it, but the pack was too bulky. If she shoved any harder, the ink bottles would surely break.

So Adaris left her pack and belt of pouches behind. She took only her book, daygem, and quill. Pressing herself through the crack—breathing out to squeeze through a particularly tight space—she all but fell out the other side again. She slid down a short incline to the bottom of the most unique room she'd ever been in. Spherical and almost entirely made of red glass, the room seemed to glow with a crimson light even without the added illumination of her daygem. Warmth washed over her, a welcomed heat after the chill of the cave she'd just left. She found the source of this heat and light by her boots, a single shard of red crystal. A crystal no bigger than her thumb. The air around it shimmered, like the air around a flame.

Adaris' eyes widened. "It can't be."

She recognized the crystal from stories. A goddess shard, or splinter of the ages. A crystalized legend. They were *supposed* to be a tale drunkenly shouted in taverns and whispered in secret in temples and sought after by the unlucky few spurred on by their deities to achieve greatness. Adaris hadn't believed the tales. She couldn't.

Until now.

Surely this is a thing of legends.

Using the hem of her cloak, Adaris grabbed the shard. She gasped at the intense heat penetrating the layers of fabric and pulled back. Unclasping her cloak entirely, she folded the dark cloth and picked up the shard, wrapping the edges around the shard again and again and again. The bundle of cloth still radiated heat, but at least Adaris could touch it without getting burned. Curiously, it didn't set the fabric aflame. Something else to note in the history books. Mind swimming with possibilities, Adaris crawled back up the sloped edge of the room to the crack. She whispered, "Thank you," to the bug wherever it might have gone, and pushed herself through, dragging the bundle of cloth behind her.

As she bent to gather the rest of her things and turn on the daygem once more, something hard smashed against her back.

Pain burst in her spine, radiating up to her neck. Her vision went white. She collapsed to her knees just as a blow to her head knocked her sideways. Her shoulder collided with the rocky floor. The world blurred. Swam. Four men in traveling gear towered over her. Then with a flicker of pain, she fell into darkness.

Chapter Three

ADARIS CAME TO, BLINKING against the harsh flame of a candle. Her back and side hummed with pain. She lay on a chilly, cracked stone floor, surrounded by stone walls with crates on either side of her. Rough rope bound her hands, and a pebble jabbed into her wrist. In her peripheral vision, she could see a book opened, facedown, with a plate of crumbs next to it.

She was back in the storage room. Candles lined the walls, flickering as the four men moved through the space. The same men she had seen earlier—two short, stocky fellows; one lanky man, whose head nearly brushed the ceiling; and one of medium build, though the huge muscles in his bare forearms gleamed. All were decked out in traveling gear, and all were Elu, even the tall one. Each one had the telltale scars from using their crafting.

Her useless clenched fists shook as they tipped her bag over, the books and papers she had stolen thumping to the floor. The sun goddess worshippers had caught her. Her whole body trembled. *They'll probably burn me alive.*

The lanky man kept rifling through her bag, unlatching the inner compartments, then tossed an apparently uninteresting item over his shoulder. A jar of sweet jam rolled across the stone floor, coming to rest on the edge of the circular design etched into the ground.

"She stole our books!" a stocky one said.

"Obviously." Another picked up the jar, twisted open the top, and stuck one thick finger inside. "See what else she took. Empty all her pouches."

They seemed to be intent on going through her things, so Adaris slowly shifted to a sitting position, awkward with her hands bound. The crates half hid her from their view, but fear lashed itself around her torso and squeezed. She winced each time one of her ink bottles smashed on the ground—those weren't cheap—and eyed the spare quills that fluttered to the floor. Thankfully, her own book and quill were safely tucked into the waistband of her pants.

The muscular one ripped open a small bag of fish jerky and stuffed all the contents into his mouth, as the taller one picked up her tek with care, eyeing the spiral blades that circled the bracer, before putting the weapon next to a crate on the other side of the room.

"That's everything. Go put the books back," the one slurping jam off his fingers ordered.

Headache still making her wince, Adaris' gaze skipped from the three men divvying up the books to carry into the library to the fourth, now licking the jam jar, to the archway leading outside. *I have to get out.*

Her Blood crafting answered her anxiety, warming her from the inside like an ember. Only one man remained in this room with her, and he seemed intent on licking the jar clean. She could use her crafting on him...if she could get her hands free. While she couldn't kill a person instantaneously like other Blood crafters, she could at least weaken him enough to get away.

She flexed her legs. At least the impromptu "rest" had given her bum leg a chance to relax. She might be able to run on it some. The head of a nail stuck out on one of the crates next to her, so she scooted closer. A string of curses came from the library, and the jammy-fingered man groaned. When he disappeared behind the archway, Adaris took a chance and sawed at the rope. Within moments, she had snapped the fraying cord off her shaking wrists.

"Thinking about going somewhere?" A voice whispered above her.

Adaris' gut lurched, and she glanced up to find two women dangling from the top corner of the room, their eyes glowing orange. Only one of each of their hands touched the stone, and from that they held their entire weight. Impossible. Arachnid-like insects with violet, bioluminescent legs skittered across their cheeks and foreheads, crawled over their hands and wrists, and wound down the fabric of their shirts. *Not impossible. Vagari.* Her earlier attempt to talk to the beetle-like bug floated through her mind, pitiful in comparison to what these women could command.

A panicked chuckle bucked in her chest. "I have to try."

She pushed herself to her feet and rushed across the empty room, angling toward the archway, her rolling gait covering the distance in a few strides. A giant asibik blocked the hallway, its bulbous body covered in thick, hairy spines. Adaris ground to a halt, heart hammering with fresh terror. Ten glowing, violet legs curled under its round form, and thousands of violet eyes glinted in the candlelight.

A parent to the mini ones scurrying about over the women.

"Depths!" Adaris swiveled, a sharp pang thrumming up her bad leg with the sudden shift in direction. A second giant asibik filled the other archway, too, the one leading to the library. Clearly, they had planned for her to try to escape.

She headed to where her tek rested against the crates. Her rolling gait had become an aching limp, but she kept moving. Fingers shaking, she slipped her arm into the weapon's gauntlet and swung around. The spiral edges hugged her forearm, so she could use it as both an offensive and defensive weapon, but she couldn't actually fight. Not with her leg the way it was. She had to favor it, so her balance was always off. The tek was more for show. She also couldn't stop them both with her crafting alone. Still, she had to try. Pulling her other hand back, her Blood crafting washed over her, through her, from the top of her head to the very tips of her toes. The familiar ember-like warmth calmed her trembling...but only a little.

Both Vagari came to a rest in front of Adaris. One of the women clapped. The sound echoed off the stone. It was only then that she noticed the second woman only had one arm, the other cleaved clean off her shoulder. Other than that, they looked so similar they could be siblings, twins even.

"Impressive," the first one whispered with a curling lilt. Her teeth flashed in the light, twin fangs peeking past her lips. Close-cut, matted black hair stuck to her head, and her eyes had dimmed to almost entirely black. Her traveling cloak swayed around her, but it took a few moments for Adaris to realize the woman wasn't actually moving; even more asibik babies wandered her body and caused the cloth to shift. Adaris shivered.

"Indeed." Her one-armed twin nodded, fingering a terribly familiar looking ax on her belt and grinning. "Are you going to try to fight us, little thief?"

Adaris' stomach seemed to drop like a stone. If she could at least slow one of them down with her tek, perhaps she could immobilize the other with her crafting. It wasn't a good plan...but it was something. She lifted the weapon. The metal flashed in the candlelight.

"Very well." The twins echoed one another. The one-armed twin pulled from her belt a long-handled ax, the other pulled a short spear.

Even Adaris' Blood crafting couldn't stop her from trembling. The ember warmth burned in her chest, longing to be free. Before she could even think about who to attack first, the one-armed woman lunged with the ax.

With a shout, Adaris stepped back, the ax just missing her face. *Depths!* The woman swung again, aiming for Adaris' chest, but Adaris lifted the tek and the ax clanged. One spiraled edge shattered under the blow but deflected the ax. The woman lost her balance, and came within reach.

Adaris grabbed her attacker's wrist. Fingertips met flesh, and she sank into her crafting, trying to pull life from this twin. The woman's eyes grew wide, horror flashing clear in them. Adaris' vision glazed white, like a fog clouded the area. Energy seeped into her, but she barely felt the twin's life energy—hotter than hers, like boiling water sleuthing through the veins in her hand—before the one-armed twin yanked her wrist free and moved back, away from her touch. A headache started in the back of Adaris' skull. Cursing her limited powers, she let her crafting go. The white haze vanished, and true colors seeped back into the world.

The short-haired twin had slipped behind Adaris and jabbed with her spear. The point collided against Adaris' thick, scaled armor but the scales held and the point didn't meet flesh. Even so, the impact caused Adaris to stumble. When she swiveled to face her attacker, white-hot agony spiked from her hip to her ankle. Her leg buckled beneath her, and she went down, hard.

The large asibik to her left spit out a gooey white web that covered her leg—from her knee all the way to her boot—and stuck her leg to the stone floor. The second asibik followed suit and spit out a web that stuck Adaris' broken tek to the ground. As much as she struggled, she couldn't free herself. Couldn't free her weapon.

The twins towered over her. The one with the spear chuckled and twirled her spear in a lazy circle. The one with the ax shrugged and called over her shoulder, "Do we need to keep this thief alive?"

Male voices floated toward them from the library room. "No."

No? Adaris made a strangled noise. If only she had been faster. A stronger crafter could've killed that one-armed twin with that simple touch to her wrist. Adaris couldn't even pull enough life energy from the woman to slow her down. *And if only my damned leg hadn't buckled.* The throbbing pain seemed to spread through her very bones.

The twins laughed. Each of them grabbed a candle, holding them over Adaris. "Did you know asibik webbing is highly flammable?" the short-haired one asked, a crooked grin twisting her lips.

Adaris couldn't breathe. All thoughts scattered from her mind, and the walls seemed to close in on her. All she could see were the bright candle flames flickering above her and the glinting eyes of the twin Vagari sisters. Her Blood crafting welled inside her, spreading through her, and she let it engulf her once more.

She lifted her free hand toward them. Bright white crafting followed the veins in the back of her hand as it traveled to the tips of her fingers. A white haze slid over her vision. “Wait!”

Amazingly, the women cocked their heads in an eerily similar fashion and paused.

“My…my family is powerful in Marion. They have wealth. They can give you anything, if you just let me live.” The lie poured from her. She came from a fishing family, and a rather poor one at that.

The women glanced at each other, then stared at her. Adaris held her crafting, heart thudding painfully, but as always, her crafting took its toll. Red lines of pain wormed into the fog over her vision and blackness started at the edges of her mind. She had to stop. Dropping her crafting, she braced herself for their reaction.

The short-haired twin who wielded the spear pulled her candle back. She nudged Adaris’ book with her boot. It had come free at some point during her struggle and now lay next to her quill on the cave floor. “And you’re a scribe?”

Adaris nodded, wondering if she had just saved her life or ended it.

“We might have a use for you yet.”

The one-armed twin put her candle back in its holder, then directed her gaze to the large asibik blocking the exit to outside. The asibik seemed to almost bow before coming forward. One of its thin, spiny legs pushed itself under Adaris’ knee and popped it free of the webbing, while another leg did the same with Adaris’ tek. With a snap, the remainder of the already broken spiral came off the weapon, as the asibik ripped it from the floor. Adaris’ shoulders slumped.

She slipped her hand out of the gauntlet and let the useless weapon fall to the stone as she rose. Grabbing her book and quill, she tried to limp back to the cave wall. Her leg trembled, barely supporting her weight. An arched eyebrow from one of the twins forced her to stop moving. *I’m not escaping this.* She knew it had been a mercy to keep her alive, and the lie she told to convince them burned in her throat. If these people went after her family—her brother—because they thought riches awaited them, Adaris would never forgive herself.

But the lie was the only thing keeping her alive.

“We’re heading back to the Sunglade,” the one-armed twin shouted over her shoulder toward the library.

The Sunglade? How could they be going there? According to myth, it was a deadly and barren place, where the battle between the goddess sisters had culminated. And it was across the ocean, on an entirely different continent. Adaris had never really believed the goddess part, never believed in the deities at all, just thought that the continent had become unlivable by a force of nature. A fire, probably.

She had also never believed in the goddess shards, yet she had just found one. Adaris' throat tightened. *Where did the worshippers put the shard I discovered?*

The short-haired twin poked Adaris in the gut, drawing her attention while also keeping her at arm's length. "And we're taking you with us, little thief."

Adaris gulped, terror crawling up her throat. Scribes had tried to go to the Sunglade before, attempted to glean stories from the broken landscape, to record their sightings and piece together the chaos that had ruined the land. So many black quills—the best of the best—had been sent across the ocean to suss out the mystery there.

None had ever returned.

Chapter Four

ADARIS' STOMACH FLIPPED LIKE a fish out of water as she followed the twin Vagari sisters toward the mouth of the rock tunnel. Her whole body seemed to tingle—excitement and dread warring within her. *I'm going to the Sunglade; it could be my chance to tell a story no one has ever told before, but no one has survived yet, either.* Sunlight sliced into the cavern opening, bouncing off the lighter stones and making Adaris wince.

One of the Vagari strolled into the sunshine while the other stayed by Adaris in the shadows, spear at her back pressing her forward. Twisting the hem of her cloak, she paused and eyed the harsh line where the fiery light began at her boots. She had a fleeting thought to run, skirt past her captors and dart away. Her leg might crumble beneath her, but she should at least try. *But where would I go?* Certainly not back through the tunnel to their hideout. And not outside in the sunshine, either.

A jab to her back made her stumble forward and fall to her knees. She caught herself with her hands, pebbles jabbing into her skin. Adaris gasped, trying to scramble back into the darkness behind her, but the spear tip at her spine halted her.

The short-haired twin holding the spear chuckled. "Go on then."

The weapon pressed harder. Adaris' armor was the only thing keeping the point from drawing blood. *Use your crafting. Run away.* She had a fleeting thought of weakening the short-haired woman, but the spear held Adaris too far away. People feared Divus, feared their Blood crafting, feared the power they had to drain life. They always kept Divus an arm's length away. Or in this case, a spear's.

Adaris couldn't use her crafting, she couldn't turn around and go back into the safety of the shadows, and her armor wouldn't last forever. There was nowhere else to go but into the fiery sunshine. She stood on trembling legs and stepped outside. Light slammed into her whole body, glancing off her black scaled armor and picking up the lighter embroidery on her long, dark sleeves as she clutched her book and quill to her chest. The heat almost burned the pale, near-translucent skin on her shaking fists.

Dipping her head, Adaris closed her eyes. Her heart thudded so loud, she was sure the woman behind her could hear. *Depths, it's midday!* The highest point of the sun was the most dangerous time to be outside. She'd had too many close calls in the dusk and dawn to believe something wouldn't try to kill her now. Just like in her youth. Just like when she'd lost her parents.

She took comfort from the thick binding of her book and the reminder of the many stories of bravery and adventure tucked within its pages. She'd woven many tales from the strength and nerve of others.

A tense moment passed. Then another.

"Can't hide from the sunlight forever, scribe. My sister is ready to transport us," the Vagari said behind her.

Her legs had turned to stone beneath her. She couldn't even open her eyes. Sunlight burned across her, already making her pale skin turn slightly pink.

White-hot pain went shivering down her spine, as another sharp jab found a joint in her armor. Adaris grunted, eyes flying open, as she limped to where the one-armed twin waited.

The one-armed twin lifted her eyes to the cloudless sky and chanted. Even though Adaris was half Vagari and knew of her mother's native tongue, she didn't understand these words except for one, Ponuriah. Her insides clenched. Of course, this woman was praying to the sun goddess.

Adaris lifted her eyes to the sky, half expecting to see the mola suncreature swooping over them. When she was younger, her family's fishing boat had encountered doldrums, stuck at midday. A mola suncreature with white wings as wide as their boat had attacked them.

The chanting grew louder. Faster, too. Bile rose in her throat as the searing memory of her childhood slapped into her like seawater. She remembered the white-hot pain of the suncreature's talons on her leg, the freezing water, saltwater clawing at her nose and throat. She'd resurfaced to find her brother mortally wounded and her parents dead. The only thing she could do was dip into her crafting and use it all to heal her little sibling, forgetting her own wounds and leaving her Blood crafting forever weakened because of it.

The too-bright yellow sun glared back at her as the woman lifted her ax to the sky. For one horrible moment, Adaris thought the weapon was meant for her—meant to kill her—but the woman swung down and buried the blade deep into the grass between her feet.

Nothing happened. The twins waited with bated breath, their eyes fixed to the sun in a way that should blind them but didn't. They seemed fully entranced in the sunshine.

Instinct told Adaris to run, but curiosity held her in place. She didn't know what to expect from this display of worship, and she certainly didn't expect anyone to answer the prayer, but she expected...something to happen.

A flash of white light engulfed her. Feather light pricks tingled across Adaris' skin. The light brightened so intensely it hurt. She closed her eyes and tucked her face into her elbow, still seeing the white glow as if the power was burning through her flesh and bones. Then, as suddenly as it had appeared, the light dimmed.

Adaris kept her face covered as the twins muttered words of thanks to their goddess. The muttering stopped, taken over by the sound of waves swooshing against the shore. Warmth pressed in on her. A salty breeze drifted her way, lifting strands of her hair and winding under her cloak. Slowly, she opened her eyes.

She wasn't in the valley anymore. The grassland and mountain had vanished and the harsh sunlight was gone. In its place, a glittering ocean reflected the moonlight, and waves sank into the dark sand beneath her boots. Adaris looked around, mouth agape.

The one-armed twin leered. "This is nothing, little scribe. It's time to see our leader. He'll show you the rest later...if he lets you live, that is."

Numb to the threat, Adaris stumbled forward. The twins pushed her along the beach toward giant columns of pale rock that stretched far into the sky. She took in the sight: water on one side, rock columns on the other, and a strip of black sand beach in between. A set of stairs had been carved into one of the columns. The twins prodded her up, Adaris' rolling gait awkward as she climbed. She was tired before they even reached halfway, her leg protesting the ascent.

At last, they crested the top. A wide-open plateau stretched out before her, glinting in the moonlight. Her boots scuffed over the cracked, pale stone that formed the ground. Stone lanterns with flickering candles brightened the area. They dotted a broken pathway leading to curious, bubble-like structures made of an off-white stone similar to the cracked ground. As she got closer, the flickering light brightened a singular circular path, with the structures ringing it on the outside and an open space in the middle. Adaris tried to make out the odd, stone structures as they passed. The rock seemed to bubble upward, parting in the front in a kind of open archway. Some had fabric across the opening, others didn't. Flickering candlelight spilled from each of the openings. *A village.*

"Who are you taking me to?" Adaris asked, voice hitching in fear.

"Tikova," the short-haired twin answered.

"As long as he's not sleeping." The other laughed.

Sleeping? Adaris lifted her gaze to the moon. *Who would sleep during the safest part of the night?* The answer came to her almost immediately. Sun goddess worshippers, of course.

They pushed her through the village at a fast clip—so fast Adaris' leg throbbed—before stopping at one of the larger bubble-stone huts. She couldn't see an opening on this one, but candlelight flickered toward the side, brightening part of the pale rock. Like a seashell, the door curled in upon itself...privacy reasons perhaps, if this Tikova was their leader.

As if he'd sensed their arrival, the light darkened. A tall man stepped out of the home, dressed in thin, white pants cut at the knee. He wore a necklace with a cracked, white eggshell on it and nothing else. The man leaned on the rock wall.

"We found this thief in our hideout," the one-armed twin said by way of introduction.

Adaris cleared the panic from her throat. She needed to be strong, stand up for herself, make this man believe she was worthy to be kept alive. "Tikova, I assume."

The man nodded, arching an eyebrow at her unsolicited words. "My name is Tikova Lis'u. Yours?" Tikova's voice was smooth, like fine mead.

"Adaris Kavari."

He eyed her with a weary gaze, sea-blue eyes bloodshot orange. A Vagari, then. A frown pulled on his lips, but as soon as he noticed the thick book in Adaris' hands, his weary visage ebbed. He arched a white eyebrow.

"Ah, a scribe, now that's wonderful news." Without warning, he snatched the book and quill from her, then turned to the twins. "It's too early for this conversation. Put her with the painter. We'll talk more in the morning."

My book! She grabbed for it, but Tikova had already turned away. He disappeared into his hut, leaving her with the twins and her fear.

Before she could say anything further, the twins marched her toward the edge of the village, where the candles ringed another structure, this one looming higher than the rest. A crisscross gate of stone and metal barred the dark opening, clearly meant to keep whoever was inside locked away. A prison. Adaris stumbled, reality sinking in a little deeper and making her legs heavy.

"Wait just—" she began.

The short-haired twin jabbed her in the back with her spear, ending Adaris' protest. The other fumbled with the large, rusted metal lock. The door swung open with a loud creak, and the twins shoved Adaris forward. She spun to face them, eyes on the spear tip still pointed at her.

One of the twins gazed past her into the darkness of the prison. "I see you, painter, don't even think about it."

"Welcome to Slagrock, scribe," the one-armed woman said. With that, the twins closed the door with a clang, locked it, and disappeared into one of the nearby huts.

Adaris shook on wobbly legs. Though she'd been ignoring it, the headache from using her crafting still lingered in the back of her skull. Her breaths came in quick gulps of air, too fast to be comfortable, but she couldn't slow them down. She turned to face her prison. Moonlight glowed through the bars, highlighting the rock room in ribbons of pale light. She still couldn't see much. Rock curved above and around her, over the solid ground beneath her boots. Trapping her.

Something moved.

A figure shifted into the moonlight so fast Adaris couldn't see them until they were directly upon her. Someone shoved Adaris back into the bars with a crash, and a hand wrapped around her throat, restricting her airway.

"Who—?" she choked out. She wrapped her hands around the stranger's wrist, clawing at their fingers. Shock ripped through her. No one ever touched a frightened Divus by force, flesh on flesh. No one would willingly risk being killed themselves. As it was, Adaris' Blood crafting surged within her, but her head pounded too much for her to grasp at her power. The figure didn't know that, though, and still tightened their fingers around Adaris' neck. Adaris struggled. "Let me go!"

"My name is Rhonwen Kia-Laryu." Sharp eyes glared at Adaris as the woman leaned closer, her voice barely above a whisper. The name tugged at a memory. Before Adaris could grasp the thought, the woman clenched her grip tighter, banishing the familiarity away. "Who are you?"

Adaris choked, unable to breathe, let alone speak. The woman—Rhonwen—loosened her grip slightly. Not wanting to incur more of this woman's wrath, Adaris answered, "Adaris Kavari."

Rhonwen's moonlit eyes widened. "Kavari? The scribe?"

Adaris nodded.

"Winter's breath," Rhonwen sighed. "Of all the people they decide to imprison with me."

How does this stranger know I'm a scribe? "How—"

"Listen," Rhonwen interrupted. "Did you happen to see a slyther on the way to this prison?"

The image of a half bird, half serpentine-like creature with six wings came unbidden into Adaris' mind. She blinked a few times, searching her memory of the fast walk through the village. "No."

"Useless." Rhonwen released Adaris and turned away, stalking through the strips of moonlight into the darkness beyond. Her voice floated back. "I have to continue my rest, Kavari, don't talk to me until the morning."

Too tired to challenge the woman further, Adaris rubbed her neck, massaging the phantom fingers away and muttering, "What did I ever do to you?"

Exhaustion pulled her to the floor. She leaned back against the prison door, as far from her prison mate as possible. Away from the sea breeze, the warmth pressed in on her, like a blanket wrapped too tight. She shoved up her long shirt sleeves. The thought briefly crossed her mind to take off her armor, too, but she decided against it. She twirled a piece of her hair between shaking fingers, wishing she could write all of this down. Jotting down her thoughts always calmed her. *I have to get my book and get out of here.*

Her gaze skirted to the darkness in the far curve of this strange room.

Rhonwen Kia-Laryu. Adaris rolled the name around in her mind. It seemed...familiar, but they'd called her a painter. Adaris didn't know any painters, personally. She sighed, closing her eyes and allowing her head to loll to the side.

Adaris jarred awake. Her back slammed into the ground as the door creaked open behind her. Sunlight brought tears to her eyes, and she yelped, throwing an arm up to shield her face. Panic skittered across her skin, tightening her muscles and making her want to run. She opened her eyes to discover a fishbone trident pointing at her.

Tikova held the weapon, his large hand steady. "Hello there, scribe! Let's continue our earlier conversation, shall—"

The frantic beating of her heart blocked out the rest of his words. His white vest and cropped pants gleamed. The trident glinted. Adaris' gaze skipped to the cracked ground shimmering from the heat to the sun perched high in the cloudless sky. Sweat beaded across her forehead and stuck her hair to her neck. The edges of her vision tunneled.

"Come with me." Tikova shoved his fishbone trident toward her, forcing her to her feet, and motioned to a different hut nearby.

Hidden once more beneath the sheltering rock, she let her eyes adjust. Daylight reflected into the hut from the open archway, but since Adaris was inside, the light didn't bother her much. Her pulse slowed a little. Tikova gestured for her to sit at the stone table, and her legs nearly buckled underneath her when she did.

She pressed a shaking hand to her forehead. She knew it was irrational—this terror of sunlight—but she couldn't help it. She blinked back the memory of her family's boat.

"I take it you fear the sunlight," Tikova murmured. "Most of your kind do."

Adaris took a deep breath. "My kind?"

"Yes, those who do not worship Ponuriah usually fear the sun." He steepled his fingers. The gemstone set into the ring on his finger glowed blue.

The mention of sun worship jolted Adaris back to her situation like a blanket pulled off in winter. Her fingers and toes went cold. She sat across the table from a zealot, a Ponuriah worshipper, in the middle of a community of worshippers. She didn't even know where she was. *Focus.* Maybe if she went along with him, answered his questions, she could get out with her life still intact. She'd prefer not to end up like those burnt bodies or the man with the ax to his head.

"I prefer moonlight," she finally replied.

Tikova gave her a gentle grin that she didn't believe. He brought out her book and quill and flipped through it. He scanned page after crinkled page, as if reading. He had probably read every word in that book already, or most of them, at least. This had to be for show.

"You have three options, scribe," Tikova finally closed the book, pressing down on the cover. "Remain in captivity forever, join our side, or die like the others."

Die like the others? Adaris leaned back, her throat tight. She couldn't bring herself to talk about that last option. "Join your side? I don't believe in the sun goddess, or any deity. I never will."

"You wouldn't have to believe in Ponuriah, though most do once they learn our ways. I care not about your faith. I'm more interested in your career. You're a scribe, and I would like you to record our time here at Slagrock, our accomplishments, our history. We're doing great things in the community, and on Sunglade proper, and I'm afraid all the other history books tell our tale wrong," Tikova replied easily, though the glint in his sea-blue eyes betrayed his fervor.

"Surely one of your...kind...knows how to write?" Adaris stared at the colored scraps of paper tucked in her book, marking each new story. Had Tikova torn out any of the pages or smudged the words? She hoped not. "Why do you need me?"

"None are recognized by the scrollkeepers at the Athenaeum of the Ancients. We haven't been able to keep a scribe here long enough to get it all down." Adaris wondered if not keeping a scribe long enough meant that the other scribes had died or been murdered. Tikova tapped the scrollkeeper emblem emblazoned on the cover of her book. "Perhaps you will be the one to stay."

"And what happened to those who chose not to?"

"You already know the answer." Tikova spread his arms wide. "Which one shall it be?"

Her mind turned over the possibilities. *Did anyone actually choose death, to be killed?* Yet she doubted they'd keep her captive forever. That meant there weren't three choices as he claimed, just one.

"You say you'd want me to record the stories of your community, but for everyone to read them, I'd have to go back to the Athenaeum," she said, biding more time to gather her thoughts.

Tikova grinned. "We'd get you back to the library, yes. Eventually."

Eventually. How much time would that be? In the deepest part of her heart, she always knew that information was the most valuable tool she could offer, and she could gain some very valuable information by staying in Slagrock. The Ponuriah worshippers had continued their goddesses' fiery warpath for generations—burning everyone and everything that got in their way. She knew from the Moon Knights' tales that the attacks were getting more intense, like the worshippers were building to something. The hideout she'd discovered seemed to confirm as much, with the attack slated for midsummer.

To her shame, she never really cared too much about the war after being rejected by the Moon Knights. She did care about her family and friends, about her job as a scribe, about her life back home. All of that would change if the fiery worshippers won the Nemora homeland and took over all the Groves.

She could even help turn the tide against these sunsick fools.

Adaris rubbed her sweaty hands over her pants. Her gaze flicked back to her book and the quill resting beside it. Her white quill. Record their stories. That was what she had wanted, after all. A good story. And a teal quill...if she survived.

Staying is the only option I have. She looked at Tikova and forced a grin. "I would be happy to record your life here. Record this...community. It will be a story for the history books indeed."

Now she just had to figure out a way to survive.

Chapter Five

"I'LL RETURN FOR YOU at nightfall, so I can show off my community when the sun sets." Tikova winked and pushed Adaris' book and quill to her. He left a bottle of ink and a small, brown bag with her as well. When his vest flapped open, the light glinted off sky-blue scales that curled around his pale sides. "In the meantime, I'll have someone bring you food and water. We can't have our new scribe going hungry."

His long, white hair flowed in sheets like water behind him as he left. She was alone in the strange, spherical rock room. Bent over the stone table, she went to work. She filled two entire pages, front and back, with the brief fight in the cave before transporting to this community. Heat pressed in on her, making her throat tickle and the ink dry on the page almost instantly. She didn't want to forget even a single moment of her encounter.

Writing helped. It always did. Her fear bled onto the page and out of her system, if only for a brief moment.

A plate and cup carved from stone clattered onto the table next to her book, shattering her concentration. The man didn't even stop to say a greeting before heading back outside. She examined the sun design tattooed into the nape of his bronze neck and down his broad shoulders as he left. Ponuriah's symbol. He, too, wore an artifact, an armband that glowed orange. She marked that down in her book, along with a rough drawing of the tattoo and armband for reference later. Would they demand she get tattooed as well? The thought sent a chill over her heated skin. And what was the glowing jewelry for? She almost felt like she'd seen something like that before.

Her stomach rumbled. The plate of food looked tempting—a half sphere of a spiny tuber with pale yellow flesh. A piece of blackened fish sat next to the vegetable, still steaming. Spices hit her nose and made her mouth water. *If this is how they treat prisoners, perhaps my stay won't be so bad.* She devoured the whole plate of food, groaning when the flaky fish all but melted on her tongue and the yellow tuber burst with a surprising sweetness. The water was slightly too warm for her liking, but it was a good meal, and she was honestly surprised by their hospitality.

Leaning back, Adaris eyed the two guards who shadowed the archway. People walked outside, sunlight glinting from their hair and shoulders. Snippets of conversation, a crunching noise as something was dragged against the path, and the sounds of a bustling community made Adaris curious.

The whole community seemed to be awake. The itch to investigate, to gather stories, made Adaris yearn to go outside, but the too-bright sunlight slicing into the room stopped her. Even without the guards keeping her inside, she wouldn't risk it. Dusk slowly approached. The vibrant yellow sunlight surging into the room ebbed toward orange, then red, then settled into calming blues and purples. The noise outside quieted.

Tikova appeared in the archway, lean frame backlit by the dusky light that remained. He extended his hand. "Come. Let me show you the community."

"Yes. Let's." Curiosity and excitement pulled at Adaris as she slipped the bottle of ink into the small bag he'd given her. The bag hung awkwardly at her side; she immediately missed her belt pouches. She didn't take Tikova's proffered hand, instead lifting her book and quill. "I'd like to take notes."

He smiled, guided her out of the spherical hut, and paused to give Adaris her first true sight of the community he spoke so highly of. *Slagrock.* The huts were all made the same way, as if the rock had been pulled from the stone plateau and formed into globes. A Hallr Nemora must have made them. Only the makers and breakers of stone could craft such unique structures.

A pathway of dark stone formed a perfect circle, with the huts dotted along the outer ring and forming a nearly empty gathering place in the center. A looming statue stood in the very center, but it was a bit too far away for Adaris to make out any details. Lit candles set along the pathway formed brighter patches in the shadows left by the dying sun. Some glowed freely; others were contained in glass and rock lanterns. The candles seemed wasteful to Adaris. Wax melted, whereas daygems rarely dimmed. Tikova led the way, and though the place seemed almost empty, a guard followed a few paces behind Adaris, bone trident at the ready.

Tikova pointed to the left. "Here you'll find the gardens and those who tend them, as well as storage for the necessary seeds and tools."

A trio of the strange rock huts stood together around a raised garden, if it could even be called that. Dark stones held dry, dusty dirt that desperately needed water. It was a decent-sized area—forty paces wide and long—but only a third of it showed signs of life. Green stalks clustered in one corner, surrounded by vibrant red leaves with pale yellow lines. She recognized the coloring on the leaves and knew a crimson vegetable sat beneath the soil, but she couldn't recall its name.

"The kizomi seeds were delivered to us a short while ago and took to our environment even better than I would have hoped," Tikova continued. "Quite frankly, it's unbelievable the trader even found the outcropping."

Kizomi. That's what it's called. From her readings, Adaris knew that the rare plant grew only near volcanoes. She wiped a hand across her sweaty brow and wished she could take off her armor. Even though she saw no volcanoes on the cracked flat rocks around her, it certainly seemed hot enough, even with the sun down. She jotted down her notes, while Tikova guided her away from the garden, still talking about the vegetables.

"You'll note we have a rather limited supply of food here—repetitive, really. All we have consistently are fish and tubers. A spare flying creature, once in a harvest moon, if I can see it. Sometimes, if we're exceptionally lucky and the Vagari who works with me is feeling up to it, a lagi."

Adaris shuddered. Lagi were giant fish with huge teeth and a tough, scaled hide. Adaris eyed Tikova. He was a head and shoulders taller than her. Perhaps his Vagari blood was of a lagi line. If so, his companion animal would be a lagi, and he'd have some features that mirrored it.

She gestured to the scales on his bare chest. "You would eat your own?"

Tikova blinked a few times then chuckled. "Keen eyes, but not keen enough. My bloodline isn't lagi." He gestured to his small, pointed ears—which didn't match the lagi bloodline traits—then to hers. "You seem to have some water kin in you as well."

Adaris lifted her chin, feeling his gaze on the twist at the tip of her ears. "Keen eyes, but not keen enough," she retorted. Her mother's bloodline wasn't water-based; it was air.

Tikova smirked, but didn't rise to her jab, nor guess at her bloodline. "I'd like you to take note of the plants that grow here, as not many do." He pointed to her book. "There are no trees or grass or any real vegetation here. That's true of this side of the continent. But I have successfully grown some plant life. That's worth noting. I had hoped it would draw more people here, entice them to stay."

Adaris nodded. "How many people live here?"

"Fifty, perhaps a little more, depending on the day. Slagrock is mostly a research community, though pilgrimages to the other coast do start here."

She marked the garden page with a slip of paper to return later on, so she could, indeed, write down all the vegetation. They continued their tour. Her bad leg held up surprisingly well, her rolling gait easier on this stone path.

This community wasn't what Adaris expected at all when she got to the Sunglade. This ruined continent wasn't thought to sustain life, yet a whole village had sprung up here on the coast. The community seemed confined to this one path—on one curve were the columns, the beach, and the ocean; on the opposite was flat rock and darkness. *Could I make a run for it?* Adaris stared into the dark as they walked. She shivered. If she went inland, she'd just be going deeper into their territory—sun goddess worshipper's territory. They paused by a rock-fenced area lit by only a single lantern perched high on a stone pillar. "This is our beast enclosure, though we rarely have any natural beasts. Only one currently. Still, it's nice to be prepared."

Only one? Adaris stared into the shadowy pen. A rock cage about the size of a two-story house was tucked in the far corner of the fencing. Something moved inside its pen. A flash of scales, of wings, caught her eye. *A slyther.* That woman—Rhonwen—asked if she had seen one. Was it hers?

The shadows in the other corner of the pen shifted, brightened with crimson and pure yellow light, as something else moved. Bright-red eyes cracked open. In a flash, the corrupted creature slithered toward her. When it opened its maw, orange saliva dripped off its many fangs.

Adaris didn't have time to react, only gasp. The tip of a trident appeared over her right shoulder, pointing directly at the suncreature. The serpentine beast stopped moving, but it was close enough that Adaris could feel its fiery breath against her face. When it snapped its maw shut, the blast of air brushed Adaris' hair off her shoulders and singed her skin. She stumbled back. The guard positioned between the suncreature and Adaris gave her no reassurance. *A suncreature. And it's loose.*

She rounded on Tikova. "That beast isn't natural."

The Vagari actually beamed. "The suncreatures are part of our research, as I'm sure you'll note more of later on. You'll see far greater things here than you could ever imagine, and I want you to record them all."

Research. That shook something loose in the back of Adaris' mind and she had to turn away from the shadows and crimson eyes to think properly.

She'd heard of a Vagari who could turn beasts into suncreatures—a scribe had discovered that keystone story in Rok on the southern coast of her homeland. Something about Blood pendants and new crafting skills, the building war, and the ability to be transported away in a flash of white light. Misti Eildelmann's story. She'd been surprised to read about it because she'd met Misti before, once and—

It came back to her in a rush. *The white pendant glowing around Misti's neck.* That's why the jewelry seemed familiar. She'd seen it before.

The scribe who recorded Misti's entire tale had been elevated to the black quill almost immediately for discovering something so valuable.

This place...it might actually be a keystone story all its own. The one she needed to advance in her ranks—if she survived the task. Adaris' hand shook as she made a few more notes in her book.

"Your hut is over there." Tikova pointed to a larger spherical structure in the distance, slightly away from the main ring. The prison she'd been held in earlier. Candles lit the way, glinting off the stone and metal bars.

Your hut. She almost laughed. The prison was as much hers as the ground she walked on. That is to say, not hers at all. But was Rhonwen still in there? Adaris hadn't seen her, though to be fair, she hadn't really kept a look out either. "Am I free to come and go for my research, or am I a prisoner?"

"A guard will take you each day to do your research." He gestured to the guard still shadowing them. "Like the painter."

I am a prisoner then. She paused and shifted her weight to her good leg, wanting to give herself a little break from this tour. A sharp sting radiated through her knee. The tour was getting long, but Tikova didn't seem to want to stop. "Why are you keeping her?"

He looked at her as if she were a small child and sighed as if it were obvious. "I need a visual recording of this place, too, of course, reflections of our research and our accomplishments. Slagrock is a marvelous community doing great things, and it should be recorded in more ways than one. Rhonwen is well known in her field of study, and I wanted the best."

Well known? Adaris wondered if that was why Rhonwen's name seemed oddly familiar.

Tikova's gaze raked over her. "We have crafting that could heal your leg, by the way. So you don't need to pause so often. I like my scribes...active."

Adaris stilled. She'd been a mere child when the accident occurred. They had crafting that could heal a lame leg even numerous seasons after it happened? Unheard of.

They moved on. Someone was watching her, though. Adaris felt eyes on her. When she glanced behind her, a triple set of crimson eyes stared back. *Another suncreature.* Tikova ignored the beast, as did the guard, but Adaris couldn't. The suncreature skittered past them, too fast for Adaris to see what kind of beast it mirrored, and curled up in the shadows of a cluster of huts overlooking the ocean. Perhaps, when the suncreature left, she could slip out that way in the future. Take to the ocean.

"Our accommodations," Tikova mentioned with a glance. "We sleep when darkness falls."

And a suncreature sleeps next to them, Adaris realized with a jolt. She knew the suncreatures were weaker at night, mostly slept the starlight away, but it didn't dim the anxiety clutching her heart. These people not only researched suncreatures, they lived with them. No sane person would do such a thing. Suncreatures were vile and dangerous, led by the need to destroy and kill and nothing else.

A foul scent of rot and death hit her nose. Ahead, a pile of at least twenty bodies reflected the lantern light. Nausea swept through her, and bile rose in her throat.

Yet as they passed it, Tikova nodded as if it were the most common thing in the world. "We burn the ones who disrespect our goddess at night, then take them to the river of lava nearby."

A man she hadn't noticed before heaved another body onto the pile. Adaris' gut heaved with it. "There seem to be many who disrespect your goddess," she said dryly, holding a hand to her mouth to keep from vomiting.

"Yes," Tikova agreed without even a hint of remorse. "Ponuriah is quite clear on what we do to those who do not respect her."

"Is that why you're here?" Adaris turned away from the bodies. She had to, or she would've lost her meal. Her hand trembled as she gripped her quill tighter. "To deal with those who don't believe in your goddess?"

"I'm here because I am trusted," he replied easily. "We often bring prisoners from the other continent here...to see if we can change their minds to our cause or use them for other means. I have a husband back home, but I was chosen for this task, and I took it willingly. I will make this community a shining ray of Ponuriah's light!" His voice lifted in excitement, wide eyes shining in the flickering candlelight, and a smile curling his lips. "Ah, I'd like you to meet our researchers, but they'll be sleeping now. You'll have to make their acquaintances later, during the daylight. Which I expect you to be more comfortable in, by the way."

Adaris shivered. She doubted she'd ever feel comfortable in the sunlight.

If Tikova found her silence questionable, he didn't mention it, gesturing to his community. "What do you think of what I've built here thus far? We still have the oceanfront to explore."

But her leg had nothing left to give. She needed to sit down. "Could we explore it later?" Adaris lifted her book. "I have quite a lot to write down already, and I need the time and space to do it properly."

She also wanted to get out from under Tikova's watchful gaze and overly cheerful manner. Her head spun with all she'd just seen. The longer she was at Slagrock, the more she realized how precarious her position might be. He obviously adored his goddess, and her need to tour in the darkness seemed to affront him. She had to find a way out if things got too dangerous.

"This way." Tikova guided them to the center of the community, a wide empty area probably meant to be a gathering space. A carved, red stone statue of a woman in a fiery dress with flames for hair and crimson gemstones for eyes had been erected there. Tikova went over to the image of Ponuriah and patted a rock seat tucked next to the statue. The top of the seat was smooth from use. "You can work here."

A small stone bowl, directly in front of the statue, caught Adaris' gaze. Her insides clenched as she saw what it held. Dried blood—blue, white, brown, and orange—crusted the bottom of the bowl. Some kind of sacrifice? Adaris looked away and caught Tikova staring intently at her.

"Do your writing here. During the day, since that's when most of my people are awake," he said. "Your guard will protect you from any harm."

"And keep me here?" Adaris said, settling gratefully down on the smooth stone seat. She rubbed her thigh, massaging the building twinge away. Her bad leg finally decided to show its spines.

"Of course. Your guard will take you back to your hut when you're ready." Tikova grinned, then walked away. His tall form ducked into a hut nearby, leaving her with her guard and her thoughts.

Tikova wanted her to do her research during the day, record their stories in the sunlight. It made sense, but Adaris didn't know if she could actually do that. She could barely stand in the sunlight the day before and wasn't faring much better after the tour.

She felt eyes on her again. The hairs on the back of her neck stood up, and she swiveled on the stone chair. Three sets of crimson eyes stared at her. It seemed like the suncreatures stood guard as well. *How will I be able to concentrate?*

Chapter Six

NOT MANY PEOPLE LINGERED during the night's passing. The ones who were dealing with the pile of bodies hauled the dead away and didn't return. That was a sliver of good luck, for now at least, for the stench in the air cleared.

That only left Adaris' guard—whom she described in detail in her book. *Light brown skin, short and stocky. Bald. A firm jaw and deep-brown eyes.* One of his forearms had what looked like a bracer. When she looked closer, it wasn't made of metal or leather. The tan-and-white patterned shell was actually part of him. Another shell on his opposite shoulder covered part of his neck and disappeared under his tunic. Obviously Vagari. A sun design made from black ink colored his other shoulder.

He wore a sleeveless tunic, baggy pants cinched at the ankles, and sandals—all pure white—which surprised her a little. She had always seen sun goddess worshippers in heavy white robes, with crimson scarves tucked round their necks and faces. The heat in Slagrock probably dictated his clothing choices, for it was still oppressive and heavy even with evening's dark. When the moon crested and the air cooled ever so slightly, the guard unrolled a heavy robe cinched to his belt and pulled it over his head—one that better matched the others Adaris had seen.

He never left her side, never waivered his passive expression, and never said a word. He kept his trident pointed at her. As if cut from stone, he simply stood next to her...all night long.

When the moon drifted low against the horizon and dawn spread like a bruise across the sky, Adaris stood and stretched. The rock chair hadn't been comfortable, and she'd sat there all night, absorbing everything about her surroundings and spilling them onto her paper. If this was to be a keystone story—one to connect others—she had to get every detail she could. The map of the community she'd sketched earlier was adequate, though she needed to walk around more to add the smaller details.

And to find a way out when the time came.

"I'd like to get some rest," she said to her guard.

The guard nodded and nudged her with his trident, keeping her at arm's length like people always did around Divus. They walked in silence to the larger hut at the crest of the circle, furthest from the ocean. Her hut, Tikova had called it. The prison. This time, Adaris didn't resist. She needed to get some rest and perhaps food, and at least the prison would be out of the coming sunlight. Her stomach clenched as she thought of the fiery orb and the suncreatures that would awaken with it. She knew she'd have to come out before the sun set, when more people were stirring, to gather more stories for Tikova.

Her guard took out a key from his belt and opened the door with a creak.

"Does everyone have a key to this place?" Adaris asked.

In silence, the guard motioned her inside with a flick of his trident. He locked the door behind her, then stood by the prison, facing away.

Sighing, Adaris surveyed her prison. Early dawn spilled inside, pooling like fire on the cracked stone floor and painting the smooth rock walls orange and pink. The empty space loomed around her. The painter must be somewhere else, though Adaris hadn't seen her outside either. The circular room was perhaps thirty paces across. On one curve, a stone table and four stone chairs had been created out of the rock floor. *Perhaps a family once stayed in here.* A single stone bed sat on the other curve of the room, gray blankets and a pale, cream-colored pillow folded on one end. The stone framework held a thick layer of black sand instead of a mattress—a sad attempt to make the rock more comfortable. Adaris grimaced at that; she hated the gritty feeling of sand, so the painter could have that bed for herself.

Tucked toward the final curve of the room was a stone desk littered with papers and paint, and an easel. Crimson and pink paint splashes, long since dried, created an attractive pattern, almost like layers of waves. Paintbrushes soaked in multiple colors were set out on the desk.

Rhonwen's area.

Adaris rubbed her throat from where the woman had grabbed it the night before. She made her way to the desk, picking up a bright-green tipped paint brush. The handle was smooth and nearly white, a material she'd never encountered before.

"Do not touch anything of mine unless I state that you can," a familiar voice snapped.

Adaris spun, paint brush still clutched in her hand.

Rhonwen stood by the door, dressed in an elegant, yellow tunic and matching flowy pants. In the growing pool of light, Adaris could get a better look at her prison mate. Dangerously thin, her bright-yellow eyes seemed to burn into Adaris, like fire rested in the woman's soul. A fresh orange bruise spread up the side of her brown neck, a matching one blooming on her cheek as if someone had held her throat and slapped her. Uncomfortable, Adaris shifted her gaze from the sight.

"And I certainly didn't give you permission to hold that one," the woman continued, tilting her head at the paintbrush. Her waist-length, gray hair slipped over her shoulder and turned white at the tips. Sword-straight. A few tiny feathers caught the light, adding pops of rainbow coloring into the long strands. Surely a mark of Rhonwen's Vagari bloodline. "Do you know how expensive bone brushes are? And that has asibik spines woven into its bristles, hard to find and even harder to buy. You could never afford it."

Adaris blinked her shock away. She held out the paintbrush. "This is a bone-handled brush?" she said, feeling vaguely insulted. She had never seen one before.

"It is." Rhonwen strode toward her and snatched the paintbrush from Adaris, then possessively gathered up the paintbrushes on the desk. She knocked them together in her hands once and put them back on the desk behind some papers.

"How do you know what I can and can't afford?" Adaris said.

Rhonwen turned to her, arms crossed. The light danced on her ochre skin, warm brown like the color of golden sand soaked with saltwater. "I know scribes with your kind of reputation simply can't afford nice things."

"My kind of reputation? That's bold," Adaris replied. *Does this painter woman know about my lie?* "Who do you think you are?"

Rhonwen scoffed. "I'm Rhonwen Kia-Laryu, of course, one of the best painters in the north. I have numerous works in the art district in Cahoma, by the Ratnaa Grove. Surely, you've heard of me."

Adaris knew of the Cahoma art district. Only the very wealthy and popular could afford to make their homes there, but she didn't know of an artist named Rhonwen.

"Never you mind." Rhonwen rolled her eyes. "I wouldn't expect a useless scribe like you to recognize the finer things."

"Useless scribe?" Adaris yelped, anger flaring hot on her cheeks. "Says the painter. I'm recording history. You're...what...drawing waves that aren't even the right color."

Rhonwen arched an eyebrow. "Art tells a story, too, scribe, but I don't expect you to appreciate that. You might not know me, but you do know my mother."

Mother? Adaris was so busy being insulted that, for a moment, it didn't hit her. Then the memory came sharp and clear as ice. *Damned to the depths.*

Kia, the chief stargazer of Celestial Abbey.

"You're Mica Kia's daughter?" Adaris had claimed to have gotten the real story from Mica and then blatantly lied about how she got to where she was. How Mica poisoned the other stargazers to gain her status. That's why Rhonwen's name sounded familiar.

"You ruined my mother's reputation with that lie. It's a great comfort to see that it also ruined yours." The painter's striking yellow glare could have curdled milk. She glanced pointedly at the white quill tucked into Adaris' belt.

The truth in her words stung as sharply as a quill prick. The room's air thickened with the silence stretched between them. A heavy lump formed in Adaris' throat. That lie. It had been idiotic, but it hadn't stopped her from lying again. She'd bent the truth in order to talk to Knight Lista, just a few nights ago, before being kidnapped. Depths, she'd lied about having a rich family, too.

"You have no idea what kind of avalanche that lie started in the abbey." Anger simmered in every facet of Rhonwen's expression, twitching in the muscle by her temple. "Why are you part of the scrollkeepers? You should have been dismissed. Isn't it your organization's mission to be truth-tellers, record history as it actually was, weave stories together to form the true tapestry of our lives?"

"We do record the facts," Adaris snapped, finding her voice along with her anger. She had to defend her fellow scribes. Not all of them lied like she had.

"Then why didn't you?" Rhonwen asked.

"I had my reasons," Adaris replied, doggedly. *My brother. My lack of crafting. My family's boat.* Shame coiled within her, but she couldn't bring herself to say the words aloud.

Rhonwen glared at her. "Oh, so you scrollkeepers supposedly write down the true history of others but can't admit your own?"

The barb stuck, twisting in her heart. Her brother's cough rattled around in her mind, his body gaunt and weak from it, but she shoved it away. This wasn't the time to think about her past. Still, she felt for Rhonwen. That lie had destroyed this woman's family, and Rhonwen deserved some explanation. Adaris took a moment to collect her thoughts. "I knew the story about your mother would earn me the black quill...if there was a new twist to it. Mica Kia's story was formidable, but it needed more to earn me the highest respect as a scribe. The master scrollkeeper only gives out a few each season, time was running out to gain one. Along with the quill comes a large sum of coin."

Rhonwen sputtered. "So you ruined my mother's career because you were greedy? Lovely." Before Adaris could protest, the painter barreled on. "Ma Le'Shawn would tell me to put the past behind me and be calm, but this one is going to take some help." Digging through a pouch in her belt she palmed something into her mouth, chewing furiously, then rubbed a thumb over her eyebrow in a rather curious manner. Her piercing gaze found Adaris. "You're not a sun goddess worshipper, and our present circumstances are dire. We should try to work together. No matter how...difficult it might be."

She released a deep breath. A strange glaze came over her yellow eyes, and she rolled her shoulders. Backing gracefully into the stone chair by the desk, she motioned for Adaris to do the same. "Did Tikova give you the grand tour of his prized community?"

For a moment, Adaris didn't reply. No one could quell their anger so easily. A swelling tide of tension still rolled thick between them, and Adaris knew the wrong word might cause it to crest and break. She had to be careful. This was the only person she could possibly trust, the only person she'd seen thus far who'd been kidnapped just like her.

"He did. I took some notes," Adaris replied, catching the roll of Rhonwen's eyes. *So the anger isn't all gone.* There weren't any other desk chairs, so Adaris took a seat at the table. She put her book down and placed her quill reverently atop it. Wanting to smooth things over, even if only for a moment, Adaris thought back to the cramped, stone cage they were keeping the slyther in. "I saw your companion animal."

Rhonwen leaned forward. "Where was he? How did he look? Are they treating him with dignity?"

"Your companion is...safe, at least. In a rock cage by the animal yard. They also have a suncreature that seems to enjoy hanging around."

Rhonwen didn't seem the least bit disturbed. "A few of the sun goddess worshippers' companion animals were turned into suncreatures to guard the community. I believe they were going to transform more, but I heard it's powerful crafting, so they can't do it very often."

Companion-turned-suncreature? Adaris remembered that from somewhere. Flipping back through her book, she found the scrawling notes she had taken at their last official scrollkeeper's meeting. The master scrollkeeper had told all the scribes how a group in the Ravenlock Woods had somehow altered Animal crafting to transform creatures into the corrupted version of themselves, but the master scrollkeeper hadn't known how that was possible.

Maybe Adaris could find out. The story was missing the final element of how the group could do such crafting. If Adaris could figure it out, it would be worthy of a teal quill for sure.

She dipped her white quill into the ink bottle in one of her pouches and started to write. "Have you seen the suncreatures interact with their Vagari companions?"

"Of course. Many times." Rhonwen waved her hand dismissively, as if being in the same place as a suncreature was normal, natural even. "It seems like the suncreatures recognize their companions and protect them, but I'm not sure if they can still communicate."

Adaris rubbed the spiral tip of her ears and thought back to her mother and her companion animal—a bitterroot flier. The fluffy, fur-covered creature had a long tail, four tiny limbs, and long ears that ended in a twist. Her mother loved her companion and vice versa. They were linked and fully bonded.

Having their companion animal corrupted would be terrible; their bond would be lost, the communication severed. No Vagari could communicate with suncreatures. Her mother always told her that a Vagari would get a massive headache and bleed from their nose if they even tried to connect with a suncreature. Some had even died.

But perhaps for sun goddess worshippers, being turned into a suncreature was what both of them wanted. To serve Ponuriah. She jotted down the thought.

Rhonwen rifled through the papers on the stone desk, pulling one sheet from under the rest. "One of my first paintings for this community was their attempt at communication."

Rhonwen laid the paper over her knees, and Adaris gaped. A terribly long, white-scaled, serpentine suncreature coiled again and again and again around a green-scaled Vagari with a tight expression. The suncreature took up almost the entire sheet, its scales a faint orange where they bent away from the body and covered almost the whole woman. Yellow-orange saliva dripped from its razor teeth. They had locked eyes—one pair glowing a suncreature crimson, one pair glowing a Vagari crafting orange.

Rhonwen ran a loving finger over the image's glimmering scales. "I used the last bit of gemstone dust I had for this painting. I had assumed, if I made the best painting possible, my life would be spared and I would be set free." Without warning, she rolled the painting into a tight coil, lashed it together with some twine from her pocket, and tossed it onto the desk with the other papers. "I just hadn't realized they meant I had to keep painting to stay alive."

Adaris eyed the thick stack of papers on the desk, the canvas with the red waves in the corner, the numerous cans of paint and bone brushes. "How long have you been here?"

"I got kidnapped during our winter celebration of the frost moon," Rhonwen replied, "and I've seen fifteen full moons since then."

Frost and full moons? Shock rippled through Adaris. Rhonwen used rural terminology instead of the standard crescent and cycle, season terms, which sounded strange coming from such a wealthy person, but Adaris couldn't judge. She did some quick calculations in her mind. "You've been in captivity for over six hundred nights?"

"I suppose." Rhonwen frowned. "But it's felt like much longer."

Adaris remembered the moment when they had first met, the tight grip around her throat. "You seem to be very capable of holding your own, and your slyther...aren't they known for slipping into and out of small places, for being so flexible they can bend over themselves with ease? For being silent and fast? Haven't you tried to get free?"

"Of course I have." Rhonwen flushed, a deep orange tint spreading across her neck and chest. "I can slip my arm through the bars on the prison door easily, but that doesn't mean I'm fast enough to grab the key for the lock. And the first time my guards discovered I was trying to escape, they locked Spectrum up. I can't leave without him." Rhonwen ran her fingers through her hair, fingers straying on the pops of downy feathers catching the light. Adaris wondered just how soft those feathers were, but she pushed the thought down, caged it like the slyther. This wasn't the time for feelings like that, at all.

Rhonwen continued with a sigh, "Winter's breath, I've tried sneaking away from my guard so many times that now they have a guard follow me into the washroom. It's humiliating, having someone stare at me while I perform my daily ablutions."

Adaris shook her head, thinking of her guard with the trident and how closely he'd watched her. Now it made sense. "That's terrible."

Rhonwen's lips tightened, and she eyed the white quill clutched in Adaris' hand. "I would rather not have my failures noted in the history books, if you don't mind, nor my daily ablutions."

Adaris stifled a laugh. "I'd skip the ablutions, and I don't need to write it in my book if you'd rather not have your story told, but tell me so we don't try the same things twice."

They spent the next little while trading stories. Rhonwen talked while Adaris prodded gently for more details, or paused to interject her own findings. Rhonwen had tried some truly bold things to get free. She'd poisoned her guards, put a stolen knife to a community member's throat, threatened a suncreature—though how she'd managed to get close enough to accomplish that, Adaris couldn't imagine. After over six hundred nights of trying, any sane person would probably crumble, but the increased captivity seemed to only anger Rhonwen more. Adaris respected her privacy and didn't write anything else in her book about the painter, but Adaris knew she would remember it all. And maybe, maybe one piece of those stories would lead to her own freedom.

Chapter Seven

ADARIS STARTLED AWAKE, JERKING her sweaty cheek from the corner of a piece of paper with a slight rip. She still sat at the table where she'd been talking to Rhonwen and blinked at the pale pink sunlight piercing through the bars of her prison. She'd slept through the night. Worry wormed its way into her belly.

She rubbed the sleep from her eyes and looked down at the table, expecting to see her book open to a torn page. Her book sat next to her arm, closed. A slip of paper rested under her elbow. Smoothing it out on the desk, she read the words written there in obsessively neat and curly script. *Don't be useless.*

Adaris could almost imagine the muscle in Rhonwen's temple twitching when she wrote those words and the roll of her eyes as she left, but what could she mean by them?

Alone in the odd rock hut, Adaris had no doubt the guard hovered outside, bathed by the light of the rising sun.

The heat was already oppressive, even in this stone room. She wiped her temple and thought for a moment, then tugged off her armor. She wouldn't be able to concentrate with all her layers on. And Rhonwen had a point about being useful.

After stripping to her dark, long-sleeved shirt and pants, Adaris considered her boots. They were thick soled, good for traveling, but were already making her feet sweat. They'd be nearly unbearable outside. If she didn't wear them, the sharp stones and cracked rock would tear her skin bloody. Divus were thin skinned, after all. She needed to protect her feet, so she left them on as she headed to the door. Unease tingled over her arms from the lack of armor.

As expected, her guard waited on the other side. He opened the door, and she inched her way outside. Dawn approached, but luckily the sun hadn't breached the watery horizon just yet. Adaris could survive by keeping to the long shadows around the huts, if it meant getting more stories.

If it meant finding a way out.

Her guard, true to form, said nothing as they walked the single broken-stone path that formed a large circle. Leading him from shadow to shadow, Adaris idly wondered if he was mute, perhaps deaf, or simply shy. She didn't ask, her attention on the bustle of the small community.

Vagari, Divus, Nemora, and Elu all lived in the village. She counted maybe forty outside. Some prayed at the Ponuriah statue or gathered in small groups to eat. Others were harvesting from the gardens or heading to the edge of the rock columns with some clear purpose Adaris didn't know of. All wore similar clothing—light airy fabrics, baggy and loose to let in airflow. The shades of white reflected the heat. Most of them had a circular sun design somewhere prominent on their exposed skin, proclaiming them as worshippers of the sun goddess. And all of them wore glowing jewelry as well.

Keystone or not, these stories would probably be the most valuable stories she would ever record. Her fingers itched to write it all down.

But danger lived here, too.

Adaris picked up her pace as they passed the animal pen area where that terrible mystery suncreature had lurked. Her leg protested when she hurried even faster past the area where they kept the bodies. She couldn't help it as she eyed the pale, cracked rock. The bodies were gone but blood—blue, white, orange, brown—seeped into the cracks like strange multicolored veins. Not as much blood as she would've expected. She'd have to record that as well, but she didn't want to look.

On her wander, she searched for an opening to slip away from her guard, but his attention never waivered. He stuck to her like sand on wet skin, always an arm's length away, but his trident lifted as if he expected her to run. *How much trouble did the other scribes get themselves into to make him so cautious?*

Wanting a glimpse of the ocean, she tried to stray from the curved path. A flash of white light had transported her to Slagrock, but perhaps a community by the water had boats. Boats, she knew. Her boots had barely left the circular path, when she felt three sharp points press into her back. Her guard. She froze and looked back. "I'm not allowed to leave the path?"

Her guard shook his head, then guided the trident away from her back to tap the book at her waist, an obvious indication of what she was supposed to do. She went back to the path, shoulders slumped. She tried to deviate two times after that. Each time, her guard nudged her back with the tip of his weapon. Not hard, not painful, just...always present.

Sighing, she turned back onto the path, following the gentle curve, aiming her attention on the community members around her. Maybe it was time to get a few of these stories. Adaris stopped a squat Vagari and lifted her book and quill.

"Another scribe, hmm?" the balding Vagari muttered. When he straightened his vest, Adaris caught sight of a metal pendant glowing softly white against his pale chest. "Must be Tikova's doing."

"Yes," she replied, noting the curious jewelry and wondering why the man was so dismissive.

The man bent over to shove a few tubers into a thick bag by his sandals. While he did, Adaris eyed the metal pendant, her gaze flicking up to a nearby Nemora woman wiping the sweat from beneath a glowing blue circlet that held back her white hair. Everyone had a piece of jewelry that glowed. Pendants dangled around their necks, rings decorated their fingers, or circlets adorned their heads.

These pendants were all different colors. Orange. Blue. Brown. White. Perhaps the coloration meant they had different types of crafting locked inside.

A familiar thrill lifted her stomach, curiosity washing through her like it did when she caught the tide of a new story. She wanted to know more about those artifacts, know how they worked, what they demanded of the crafter. See one used in person.

Finally the man straightened and arched an eyebrow, as if surprised to still see her there. "Fine, I'll talk to you, but I don't expect you to live long enough to gather all the stories Tikova wants."

Adaris' gut flipped, remembering the bodies. She wouldn't be one of them, even if it meant playing along with Tikova's requirements. "How do you like living in Slagrock? What do you do?"

"Always the same questions." The Vagari rolled his eyes, pulling a dried fish from his pocket. He crunched down on the head. Bits of broken bones spat from his mouth as he talked. "I'm one of the harvesters. I pick the tiny amount of vegetables we can grow on this broken rock, plant the seeds, and try to coax more into growing."

"The garden looks—"

"Garden?" The Vagari interrupted. "Fancy word for a patch of dust that doesn't grow anything. It's too hot here. We have nothing—no real fruit or meat. The only animals are suncreatures. Maybe a sea creature or two if we're lucky." He waved his piece of fish around. "But once we capture the Nemora homelands, we won't need to scrounge around for a piece of bread. We'll be able to expand, thrive even."

Adaris scribbled in her book. The need for resources made sense, and was a far cry from the sun goddess worshippers' lust of blood and fire she'd been taught as a child. The Nemora controlled all the natural resources in all of the Groves and traded fairly with Adaris' homeland. If these people on the Sunglade had no access to the Groves or to the trading system, it would be hard to survive. No one could grow crops like the Nemora.

"So, you mean to capture the Groves by force?" There were seven in the center of Adaris' homeland, each one focusing on a specific natural resource, like trees, fungi, shrubbery, or gemstones. "All of them?"

He shrugged. "They have the lands we need. We have the means and the ability to take them."

"But if all you need is food, you could try talking to the Nemora leadership? Make a truce with them. Talking could prevent war and save lives on both sides." She knew it was a hopeless dream even as she said it—these worshippers had done too much damage to the people of Adaris' homeland to talk their way into a deal.

He scoffed. "When you have the superior crafting, talking is unnecessary."

Superior crafting. "What will you do to the people in the Groves, to the Nemora who live there? To everyone else on that continent?"

"Form a new world order, of course. One our goddess will be proud of!" the Vagari slapped the sun design scar on his forearm. "We deserve a continent better than this one."

Adaris moved on. A tall Nemora, who was fixing a fishing net, turned out to be far more chatty than the Vagari had just been. The Nemora described the Sunglade in detail Adaris had never heard. She scribbled madly to keep up, hoping she had enough ink.

Apparently, there wasn't much on the Sunglade at all. Most of it was uninhabitable, claimed by suncreatures even the sun goddess worshippers didn't want to face. While the tomes back home had little to no information about the Sunglade, it seemed to be common knowledge among these people that this continent had four distinct sections.

The community of Slagrock was formed on one region—made entirely of cracked rocks, columns of cooled lava, and black sand beaches. Rivers of lava flowed close by, heating the area from within.

One entire portion of the land was a massive active volcano, unlivable save for a few Nemora or Vagari who could stand the unbearable heat. Fruit and vegetables grew lush there, but not many made the trip across the lands because the continent was so vast. The volcano was on the other side of the continent, the farthest area from Adaris' homeland. Those who wanted more power from Ponuriah made the pilgrimage to the temples there.

The northern section was gray, ashy, and burnt to ruins, filled with strange and vicious suncreatures. One community member even likened it to the Ravenlock Woods and Cinder Forest back on Adaris' homeland. Those petrified forests teemed with twisted and strange suncreatures. The leadership—the doyen as Adaris learned—claimed that area for their own, because it seemed to be the most protected area from an outsider attack. The most dangerous for the Moon Knights to capture.

The southern section of the continent seemed to be a desert and salt flats.

"No one lives on the salt flats," the Nemora muttered with a wave of her hand. Her mesh wristband glowed a distractingly vibrant blue. "No food grows there at all. All the fresh water has evaporated away. Nothing but sand and salt and an endless stretch of the horizon. No one goes there. It's why we need the Groves, scribe. Our goddess demands that we raze the Groves to the ground and start anew. So that's what we'll do. I'm tired of eating nuts. You will be too if you live long enough."

If I live long enough. Everyone seemed to doubt her longevity. Adaris stopped writing, afraid her shaking hand would ruin the page. She thanked the Nemora and stood, moving deeper into the shrinking shadows near the garden.

It seemed everyone was obsessed with the Groves. Did they not realize that unless they worked together with the Nemora, the Groves would be rendered useless? The Nemora cultivated the lands to perfection, but they were also linked to their territory. Connected to them, like Vagari were tied to the beasts of the world.

Razing the ground—burning it to ash—simply wouldn't work unless the sun goddess worshippers had many different Nemora who could command the lands.

Adaris reviewed her notes, trying to connect the stories and flipping through page after page of ink. The frantic scribbles made her wince. She'd have to make them more coherent later on. Her guard stood beside her, silent as ever, while she watched people passing, toiling, sweating. All in the name of their beloved Ponuriah.

She remembered reading about the planned attack at midsummer, how the worshippers were preparing a large-scale attack on the Nemora Groves. The possibility had alarmed her then, but not as much as it did now. The glowing jewelry worried her. The master scrollkeeper only knew about the one white Blood pendant. They suspected a few others, of course, but every person in Slagrock seemed to have one. If the jewelry held crafting power, as she suspected, the sun goddess worshippers were far more prepared for the coming battle than anyone probably thought.

She needed to see what these new artifacts could do. Learn their abilities, their weaknesses, and bring that information back home...if she didn't die like all the other scribes before her.

Chapter Eight

SITTING BESIDE A HUT, Adaris leaned back, wiping the sweat from her brow and noticing the way heat shimmered on the ground. Her shadow had shrunk to almost nothing beneath her, and fear took over. She gasped and scrambled to her feet before darting into a nearby hut, her guard following on her heels.

A mound of dirt sat near the entrance, and a few metal boxes rested in the far curve. A single window let in light, which slanted onto the ground. *A storage area for the gardens, perhaps.*

A small bald boy sat on one of the smaller boxes, using a taller one for a makeshift table. He barely glanced up. The boy's whole being seemed intent on a gemstone that rested in a large, metal cooking pan. His eyes glowed a deep-brown as he leaned forward and pressed his hands onto the metal box beneath him. *A Nemora then, studying the gemstone with eyes glowing like that.* His dark green skin mottled to a lighter shade on his arms. Her gaze slipped off the child and onto the gem. As large as two fists, blue-green in color and faceted, the gem was pretty but plain as well.

Pressing a shaking hand to her chest, Adaris sat on a smaller crate across from him. The metal felt too warm, even through her pants. A small pile of white nuts sat next to his hand. Her stomach growled. She hadn't eaten yet, but she certainly wouldn't want to eat those. Drugs wouldn't help her right now.

Placing her book and quill on the crate between them, Adaris eyed the boy. The crystal pattern on his shoulders marked him as a Ratnaa Nemora, a caretaker of gemstones and the rare minerals. Ratnaa Nemora often did such things as his intent study, almost absorption of the gem to help them find more of the same kind in the local area. The boy didn't seem keen to start a conversation, so Adaris did. "You must be the youngest member of the community I've seen."

The Nemora blinked his Nature crafting away, and the deep-brown glow emanating from his eyes vanished. He lifted his head, then got to his feet to edge his makeshift chair away from her—just out of arms' reach. Adaris didn't mind.

The sharper angles of the crystal pattern decorating the boy's arms caught her attention. He was past the Choosing ritual every Nemora went through and had chosen to stay male. The Nemora only went through the Choosing ritual after a time of nox—fluidity of gender—when they could explore who they wanted to be. They made their choice after they had enough life experiences, but he looked so...young. Short, too. A boy, not a man. Most adult Nemora were tall. This one looked to barely come up to her chest in height.

Adaris shook the thought away. The Nemora could live for hundreds of seasons, after all. She wouldn't judge.

"What's your name?" she asked gently when the Nemora sat down again.

He bit his lip. "Berhn."

"Well anoc-suna, Berhn." She hoped using the Nemora word for hello would help him relax. "Nice to meet you. My name is Adaris." She patted her book. "I'm a scribe. I'm supposed to record your lives here, and I'd like to know more about you. What are you working on?"

"I...look for these gemstones." Berhn motioned to the bright gem resting in the pan, as if Adaris hadn't already noticed it.

Shy, Adaris realized. She gave him an encouraging smile. "Why?"

A dark-brown blush rose to his green-skinned cheeks. He glanced away, not speaking. Then he tossed a couple of nuts into his mouth and chewed. Adaris expected a glaze to cover his eyes, like the cloudy film that covered Rhonwen's, but his eyes stayed a clear and bright green. A moment passed, then another. Finally the boy—no, the man, Adaris corrected herself—gulped some air and said, "I find them in the mines for Sroc. For her research. The gemstones are important."

He motioned outside, and through the oval window, she saw a few large boulders on the outskirts of the community. She hadn't yet wandered that way, but it must be where the mines were located. She flipped her book open, scratching some notes onto a blank page. "I haven't met Sroc yet. Do you happen to know what research she's doing?"

Berhn's gaze fell to the open book and the quill resting in Adaris' fingers. He shook his head.

"That's okay," Adaris replied.

"All the scribes around here die," he mumbled, tugging on the sleeve of his white tunic.

"I've heard," she replied, trying to keep her voice steady. Nearly every person she'd spoken with had told her that. Never why or how, just that the scribes didn't survive. It scared her to the depths of the oceans and back, but information could help quell that worry. Maybe Berhn would be more forthcoming. "Can you tell me why?"

"No," Berhn replied quietly, focusing on the stone once more. "The others in the community don't really talk to me much. They feed me and clothe me. Let me and my parents work."

Parents. She hadn't seen any other Ratnaa Nemora, yet. After the choosing, it was curious that he'd even stick with his parents anyway. Most Nemora found their own way. He must still be young in their eyes. "Your parents live here, too?"

He looked up at that question, finally meeting her gaze. "Yes."

There. A spark in his eyes. Adaris could always tell when she picked the right topic to get a person talking. She made a note in her book. "What do your parents do here?"

He shrugged. "They're elderly, so they cook our meals."

"Did they give you that pan?" She nodded to the thick, heavy metal pan the gemstone sat in, glad to see him opening up.

A small smile twitched Berhn's lips. "Yes. It's useful for putting stuff in, and you never know when you need to cook something. My parents always say that."

Berhn was adorable, and Adaris couldn't help but laugh. "Your parents must be quite smart."

"Berhn, enough frivolity. It's time to work." Tikova's frame filled the open door, silhouetted by the vivid rays of midday. "And Adaris needs to eat."

Berhn stood. He grabbed the gemstone in one hand and the pan in the other, then slid the pile of white nuts to her with his elbow. "You can have those," he said.

He slipped around Tikova and vanished into the sunlight. Tikova's head nearly brushed the ceiling as he walked to one of the metal boxes and pried it open with a small creaking noise. He stuck his hand inside, retrieving an oval melon with pale, purple skin.

Giving her a wink, he plopped it onto the crate in front of Adaris. "Don't tell anyone about my stash. These arrived from the mainland a few days ago, and I'd like to keep it between us for now."

"You're not sharing it with your community?" Adaris arched an eyebrow. "And wouldn't they go bad in the heat?"

"Oh, they will." Tikova waved a hand at her. "We're having a celebration soon, and I plan to share with everyone then, but one sample can't hurt."

He flourished a gleaming white knife from somewhere on his person and cut the melon in half. Much to her surprise, the melon was bright yellow on the inside and still juicy. Setting the knife on the crate, Tikova palmed one half and offered her the other.

For a fleeting moment Adaris thought about grabbing that knife and stabbing him, but her courage gave out and she took the melon instead. After her first small bite, bright tartness flooded her mouth, the flesh all but melting down her parched throat. She ate the rest ravenously, even the slightly chewy rind, letting the sticky juice run down her palms, wrists, and arms.

Tikova languidly enjoyed his melon, eyes on everything but her. He seemed unconcerned to be in her presence, so different from the other people in the community. Everyone else held her at arm's length. She supposed their actions made sense; as a Divus, she could use her Blood crafting to kill them with her touch. Or rather...other Divus could do that. Not her.

But they didn't know that.

Tikova, however, didn't seem to mind being close. Like he challenged her to do something. It unnerved her.

Her gaze flitted to the knife still on the crate. Entirely made of a white material, the handle didn't have a guard of any kind, and the blade curved slightly at the tip. "That's a fine blade you have. What is it made of?"

"Squallizard tooth. Their fangs make great blades. Lovely tridents, too." He patted the trident strapped to his back, then gestured to his knife. "That tooth belonged to my companion's sire."

Squallizards were massive, reptilian-like sea creatures, with long teeth and even longer claws. Their powerful fan-like tail could create great gusts of wind. Fisher families liked them for that very reason, and pirates often harnessed those gusts for nefarious purposes. Adaris shook her head.

"A squallizard tooth? Interesting." So Tikova's Vagari bloodline was squallizard. Adaris scribbled it down, connecting some pieces together, other questions splintering through her mind. Where did the creature live—by the sea? What powers did that bloodline gift him? It had been many seasons since she'd seen a squallizard—probably not since she'd been out with her family as a child. She had to see Tikova's. "Did you battle your companion's sire to acquire it?"

"He was killed during the War of the White Fields," he said in an offputtingly friendly tone. "And I wanted to honor him for my own parents."

White Fields was a small coastal town, one that had been overrun by a hidden band of sun goddess worshippers over twenty seasons ago. According to history, as she remembered it, the worshippers had lived and worked in the city, but hidden their relation to the fiery goddess until they suddenly attacked. The land had been devastated, turned into ashy ruins.

"Did your parents survive the attack from the sun goddess worshippers?" she asked.

"The sun goddess worshippers' attack?" Tikova picked up the blade and twirled it slowly between his fingers. "Is that what your people teach you?"

Adaris nodded. "The attack was unprovoked. Your people burned it to ashes. We call it the Coastal Ruins now."

Tikova's features hardened. "Unprovoked." The word slipped past clenched teeth. "What little you know, scribe. This is why you need to be here. Recording things the way they actually are."

Adaris knew better than to argue. She told the truth, as far as she knew it. The sun goddess worshippers attacked and burned the city to the ground. Fields of harvest, gone. Buildings ruined. Everyone, women and children included, slaughtered like animals. That's what the books said. "So what's your version, then?"

Tikova slipped the blade into his belt, then smoothed one eyebrow with his fingertips. "We need better crafters here at Slagrock. You may have noticed in your walk through our community that Blood crafters, in particular, are in short supply. How powerful are you, scribe?"

Apparently, the conversation about White Field was over, whipped away in place of a new one. Adaris put down her quill, frustrated. She had noticed only one other Divus during her conversations with the community members. People needed Blood crafters. Needed healers, but they probably needed more powerful ones than her. *The power ebbs in me.* She couldn't say that, and if she lied, they might catch her in it.

"I'm an...okay crafter," she finally said, but didn't elaborate.

Tikova steepled his fingers and nodded. "Having some Blood crafting is better than having none at all. Tomorrow, I'll have Sroc visit you. She could use your crafting skills, and you can record her stories as well."

Adaris' gut clenched. Her weaker Blood crafting would be painfully obvious the moment Sroc put her to work. She couldn't mend broken bones. Gaping wounds made her gag. Other Divus had life energy to spare and readily healed others, but the ache in her leg always drained her small reserves. *Depths, I can hardly knit a few scratches on my arm without suffering a headache!*

They spent the afternoon in each other's company—her reviewing her notes, him watching her. The silence grew thick, but she refused to break it.

Rhonwen cornered Adaris the moment her guard shut her into the prison that evening. "You were out in the community the whole day. Did you find anything interesting? A way out perhaps?"

"Hello to you, too." Adaris clutched her book to her chest. She'd learned plenty of interesting things but hadn't found an escape route. "My guard was too alert during this first outing. Perhaps after some time in the community, he'll relax."

"Don't count on it. Your guard is the keener type," Rhonwen muttered. She limped to the stone chair by her desk, tucking one foot under her knee, and sighed. Her elbow bumped one of the paintbrushes, which clattered to the ground. Sighing, Rhonwen immediately bent to pick it up and tucked it protectively into her belt. "He used to be assigned to me. They wanted me to paint the lava river where they dispose of the dead. I did...then I attempted to shove that guard into the lava. Obviously, it didn't work, and the guard spoke to Tikova to get reassigned to a new prisoner. I have a different guard now."

"Bold to try," Adaris snickered, eyeing her thin frame and the thinner almost gossamer white dress that draped over skin. It looked like the painter couldn't even push open a heavy door, not to mention shove a guard. She sank to the floor. "I would've liked to see that. See you in action."

Rhonwen shrugged, a lift of her shoulder, as if shoving an armed guard into a river of molten lava was an every-night occurrence. In the flickering candlelight, a fresh cut on the top of her shoulder glimmered with orange blood. It was thin and as long as a finger, but the painter seemed to ignore it. "I'm honestly surprised they haven't killed me yet. They must desperately need my paintings." She cupped her chin in her hand, gaze drifting to her art supplies.

"They probably need your name more, since you're apparently famous somewhere." Rhonwen bristled, but Adaris gave her a wink to let her know she was teasing...and flirting, Adaris realized too late. Depths, she was trying to flirt with someone who still hated her. With reason, too, she hadn't yet told Rhonwen the whole reason why she'd lied about Mica Kia. Rhonwen arched an eyebrow at the tease and heat burned Adaris' cheeks. "Tomorrow, I get to meet a woman named Sroc. A researcher, apparently."

"Sroc?" Rhonwen's spine stiffened and her eyes narrowed. She lowered herself to the floor next to Adaris, close enough their knees brushed, and stuffed a hand inside the bag by her chair.

It occurred to Adaris that Tikova wasn't the only one who didn't mind getting close to her, Blood crafting and all the communal fears about the powers be damned. Unlike Tikova's nearness, Adaris definitely didn't mind Rhonwen.

"Most of the scribes have died after seeing her. Here, take these." Rhonwen held out a palm heavy with those curious white nuts. "They're called aca nuts. They'll calm your nerves. You'll need it, facing Sroc."

Adaris accepted the nuts, but her gut twisted. "Do these grow here? I've seen similar ones around the community."

"One of the Nemora cultivates them by the lava river. They're one of the only things that grow with reckless abandon on this side of the continent. I should tell you they're addictive, highly so. Only use them if you need them."

"Why do you think I'll need them with Sroc? What is she researching?"

Rhonwen tucked her knees to her chin, wrapping her arms around them. This close, Adaris could see a large bruise welling on her ankle, the reason she was limping, probably. Every time she saw Rhonwen, the painter had more injuries decorating her skin but none of them seemed to really faze her. Perhaps after so many nights of abuse, she had just gotten used to it.

But she seemed...scared, almost. Like the mere mention of Sroc's name frightened her, a curse that would kill them all. "I haven't the faintest idea what Sroc is researching or what the scribes do or discover when they're with her. I only know that some scribes haven't come back at all."

"Lovely. How am I supposed to get to sleep with the possibility of dying tomorrow on my mind?" Adaris' tongue grew sharp with her rising anxiety.

"You should always live as if you're going to die tomorrow, sleep like that too. I do. Here, especially." As if a gate closed on their conversation, Rhonwen stood and went to the single stone bed. "I can give you a spare blanket if you'd like. It's too sweltering for me."

Adaris bit her lip. "It is too hot for a blanket, but I could use it as a cushion."

Rhonwen tossed the blanket to Adaris, then shifted some of the sand around to her liking. After flopping over rather ungracefully, her eyes fluttered closed.

The painter's lithe form sent a kick through Adaris, and glowflies fluttered through her. *Depths! Stop it, girl, she hates you.* Adaris turned away.

Tired as she was, she moved to the stone table, brushing away the sweat from her brow. The reflected sunlight on the walls faded, and she was forced to light a candle. She reviewed her notes again, rewriting everything she'd learned in a more coherent manner, stringing details together like gems on a necklace, and adding words to her sketches. Obsession pushed her onward, grinding her to get every last detail. This could be a keystone story, after all. She had to get it all down.

"Could you do that later on perhaps? The scratching sound of your quill grates on my ears." Rhonwen groaned. "I thought you spent the afternoon with Tikova, recording your thoughts."

"I did but—"

Rhonwen interrupted her, judgmental gaze finding hers. "It's been a long day, scribe, and we both need sleep."

Adaris frowned. "Well, *painter,* if I don't record everything I die. Tikova has said as much. Do you want me to die?"

"If you keep up that noise when I'm trying to sleep, I'll kill you myself." Rhonwen dug into a pouch on her belt and stuffed a handful of the aca nuts into her mouth.

"Those are highly addictive you know," Adaris muttered.

"I wonder where you learned that," Rhonwen snapped. "They take me to a better place, which is what I need if you're going to continue making noises when I'm trying to sleep." She flipped over and faced the wall, the movement sending a pile of sand to the floor.

Adaris huffed. She blew out the candle, letting darkness surround her, and settled on the floor next to the table. The rock made for a terrible bed, even with the folded blanket beneath her. Adaris wouldn't consider herself old in her thirty seasons around the sun, but the rock made her bones throb. A pebble poked her back, and she stuffed her armor under her for some semblance of comfort. Still terrible, but even if she'd been comfortable, she wouldn't be able to sleep. Worries about tomorrow—about Sroc—pressed into her mind like clouds rolling across the horizon. She adjusted her lame leg, wishing the air wasn't so hot.

A rolled-up blanket landed in a flop next to her head. "For a pillow," Rhonwen murmured. "You'll need your head for tomorrow."

"Thank you." Adaris squinted through the darkness. "Rhonwen, how many scribes have come before me?"

The silence stretched for so long, Adaris thought the painter had gone to sleep. Then Rhonwen's clear, quiet voice floated to her. "I stopped counting after thirteen. Refused to talk to them after that."

More than thirteen. Adaris' heart crashed like waves inside her chest.

"Why did you tackle me when I first got here, then? Why are you talking to me now?" She stared into the darkness. "Depths, I ruined your mother's career! Why even help me at all?"

"Because you're a liar and none of the others were," came Rhonwen's soft reply. "The truth couldn't save us, but perhaps a liar can get us both out of here."

Adaris turned the words around in her mind, grateful for something else to think on. A lie to save them. Now that was a curious idea indeed.

Chapter Nine

ADARIS STARED AT THE figure waiting at the prison door. For some reason, she had expected Sroc to be a wizened, silver-haired woman bent over a cane. Such a great researcher—one who demanded so much respect—surely should be old and wise. Instead, a child stood before her who had not yet reached her teenage season. So few trips around the sun, yet these people regarded her so dearly.

The researcher was terribly thin. Bones jutted out at odd angles and sharpened her youthful appearance to points. Her nose and chin and cheekbones were prominent on her sickly pale face. Almost bird-like in appearance, yet her clothes seemed too tight. Strips of dark leather wound around her entire body like a serpent. A Divus for sure, with clothing like that, though odd for a place this hot.

As Adaris approached her, Sroc pushed back a thin lock of black hair from her eyes. "Follow me, please." Her voice was a quiet, breathy whisper, as though speaking was an effort. Sroc left the prison door and headed down the curved pathway without seeing if Adaris would follow.

Of course, Adaris would. A trickle of fear dripped down her spine as she scrambled to catch up, her guard following close behind. Night pressed in on them. Thick clouds blocked the stars in the deep, blue-black sky on the distant horizon. Sroc seemed fine working at night when others in the community usually slept. Adaris was thankful, even though still on edge.

Rhonwen's warning echoed in her mind. *"I only know that some scribes haven't come back at all."* This would be a test; Adaris was sure of it.

The researcher walked in silence, just like Adaris' guard, so Adaris followed suit. They strolled down steps cut into the rock columns close to the sea. Sroc was sure-footed on the steep steps. Adaris kept one hand on the vertical column jutting to the sky. A pair of crimson eyes on the beach caught her attention, and she stumbled over the final step. A suncreature. Many pairs of eyes opened—all crimson. Her gut kicked. Too many suncreatures were resting on the sand, but thankfully, Sroc went the other way. They turned right, to curl with the columns, instead of left to the endless sandy beach, and left those creatures behind.

Adaris concentrated on the ocean instead. Water ebbed and flowed onto the black sand. She had finally relinquished her boots in favor of cooler footwear, and her sandals sank with each step, the cool sand filtering between her toes. The chill felt good after the intense heat of the day.

She had changed outfits completely. She wore a pale, sleeveless tunic and airy pants that cinched at her waist and ankle, but billowed out around her legs. A bag over her shoulder carried her book, quill, spare bottles of ink, and scrap paper. She thumbed the nuts in her bag as they walked, wondering if she should eat one.

Even with lighter clothes and the coolness of the sand on her feet, sweat poured down her neck and back in rivulets, making the cloth stick. *What I wouldn't do for a glass of ice water right about now, or a cold bath.* "Where are we going?"

Sroc didn't answer, didn't even look back as she curled their path around the beach, keeping close to the rock columns until they reached a small hut nestled among the rocky protrusions. Stinking guts of fish for bait filled metal crates beside trident spears propped up against the rock. Fish bones littered the beach. *A fishing hut.* She even saw a few rafts beached near the water.

For a moment, Adaris felt like she was home.

Sroc went around the hut and slipped into a hard-to-see break in the rock columns. Adaris' brief sigh of relief seized in her chest.

Whatever waited inside the columns couldn't be good. A lump formed in Adaris' throat. Consumed with a sudden urge to flee, she took a step back. Her guard stopped her with the tip of his trident. The time to run was over.

In an attempt to calm her shaking nerves, Adaris popped one of the aca nuts into her mouth. She chewed the bitter flesh and waited for numbness to wash through her before she followed Sroc's fading footfalls. Despite the effect of the nut, her pulse pounded in her ears. The moonlight that filtered in behind her lit a small, secret cave. If she stretched her arms wide, her fingers could brush either side of the rock walls. What could anyone do in an area this cramped? She wished she had her daygem, or any daygem, in fact. Her guard didn't follow her in, and she suspected it was because the space was too small to fit them both.

Adaris peered around. She could barely see.

"This way, scribe," Sroc whispered from somewhere in the darkness.

Adaris started at Sroc's voice, taking a step back that twisted her bad leg. Pain shot up her leg. Shoving a hand in her bag, she found another nut and hoped it would dull the pain.

Something scratched and a candle brightened a corner of the space with pale, yellow light. Sroc waited for her, partially inside a stone hatch in the floor that Adaris hadn't noticed. Sroc lowered herself, the flickering candlelight following her.

Adaris knelt, peering into the hole at the ladder and the top of Sroc's head swaying as she descended. It was a dungeon, surely, or a torture chamber, or another prison of some kind. It was a stupid idea to follow...but curiosity pushed Adaris forward anyway.

The aca nuts had started to take a firmer hold, and an odd calmness wound through her, like she'd drunk too much. It wasn't bad...just strange. Rhonwen had said that aca nuts steadied the nerves. Adaris shuddered to think what a handful could do, if two affected her this strongly.

As she lowered herself onto the ladder, her guard came into the cramped cave, obviously still keen on following her. Adaris climbed down. The unfamiliar movement jarred her leg and jolted pain up her calf. She clamped her teeth around a groan and concentrated on the damp stone rungs of the ladder and the scent of briny sand that fell like snowflakes around her. The guard was starting his descent down the ladder. Finally, her sandals hit level ground and she turned to face Sroc.

A grin curled the child's lips as she gestured around. "Go on. Take a look."

In the meager candlelight, Adaris saw a too-smooth rock floor and walls. She suspected the place was not a natural cave, but crafted by a Hallr Nemora. At the far reach of the candle's light, she saw the edges of a stone table, perhaps a stone bookshelf, but the room felt much larger than that. She noticed an odd dip in the floor at the very edge of the candlelight.

"I can't see very well in the dark," Adaris admitted. "Can we—"

Light burned behind her, and her guard handed over a stone lantern about the size of her palm, with a squat candle burning inside. He motioned for her to stay put, then wandered into the darkness. One by one, he began lighting candles and lanterns around the area.

With each new light source, the room revealed itself to be an oval shaped space that was cramped on the sides but open in the middle. On one curve, there were tables strewn with books and crammed with papers. On the other, bookshelves lined the walls, stuffed full of heavy tomes. On the far end, more bookshelves held rings and pendants, circlets and armbands. Artifacts, she realized. Like the ones so many people in this community wore. Curiously, none of them glowed. In the center of the open area, a terribly thick book sat on a podium, as if it were better than all the others.

It slowly clicked in Adaris' mind. This wasn't a dungeon or a prison...this was a research lab. Adaris immediately went to that podium, curious about the thick tome. She stumbled a little on the odd, bowl-like dip in the floor.

Sroc got there first, flipping the book closed before Adaris could see the markings inside. "You're not ready to read out of that book, scribe."

"What did you want me to see here, then?" Adaris asked, gesturing to the shelves around her.

"These. I want you to record these." Sroc wandered toward the artifacts, and Adaris followed. Sroc picked up an armband with a white gemstone. "Do you know what these are?"

"I've seen jewelry like that around the community, but I don't know what they do," Adaris replied.

That wasn't completely true. The master scrollkeeper had told her about Misti's Blood pendant, which could suck life from people and transfer that life—their energy and strength—into the wearer to heal them, exactly the way a Blood crafter wielded their powers.

"I could tell you, but it would be much more fun to show you." Sroc's giggle sounded off-key somehow.

Sroc took off one glove and wiggled her fingers. Each had a plain, metal ring set with a glowing gemstone. She raised a thumb circled by a silver ring that shimmered white, and a pulse of white energy radiated outward like a shockwave.

Adaris barely got her arm up in time to cover her face from the blow. Exhaustion swept through her, as if she hadn't slept in nights. Her bad leg buckled, and she had to catch herself on the bookshelf to keep from falling.

The sensation subsided as soon as it had come.

Sroc grinned. "Blood crafting, obviously."

Though Adaris had her strength back, she still felt weak from the shock. Wobbly, yet the power was fascinating. Her curiosity and the strange calm from the aca nut nudged her concerns aside. The ring harnessed Blood crafting, just like she could. That such a little object could pull so much from her was astounding. Adaris wondered whether this white ring amplified Sroc's Divus Blood crafting or was separate from it.

Sroc raised her index finger, which had a ring with a glowing blue gem. She pointed her finger at Adaris, and a wall of cobalt light shimmered between them.

A shield. Adaris' eyes widened. A trident flew past her head and bounced harmlessly off the shield, clattering to the floor. She spun. Her guard shrugged and went to pick up his weapon, as if demonstrations like this happened every night.

"Moon crafting," Sroc explained, as if Adaris didn't recognize the signature blue glow.

Before Adaris could speak, Sroc lifted her middle finger, wrapped in a copper-colored glow.

The stone beneath one of Adaris' sandals melted, the molten rock capturing her foot before hardening again. She gasped and caught herself against the bookshelf once more, staring at the place where her ankle seemed to vanish into the stone, shocked that it didn't hurt. She felt the pressure of the stone around her foot, but not pain. The ground liquefied again, and Adaris yanked her foot free.

Amazing. Unheard of. One person wielding three kinds of crafting. Even Adaris, with her limited use of her two abilities, was an oddity and lacked strength in either craft, but she'd just witnessed fully harnessed crafting. Full strength in each of the three crafts. It couldn't—it shouldn't—be possible, yet proof glowed clear on this child's fingers.

"How?" Adaris gasped. "How do you harness the crafting like that? Can any—"

"I'm not done yet." Sroc interrupted. Two more rings left—one orange and the other crimson. One was surely Animal crafting, but what was the other?

Sroc sank to the floor. She touched the ground with her finger and stared at the bookshelf. Adaris bent to look at where she was staring. Unlike the others, this bookshelf had no back. Instead, dark sand created the wall.

The black sand crumbled, and a crustacean burrowed its way into the room, followed by three others. A gush of seawater came with them and followed a curve into a hole in the floor, probably to seep back into the ground once more. About as long as Adaris' arm, each creature had a hard protective shell, eight skinny legs, and a long, segmented tail that curled downward in a tight spiral. Their shells were bright blue on the top and brown on the bottom. Adaris recognized them from her childhood, karks. Seabugs, her brother called them. The crustaceans littered the deep sea, and her family would eat them whenever they could catch them.

"Our special dinner's arrived," Sroc murmured, reaching out a hand to stroke the ten long antennae sticking out of the first kark.

Adaris' guard clumped back down the ladder. *When did he leave?* So entranced by Sroc's demonstration, Adaris hadn't even noticed. He was carrying a thick mesh bag clearly taken from the fishing hut. He scooped up the four karks in his arms and stuffed them all into the mesh bag.

"One more ring left," Sroc said.

Adaris tore her gaze from the karks, not wanting to miss whatever the final ring could do. *What kind of crafting is crimson?* Even in all her seasons of study and searching, she didn't know.

Sroc laughed with that same blood-curdling giggle. "This one's just for show. And because it's pretty."

"But it's glowing."

"It's a daygem, made by a powerful Elu on the eastern shore."

Disappointment made Adaris' shoulders slump. "Well, then what are the jewelry pieces called?"

"Bound artifacts." Slipping her glove back on, Sroc tightened her fingers into a fist. "And that's where you and your crafting come into play."

My crafting. The words sank into Adaris. Her crafting was terrible; the child could probably heal better than she could. The last thing she needed was this sunsick researcher deciding she was useless. *Focus on your work, scribe. What the depths is a bound artifact?* Pulling out her book and quill, Adaris leaned on the bookshelf as nonchalantly as her racing heart would allow. She started a new page. "You wanted me to record these artifacts. Well, I have some questions. How many bound artifacts do you have?"

Sroc gestured at the artifacts—the bound artifacts. "These, the ones in the community, mine."

"How do you bind the crafting to those artifacts? Can anyone use them?"

"I create them, and anyone can use them. Once I perfect them, we send them away so our people can use them to better Ponuriah's cause. Our cause. I create more as resources allow." Sroc plucked a stray, orange gemstone from the bookshelf and scowled. "My best work fell to our enemies, two crimson crystals that harnessed Nature crafting to become completely invisible. The foolish twins who smuggled them for us decided to double cross us." She set the gemstone back on its shelf, a grim look painting her face. "We won't let them live for long."

Adaris shuddered. She didn't want to think of what the sun goddess worshippers would do to someone who betrayed them. Unbidden, the burned dead body in the hideout came back to her. *Twins, though, and crimson crystals that made the wearer invisible.* The idea broke something loose in her mind, something she had read in the library, but she couldn't quite remember it.

"But that's neither here nor there, scribe. You're a Blood crafter." Sroc leaned forward, touching Adaris' hand with the tip of her finger. "And we need Blood crafters here."

Adaris' legs felt like stones, her body frozen. Like any Divus, this child could kill her between one heartbeat and the next. "Yes, I'm...an adequate Blood crafter."

"Adequate can mean a good many things. Let's test it, shall we?" Sroc selected a thin piece of glass from the bookshelf and smashed it onto the stone. The glass shattered into hundreds of tiny glittering shards. Calm as a winter's night and just as cold, Sroc pressed her palm into the shards and dragged her hand around. She thrust her injured palm in Adaris' direction. The glass shards glittered in the candlelight. "Heal me."

Depths! Adaris gaped at the injury. The glass had embedded itself into Sroc's skin like a starscape. It would take some skill to remove all those shards. Skill she might not have.

This was a test, and she knew she had to at least try.

She could be killed if she didn't.

Sinking into her crafting, Adaris welcomed its familiar warmth, a calming sensation that went far deeper than the aca nut did. White fog washed out the true colors of the world.

Pressing one hand on the back of Sroc's hand and the other on her wrist, Adaris pooled her crafting. The white light traced her veins and sank into the young researcher, then brightened the cuts. Adaris focused, narrowing her gaze on the glittering shards, directing her crafting to push them out of Sroc's flesh so she could heal the wounds. Like vines, her crafting pushed the shards out, one by one.

The process was terribly slow, and all too soon, the headache started like a pin pushing into the back of her skull.

She probably could've plucked the shards out faster with just her fingers, but Sroc had told her to heal the wound, had wanted to test her crafting. So Adaris kept at it. One by one by one, the glass fragments popped out of Sroc's skin, dropping like rain to the stone floor. Adaris' headache pushed deeper into her skull, and her energy flagged as she poured more of herself into her crafting.

She tried her best to hide how much the effort took from her. She kept her breathing slow and sure, even as it felt like daggers sank in her mind, even as darkness pressed in at the sides and she desperately wanted to go to sleep.

One by one by one, the glass slipped free.

Finally, when all the glass was out of Sroc's palm, Adaris used her crafting like a needle and thread, stitching up the cuts and leaving only mended flesh behind. It would leave a scar, but at least it was healed.

"Done," she said, letting go of Sroc.

The young researcher flexed her hand, closing her fingers into a fist to examine a few glass shards Adaris had missed, glinting like stars next to her thumb. "Adequate enough," she sneered. "You'll do, for now."

Adequate enough. The words rang in Adaris' mind. She let her crafting go. The fog rolled away, and her headache dipped to a mere pounding. Tired, she leaned on the bookshelf. *I did it. I passed their first test.*

Sroc brushed the glass shards away, then picked up a ring with a blue stone set into it. Her smirk sent a chill down Adaris' spine. *What does she want me to do now?*

Chapter Ten

THE CHILL FROM SROC'S smirk wouldn't abate, any more than the echo of Rhonwen's words. *"I only know that some scribes haven't come back at all."* Scribes had died in this cave. Adaris eyed Sroc, expecting the young researcher to command her to do another test, to prove her worth.

Sroc ignored her. She seemed wholly intent on examining the ring with the blue gemstone...silently. The ring wasn't even glowing. "Why are you so fascinated with that?" Adaris asked, probably more bluntly than she should have. She held in a breath, waiting for a reprimand and almost expecting another wave of Blood energy to pull life from her. The researcher didn't reply or even look up from that little ring.

Adaris chewed on her cheek. *Is this another test?* If so, it seemed like a pointless one. The long silence carved jagged paths into Adaris' already tenuous calm. "Can I leave then?"

Sroc waved her hand like she was swatting away a bug. "Count the unbound jewelry, as well as those jars. Note how many I have of each."

What? Adaris tilted her head. That had nothing to do with crafting or even research, as far as she knew. Adaris stared at Sroc, trying to tell if the researcher was serious. One look from those bright purple eyes told her she was.

So Adaris did as she was told. She counted the artifacts on the various shelves—thirty in all—before moving on to the jars of colored liquid she hadn't noticed before. The jars, in particular, were irksome, since they were scattered about in a haphazard fashion. Some were tucked behind books, others shoved under the long table. She even found one behind the ladder they'd climbed down. At least her guard had helped her find that one, nudging it out with his sandal into her view. Her stomach turned over at the thick, white, viscous contents. She desperately hoped it wasn't blood.

She tripped over the curious dip beneath the podium more than once, and her bad leg complained with each crossing of the room. The air was heavy and stifling with what was probably midday heat from outside. Sweat poured into her eyes and down her neck. The air grew stale, and the work was mind numbing, but she finished the job.

Between death and cataloging, she'd choose cataloging any night. And having notes of this lab and its contents might be useful to the people back home...even though she didn't know what any of the items were for.

"Gather the paper, ink bottles, and quills," Sroc said with another wave of her hand.

A curious request, but Adaris started doing that, too. It wasn't as if she had any choice. At least the young researcher didn't ask her to do any more crafting. Exhaustion seeped into her bones, settling in her soul and calling her to sleep.

While Adaris was busy gathering the quills, Berhn all but fell into the room, barely clutching the ladder on his quick descent. Gripping a blue-green gemstone, he darted over to Sroc. His metal pan thumped next to his hip. Apparently, the Nemora always did carry that with him.

"I found another one!" Berhn exclaimed. He lifted the blue-green gemstone. It was small, only as big as one of his fists, but he looked like he'd found the most precious thing in the world. "This one was closer to the lava river."

Sroc palmed the gemstone, nodding. "Excellent."

"I sense another one close by." Berhn puffed his chest out a little. "I'll soon find it for you."

"You will," Sroc replied. She nudged him back toward the ladder. "Well, what are you waiting for? Go on then."

Berhn waved at the guard, who grinned broadly in return. Berhn flashed a shy grin at Adaris and scurried up the ladder and out of sight.

It actually shocked Adaris that her guard could smile; his stoic expression hadn't changed since she'd met him. The guard and Berhn had to be friends.

"Wonderful." Sroc lifted the gem to the candlelight, drawing Adaris' attention. Running a finger around each beveled edge, Sroc tilted the stone this way and that.

"What's that for?" Adaris asked. Her curiosity always pushed her to get more information. She set the handful of quills she'd gathered on the stone desk. Her leg burned, so she sat on the floor to rest.

"I need these to do my bloodbinding." Sroc's gaze was locked on the gem. "Berhn is the best at finding them."

Bloodbinding? Blood crafting Adaris knew, but bloodbinding was a curious turn of phrase. "And what is bloodbinding exactly?"

"An ancient crafting, scribe. Similar to how Elu can lash light to daygems, but better." A wry grin split her face. "I learned how to do it from that book." She wandered to the podium and flipped through the pages of the thick tome that had caught Adaris' interest before. "This book survived the Great Rift. It's the last remaining tome of those ancient civilizations that were quelled under Ponuriah's fiery wrath."

Adaris started at that quiet revelation. A tome of the ancients? A book like that would be worth its weight in coin. A keystone story all itself, and history unseen in a hundred generations. How the depths did these people find it? And where? The old races could supposedly command all four crafting abilities—Blood, Animal, Moon, and Nature—perhaps that book could explain how. Maybe it even went into why they lusted for more power, how they overused it. How they destroyed their world with it.

It's why the crafting powers split after a great firestorm, and why that crafting ebbed and flowed in people. Nature—the great equalizer—created balance again. That's what she'd always believed anyway.

Her fingers itched to touch that book's ancient pages. "I always thought everything had burned."

"Nearly," Sroc conceded. "But we were born from those cinders, you know, from the ashes of the past. Aluriah, the cold and distant moon goddess, couldn't have created us herself. She needed her fiery sibling and those cinders of the past." Sroc took a deep breath and barreled on. "Yes, Aluriah split the crafting and built our four races as a reflection of what once was, but she couldn't betray Ponuriah's wishes entirely, not her sister. Her elder. The moon is a mere reflection of the sun, after all. The goddess sisters rebuilt the world anew, just like Ponuriah wanted! The moon goddess needed the destruction—ordered it even. You write that down, scribe. Write down the real history of the ancients and of us."

Aluriah ordered the destruction of the world? Adaris stared at Scroc, shocked. She'd never heard such ludicrous beliefs. The researcher must be mad. She'd spent too much time in the sun and it had burned away her reasoning. *Born from the cinders.* If that was the case, the entire Sunglade should be teeming with life. Instead, it was some barren rock full of lava and salt flats. As mad as Sroc may be, her ramblings might be of use. Adaris started writing, the scratching from her quill filling the room. When she lifted her gaze, Sroc was staring at her.

Sroc leaned forward, eyes wide, as if she was spouting the truth of the universe, not some deity-dripping fallacy. "The fire allowed the rebirth, allowed everything we know to exist, and a great fire will do it again. We will call Ponuriah down to burn the world and reshape it into something new."

Adaris bit her tongue. *Truly mad.* Sroc's ramblings had gotten more frantic and, quite frankly, more cult-like. But there might be some seed of truth to these insane ramblings. Though Adaris might not believe in the deities, she did believe in a great fire. Calling down a goddess might be Sroc's way of saying the sun goddess worshippers were going to create a great firestorm in order to cull the innocents. Burn their way to the Groves, perhaps?

Adaris shakily cleared her throat. "You'll call Ponuriah down? How? When?"

Sroc blinked a few times, her shoulders relaxing as her frenzy seemed to ebb. "When we get enough shards to pull Ponuriah's power down, of course. To channel Ponuriah like she commands we do."

She said it so matter-of-factly, Adaris stopped writing. Sroc truly believed she spoke to Ponuriah on a regular basis, like the goddess was real. Commanding them. *Impossible.* Adaris shook her head.

"But I digress. I get...passionate when I think about our goals. What we're going to achieve soon." As if just noticing Adaris was sitting, she asked, "Are you done cataloging my lab?"

"Yes." Adaris flipped back a page to her cataloging, then swiped a hand across her sweaty forehead. If she wasn't going to get to read the book or learn about bloodbinding, at least she could try to get some fresh air. "May I leave now?"

Sroc shrugged again. "If you've already noted what I asked, you can go. Tikova said I should only show you my bound rings. For now...."

That demonstration felt like ages ago. "Then why have you kept me here?"

Adaris had left her book open on the floor next to her, making sure the ink dried in this hot, humid room. Sroc leaned over to scan the page. Without any warning, her small fingers gripped the corner of that page and ripped it entirely out of Adaris' book. Adaris gasped, grabbing the book from her.

"Because I needed my lab cataloged," Sroc replied with a smirk. "And who better to do it than a scribe?"

No one had ever—*ever*—taken a page from Adaris' book without her permission. She checked to see if the young researcher had pulled any surrounding pages loose. Thankfully, the others were undamaged. The researcher merely smiled at her, holding the page behind her back and humming. A game, Adaris realized. This had all been a game.

Annoyed, Adaris rose and started for the ladder. "I'll take my leave then."

"Wait." Sroc heaved a sigh. "There is one other thing."

Adaris froze. Rhonwen's warning came back full force, a wave crashing through her. *What if I overstepped?* She paused, then turned, expecting another test.

"Tikova mentioned you have a limp," Sroc said. "It's obvious, so don't try to deny it. I assume you got it in your youth?"

Of course her limp was obvious, but it seemed like this woman was fishing for her story, and Adaris didn't want to give it. "We didn't have enough healers," she replied.

"As a show of good faith, Tikova wanted me to show you this." Sroc went to her desk and lifted a simple metal band that looked large enough to fit around someone's ankle. The silver metal glimmered in the candlelight; orange crystals had been pressed into it like stars.

Adaris eyed the band, fear swelling in her chest and making it hard to breathe. Despite the young researcher's words, Adaris couldn't shake her fear. Was this anklet a torture device? She wouldn't be surprised. The researcher had ground shattered glass into her own hand. And Adaris hadn't even gotten all the shards out.

"Don't look so miserable. You have nothing to worry about." Sroc twirled the band around her finger. "In exchange for you recording our history and helping me whenever I ask, you will get to wear this. It will make your gait easier. Pain free, even."

Pain free? Adaris' thoughts about a test and fears about being killed were instantly quelled. Pain free. The words might as well be a myth to her. She hadn't walked without pain since the accident. She got up, leg aching from just that small movement, and reached for the band.

Sroc pulled it away. "You'll only get to try it now, not keep it. You'll have to prove your worth first. To Tikova and to me."

Adaris didn't like how Sroc kept mentioning herself—*How would I be any use to the researcher?*—but she assumed there would be more tests. She nodded. Perhaps she was agreeing to more than she knew, but from Sroc's demonstration, Adaris knew she'd have to try that anklet on just to see what it did.

Sroc dropped the band of metal into Adaris' open palm, and Adaris immediately knelt to put it on the ankle of her bad leg. The piece clasped firmly together, the metal bright on her pale skin. "How do I activate it?"

A grin curled on Sroc's lips. "Dip into your crafting. You'll see."

Adaris' stomach tightened into a knot. Her crafting was already tapped, her energy low, and the throbbing in her leg pulled her attention there instead of within. As she called on her crafting, white fog covered her vision, and the familiar ember-like warmth filled her. She waited, expecting to feel something different. Something new. A quiet headache started at the back of her skull.

Biting her lip, she concentrated harder, nudging away her apprehension, trying to ignore the pain. She slowly pooled her crafting at her ankle, as if there were a wound to heal. There. Something brighter answered her. Something hot. The anklet activated, gemstones glowing bright orange.

Bands of heat wrapped themselves around her bad leg, curling around her hip, fortifying her knee, sliding down her bones. The low-level pain constantly thrumming in her leg—one she was able to mostly ignore—vanished instantly. She took a few steps. Her gait didn't roll. Her leg held her weight perfectly. Her heartbeat pounded in her ears and her skin tingled. Excitement and curiosity warred within her. *How the depths is this possible?*

On a whim, she jogged from one side of the room to the other, something that would normally cause her leg to buckle with spikes of agony. She felt nothing. Blissful nothing.

Amazingly, her headache didn't build to pounding like it usually did. In fact, it dimmed.

"How?" Adaris asked. Colors pushed through the white fog over her vision. They seemed brighter than before, though that could just be her excitement. "What kind of crafting is this? Animal, surely, from the color of the gemstones, but what kind of beast can heal a broken leg?"

Sroc waved her hand. "Tikova likes to exaggerate when he talks. This bound artifact hasn't healed your leg, merely buffered the pain and strengthened the bones. The crafting is from a type of sea creature who lives deep in the ocean and deals with the intense pressure of the water."

A sea creature. Adaris was familiar with all kinds of creatures, including ones that lived in the deep oceans, like karks, but how did they lash that beast's ability to this anklet? It must be that bloodbinding Sroc talked about. Adaris had to know more.

Sroc held out a palm. "Now give it back."

Reluctantly, Adaris broke out of her crafting. The bands of heat vanished, the white fog in her gaze completely ebbed away, and the usual dull pain in her leg returned. "What do I have to do to keep this?" she found herself asking, even as she bent down to remove the anklet.

Sroc snatched the jewelry from her. "Prove you're loyal to us."

Adaris swallowed but nodded. Deep inside, she knew this was a ploy, a trick to keep her compliant to their curious demands, to do all the tests they deemed necessary, but she couldn't help herself from fixating on the comfort the anklet had brought, a seeming miracle. Between death and rambling and cataloging and the anklet, she'd choose the anklet over anything else. If it meant she could live without pain, even walk unhindered, she'd do almost anything they asked of her.

Chapter Eleven

ONE MOONLIT EVENING, AFTER most of the community had gone to bed, Adaris sat with Berhn under the Ponuriah statue and pored over her notes from the past couple of interviews. Her guard shifted beside her, dressed in his long white robe again and sighing as he looked at the darkening sky. She still couldn't bring herself to be active during the day, but had been talking to people every dusk and dawn for a few nights, trying to gather enough stories to satisfy Tikova.

Even without the lure of the anklet, Adaris found that a sickening fascination with the place curled within her. She needed to know more about the strange happenings in Sunglade, needed to stay. There were so many stories to collect. These lives were so different from hers, from anyone's back home. She had the opportunity to record them all. Her curiosity lashed her to Slagrock. If she wasn't going to escape right away, perhaps she should try to earn that anklet. At least she'd be comfortable while she recorded.

A twinge started in her neck, and she sighed, rubbing it away. *Depths, my whole body aches.* The hardness of stone furniture showed in the ever-increasing rolling of her gait, in the weakness of her knee, in the thrumming pain shooting up and down her leg with each step. Her mind kept returning to those fleeting moments with the anklet when she'd been pain free. She wondered again about Sroc's research, bloodbinding, and the curious gemstone Berhn had brought down.

She glanced at Berhn, eyes glowing copper as he focused on his gem. The child was quiet, but sweet. Berhn proved a good sitting companion when Adaris got tired. Or lonely. Rhonwen had left a few nights ago, with her guard and a whole lot of paint.

Berhn opened his mouth to speak—

A loud Vagari curse broke the silence before he could.

In the dim candlelight of the Ponuriah square, four figures appeared. A gray-haired woman thrashed against a larger man who held her. Behind them, two others carried armloads of colorful paintings and small metal buckets. The three men wore white robes, but the woman wore filmier fabric that floated around her like a cloud.

Adaris' gut clenched as she recognized the woman in his grasp. Dark-orange blood dripped from a cut on the woman's forehead and stained through a piece of cloth wrapped around her arm. "Rhonwen?" Adaris turned a furious glare on her captors. "What's this all about?"

Rhonwen tugged harder against the man's grip. "Let me go!" The painter dragged her nails across the man's arm, drawing blood.

The man grunted, closed his free hand into a fist.

His punch slammed Rhonwen into the ground. Pebbles sprayed out under her from the force of the blow. She groaned as the man grabbed her and hauled her to her feet.

Adaris rose, tucking her book into her belt. She wanted to help, stop things before someone got hurt any worse, but she was a prisoner, too. What could she do?

Rhonwen's eyes glowed bright orange with her Animal crafting. Her arm shimmered a matching hue, then slipped from the man's grasp. The man cursed, tried to catch her. Missed. Rhonwen darted to the statue and gripped Adaris' hands in her own. Her crafting light dimmed, and pain shimmered in her yellow eyes. Cuts webbed around the delicate skin around her eye from the blow to the face. "Help me!"

"What happened?" Adaris asked. The guard who had held Rhonwen approached holding a small dagger, but Adaris pulled Rhonwen behind her. "What did you do to her?"

"What she deserved," one of the other men snarled. Cobalt blood dripped from his scraggly beard.

"No one deserves to be dragged around like that," Adaris snapped back, the shock of it all making her feel braver than she actually was. She turned to her guard, imploring him with her eyes. "Can you take us back to the hut?"

Her guard gave the men a hard look, then jerked his head toward the direction of the prison hut. Adaris guided Rhonwen while her guard kept pace between them and the men by the statue. A shocking wave of gratitude rushed through her. While she didn't exactly like being guarded, she appreciated his presence. He opened the prison hut door for them, and Adaris pulled Rhonwen inside.

The prison door sighed closed behind them, and the lock clicked firmly into place. Moonlight created pale ribbons of light through the bars, but they needed more. Adaris lit candles until a soft yellow glow soon infused the area.

Rhonwen had shrugged off the cloud of white fabric—a robe, Adaris realized—and now collapsed on the bed.

Adaris moved toward her. "What happened?"

Pushing a trembling hand into her pocket, the painter drew out two aca nuts and chomped on them.

Adaris expected the nuts to calm Rhonwen down, but when their gazes met, Rhonwen's eyes read nothing but fury. "Tikova instructed me to paint the lava river, so I went along with those idiots to get the task done. It's a half-day's journey there. I spent three days working on the painting, getting the shadows and contours perfect, the glossiness of the cooled lava rocks on the embankments, the fiery brightness. I captured the energy of that river. A masterpiece really." Her teeth bared. "Those fools ripped it up!"

"Why?" Adaris asked, setting a candle on the nearby desk. "Tikova instructed you to paint the river. Why destroy it?"

The creamy sleeveless tunic and shorts Rhonwen wore had splashes of color on it. Vibrant orange and crimson. Thick gobs of yellow. A streak of black decorated the painter's chin. "They said it wasn't raw enough." Rhonwen bit off the words as if they were poison. She gestured to the crimson-wave painting leaning against the far curve of prison wall. "It's not the first time I tried to paint the river, and I assume it won't be the last."

Adaris didn't know the art of painting well enough to talk about a painting's rawness. She knew rawness in the stories she recorded—emotions cracking clearly through the storyteller's faces, their eyes most of all—but in gobs of paint? There wasn't a single painting she'd ever seen that seemed "raw" to her. "Tikova must have given them...specific instructions on what he wanted," she offered lamely.

"Well, he should have been there to judge the painting for himself, not get his lackeys to do it. Or simply informed me of what he wanted in the first place!" Rhonwen scowled, pulling up her legs and crossing them. She lifted the piece of cloth away from her arm to inspect the wound underneath and winced. "At least I got a decent hit on one of them in return." Her fingers trembled, and she sighed. "I may have broken my hand doing it though."

"Are you all right?" It was a stupid question. The woman had a gash on her arm and a wound to her forehead. Maybe broken bones, too. Of course she wasn't all right. Rhonwen arched an eyebrow. "I mean, did you want me to heal you?" Adaris had said the words before she realized what she was asking—the offer slipping off her tongue as easily as a lie.

"That would be nice," Rhonwen replied a little too curtly.

Hoping she could actually mend the painter's injuries, Adaris knelt in front of her. As she focused her crafting, the familiar white fog rolled over Adaris' vision. She took note of Rhonwen's injuries. The cut on her forehead. The blow to her face cutting the delicate skin by her eye and making the area swell already. The broken bones in Rhonwen's hand. The gash on her arm. Adaris' crafting warmed to embers inside her, and she gently pooled the power in the veins in her palm.

Rhonwen had become very still, eyes on Adaris in a way that made it seem like the painter could see through Adaris' soul, yet she found she didn't mind the scrutiny.

Reaching out to touch Rhonwen's hand, Adaris pushed her crafting forward, centering it on Rhonwen's fingers and mending the fractures she discovered there. A familiar needling started behind Adaris' ear, a headache building, but she tried her best to ignore it. The painter needed her hands, especially when painting was the only thing keeping her alive. Adaris aimed for the larger gash on Rhonwen's arm next, the worst injury by far, and started to mend that as well. The ember warmth inside her dimmed. She cursed herself for kneeling, because that intensified the fire in her leg and split her focus.

Still, she tried.

Her crafting glowed inside the wound, knitting it up, a thread of light pulling back and forth, back and forth over the gash, but the cut was too deep and her crafting too slow. Her headache brightened. Her vision grew blurry. She closed her eyes, panting and trying to remain conscious, trying to keep healing—

With a gasp, Adaris slumped over.

Rhonwen's strong grip caught her just before her head hit the floor. "You did enough," she said. "I don't need you collapsing on me."

Adaris blinked a few times, the white clouds breaking off her vision and true colors returning once more. She let her crafting fall away and leaned back on her hands. Her headache ebbed to needling, but her leg throbbed as if someone had stabbed it with a rusty knife.

Rhonwen's wound still oozed, dark-orange blood welling, though slower than before. Her shoulders fell. Adaris whispered, "I'm sorry."

"It's not as deep anymore." Rhonwen tore a strip of the blanket and wrapped it around the cut. "And it doesn't hurt as much, so that's good enough for me. I've read how difficult Blood crafting is, so thank you for the effort."

The kind words surprised Adaris. She had expected more bite from the painter, angry as she'd been, but then she wondered how many cuts and bruises Rhonwen had dealt with, if the gash didn't faze her much. "A more skilled crafter could have healed you completely," Adaris admitted, ducking her head.

Rhonwen seemed to notice her embarrassment and changed the topic. "Tikova makes me go away from the community all too often. I think it's so I'm not near my companion animal, so I can't try to set him free."

Guilt twisted like a dagger in Adaris' gut. Spectrum, Rhonwen's slyther. She hadn't even looked at the creature while gathering her stories.

Dipping her voice lower, Rhonwen whispered, "I'm honestly surprised to see you, after you met with Sroc. Most scribes don't return. You've been around the community...have you noticed a way out yet?"

The dagger twisted again. "There's something I need to get first. An artifact."

"What kind of artifact?" Rhonwen asked.

Adaris lifted herself off the floor and sat in the desk chair instead, needing the back brace. Her body trembled from weakness, and she cursed herself for it. "It's...something to help with my leg. Sroc allowed me to wear it and it worked. The pain in my leg vanished!"

Rhonwen's eyes darkened. "And what did Sroc ask of you in return?"

"That I do what she asks, listen to Tikova, and record their stories."

Rhonwen looked at her as if she were crazy.

"Which I was going to do anyway," Adaris hastily added. "I am a scribe, after all, that's my job."

"Not when you get kidnapped by people who burn you alive for a single misstep," Rhonwen snapped. She sighed, rubbing her finger over her eyebrow in the same curious gesture she used before. "Why must I be kept in a prison with someone so clearly swayed? You do know why they're dangling that sweet winter berry in front of you, right? You must know it's to keep you here. To keep you bending to their will."

Adaris bristled. "I know." And she did. It would be foolish to think otherwise. "But the anklet would change my life."

Rhonwen scoffed. "You're already recording their stories, though. What will they ask of you next? And what will Sroc ask you to do? She's dangerous!"

Sroc was creepy, yes, but dangerous? She was basically a *child*...how much harm could she do? Anger made Adaris' neck flush. Her whisper slipped from her like a knife. "I know what they're doing, but I think we should keep doing what they ask. Follow their rules until we come up with a plan. And we still don't know how to get Spectrum free, anyway."

Rhonwen blinked. "You remembered his name."

"Of course." A plan was unrolling in her mind. "You keep struggling against them, like you've been doing so we won't look suspicious. Though maybe tone it down a little." She nodded at the covered gash on Rhonwen's arm. "I'll keep recording their stories and doing whatever Sroc wants, and while I have access to the community, I'll look for a way to free your companion. Could your slyther fly us out of here?"

Rhonwen wilted a little. "I've been here for six hundred nights, and Spectrum hasn't been let out of his cage at all, as far as I know. He could if he was at his full strength, but he..." her voice cracked. "He's so weak. Too weak."

"Okay." Adaris pivoted the conversation, she didn't want the painter to get too upset. "So we'll need a boat, perhaps. Even a small one would do, at least to get us out of here, and then maybe your slyther could ask the animals for help getting us across the ocean."

"A boat?" Rhonwen canted her head.

"Or even just a raft! In the right hands a raft can take you anywhere. If we can sneak away on one, I'm sure I can get us out of here. Tikova wanted to show me the ocean anyway." Her confidence grew with each word until it nearly overflowed. With a boat, she could get all three of them out. She was sure of it. "But only after I get that anklet."

"I don't think—" Rhonwen started, but Adaris interrupted her.

"I'm not going anywhere without the anklet," Adaris warned. She knew it meant more time in the community and more time in danger, but it also meant more time to gather stories. "Think about it, Rhonwen, they want me to gather stories in exchange for the anklet, and the more stories I get, the more damning it becomes. They're telling me their secrets, and I can bring those secrets back home. Do you know what Sroc is doing in that research lab? What she's creating? Bloodbinding. I don't even know what it is, but it's how she creates the glowing artifacts. And do you know they're planning on attacking the Groves? The information I gather can help prevent that, turn the tide in our favor. This is how I can help. This is the only way I'll *ever* be able to help. And I can do so much more with that anklet than I can do without. Now go to sleep. You need to heal, and rest always helps."

Even though Rhonwen gaped at her, Adaris turned away, ending the whispered conversation. A plan rooted firmly in her mind. She blew out the candles and heard some crunching noises that she suspected meant Rhonwen was eating more of those strange, calming nuts, then finally silence as the other woman slowly fell asleep.

Adaris' thoughts deepened the roots of her new plan. Following their orders about gathering stories meant she'd be out in the community. It also meant she had more chances to slip up, to get injured like Rhonwen, or killed. If only she could figure out what bloodbinding was, uncover more of their plans for attack, discover what they were doing with the sun goddess shards...then they could escape... Her mind wouldn't quiet.

Adaris sighed and took a few of those aca nuts out of her bag. One had calmed her down, two had dulled the pain, what would more do? She popped three into her mouth and lay on her back, waiting. Moonlight drifted into the hut, banishing the darkness with its silvery light. The bitter taste of the nuts lingered on her tongue. For a heartbeat, Adaris wondered why these nuts were so popular, why Rhonwen kept taking them. They didn't seem to do much—

The ceiling canted sideways. She blinked, her vision unraveling at the edges. An overpowering calmness barreled through her, wiping all else away. She no longer cared that she was in a prison, or surrounded by sun goddess worshippers, or far away from home. Her body seemed to float, held aloft by the coolest ocean waves. She couldn't tear her gaze from the moonlight pooling on the rock floor next to her—its silvery light turning almost prismatic at the center.

With the serenity came truth as well, her own words reverberating back to her. The only thing she *could* do was gather information. The realization whispered through her. She could never be a Moon Knight, defending the towns and villages from their enemies, but she could be a damn good scribe. Knowledge was power, and she could get so much of it here.

Chapter Twelve

ADARIS LEFT THE PRISON hut as soon as the sun set over the horizon, heading for the center of the community. She'd slept the harsh light away, and the last dying rays of the sun bent around the huts, casting long shadows that Adaris felt comfortable walking in. As comfortable as her twinging leg would allow, that is. Footfalls followed behind her, her guard the ever-present shadow.

She reached the stone-fenced animal enclosure and paused, looking at the large cage in the far corner. A gaunt creature coiled inside, looking more skin and bones than muscle. The back half serpentine end glinted a pattern of rainbow-colored scales. Shiny black feathers covered the front part, with six black wings pressed tight against its body. A patch of multicolored feathers formed a crest on its head, and its bright, yellow eyes locked onto hers over a narrow, black beak.

Spectrum.

The cage had no lock or chains. No hinges. Not even a door. The stone bars were made of one continuous piece of rock, probably crafted by a Hallr Nemora, with spaces no bigger than a finger. Slythers were nimble and could squeeze through tight cracks, but obviously, those cracks were too tight a space for Spectrum. The bars would have to be broken somehow, then the slyther could be freed.

Adaris moved on, not wanting to rouse suspicion from her guard.

At the Ponuriah statue, cobalt and orange blood dappled the ground, dried from the evening before. Adaris' stomach churned. She hadn't checked on Rhonwen before leaving. But a part of her wished she had, just to make sure her wounds were healing properly, but the painter was sleeping when Adaris left, and she didn't want to disturb her. Her guard stopped behind her, waiting.

"Thank you, for yesterday." Adaris shifted her gaze from the blood to her silent guard. "I appreciate you being there for us."

He nodded, curling his free hand into a fist and tapping over his heart twice in a gesture Adaris hadn't seen before. Suddenly, Adaris needed to know more about him and his story. What his *name* even was. This man had followed her around and not spoken a single word.

She'd heard him talk to the other guards before, so she knew he could speak. He just chose not to around her.

"We've spent days together, and yet I don't know anything about you. Where are you from? Where's your companion animal? What's your name, even?" Questions flowed out of her.

Her guard grinned, flashing a set of white teeth. "You need to gather the other stories, Adaris. Not mine."

She blinked. She'd half expected him not to answer. He'd not only spoken to her, he'd used her name. Most people called her scribe. "But you will tell me your story, eventually?"

The guard nodded again.

"Can you at least tell me your name?"

"Kye."

Adaris wrote that down in her book next to his description. "Thank you."

A horrible screeching noise made Adaris' fingers slip, and ink scratched across the page in a thick, dark line. *Depths!* She turned, and her body went cold.

A suncreature nestled its white-shelled body into the sandy area of the animal enclosure, crouching close to the cage Spectrum was in and digging its twin pair of pincers into the black sand. Two narrow segmented tails, each ending in a stinger, curled over its back. Every movement made crimson-orange light pour from the seams between the creature's segments, brightening the area in a terrible glow, until the beast finally found its resting place. Curled in the black sand, motionless, its white body looked like a boulder. Like it had always been there.

Each of its many pairs of eyes opened to gaze directly at her.

Adaris trembled. "Is that a companion?"

"That is." Kye stepped between the suncreature and Adaris. He turned his back on the creature and shifted his trident from one hand to the other almost lazily.

Adaris forced herself to look away from the suncreature. "Yours?"

Kye shook his head. "No." Adaris thought she saw a flash of pain in the man's eyes, but it was gone too fast for her to be sure. *Was his companion even one of the suncreatures that lived here?* It seemed to be a sore spot for him, judging by his expression.

"How do they transform the companions into suncreatures?" she wondered aloud.

He shifted from one sandal to the other; the man actually looked uncomfortable. "Sroc's research assistants would be able to help. Not Berhn..." Kye paused, lost in thought.

Berhn. She hadn't realized the Nemora was an assistant. He seemed too young. *But Berhn's not a boy.* He had chosen male, after all, so no matter how young or childlike he appeared, he was a man in his people's eyes.

"Berhn's your friend, right? The Nemora man with the gemstone and metal pan?"

"Yes," Kye nodded, a smile tugging his lips. "A good friend. Ah." He snapped his fingers. "Celli is the one you need to talk to."

Celli. Adaris hadn't heard that name yet, but she did need to learn more about the suncreature research. "And where can I find her?"

"I see you're still gathering stories at night, scribe." Tikova's familiar voice startled her from her pages. She hadn't heard the man approach, but suddenly he stood almost next to her. "I assumed you would have broken free of that particularly vexing custom after spending time here."

I've only been here ten nights. Did he expect me to shake a lifetime of fear overnight? "I haven't tried yet."

A grin lingered on his lips, but his eyes hardened. "Most of my people work during the daylight. You must as well."

Adaris' gut twisted at his quiet threat. "I will." She forced a change of topic. "So, where have you been?"

Tikova shrugged. "Oh, there was an incident that needed tending. A handful of knights almost crossed the ocean lines. We dispatched them."

"Knights?" Adaris' heart leapt into her throat. The Moon Knights knew this location? And Tikova called it *an incident*? "How many knights? And how did you dispatch them?"

"Only five, and my companion took care of them easily." He lifted a hand to his lips as if just realizing something. "Ah, you haven't met my companion yet. I need to introduce you to her."

"I'd like to meet her," Adaris replied quickly. She'd also like to see the ocean again, see if there were any boats to steal when the time came to escape. The nearby suncreature shifted, orange-yellow light spilling from between its segments again and catching Adaris' eye. Her thoughts turned back to the suncreature research. "I was just thinking about how you turn companions into suncreatures. I was told to speak to Celli. Do you know where she is?"

He nodded and spread his hands. "Come with me."

He led the way to a hut Adaris had noticed before but never entered. It was a larger stone structure than the others, the rock forming a pointed dome. Without waiting, Tikova went inside.

Adaris slipped in behind him, quill and book ready, a thrill of excitement pulsing through her at the possibility of new knowledge. Even after so many seasons of being a scribe, her curiosity never wavered. The entryway opened into a wide sloping space filled to the brim with books and jars of curious liquids. Scales, fur, and feathers littered the ground. Some pure white, others colorful. The hut had no windows, but candles decorated the space, sending yellow light flickering over the cracks in the stone.

An elderly woman hunched over a stone desk, frantically scribbling something in a notebook. Something orange had splattered the back of her smock. Adaris hoped it was paint, but judging by the golden feathers stuck in spots, she knew it wasn't.

Blood caked the floor in placesm, too. For the first time, Adaris' curiosity faltered. She liked animals, bonded with them. She had beasts growing up; a horde of bitterroot fliers—her mother and brother's bloodline—often joined her family on their fishing jobs. Often, she cared more for animals than she did people. Suddenly, research on turning beasts into suncreatures didn't sound so fascinating anymore. It sounded cruel.

She realized Kye had remained outside and swallowed.

"What do you want now, Tikova?" the woman snapped without turning around. Scratching sounds filled the hut, the woman still writing.

"My dear Celli, I'd like to show Adaris the power of the goddess shards." Tikova seemed unfazed by this woman's anger. "Yours, specifically, since she was asking how we can turn beasts into their true forms."

True forms? Adaris worked to keep her face impassive. The guy was cracked, baked too long in the sun to think that the suncreatures were "true forms" and not some base corruption. The mention of goddess shards had pricked her ears though. Dipping her quill into the ink bottle in her bag, she asked, "Is this where the goddess shard I found ended up?"

Tikova pointed to Celli. "Well? The question really is for you, Celli."

Giving an exasperated-sounding huff, the elderly woman spun around, clutching her quill with long spindly fingers that looked more like talons than anything else. A familiar looking crimson shard, wrapped in cord, dangled from a leather band wrapped around Celli's wrist. The goddess shard. Oddly, it didn't seem to give off any unbearable heat like it had in the glass sphere where Adaris found it.

"Yes, I have the shard. Finally," she said, her voice sharp as a knife. Wrinkles lined Celli's face as she scowled. A circlet with a glowing, dark-brown gemstone sat in her graying hair. Her white eyes caught Adaris' attention the most. Not the white of a Blood crafter—the woman was blind. "I suppose now is as good a time as any. If you want to see me use it, little scribe, stick around."

Adaris leaned a little closer to the desk, trying to see the ink scribbled on the open pages. How did the woman write while blind?

Celli slammed her notebook closed, snatched a stone cane off the table, and shuffled to the back wall. There, she swung the cane upward and smacked the stone in a dark curve of the hut that Adaris couldn't quite see into. A squawk came from the darkness, and a few golden feathers fell into the candlelight.

"Come down, my sweet," Celli called.

A gold-feathered thunderclap fluttered to the table, then tucked its head under its wing. The bird looked ill. Feathers were missing in some places, and a small cut on its neck oozed orange. Judging by the overgrown nails and darker leg feathers, this looked like an adult bird...but an incredibly small one for its kind.

Adaris' inquisitiveness rooted her to the spot, but she didn't want anything to happen to the golden bird. "I don't—"

"This is my companion. She was one of our best scouts, found this piece of land for our community in fact. But she's sick, been sick for a long time, and my healing only lasts for a short while before the sickness returns with a vengeance." Celli came back to the table and ran her fingers over the bird's crest. Her voice softened. "We can't find the right blend of herbs I need to help her keep food down. Ran out of them three days ago, and the ship doesn't come for another twenty."

Adaris wrote all of that down. "What kind of herbs?"

"Shadowlock, pinkbells, yellow jaho, a few others."

Yellow jaho Adaris knew, but shadowlock and pinkbells she didn't. "I was transported here in a flash of white light. Couldn't you use that to bring whatever herbs she needs back here?"

Celli shook her head. "I need too large of a supply of the herbs to keep her going. The light only brings people and some small things—smaller companion animals, clothing wrapped tight, sometimes food if we're careful enough. We depend on the ships for the rest, or the other side of the Sunglade. Both of which are too far away. She won't last another day." The woman quivered, as if nervous. "But the shard can save her."

"How?" Adaris moved a little closer to the pair.

"By turning her into a suncreature, of course," Celli replied.

"Her true form," Tikova murmured. "And we need all the research we can get on the power of the goddess shards. Celli is learning what the shards can do for a Vagari."

"Research, yes." Celli kept petting her companion, down its neck and chest, over the worn talons. Her voice cracked. "And it'll allow her to stay with me for a little while longer."

Adaris felt compassion for this elderly lady and her sick bird. The companion bond was the strongest in the world, the Vagari and their companion essentially one, their crafting and powers bound to one another. The corruption had to change the companion animal in some way, but having a suncreature companion must be better than having no companion at all. "I hope it works," she said, the truth falling from her lips.

The elderly woman's snow-white eyes began to glow a vibrant orange as she dipped into her Animal crafting. She put her forehead against her companion for a moment, staring into its beady eyes, then she kissed its feathered crest.

"Give us some room," she spat, waving her arms about her, reverting to the impatient woman from earlier. A shield for her worry, Adaris realized.

Raising both hands, she put one on her companion's neck and the other on its talons. "Come back to me, my sweet," she whispered.

The crimson shard on the band around her wrist glowed brighter. Crimson light filled the space, so brilliant, Adaris had to squint. Just like when she'd found the shard, the surrounding air grew hot, then hotter. Her eyes itched and her mouth grew dry. Sweat beaded at her brow and ran down her neck. She took a step back toward the exit.

Celli's eyes darkened, the vibrant orange from her Animal crafting growing deeper, richer.

Redder.

Her veins illuminated, the crafting flowing outward into her wrist, hands, fingers, and then diving into the sick thunderclap.

The thunderclap trembled. Screeched. The bald patches in its feathering flared crimson before fresh feathers sprouted to cover the damaged flesh. White feathers with red tips. Like a droplet into calm water, its black eyes rippled until they, too, glowed the signature suncreature red.

The crafting dimmed. The heat dissipated. Only the light from the candles, and the crimson shard, and the suncreature's eyes filled the space.

Depths! Adaris blinked away the shock and wrote, her quill flying over the page. She knew it was possible—the master scrollkeeper had told her as much—but seeing it...

So many questions flashed across her mind, each one more important than the last, but she didn't ask. She focused on writing down what she'd seen before she forgot a single detail.

Celli leaned closer to the suncreature. "Are you still there, my sweet?"

The companion-turned-suncreature tilted its head at her, feathered crest rising higher than before. Clicking its white beak, the suncreature nuzzled into Celli's neck, coo-ing with pleasure.

The sight, though sweet, made Adaris' skin crawl. Having a suncreature so close was terrifying.

Laughing, Celli hugged her feathered friend. Tears leaked from the corners of her eyes. "You are! How do you feel?"

The suncreature fluffed out its feathers and shook its head. It dipped its head low and darted to the edge of the table, stretching its wings out. The bird swooped into the air, flapping its long wings to gain height to the very top of the ceiling. Its presence banished the darkness away, each flap of its wings causing its skin to glow under its feathers.

It turned its beady crimson eyes to Adaris and cawed, diving toward her with incredible speed. Claws outstretched, it aimed for her head.

Adaris gasped and stumbled back and away. She clenched her book to her chest and covered her face with her elbow.

The bird missed her, swooping around once more to aim for her face.

"Veris!" Celli snapped, and the suncreature squawked. It changed trajectory and landed on the stone table next to its Vagari companion. "Good girl."

Adaris lingered by the door, keeping a wary eye on the suncreature. It seemed happy now that Celli was petting it. Pressing a hand over her racing heart, Adaris took in a few deep breaths. Nerves skittered under her skin. The scrollkeepers had a record of a Vagari turning a beast into a suncreature, but they didn't know how that was possible. Perhaps she had just made that discovery. Perhaps that Vagari had used a goddess shard.

She tried to distract herself by asking questions. "How did you figure out the goddess shards could do that? Is that all they can do?"

"We had many trials to see what the shards could do. Quite a lot of error, too. We honored those who gave their lives to it." Celli petted her companion's feathered crest. The bird locked eyes with Adaris, its crimson gaze making her squirm.

Adaris resisted the urge to step back. "How many shards do you have?"

"Five, before the Cinder Brigade took them to the salt flat region to test them out," Celli murmured, eyes still on the suncreature.

"We Vagari discovered we could create suncreatures, bend even more creatures to our will than ever before, command even the largest and most dangerous beasts." Celli stroked her companion's feathers, attention wholly on the bird. She seemed happy to talk, now that her friend had survived. "The goddess shards amplify the crafter's powers. So whatever you can do, it heightens to an immeasurable degree, but it's more impressive to show her, Tikova."

"I plan to." Tikova's smile widened and excitement sparkled in his blue eyes. "First I must show her the ocean."

Celli let out a hacking cough that may have been a laugh once, but seemed full of rocks. "You want to show off Pebble?"

Tikova made his way to the entryway leading outside. "But of course! Come, Adaris."

Adaris didn't move to follow him like she usually would. She lifted her quill, eyes only for Celli and the bird. She didn't want to see the ocean any longer. She wanted to see what else these sun goddess shards could do, learn more of their abilities. "I have more questions for Celli."

"You can return later, after she's spent some quality time with her companion."

"But—"

Tikova's voice lowered in warning. "I can very easily get another scribe if the current one doesn't listen."

The threat skated down Adaris' spine, pulling her nerves tight. She remembered the dead bodies during her first tour. How Rhonwen had been injured. Her notes would be useless if she never made it back, so Adaris followed the man out, glancing longingly toward where Celli still stroked the white-feathered bird.

Outside, Kye was still waiting. He trailed in their wake as they made their way through the community to the rock columns. Each step made Adaris' heart pound faster, though not with fright, she realized, but excitement. She had just seen an amazing demonstration of the legendary goddess shards and now she was heading to where she might find a boat to help them escape. Even the constant misery of her bad leg couldn't keep her excitement down.

"Can...anyone work the shards?" she asked, filling the awkward silence that had shadowed them since Tikova made the threat.

"Only those who believe in Ponuriah can work them, those who are her avatars, like Celli." He led the way down the rock stairs tucked behind the stone columns. "Most people in the community can wield the shards, but they work best when wielded by the strongest."

"Why didn't you keep the previous five?" Adaris asked.

"We're merely a research community. The Cinder Brigade has to learn how to use them for the war on the Groves."

She scribbled furiously as they walked. She'd filled six pages with what she'd seen in Celli's hut. That demonstration was exactly the kind of information she wanted to bring back home. No one in her homeland had ever found the goddess shards before. She'd not only found one herself, she also knew how many shards the Ponuriah worshippers had and what they could do in a Vagari's hands. The people of Slagrock wore their secrets like jewelry, showing them off instead of hoarding them, and it was something Adaris would make sure they'd regret.

Chapter Thirteen

THE OCEAN SPARKLED IN the dying light, and Adaris' sandals seemed to sink into the black sand, stabbing white-hot daggers into her knee with every step. Adaris tried to ignore the pain and kept following Tikova. Kye followed close behind her.

The sun had set, but the night air still felt heavy and thick with warmth. Each time the slightly cooler seawater slushed over her toes, a satisfied chill ran up her spine. The Moon Knights had been out there, trying to get to shore, maybe even trying to get to Slagrock to attack this community. The ocean had been her family's livelihood; perhaps it would help her again. Perhaps more knights would come.

"Celli mentioned cargo ships," she said. "Do you keep any here at the community or do they only stay long enough to unload their cargo?"

Tikova glanced at her, blue eyes glinting. "Only long enough to unload. The trip to the other continent takes a while, and we have no need for the larger ships here."

"So you just use the rafts for fishing then," Adaris replied. When Tikova confirmed it with a nod, Adaris' hopes sank just a little. Yes, she could get her and Rhonwen off Slagrock by raft, but a small sea-worthy boat would have been better suited for the trip. They'd need to gather enough water for the trip and navigation would be challenging. Spectrum would probably be of no help, weak as he was. A raft would get them off this continent, but making it home would be a different story entirely.

The rafts she'd seen earlier were cracked and fraying. Her father had taught her how to build rafts when she was a child. She knew she'd be able to lash together a better one. Given the chance, she could make it wider, sturdier. She only needed to find a way to gain access and opportunity.

Swallowing her hesitation, she said, "If you give me some planks, I could make your rafts stronger. I have some experience fishing."

"A scribe from a wealthy family has experience fishing?" he asked, shock clear in his voice. "How curious."

Depths. Of course a wealthy scribe wouldn't be fishing...that was poor people's work. Her family's work. She had to cover her tracks. Right now. She forced a laugh and rolled her eyes. "One of my first duties as a scribe was to record the story of a fisher and his family. I lived on their vessel for a time."

The lie slipped easily off her tongue, but did he believe it?

"A quick study, then. I appreciate that." Tikova rounded a pale boulder that jutted out from the dark sand and followed the curve of the beach away from Slagrock.

Adaris relaxed a little and limped along behind him.

"Ah, here we are," Tikova murmured.

Adaris looked around. There was nothing noteworthy about this stretch of beach. Same waves, same black sand, same rock columns tucked further back on the beach.

Tikova took off his sandals and waded into the ocean. His vest floated out behind him like cream-colored wings. When he turned to her, his long hair drifted around him, bright white strands in the dark blue ocean.

"I'd like you to meet Pebble." Tikova lifted his hands. The sky-blue scales along his chest flashed in the moonlight.

A trail of bubbles approached Tikova, then swirled around him like his own personal whirlpool. The water swelled, then broke as a large reptilian head surfaced. A squallizard with pure-white scales. The creature had four deep-red, glowing eyes and a pearly scaled snout. Its enormous body curled around Tikova.

Adaris stumbled back a step, bumping into Kye.

"I will not let her harm you," Kye whispered from behind her.

Her hands quaked, and she clutched her book and quill to give them something to do.

To her horror, Tikova started walking toward her, one hand on the water's surface, the other on the head of his companion animal.

Saltwater poured from the creature's slender body as it emerged onto the sand. It drew its powerful, fan-like tail out of the water, curling it around its body, then whipping it to the other side. A gust of wind bombarded the ocean, shoving the waves back far behind Tikova, and he laughed.

"She's a showoff," he said, and Adaris was sure she saw the squallizard's long mouth curl in a smile. Tikova looked to Adaris, waiting for her to approach.

She couldn't. Her legs locked into place, knees trembling. All thoughts of the Moon Knights scattered from her mind in the face of this corrupted, glowing beast, who locked all four eyes onto hers. Pebble was the largest ocean creature she'd ever seen.

Kye shifted behind her. Out of the corner of her eye she saw him lift his trident and gently tap the blunt end to her calf. The gentle tap helped pull her back to reality. It was rude not to greet a Vagari's companion when one was introduced. *Say something.*

"Pebble," she whispered, forcing her body a step forward. Her heart thundered in her chest. "Nice to meet you."

Pebble opened her long jaws, bathing Adaris in a blinding, yellow-orange light. Pebble closed her mouth with a snap, and Adaris' hair blew back in the wind. She had to clamp her lips shut to keep from yelping.

"That's her saying hello," Tikova said. He ran his hand over the creature's curved forehead, down her cheek, fingers lingering by her neck. The water puddled beneath the creature was tinted yellow-orange by blood.

"She's hurt," Adaris replied in a rush, hoping her voice didn't shake. "From the Moon Knights?"

Tikova nodded. "A lucky slash. I need to spend some time healing her."

Healing her. But no one could heal suncreatures back home. Her mother said they'd get a piercing headache each time they even tried to connect with one. And why would they even try anyway? Suncreatures were corrupt and dangerous. Deadly. But she had new knowledge now, and these suncreatures weren't just suncreatures, they were companion animals. Adaris swallowed, opening her book to the notes she took of Celli's demonstration. The bond between Celli and her thunderclap was still in place even after the transformation, and obviously Pebble and Tikova's bond held as well...so maybe they could do more than just corrupt their companions, perhaps they could actually heal the suncreature versions as well.

"Sit with us while I do, why don't you? Tell me about the stories you've gathered."

The stories. Adaris was glad for anything to distract her from the fear trying to claw up her throat. Anything to get her away from the suncreature standing so close to her she could see the glow of each individual scale.

"I—I have quite a few, but I'd like to know hers as well. What does she do for the community? And I'd like to know about the attack that injured her."

"Of course." Tikova moved further up the beach, away from the waves and the puddles of water. He sat cross-legged in the sand, and Pebble set her massive snout in his lap. He dipped into his Animal crafting, eyes glowing orange, and rested his palms on his companion's scales. "But you first. Tell me, what do you think of this fine community?"

Settling on the sand, Adaris focused on her book. The sun had completely set, and the pages were hard to read in moonlight alone. Kye, seeming to sense this, brought out a small lamp and a dagger, lighting the candle with an expert strike of flint to the dagger's edge. Yellow light illuminated the area, wavering in the sea breeze before Kye closed the candle inside its lantern.

"Thank you," she said.

Kye merely settled next to her, his trident resting on his knees, barbed tips pointed at her.

Thumbing through the pages, she went back to the first note about this community. Adaris stared at the ink on the page, gathered her thoughts, then began. From page after page, she told Tikova everything she'd recorded, leaving out her own thoughts and interpretations. Facts were all she'd written down, and facts were all she'd give him—scribes were trained to be neutral. She spoke quickly, wanting to ask him questions about his companion animal instead. Deep down, she also hoped she had recorded enough to get the artifact that could make walking easier.

Tikova remained quiet, still as a stone in deep waters. Amazingly—no, impossibly—the orange-yellow blood seeping from Pebble slowed, then stopped entirely. The suncreature closed her bright-red eyes, completely relaxed on the shore. Somehow, Tikova had broken barriers and crafting laws and healed his companion-turned-suncreature. The companion bond had to be the reason he could do such a thing.

Once she finished reading, Adaris inhaled deeply, letting the briny air fill her lungs. "I'll be able to record even more of this community if I don't need to worry about my leg. Sroc showed me an anklet..."

That brief moment she'd been pain free came crashing back on her. Her emotions grew thick in her throat, stopping her words. She remembered how powerful her steps were, how sure her stride without the pain hobbling her. That tiny anklet had given her a moment of freedom. She wanted it so badly. Adaris cleared her throat. "She said, once I'd recorded enough, I could have it. I know an item like that would help me better record your community."

Tikova's eyes dimmed to their usual sky-blue coloring as he released his Animal crafting. "Participate in tomorrow's sunlight celebration and show your budding devotion to us. Perhaps that will be enough to earn the anklet."

A sunlight celebration? She didn't want to ask what a sunlight celebration entailed, didn't want to seem ignorant. She knew, at the very least, it would mean standing out under the sun, fully exposed. Without the anklet, she couldn't run. Her fingers stiffened around her quill.

He leaned back on his palms, eyeing her. Waiting for her.

Testing her, Adaris realized.

He knew she didn't want to stand in the sunshine, that the daytime frightened her. He knew.

Her gut flopped. Tikova was forcing her hand, making her participate in this sunlight celebration, dangling the anklet as a motivation. She knew it, but she wouldn't back down. The anklet would change her life. Perhaps Rhonwen would know more about what to expect.

And it wasn't like she could do anything else but agree when death was the alternative.

"I will," Adaris replied, pulse thundering. When Tikova nodded, she changed the topic to something equally as fascinating, "I see you've healed Pebble. Can you heal any suncreatures, or just your companions?"

Stretching his long legs out on the beach, Tikova stroked his companion animal. "Only our companions. It's a gift Ponuriah gives to us. As for other suncreatures, we even tried to use goddess shards, thought perhaps that would amplify the healing powers, but it hasn't worked...yet." He lifted a handful of sand, then sifted it through his fingers. "We will...perform more tests."

Beside her, Kye jerked slightly and seemed to suppress...something. Adaris snuck a glance at him. The man stared out at the ocean, seeming to be on guard, but his fingers had tightened around his trident.

"Have you done a lot of tests with companion animals?" she asked Tikova, thinking of Celli and her bird.

Tikova sighed. "Many, but obviously more are necessary." He tilted his head to her, eyes bright. "Thankfully the painter's companion is still in its natural form. If we need to start from scratch, we can."

Spectrum. Adaris' chest tightened, but she held onto her passive expression. *Neutral.* She desperately searched for a way to sway the topic away from Rhonwen's companion. "Why did you name her Pebble? Such a tiny name for an impressive beast."

Tikova patted his companion's snout. "Before my parents left to join our forces in White Fields, they told me a single pebble can cause unbelievable ripples across the surface of water. One ripple is all it takes to disrupt the standard way of life. I want to do the same. Hence, Pebble."

Adaris stared at the squallizard, taking in the sheer breadth and length of the massive water beast. Pebble indeed, more like a mountain. One that Tikova would no doubt use to disrupt everything back home.

Suddenly, she had to know more of his story. "You said you have a husband you'd like to get back to, and yet you stay here at Slagrock. Surely there's more reason than for your goddess or for some grand idea of this community. Why are you really here?"

Tikova was quiet for a moment. His eyes darkened. He looked out over the horizon at the ocean and the moon tucked into the sky. "You're the first scribe to ask me that."

Silence stretched between them, until Adaris was certain he wouldn't answer.

His reply came, soft as a whisper. "My parents were discovered as worshippers of the sun goddess. The other Vagari killed them without a trial."

"Ah." Understanding dawned inside her. Her had mother taught her about that part of the Vagari culture, how they could kill a sun goddess worshipper without asking any questions and not be in the wrong. It was brutal, animalistic some might say, but not as brutal as the stories of how Vagari who worshipped the fiery sun goddess would burn their beasts in her honor. Kill their companions. Vagari couldn't accept that.

The only requirement about killing a sun goddess worshipper was that the worshipper had to be committing an obvious crime—stealing wares instead of buying them, for example. "What crimes were they doing when they were killed?"

Tikova gave a bitter laugh. "They had actually just finished helping a wounded fisher. A woman was accidentally stabbed by a fishing spear. My mother and father pulled out the barb. They got blood on their clothes and were heading home to wash up. A Vagari guard saw the blood, assumed the worst, and murdered them."

"And everyone believed the guard?" she asked. She almost didn't care, after all, two less sun goddess worshippers meant two less evils in the world.

Tikova nodded. "Of course. Who would believe a worshipper of Ponuriah?"

For a moment, she wondered if Tikova was lying to make it seem like his parents were innocent victims, but all the usual cheer had vanished from Tikova's voice. A sad, angry man sat on the beach next to Adaris. She knew he told the truth, and while she might not feel sorry for him, exactly, what happened wasn't fair.

"That wasn't right," Adaris whispered.

"It wasn't, but I'll burn each and every one of the Vagari to the ground for their offenses." Tikova pushed his shoulders back and straightened, as if steadying himself. The grin curled back on his lips, eyes bright in the moonlight. "But first, we must research here in Slagrock, we must gather our resources, we must prepare. Then, we'll attack, and we'll win!"

They sat on the beach for a long while. Tikova scratched his suncreature companion animal. Kye watched the horizon. Adaris wrote down the thoughts of a madman. Her leg hummed with pain, constant and steady as her heartbeat. After tomorrow, perhaps it would be different. Perhaps she'd have an anklet. A shiver ran through her at the thought of the sunlight celebration. Whatever it was, she'd force herself through it. She had to.

The anklet would be worth it.

Chapter Fourteen

WHEN THE MOON REACHED its highest point in the sky, Adaris made her way back to the community. She needed rest before the sunlight celebration in the morning. Her stomach gave a little flip thinking about what might be coming. Fire? Sacrifice? Her legs felt heavy and numb as she trod down the curved path to her prison, anxious thoughts shadowing her the entire way. There were no flickering lights inside the huts she passed by, so it seemed everyone had gone to sleep. Adaris' heart sank when darkness greeted her as she reached the prison hut. Rhonwen was probably sleeping, too, which meant Adaris couldn't ask her any questions about the celebration.

One person was still awake. Her ever-present shadow.

Adaris turned to Kye, trying to read anything in his stoic expression. "Do you know anything about the sunlight celebration?"

"Only that they start at midday," he replied. "I've not been a part of one."

Midday. That left some time to ask Rhonwen questions, assuming the painter was willing to talk. They didn't part on such good terms after Adaris decided to stay to get the anklet. She worried that Rhonwen might not want to help her after all.

"Thank you," she said to Kye.

Kye frowned, took in a breath as if he wanted to say something—then opened the prison door and gestured for her to go inside.

She complied. The quiet clank of the lock sliding closed whispered through the dark interior.

Adaris turned to her guard once more, looking at him through the bars. "Kye."

He had already taken up his post outside the prison, but he tilted his head in her direction. "Yes?"

"Thank you for snapping me out of my fear at facing the suncreature." She sighed. "Facing Pebble."

He nodded, gaze slipping back out toward the community. She thought the conversation was over, but then he spoke in a quiet voice, "Do exactly what Tikova tells you. Every single day. Otherwise, the consequences will be severe."

Her mind went back to the dead bodies, the threats. "Death, yes, I understand that."

His jaw tightened. "There are things worse than death."

The firm but honest way he said those words grabbed her attention. Had he experienced something firsthand? As a community member, she thought he'd be spared from threats like that. What kind of people would threaten their own? "Why did you decide to come here, Kye?"

He straightened, tightening his grip on his trident, eyes only for the community before him. "It was of my own volition. Now go to bed."

"But—"

"Rest. You'll need it."

With that, he fell silent once more, and Adaris knew the conversation was over. Sighing, she felt her way to the desk. Rhonwen snored from her bed, and Adaris didn't want to wake her. How could she make certain Rhonwen stayed in the morning, so they could talk? Inspiration struck like lightning. She pulled a spare piece of paper to her and dipped her quill into the ink bottle in her pouch, then scribbled down four simple words.

I saw Spectrum again.

She tucked the note under Rhonwen's precious paint brushes, knowing the woman wouldn't go anywhere without them, then felt her way to her curve of the room. Kye had given her a few spare blankets and her cloak a few nights ago. She'd made a makeshift bed with her cloak, across the way from Rhonwen's. The thin folds of fabric did little to cushion the stone, but it was better than sleeping directly on the rock floor.

Kye's words stuck in her chest. Something had happened to him while he was in the community. Something bad, but what? It occurred to her that she hadn't yet seen his companion animal. As a Vagari, the two should be inseparable...so where was his? She tucked that into the back of her mind for another round of questioning later on.

In the dark and all alone, she couldn't help but wonder what tomorrow would bring. Standing in the sunlight—in broad daylight like a sunsick fool—made her freeze, made her sick, made her panic so intensely she might actually black out. How could she go through with this celebration? Worry coiled within her, spiraled like a whirlpool until she couldn't breathe.

She had to stay calm. She closed her eyes, sank into her Blood crafting, and put her hand on her chest. She willed the fear away. The worry unraveled, and the pain in her chest softened. A slight headache started in the base of her skull, so Adaris let her crafting go, then quickly fell asleep.

Much too soon, something nudged her. Adaris rubbed the sleep from her eyes and groaned. Rhonwen stood over her, shoving her sandal into Adaris' ribs. Pink-orange sunlight sliced into the prison through the bars, making the room glow.

She bolted upright. *The sunlight celebration.*

"Is it almost midday?" she asked.

"No. How did Spectrum look?" Dressed in light layers of white, Rhonwen folded herself into the stone chair. A flash of pain winced through her face, catching Adaris' attention and causing her to look fully at the painter. A new, dark-orange bruise had appeared on Rhonwen's cheek, splitting open at the top by her eye, and a fresh cut sliced her leg just above the knee. *When did she get those?* Adaris' Blood crafting hummed to life. Rhonwen must've noticed her staring because she said, "These wounds are nothing compared to what they've done to me before. Pay them no mind. Tell me about Spectrum."

"He looked...alive." Adaris got to her feet and looked out the prison door instead. The sun had just crested the horizon, closer to dawn than midday. She breathed a sigh of relief.

"And?" Rhonwen pressed.

When Adaris turned back to Rhonwen, hope shimmered in the painter's yellow gaze. The anger that usually simmered there seemed gone, or at least replaced for now. Adaris took advantage of the opportunity to talk. She went over to the desk and leaned against the stone. "I didn't see any wounds, but he looked weak. Haggard. Bonier than I've seen other slythers, but he was alive." She lowered her voice to a whisper. "His cage didn't have a door or hinges of any kind. It was made of one continuous piece of stone, so we'll have to find a way to break it."

"Break it?" Rhonwen replied, just as quiet. "How? If Spectrum can't break the rock, I don't think either of us can."

"Perhaps we'll find something that we can ram into it. Have you seen any carts? If we fill something like that with rocks and slam it hard enough into the stone, it might break."

She knew as soon as she said it that a wagon full of rocks wouldn't break the stone, but Rhonwen looked so unhappy, Adaris had to suggest something. Anything to get back that glimmer of hope.

Rhonwen shook her head. "The only carts or wagons here are the ones that come by when the Cinder Brigade rolls through. Other than that, everything is hand-carried."

"Depths," Adaris said. *Cinder Brigade?* She'd heard that phrase before, but hadn't gotten anyone to talk about it. This wasn't the time. Not with a sunlight celebration looming in front of her. "We'll have to keep our eyes out for another way to break the cage."

"We'll find something." Rhonwen put a hand on Adaris', her voice softening. "Thank you for finding that much out for me."

"It's the least I can do." A small piece of her registered that Rhonwen had willingly touched her hand, that her palm made Adaris' skin tingle. Heat crept up the back of her neck. Not many people willingly touched Divus, Blood crafters, yet this painter did. But Adaris' anxiety about the sunlight celebration was louder than her reaction to Rhonwen's touch. The celebration was in a few hours, and she knew nothing about it. "Do you know anything about the sunlight celebrations they do here?"

Rhonwen pulled back, her hand sliding away and falling to the stone desk. "They had a celebration when I first arrived, but I only heard shouts. Why?"

"They're having one today."

The words set Rhonwen in motion almost immediately. She gathered her paintbrushes in one hand and pulled a blank canvas from the side of the desk with the other. "I'll have to paint it. Maybe try adding more *rawness* to it. Are you supposed to record it? Perhaps we can sit together, in the shade of course."

Adaris would have liked nothing better than to sit in the shade with this beautiful woman as she painted whatever was to come. To have Rhonwen offer that companionship, after being so angry the night before. She must be trying to mend things after their fight.

Adaris sighed, knowing Rhonwen wouldn't like her next words. "I'm supposed to be in it, actually."

"In it...as in, participating? At midday? Why would you ever agree to—" Rhonwen's words shuddered to a stop, realization dawning in her eyes. "They offered you that anklet if you do this, didn't they?"

"Tikova told me as much last night," Adaris replied.

Rhonwen rolled up the canvas and stuck it into her belt. She frowned. "He lies."

"I know, but I don't think he lied about that."

"So, after only twelve nights of doing what he's asked, you think he's just going to gift you the one thing you so obviously want?"

She had wanted to believe that. Though from the shocked look Rhonwen was giving her, doubt ebbed into Adaris' mind.

"You do remember you're not the first scribe to record their history. They killed the ones who didn't follow their rules. And you're not the first kidnapped person to be swayed to their side," Rhonwen said.

"I'm not being swayed to their side," Adaris huffed.

Rhonwen canted her head. "If you do this sunlight celebration, you might as well be."

"And how do you figure that?" Adaris pushed herself off the desk. Her bad leg pulsed from that sudden movement, and she winced. "It's not like I worship Ponuriah, or believe in their cause, or even want to be here."

"Liar." Rhonwen stood as well, gathering some cans of paint and setting them on the desk. "You obviously want to be here. You seem to be fine doing as they ask. First recording their history, now this celebration. What if it's dangerous?"

"If it's too dangerous, then I'll stop," Adaris replied.

Rhonwen sighed, running a finger over her eyebrow again. "Winter's breath, I can see how much you want that anklet. And if you want it as bad as I think you do, I don't think you will stop."

Adaris bit her lip. She wouldn't do anything terrible. It made sense to go through with this...whatever it was. The opportunity for information alone pushed her toward participating. Why didn't Rhonwen see that? "Maybe this celebration will get me more information about how these people work. About why they do it. Does it make them more powerful? More deadly to the people back home?"

"I don't know," Rhonwen replied, voice sharp as a nail.

"Of course you don't." Air left Adaris in a rush as she groaned. "That's the point. No one does! Except them. And now, maybe us, if we record it. You paint everything you see, no matter how small. What they use for the celebration, how they sit, how many people participate. And I'll know how it works from the inside. I'll see if it makes them more powerful. Maybe even figure out how to stop it."

Rhonwen leveled a glare at her that could freeze the deepest part of the ocean. "Your curiosity will be the death of you, and you'll stay here forever because of it."

Annoyance rippled through Adaris. She snatched her book and quill from the floor by her makeshift bed, not wanting to look Rhonwen in the eyes. "It's either do what they ask or be killed, so I might as well go along. I know my notes won't help anyone if I die, so I won't do anything deadly or stay here forever, but while I'm here I'm going to gather as much information as I can. Their stories are valuable. Depths, this might even be a keystone story. I could get a black quill, and the coin that goes along with it."

"Coin? Why are you so concerned about the—?" Rhonwen started but Adaris interrupted her. This wasn't the time to talk about why she wanted coin so badly.

She changed the topic to something Rhonwen would appreciate. "I already learned that the Vagari can heal their suncreature companions; the bond is still active between them. And I discovered how they're creating suncreatures in the first place, by using a sun goddess shard."

Rhonwen waved that away, as if it wasn't the biggest discovery Adaris had ever found. "They're giving you just enough information to keep their hold on you. Don't you see that?"

"No one back home knows how the Ponuriah worshippers are creating suncreatures. No one back home even knows if goddess shards even really exist. They think the shards are a myth! How can you wave that away?" Adaris bristled.

"None of that will save us," Rhonwen replied. "And it won't save Spectrum."

Adaris groaned again, turning away in a huff. "Just paint everything you can, will you? We'll figure out the rest later." She was just about to call out for her guard to unlock the door, when Rhonwen stopped her with a hand on her shoulder.

"Wait." Rhonwen turned Adaris to face her. She pushed a palmful of aca nuts into Adaris' pocket. "If it gets terrible for you, eat some of those. Maybe it'll make being in the sunlight easier."

"No, I want to be clear headed for all of this. I can't let myself sink into that place. Not like you."

Hurt and anger shadowed Rhonwen's face, and Adaris immediately regretted her words. "Fine." Rhonwen bit off the word. "Just be safe then. Like you said, you can't bring back your precious notes if you're dead."

Rhonwen went back to the desk, slamming more cans of paint onto the desk and cursing in the Vagari language. When Adaris turned away, she realized she could have asked Rhonwen how she dealt with being in the sunlight since it didn't seem to bother the painter much. If she knew of any ways to tamp down the all-consuming terror.

But Rhonwen had done just that without Adaris asking. Adaris palmed the nuts, still in her pocket, and called for her guard.

Chapter Fifteen

ADARIS SAT ON THE edge of a long, stone table in a narrow hut she'd stumbled upon a few nights ago. An eating area, judging by the single stone table and racks of drying fish. Kye plucked two from the rack and tossed one to her, munching on his piece in silence. Pale morning sunlight surrounded the hut, and the shadows outside grew ever shorter. Every snippet of conversation Adaris caught had to deal with the sunlight celebration, and worry settled like a stone in her stomach.

Berhn wandered inside. He rubbed sleep from his eyes, then stretched both hands over his head, yawning. He stopped short when he saw Adaris sitting at the table's edge.

Instead of going to the food, he came over to her. "Anoc-suna!" The Nemora word for hello fell gracefully from his tongue.

"Anoc-suna," Adaris replied.

Kye patted the stone bench next to them and grinned at Berhn. The men chatted a bit about small things—the weather, the fish, how Berhn's research was going—random things friends talked about over a meal. Adaris had never seen Kye so relaxed and open than when he was chatting with Berhn.

Berhn placed his thick metal pan on the table and set his usual gemstone inside, then turned to Adaris. "Are you recording the sunlight celebration today?"

"Yes. And I'm supposed to be participating in it, too." Adaris stared at the young man. Perhaps he'd know more about the celebration. "I'm a little nervous. I'm not sure what to expect during the celebration. Have you been in one before?"

"Yes, I've been in a few." He plopped his hands on the table, palms up, as if that proved anything. "My parents said I had to, in order to belong in the community. It's scary at first, but it's not really that bad. You just need to offer some blood."

"Blood?" Adaris' insides flopped like a fish out of water. Her thoughts pulled back to the pile of dead bodies, then to the dried blood in the bowl beneath the Ponuriah statue. Was this a celebration...or a ritual? She pulled her book and quill out and flipped it to an empty page. "Can you tell me about it?"

Berhn pulled his lip between his teeth and glanced outside. “It’s easier to show you. Come with me!”

He got up and in a few short strides walked outside. The Nemora was bathed in pale sunlight. Turning to face her, he beckoned for Adaris to follow. The crystal pattern on his bald head stood out sharply against his dark green skin, and his white tunic nearly glowed.

She didn’t follow him, didn’t move from the table. She didn’t even put her book and quill away. She couldn’t.

“Come on,” Berhn said, gesturing again.

“I don’t...I don’t like being in the sun,” Adaris replied. It probably sounded foolish to him, a grown woman admitting she didn’t like sunlight even as the young man stood in it, but it was the truth. “It’s hard for me to walk in it, like you do.”

Berhn tilted his head. “It’s...going to be hard for you to be in the celebration then. It’s happening midday, you know.”

Adaris forced out a chuckle that sounded more like a sob, trying to ignore the worry rooting her to her seat. “Yes, I know.”

“I—” Berhn stopped for a moment, glancing over his shoulder at the Ponuriah statue...or perhaps beyond it at the huts on the other side of the circle. He came back inside, stopping an arm’s length away from the table. “I can help you with that, if you’d like. I used to be scared of being outside during the day, too.”

“You?” She penned that discovery in her book. “I assumed a sun goddess worshipper like yourself wouldn’t be afraid of the light.”

Berhn shrugged. “When I was very young, I was. As a Ratnaa Nemora, most of my first nights were spent underground, learning about different gemstones and the rock they nestle in, as is our custom. Outside was too bright for me, and the suncreatures were scary back then.”

“The suncreatures are terrifying to me,” Adaris said. “They’re the main reason why I don’t like being outside.”

Berhn nodded and looked over his shoulder again. “My parents taught me how to not be afraid. I can teach you.”

He looked at her with such hope and openness that Adaris closed her book and stood, walking to the edge of the archway. Sitting on the stone bench had made her leg hurt and her back throb. She pressed her knuckles into the small of her back to loosen the knot—and to hide her shaking hands. The morning light created a hard, bright line near the archway. An edge Adaris usually wouldn’t dare cross, but she was curious as to what this Nemora could teach her.

"My parents are wise," Berhn began. "They told me that the only way to truly not be afraid of something is to face it head on. To confront it. Safely, of course."

"Wise words, but there's nothing safe in the daylight," Adaris replied.

"I'm not dangerous." Berhn shifted so he stood outside, the sunlight dappling his head and shoulders.

Adaris laughed, despite the dread clawing up her throat.

"Take my hand," Berhn replied. He lifted his hand, palm up.

The confidence astounded Adaris. "You know I'm a Blood crafter, right?" Only a few people got within arm's length of her. Rhonwen. Tikova. Everyone else stayed out of reach, even Kye. "My kind can kill you with only one touch."

"But why would you?" Berhn replied. "Come on. My parents always told me not to stall, it only makes things worse. Take my hand. I won't pull you out here, if that's what you're worried about."

"Are the suncreatures who live here nearby?" Adaris asked. Her legs were already trembling.

"They're not around right now," he assured her.

Her pulse thundered in her ears. Suncreatures move quickly. Kill quickly. Just like when they'd killed her parents, but she had to step into the sunshine if she was to participate in this celebration...*or get that anklet.* Adaris put her hand in Berhn's. The Nemora's palm was soft and smooth, like glass. Most of Berhn was in the sunlight while all of Adaris still remained in the shadow. "Now what?"

"Now you come out. As slow or as fast as you want," Berhn replied as if it was the simplest thing in the world. "Try taking a step. You can go slow, just keep going."

Adaris put one trembling, sandaled foot into the sunshine. Warmth immediately bathed her pale skin, like she had dipped her foot into bathwater. She held still, muscles stiff and bad leg throbbing under her weight.

"Good!" Berhn flashed her a smile. "See, nothing bad yet."

Adaris inhaled a shaky breath. People were walking in the sunshine and nothing bad was happening to them.

Go slow, but keep going. When she shifted her weight, half of her was in the sunlight. Her heart leapt into her throat. Her gaze shot to the unbroken blue expanse of sky. No suncreatures. No danger.

"Take the step, scribe," Kye said from behind her. "You know I'll keep an eye out as well."

Adaris appreciated the encouragement, but she couldn't make herself move completely into the light. Only sunsick fools would be out in the sunshine. Only people who wanted to be killed or maimed for life would chance that. *Of course, Berhn and Kye are comfortable outside, they live here. Damn it to the depths, they even live with suncreatures!*

She shook her head. "I can't."

Kye pressed the blunt end of the trident into her back. "I can push you, if you want."

"Don't," Berhn said quickly. "The best way to face fears is on your own terms, not someone else's."

The pressure against her back vanished. "Nothing will hurt you under my watch."

It was still midmorning. There was enough time, perhaps not to get comfortable outside but to try standing at least. How long was the celebration? How long would she have to remain exposed?

Rhonwen meandered into the community center, eyeing the statue and carrying a paint can and brushes. Two guards trailed behind her, carrying an easel and even more paint. One of the guards stopped to see the curiosity happening outside their food hut, which caused Rhonwen to turn as well. When their gazes met, Adaris' chest tightened. She wanted to be brave, not only for herself but for Rhonwen. Adaris wanted to show the painter she could manage to be in this celebration, could find more ways to get out of this prison, could maybe even save them both.

Her heart thundered, her whole skin prickled with anxiety, and every muscle tightened like a bowstring. She looked to the sky again. Clear. Her whole being screamed at her to not move any farther, to not take another step, to fear everything she always had because of course there was a suncreature out there waiting to kill—

She stepped fully into the sunlight, eyes squeezed shut. The light seemed to spear right through her flesh, making the insides of her eyelids glow. Her insides clenched. Every ounce of her soul wanted to run back inside, but she didn't. She stayed outside, panting, allowing the sunlight to bathe her entire body. Her skin warmed, then burned.

Berhn squeezed her hand, and Adaris slowly opened her eyes. The bright sunlight hurt her eyes, and she winced. He looked at her with such joy in his wide eyes, but she looked away, expecting to see a suncreature swooping down to attack. Cloudless blue still stretched overhead. Only the sun glared back at her. Her body trembled so much she was sure everyone around her could see, but she stayed outside.

She felt a tug on her hand and tore her gaze from the sky above to the grinning young man standing before her.

"See? Now, all you have to do is stay out here during the celebration. You'll actually have to stand closer to the statue, though." He pointed to the Ponuriah statue. "I can show you where the blood goes, if you'd like?"

"The blood," Adaris repeated. Berhn had mentioned it before, yet the words seemed to slam into her. *The blood. What if they use my blood for something nefarious?* She pulled her hand from Berhn, stumbling back. She'd have to offer some blood for this celebration, this ritual, this whatever it was. These people had kidnapped her. They locked her up. They hurt her. Hurt Rhonwen. They lived with suncreatures. They killed people.

What the depths am I doing?

She twisted away from the sunlight, back to the safety of the food hut. A sharp pain shot through her bad leg, traveling up her thigh, over her knee, and down her calf. She groaned, shifting her weight to the other leg, but the pain only brightened. Her bones seemed set on fire inside her.

Her whole body shuddered and clenched. Her knee wouldn't bend, her ankle refused to take her weight. Even her hip throbbed. That had never happened before. She rubbed her thigh and calf, calming the muscles, easing the tension until her leg relaxed. The deep-seated pain dimmed, replaced with uncomfortable pinching like bugs biting into her flesh, but she'd take that over the white-hot lancing any night.

"What am I doing?" Adaris muttered, eyes only for her trembling knee. Her heart thudded in her ears.

Rhonwen was right. It wasn't worth going through with the celebration. Stay to gather stories perhaps, as long as nothing dangerous happened, but this celebration? The blood? It was all too much. Her shoulders slumped.

"How can you stand being in this community?" Adaris asked Berhn, who had come back inside as well, a look of concern flashing across his young face. She needed to know. Berhn seemed so kind, open. Thoughtful. How could he stand it? "They use blood as part of a celebration. Blood, Berhn."

"It's only a few drops," Berhn replied softly. "And I like being part of the community."

"I know, but they've killed people! There was a pile of dead bodies the night I arrived." Adaris stared at the Nemora.

"I know. Most of this community believes in the..." He shifted from one foot to the other. "...scorching part of our goddess. The revenge factor of her being. But fire can be cleansing, too. It can make things better."

She flipped open her book, needing to do something to calm her nerves. She dove into the familiar waters of her research. Sroc had said something similar. She read aloud from the page, "Sroc told me, 'The fire allowed the rebirth, allowed everything that we know now, and a great fire will do it again.' Is that what you believe?"

Berhn laughed, a light and airy sound. "No, but I think Sroc believes all of it, even the revenge aspect, though I don't know for sure." He paused, biting his lip. "Did you know there are certain seeds that need to be burned in order to sprout? And that intense heat—like volcanoes—makes things sweeter, especially the vegetables and fruits that grow nearby? Sometimes, rare flowers can even grow after a fire burns the other vegetation away."

"No," Adaris replied. She wrote it down, using the familiar sounds of quill scratching the paper to calm her nerves.

"Well, that's the aspect of Ponuriah that I believe in. Fire can be good, heat can make things better, sweeter," Berhn said.

It seemed like he honestly believed in an almost gentler form of Ponuriah. It was a side of Ponuriah that Adaris had never heard of. "But...they've killed people."

"But not all believers in Ponuriah do," Berhn replied. "My parents have never hurt anyone, and neither have I."

"So, even though you don't believe exactly what they do, you like to live with them," Adaris said.

"They protect us." He glanced away when he said that, gaze skating to the sunshine and the Ponuriah statue outside. "I can guide you into the sunshine again, when it's time, like we were doing before."

Her insides roiled. She couldn't bring herself to look at the sun moving steadily to its apex.

"I can help, too, Adaris, if you'll accept it," Rhonwen said.

Adaris hadn't noticed her come inside, and it shocked Adaris to see her there, offering aid. The painter lingered next to the table. Her two guards flanked her. The paint cans and the easel had disappeared, probably stashed into some shadowy corner where Rhonwen could settle down and paint the celebration to come.

She felt like a fool for snapping at Rhonwen earlier. The painter had been in Slagrock longer than she had—over six hundred nights, for depths sake—and Adaris had foolishly ignored her warnings. She knew the community, knew how to navigate it, had survived this long...and Adaris had walked away from her.

Adaris' hands trembled as she closed her book. "Why would you help me after what I said?"

"Because you obviously need it," Rhonwen replied, though a smile softened the blow.

Rhonwen was being nice to her. It felt like the world was tipping and Adaris couldn't hold on to anything. "I'd be grateful for your help," she admitted.

Chapter Sixteen

THE SUN BURNED ADARIS' skin, its brightness making her wince. She lifted her hand to shade her eyes. Her whole being told her to stay still, to crouch somewhere in the shadows, but she kept walking, heading to the Ponuriah statue. The hairs on the back of her neck stood at sudden attention. She glanced up and saw two creatures flying overhead, shadows against the blinding sun. Gasping, she dropped her gaze to her sandals and forced herself to keep moving.

She no longer saw her feet or the cracked stone beneath them.

She saw the ice that rimed her family's boat. She felt the searing pain as her bones cracked, and remembered the swelling panic as she pushed all of her crafting and more into her brother to save his life. She saw the bodies of their parents, torn and bloodied, floating next to her, lifeless eyes staring at the cloudless sky.

Rhonwen nudged her. Sometime in the memory, Adaris had paused. She blinked the memories away. Her vision swam and blurred. She squeezed her eyes shut and reached for Rhonwen to keep her steady. Adaris felt dumb, reaching for her as if they were friends, like this woman who hated her for a good reason would actually, truly help her. The painter twined their fingers together, an anchor in the coming storm, and Adaris' eyes popped open.

"The suncreatures are far above us," Rhonwen whispered, looking at the sky.

"They could still dive down to kill me," Adaris replied harshly, trying to put on a gruff attitude to hide her anxiety.

Rhonwen squeezed Adaris' hand. "I doubt that would be part of the celebration."

Yet Adaris couldn't help glancing around like a cowering thunderfawn. Dread threaded through every piece of her, from her sore leg to the churning in her guts, to the tight muscles bunching in her shoulders.

She walked on, keeping her eyes on the ground and on the light pooling orange-red like lava on the stones beneath her sandals.

Conversation picked up around them, and Adaris' gaze rose to the white-clad people gathering at the base of the looming Ponuriah statue.

Tikova stood waiting like a proud father watching his children return home. It seemed the entire community had come for this celebration. Sroc stood next to the stone statue. The red Ponuriah sculpture rose high above her head, wreathed in stone flames.

Rhonwen and Berhn veered away from Adaris, heading to the garden area that had a perfect view of the statue. Adaris assumed they would stay there to watch. She longed to go with them but continued limping toward the statue and to the familiar leader of the Slagrock community.

Tikova's white vest lay by his feet. A calm expression lingered on his face. "I'm glad you came, scribe."

"I wouldn't miss it," Adaris replied, proud that her voice didn't shake even though her body trembled. *Because I didn't have a choice.*

He bent to roll his knee-length shorts up to his thighs, then slipped his sandals off. Adaris thought it was a curious act, but then she realized everyone around her was doing the same, rolling up their pants, taking off their light airy layers, or stripping entirely until they wore the bare minimum to keep decent.

"We do this to get the full effect of the sunlight," Tikova explained. "But if you're too modest, you don't have to strip. Sroc doesn't."

Next to him, Sroc scoffed, still in her layers of leathers. "You know I honor her in other ways."

Adaris glanced at her outfit. She definitely wasn't taking off her tunic; it was already sleeveless, for depths sake. Her exposed skin burned in the rays of the sun, but she'd heard the challenge in Tikova's voice and rolled her airy pants that normally cinched at her ankles up to her knees.

Tikova's eyes danced, watching her for a moment, then turning to the crowd. He lifted his arms. "Welcome everyone, to the sunlight celebration. Let us begin!"

The crowd of people cheered, and far overhead, the flying creatures shrieked. Adaris winced from the high-pitched noise, glad the shuffling crowd paid no notice. People formed a long line that coiled around the Ponuriah statue.

Throat tight, Adaris started to join them, but Tikova grabbed her shoulder.

"You stay by me," he ordered. "Help Sroc heal."

Not a shadow in sight, she'd be required to remain in broad daylight. Adaris gathered her courage and stood next to him. As the crowd moved, she forced herself to watch, wrangling her composure into something resembling normal. Sweat beaded on the back of her neck. It felt like hot wax coated her skin.

A shadow fell over the crowd and Adaris gasped. A huge, scaled creature thudded onto the ground, just beyond them all. A wyvern suncreature, judging by the leathery wings and massive jaws and the spiked tail. A smaller, feathered creature fluttered down next to it, one Adaris didn't recognize. One by one, the other suncreature companions arrived—the serpentine beast, the thunderclap, the hard-shelled creature that guarded Spectrum. The community members ignored them, but every time Adaris snuck a glance toward the suncreatures, one of them stared back at her. Crimson gazes locked onto hers. Unnatural. Terrifying. Shivers went down her spine.

Kye stepped between her and the creatures, and she could finally breathe again.

The first person in line—an elderly Nemora with a crystal pattern on her exposed, pale-green skin—offered her arm to Tikova. The woman looked familiar. It took Adaris a moment to realize the woman must be Berhn's mother; they had the same eyes.

Tikova pulled his white dagger from his belt and flourished the gleaming blade in the air. He lifted his eyes to the sky, to the sun. "We give our blood to our goddess."

"We give our blood to honor her," the Nemora replied.

Tikova dragged the dagger across the Nemora's forearm, slicing a deep cut into the woman's skin. He turned her wrist, and brown blood poured from the woman's arm into the stone bowl waiting below. The Nemora didn't wince, didn't gasp, didn't respond at all to having her arm cut open. She merely lifted her gaze to the sky and smiled.

The sharp, metallic scent of blood hitting hot stone reached Adaris, and bile rose in her throat.

Next to her, Sroc's eyes glowed white as her Blood crafting took hold. The young researcher put her hand on the Nemora's arm, slowly healing the cut.

What a curious celebration. It seemed almost...harmless, since the person was healed moments after they gave blood. Perhaps it was simply a bonding experience? She wished she dared to bring out her book and quill to record the ritual. *I'm here as a participant, not a scribe. Tikova made that very clear.* She'd have to write what she could remember later.

The stone pathway cracked and shifted. Milky white beetles with crimson eyes pushed up from the ground. They swarmed around the statue in an intricate dance that kept them away from the boots of the crowd. Their multifaceted eyes seemed to stare at Adaris. Her heart beat like a caged bird. Had they come for the blood, or were they someone's companion? She didn't have a chance to determine which as the next person stepped up and offered their arm.

"You take care of that one," Sroc said. Adaris nodded absently.

She automatically dipped into her Blood crafting and healed the wound. It took her much longer to heal than Sroc, but she did as she was told. They alternated healing, while Tikova conducted the celebration. Focused on her task, she almost forgot she stood in the direct sunlight, almost forgot the heat pressing down on her and the sweat beading on her brow. Almost, but not quite. And she almost, but not quite, forgot the prickling on her leg, like bugs biting into her skin.

The slight needling in her head grew to pounding. Her vision blurred, but she forced herself to stay upright. Sroc healed three times as fast as Adaris, but if the young researcher noticed, she didn't say anything.

As multicolored blood brimmed in the bowl, the line grew shorter, the coil tighter. The people who had already offered their sacrifice lingered to the side in a group.

Suddenly, the line ended. Only Adaris, Sroc, and Tikova remained. Adaris blinked her crafting away, snapping her connection to her power and wishing her headache would fade. It was hard to focus when pain danced behind her eyes and sent needles through her skull.

Tikova turned to her and lifted his hand, obviously waiting for her arm.

She hesitated. The Ponuriah statue towered next to him, the red gemstone eyes staring down at her. The heat radiating from the stone seemed to increase the longer she stood beside it. She didn't want to offer her blood, but she had to know why these people went through with it. She had to know what happened next. Everyone seemed to be watching her, waiting for her. She felt each and every one of their gazes.

"We give our blood to our goddess." Tikova's blue eyes bored into hers, challenging her.

Adaris offered her arm. "We give our blood to honor her."

The words flowed from her. While it might be true for these people, it was a downright lie for her. She'd told enough lies to make the statement ring like truth, though, and Tikova gave her a satisfied grin.

His blade bit into her skin. White blood welled over her pale flesh almost instantly. Clenching her lips to hold back a gasp, she turned her wrist downward. Her blood poured into the bowl, white spreading into the orange and brown and blue.

Sroc immediately touched her arm. The burst of heat wound through her arm, and white light knit the wound. Rubbing her mended arm, Adaris joined the other participants. They formed a very clear empty circle around her, not willing to get closer than an arm's length away. Kye took up his usual post at her side.

Tikova turned to the crowd, his eyes bright and excitement clear on his features. Sroc knelt and dipped the fingers of one hand into the bowl of blood, muttering something. Her eyes still glowed white, her Blood crafting winding its way down the veins in her cheeks and neck, under her clothing, and into her fingers. *What the depths is she doing?*

"Very good, everyone," Tikova shouted. "Are you ready to see the fruits of our research? The real reason for this sunlight celebration?"

The crowd cheered. The suncreature beetles swarmed back, seeming to make room for Tikova. Adaris stood transfixed. *The fruits of their research?* Her fingers itched for her quill.

"I need a volunteer for this demonstration," he yelled.

His gaze narrowed on the crowd before him. For a horrible moment, Adaris thought he was searching for her, but he latched onto an elderly pair of Nemora. Adaris recognized Berhn's mother. The man was a much older version of Berhn. Deep wrinkles lined his dark, green skin.

Tikova pulled him to the statue. "Reach out for our goddess," he commanded.

The elderly Nemora did as he was told, lifting his arms to the Ponuriah statue. The crystal pattern on his naked back glinted. He looked at the Ponuriah statue for a long moment, then lifted his gaze to the sun.

Tikova nudged Sroc with his foot and the young researcher rose. Blood dripped from her fingers. She rummaged around in her pocket and produced a large crimson crystal. *A sun goddess shard!* Adaris hoped Rhonwen was capturing this moment. The painting could be helpful when Adaris recorded the story in her book later.

Tikova spun. Something flashed in the light. Both of the Nemora's outstretched arms thudded onto the stone, severed at the elbows.

The elderly man screamed and fell to his knees. Brown blood gushed from the stumps that used to be arms.

Adaris gasped. *Depths!*

Berhn's terrified yell cut through the air.

The short sword in Tikova's hands dripped blood, but he looked down at the screaming Nemora with a smile.

Clutching the goddess shard in one bloody hand, Sroc put her other hand on one of the Nemora's stumps. The crimson shard glowed, and a wave of heat flashed out from it, slamming into the crowd. Adaris' eyes and skin tightened from the instantly dry air. The moisture in her mouth turned to ash, but she couldn't look away.

The young researcher concentrated, sweat beading on her brow.

Bone stretched from one of the severed elbows. Tendrils of muscle slipped out of the wound. Tendons anchored bone and muscle in place. Finally, dark-green flesh covered the limb. Sroc had created an entirely new forearm and hand for the man. She'd regrown the Nemora's limb. He looked down at his new arm, eyes bright with tears of panic turned to joy. Sroc reached over and regrew the other one.

The entire crowd was silent as awe settled over them. Adaris had never, ever seen crafting like that. Blood crafters could mend a terrible wound, the most powerful could even bring someone back from the brink of death, but to regrow a whole arm? Two arms? Only the ancients could do crafting like that. This was the fruit of their research. Adaris recalled Celli saying the community had been experimenting with what goddess shards could do. What kinds of tests did they have to do to figure out how to regrow limbs? How many errors were made before they realized its limits?

Depths, what are its limits?

The Nemora flexed his newly grown fingers, his elderly face slack with wonder. Berhn's mother rushed to him, kneeling and grabbing him into a hug, a smile brightening her features. Berhn fell at his parents' side, sobbing.

Tikova stepped forward, arms outstretched, exultant. Then he laughed. The sunbaked idiot actually laughed. The crowd started laughing, too. Like a bubble had burst, the entire community erupted into cheers and shouts of joy. Even Berhn's parents were smiling, though it didn't escape Adaris' notice that Berhn himself didn't join in.

"Who's next?" Tikova shouted. Horribly, the crowd yelled back, asking for their turn.

Nausea swooped through Adaris, pushing her back as if struck. She turned away from the Ponuriah statue and Tikova's laughter. Kye followed as she broke through the crowd to discover Rhonwen standing at the edge of the pathway. Crimson dripped from the paintbrush she clutched, easel obviously forgotten behind her. Her brown cheeks had paled.

Adaris grabbed her arm and pulled her to their prison hut in silence. If this was what they deemed a celebration, she didn't want to wait around for anything else.

Chapter Seventeen

THE PRISON DOOR SWUNG shut, and for once, Adaris was glad to hear the lock click into place. Even though it was a false sense of security it felt better to be locked in with Rhonwen than to be out there with the worshippers.

If Tikova did that to his fellow community members, Adaris didn't want to think about what he would do to her if she stepped out of line.

Rhonwen sank onto one of the stone chairs by the table, her head in trembling hands. Adaris went mutely to the other side. The moment the backs of her knees felt the stone, her legs crumbled beneath her. It felt like her lungs were paper pressed beneath a brick. She pulled her flask from her belt and drank deeply of the stale, warm water.

"What the depths was that?" She rubbed her aching leg to give her hands something to do.

"I—I can't believe they just severed that man's limbs off," Rhonwen muttered. "I can't believe the experiments worked."

"You knew they were researching how to regrow limbs?" Shock pulled Adaris upright.

A deep shiver vibrated through Rhonwen's body. She lifted her knee to her chin, angling her sandaled foot toward the light and running her fingers over her toes. Three of her smaller toes ended in abrupt and ragged stumps, the nails completely gone. "After I tried to push Kye into the river of lava, they punished me by using me as a test subject."

Adaris gaped in horror. The skin over what was left of Rhonwen's toes had puckered and turned a deep, dark orange. Blood crafters could've knit the skin back together smoothly. From the look of the area, it didn't look like they'd tried at all. Her horror twisted, turned sour, made her mouth feel like ash. "No one tried to heal you?"

"They said I wasn't worth the energy." Rhonwen tucked her foot under her knee, then dug into her pocket and lifted a handful of aca nuts to her lips.

"Wait!" Adaris put her hand out, and Rhonwen paused. "We need to talk. I have news and I...I need you to be here when I tell you."

Rhonwen blinked at her. "Be here?"

"You know what I mean," Adaris replied. "I need you to be alert."

A bright orange flushed Rhonwen's cheeks. She clutched the nuts in a trembling fist. "Listen, Adaris, I just saw a man get his arms chopped off. For show." Her voice lifted to a squeak. "I need to calm down, right now."

Rhonwen's wide eyes couldn't seem to find a purchase, and her whole body trembled. She looked...younger. Adaris' age. For the first time, Adaris actually saw the scared Vagari Rhonwen was. The woman trapped, caged, like her companion animal.

Adaris was so used to seeing Rhonwen angry, or judgmental. It shocked her to see the painter scared, and a strange urge overwhelmed Adaris, a protectiveness she hadn't felt before. "Moon Knights attacked the community," Adaris whispered, leaning closer.

"What?" Rhonwen locked their gazes. "Where did you get that information?"

"Tikova told me last night. I'm not sure when the knights attacked, to be honest, but they wounded Tikova's companion animal. He told me about it while he healed her. He has a squallizard, by the way."

Rhonwen waved her hand, nuts forgotten on the table. "Pebble, yes. I've seen her. Do you think someone's coming to save us?"

"I don't know. Tikova just said they just attacked from the ocean. Since the ocean failed, I would think they would fly here."

Rhonwen nodded, then drew a finger across her eyebrow.

Finally, Adaris realized that rather curious gesture was a calming method. Her own mother had used it to relax baby slythers.

"The knights attacked. I can't help but hope they'll do it again." Adaris leaned forward, resting her elbows on her knees. "We need to be ready."

Rhonwen paled. "We haven't gotten Spectrum out yet."

"I was thinking about that." Adaris twisted a lock of her long hair between her fingers, gathering her thoughts. "Maybe we can use one of the artifacts. I saw Sroc melt stone, like a Hallr Nemora, with one of the rings she wears. Maybe one of us can steal it...use it to melt Spectrum's cage?"

"Steal it from Sroc's finger?" Rhonwen gave a dry laugh. "Apologies, but that's highly unlikely."

"Then we look through the other items. Sroc had quite a few on her shelves. Or maybe even the other research huts."

"I haven't ever been to Sroc's underground research area, and I can't bring myself to visit Celli's hut. Every time I'm near it, I can't help but think they'll do their research on Spectrum. What about the artifacts the community members wear? Can we find out what they do?"

Adaris scrubbed her face with her palm. "That might be too obvious. We can't give any of our plans away."

"You're here to record their history," Rhonwen replied, giving her a small smile. "The glowing jewelry is a big part of their story."

She was right, obviously, but the dead bodies plus the casual way people told her she wouldn't last long haunted Adaris. Worry gnawed at her. It would be too suspicious to ask everyone about their glowing jewelry. Too obvious. "If I ask the wrong questions, I'm likely to end up like the other scribes."

Another cheer ripped through the air. Laughter followed the wind to their prison hut, only to be pierced by a shriek. Both of them winced, turning so their backs faced the door.

Rhonwen leaned closer and touched Adaris' hand. "Well, you're the first one who I think could actually get us out of here."

Adaris' hand tingled, and she hoped the painter couldn't see the heat spreading up the back of her neck. She didn't move her hand away. "Why?"

"You stepped into the sunshine and did the celebration. I honestly thought you wouldn't, even with the promise of that anklet hanging over you like a winter berry. Other scribes couldn't face their fears like you did. I don't know for sure, but I think that's one of the reasons Tikova killed them. They didn't stand up to his threats. You did." Rhonwen squeezed her hand, didn't let go. "It was quite brave."

Pride swelled up inside Adaris, a warm wave spreading through her core. She'd never really considered herself brave. Moon Knights were brave; adventurers were brave. Scribes were just...there, recording the stories and bravery of others. "Thank you."

Rhonwen's smile could rival the stars and win.

Suddenly, Adaris wanted to learn more about Rhonwen, more about her story, her background. Adaris knew about her mother—Mica Kia, the chief stargazer from Celestial Abbey—but not much else. "What's it like, being a painter?"

"Awe-inspiring. My gallery in Cahoma draws quite a lot of visitors, even from the far south and the islands. I paint mostly scenery and beasts, sometimes portraits." Rhonwen's voice lifted with excitement, seeming grateful to latch onto a conversation completely separate from what was happening outside. "I want my paintings to show people places they've never seen before. Perhaps places they'll never be able to travel to. And the coin isn't bad either."

Adaris nodded, despite a slight pang of jealousy. Rhonwen probably made enough on a single painting to purchase a whole boat, a whole season's salary of a fishing family. Adaris enjoyed her life as a scribe, but it wasn't the best in terms of coin, and having coin made everything easier. Their lives were so vastly different. Adaris compared her small stream of decisions to Rhonwen's ocean of opportunities.

"Traveling the world is enjoyable, too," Rhonwen continued. "I have the opportunity to see so many things and bring them back home. It must be similar for a scribe."

"Only for wandering scribes. Most of us stay in the Athenaeum of the Ancients, or the smaller libraries scattered about. It takes a lot of work to tend the histories and connect the stories together."

Rhonwen cupped her chin in her hand. "But you're a wandering scribe, right?"

"Yes." Adaris smiled, happy that Rhonwen was curious about her work, too, happy also to talk about anything but this community. "I wanted to join the Moon Knights when I was a child. They have the best adventures saving people. My leg held me back, so now I record their adventures instead. They do the really important work, after all."

"Recording history is also important work," Rhonwen said quietly. "And you do get to have adventures. See the world."

"It's not the same as saving people," Adaris replied, rolling her eyes.

Rhonwen shrugged. "Then save us. Put yourself in a history book."

She said it so cavalierly, as if it wasn't the most daunting thing in the world, as if they both couldn't be killed in an instant the moment either one stepped over Tikova's line, but Adaris appreciated the outlook all the same.

"I plan to do just that." Her words sounded braver than she felt.

"I'll hold you to it," Rhonwen replied. "Are all your family members scribes?"

Adaris gave a dry laugh, stalling for time. She didn't want to tell Rhonwen about her family being fishers. She was proud of her family. It was a good, honest life on the sea during her childhood, but to a painter who used expensive gemstones regularly in her work, a fishing family would be rather boring. Still, the pressure of Rhonwen's hand on her own and the open look of curiosity on Rhonwen's face made Adaris want to tell the truth.

"I come from a fishing family," she said. "I lived on our ship as a child, sailing the oceans, snagging ocean creatures when we could and selling to the highest bidder. It was a good life."

"Oh." Realization lit Rhonwen's eyes. "So that's why you're confident a raft can get us home. You said a raft can take us far with experienced hands. Your hands."

"Yes, I meant mine." Adaris bit the inside of her cheek, thinking. She wanted to tell Rhonwen the whole truth as to why she'd made up the story about her mother. Why she lied to try to get the coveted black quill. Why she ruined Rhonwen's mother's reputation in the process. *Now is as good a time as any.* But where would she even begin? "The thing is, it's not a profitable endeavor. My family barely scraped by each season when we were younger, even though my parents were very good at what they did."

Rhonwen tilted her head, obviously curious as to where this conversation was heading. "So that's why you want the black quill. To get the coin to help your family."

Adaris blinked. Rhonwen remembered that, too? The painter was smart, scary smart; she remembered conversations almost too well. "Well, kind of." Adaris' nerves bubbled up inside her, jumbling her words. It was hard to think. She had never told anyone the real reason why she lied, not even the master scrollkeeper. "My parents actually died from a suncreature attack, a long time ago, but my brother still lives."

A furrow appeared between Rhonwen's eyes. "I'm sorry to hear that," she whispered.

The genuine warmth in Rhonwen's voice made Adaris' throat tighten. "You asked why I lied about your mother's career. I did it because my brother got sick with the bixy fever. It's a rare sea-faring disease from the deep waters. It's crippling at best. Most often it's deadly. Even though I'm a Blood crafter, I couldn't heal him. I didn't have enough strength. He needed a better healer, a real healer at the medico, but the cost was sky high. I told him I could get the coin." She gulped air, emotions taking over. The truth fell fast from her lips, guilt burning across her face to her ears. "I tried. I really did, but none of my stories were worth another quill. None were important enough. So, I lied to get the black one. I deemed Mica Kia's career worthy of ruin in order to save my brother, but I got caught, and I didn't gain the black quill, and even worse, I didn't get the coin."

Rhonwen's eyes widened. "And your brother?"

"He had to sell our family's ship just to pay for the healing, but waiting so long made his condition chronic," Adaris admitted quietly. Saying it out loud hurt. "My brother has a terrible cough, now, one that rattles his lungs like a can of nails. He can't even lift a kark cage from the water, and his crafting has gotten difficult to use. He trusted me to get the coin, and because of that one lie, I sank that hope to the bottom of the ocean." She shook her head. "Lying was selfish and idiotic, and it cost much more than I might've guessed."

Rhonwen had gone quiet. Her gaze drifted to the stone table between them, to her hand still resting on Adaris'. "It must have been very hard for your brother to sell your family's livelihood."

The lie had cost Rhonwen's mother her livelihood. Rhonwen had said the lie caused an avalanche inside the abbey. *Did I ever apologize for it?* Shame stabbed through her when she realized she actually hadn't. *Depths! Even now I'm being selfish.*

She turned her hand palm up to grasp Rhonwen's. "I know it cost your mother's reputation as well, Rhonwen, and for that I am truly, deeply sorry. I wasn't thinking about her. I was being selfish."

Rhonwen tucked a lock of her sword-straight hair behind her ear and drew a breath. Stalling, just like Adaris had been. "Thank you for apologizing," she finally whispered.

"How is your mother doing? Does she still have a job at the abbey?" Adaris leaned forward. It was a question that had niggled her for many nights after she was caught.

"No, she lost her position as chief stargazer. Even though your master scrollkeeper came forward about your lie, she can't get another position there." A bitter note permeated Rhonwen's reply, one that wrinkled her forehead and creased the sides of her mouth like she had eaten something sour. "The Celestial Abbey's reputation was on the line, so they had to get rid of the tarnish. They even gave my mother a bad mark—one that says she'll never be able to work there or in one of the auxiliary locations ever again. Her entire schooling, all the training, her research, dreams. Gone. Very publicly, too. The shame made her move. Ma Le'Shawn—my other mother—gave up her position and went with her."

Adaris leaned back, guilt twisting in her gut. She'd heard that Mica had moved away, but never suspected her reputation was so completely tarnished that she'd never be able to work at an abbey. "What does she do now?"

Rhonwen frowned. “She works at my gallery in a very behind-the-scenes role. Ma Le’Shawn said they could work together, trying to rebuild Ma Le’Shawn's curator business, but Ma Mica didn’t want to drag Ma Le’Shawn’s reputation down, too. She didn’t want to work with me, either, but she needed a job.”

“I’m so sorry,” Adaris said again.

“I think Ma Mica will eventually join Ma Le’Shawn as a curator. It would be more fun for her.” Rhonwen sighed. “And the abbey is worse off as well. When other scribes descended on the Celestial Abbey to research and record the incident, they discovered a handful of missing books from the Halls of Knowledge, a drug ring run by the lesser stargazers, and even some banished folk hiding in the tunnels. Apparently, your lie brought to light some actual truths that the abbey didn’t want anyone to know about. Many other people lost their jobs, too.”

“Wow.” Adaris couldn’t believe it. *All I had to do was dig deeper for the truth and I’d have had a scribe’s dream find. Yet I chose to take the quick fix and lie. Such an idiot.*

“Wow indeed. The Celestial Abbey is in chaos!” A rueful smile twitched on Rhonwen’s lips.

“I...I don’t know what to say,” Adaris replied. Her thoughts spiraled with all this information, about Rhonwen and her mothers and how her lie had transformed so many lives.

Rhonwen lifted one finger and tapped Adaris’ hand idly. “Say you’ve learned your lesson, that you won’t lie about something so important again.”

“I did learn my lesson.” Adaris swallowed the lump forming in her throat. “But I still do lie occasionally, and I might have to lie to get us out of here.”

Rhonwen nodded. “I think we both might have to.”

A third cheer rose from outside, followed by a wail of pain. Rhonwen went pale and clutched Adaris’ hand tight.

The need to run ripped through Adaris, but there was nowhere to go. They couldn’t leave, not yet, not without Spectrum and a firm plan of escape. The cheering outside grew impossibly loud. She stared at the white aca nuts, thinking through the options, then finally pointed toward them. “Shall we?”

A noticeable wave of relief rippled through Rhonwen’s features. She lifted four nuts from the small pile and ate them, and Adaris did the same. The bitter flesh burned Adaris' tongue, so she washed it down with a gulp of water.

A calmness flowed into her, taking over almost immediately. The cheering outside dimmed. The hut grew fuzzy, and all her worries washed away. A small part of her hoped Rhonwen would stay with her at the table, but the painter released her hand and stood, seeming to float to her bed.

Sleep pulled at Adaris, too. When she stood, she felt weightless, like she could float, or fly. Settling down on her bedding, the hard stone floor actually felt comfortable. The usually suffocating warmth of the midday sun cradled her into darkness. Sleep did not come soon enough. The wind carried to her another scream. Another limb severed. The imagination was almost enough to push the dulling nuts away.

Almost, but not quite.

Chapter Eighteen

DESPITE THE HORRORS ADARIS witnessed, the sunlight celebration seemed to put the entire community in good spirits for the next couple of days. Rhonwen stayed in the prison, painting furiously, yet still too shaken to leave. With Kye ever in tow, Adaris ventured out each night, careful to head out before the sun dipped below the horizon, careful to walk in the sunshine for a little while to show anyone who was watching that she could.

And to prove it to herself, too.

She made sure to stay away from the community center, avoiding the Ponuriah statue. Nothing, not even the promise of the anklet, could pull her toward that statue. Her stomach turned violently each time she tried to go that direction, so she went a different way. She kept to the circular path and watched the ocean horizon for glimpses of sails, of hope.

She didn't see any.

Four nights after the celebration, Adaris sat outside the food hut, half in the rusted orange rays of the setting sun, half in shadows. Her face, neck, and shoulders itched and burned from the sunlight celebration. She opened a tiny jar and slathered on some yellow nut butter, the fourth application just this evening. She sighed as it immediately cooled her wounded skin. Rhonwen had given her the jar, saying she didn't need it, though Adaris did catch the darker orange spots on Rhonwen's brown shoulders and forehead.

Adaris wanted to prove to Tikova that she could stay outside, so she stayed in the sunshine, even when he didn't threaten her into doing so. She wanted to prove her worth.

She eyed her book propped open on her lap. Normally, writing helped ease her fears. She would pour herself onto the page, so she didn't have to feel, but she couldn't write about what happened. Her hands shook too much. Reliving the memories was too much. Her blood mingling with the others. The sickening squelch of severed arms landing on the rock. Berhn's piercing wail. The cheers after. *Who would cheer after such a terrible display?*

A tremble passed through her, but she clenched her jaw against the lingering panic. She hadn't seen Berhn since then, and worry tugged on her for the young man and his elderly parents. What happened to Berhn's father after his arms were regrown? Had Berhn's mother been chosen next? The tears flowing down Berhn's cheeks made Adaris hope his family didn't partake in any more of the celebration.

Her gaze lifted from her book in her lap to the statue. Tikova hadn't asked her to record the celebration, but she knew he would. And she knew she should. It was one of the reasons for her actually participating, to bring that information back home—that and her want for the anklet. That and the threat of death.

She stood and stretched, skin prickling as the warm sunlight spiked across her skin. *Go slow, but keep going.* Trying to ignore the familiar catch of breath when she looked to the sky and the thud-thud-thudding of her heart like a pyerwolf throwing itself at the walls to be free, Adaris walked into the sunshine and headed for the Ponuriah statue. Kye followed a few paces behind. She'd grown to like her constant shadow more and more. He had proven, time and time again, that he was on her side, or at least, not willing to hurt her like some of the other guards.

Despite the small comfort of her guard, each step of her numb body felt heavy. It would have been lovely if her bad leg went numb, too. Instead, her leg protested every single movement. Her leg seemed to have gotten worse over the last few nights. The pain frightened her, reminding her of the never-ending sharp throbbing in the first season after she'd been injured.

Still, she limped onward until she reached the Ponuriah statue. Her gaze settled onto the bowl of dried blood. Sighing, Adaris opened her book and began to write what had happened that day. Her gaze kept drifting to the bowl. Sroc had dipped her fingers in the bowl, that had to be important; they had to use the blood for something.

Adaris needed to find out what the blood contributed to the celebration, not just for curiosity's sake, but also for her own wellbeing. She was a Blood crafter. She had studied the art of crafting, the ebb and flow of the inner working of the body and mind. Never in her life had she seen or read a ritual such as that. To her knowledge, after blood left the body, there was no use for it anymore. Perhaps that wasn't the case. She kept writing until she'd gotten the whole encounter down on the page. It felt good, getting it out of her, and she was glad she'd forced herself to do it.

The back of her neck prickled like someone stared at her. She looked over her shoulder. People were milling about, going into the food hut, chatting and laughing, but no one was specifically watching her. She pulled a long lock of crimson hair over her shoulder and began twirling it between her fingers, then focused on her book, ensuring that she got every detail down, no matter how gruesome.

"I'm glad to see you out and about." Tikova's voice startled her.

She swallowed a yelp of surprise and looked up. Tikova was leaning on the Ponuriah statue. His grin and easy manner didn't mesh with the violence he had done during the celebration, and she couldn't help but look for the short sword he had used. He wasn't wearing it, and for that she was grateful.

"I'm glad to see you as well. You disappeared again these last few...days," she replied with a forced calm. It felt strange to say *days,* when really she meant *nights,* but the community used days to show the passing of time. "I assumed you'd want to be with everyone after the sunlight celebration. It was quite spectacular."

"I'm impressed you participated," he said with deliberate slowness. Adaris' heart leapt to her throat. He had promised her the anklet if she participated. Was he going to offer it? She made herself nod, accepting his compliment and trying not to appear too eager.

Tikova continued, "Some of our fishing equipment was damaged during the attack, so Pebble and I have been helping at the waterfront, trying to patch things up. Since you mentioned being with a fishing group for a time, I thought you could help."

Adaris refused to let her disappointment show. She wanted to see the rafts anyway, to take a closer look at the fishing area and see if there was anything they could use to escape. "Of course," she replied smoothly, getting to her feet and closing her book. "Lead the way."

Tikova and Adaris walked through the community, down the rock columns, and to the black sand beach. Adaris purposefully exaggerated her limp, rocking with each step, trying to nonchalantly remind Tikova of the anklet and the promise he'd made. If he noticed, he didn't comment.

They reached the fishing hut she had seen only once before, the familiar scent of fish guts and rot permeating the area. Her gaze cut to the jagged hole in the rock, just behind the hut, the one that led to the area where Sroc did her research. *Bloodbinding.* Sroc's term slammed into Adaris, and she rocked onto her heel. Tikova went on ahead. He rounded the curve of the fishing hut closer to the ocean and disappeared. Adaris didn't follow. Her realization anchored her to the spot. Perhaps that was why they needed blood—to blood bind. Whatever that was.

Kye cleared his throat. When Adaris gave him a questioning look, he tilted his head to the ocean. "Tikova is that way," he muttered.

"Oh, yes. Thank you." She turned her back on the rock columns and circled around the squat fishing hut to the side facing the ocean. Trident spears leaned against the walls. Her heart skipped at the sight of gleaming metal and curved hooks. They were collapsible to be portable, but with a long enough reach to capture a sea creature. She couldn't fight worth a lick, but she knew her way around that kind of tool. Her childhood had been full of such tools. *Such weapons.*

Her sandals crunched over the small bones littering the sand and stone. When she reached the front of the hut, she gasped at the shattered hole. Something had clearly crashed through. The impact had broken the stone table and chairs, severed the fishing wire, and snapped the poles. A few community members picked through the area, talking quietly to one another while they cleaned.

Tikova said their fishing area had been damaged, but she hadn't expected this much ruin. It almost seemed like the attack was targeted.

A splashing sound behind her drew her gaze. Her spine straightened, nerves slowly starting to wind up again, as she turned to the ocean. Tikova had gone thigh deep into the water and was currently hauling back a tired-looking wood raft. It was one of the first wooden things she'd seen since she arrived.

He pulled it onto the beach. "Can you fix this? It's our only one left."

Adaris took one look at the unraveling cord loosely weaving between the thick, worn logs. She shook her head at the large gaps between the logs. Someone had tried to patch up the raft with a plank of wood acting like a crossbeam, but the nails weren't long enough to secure it. His request would be almost comical—if the question wasn't being asked by someone who could outright kill her.

Adaris chose her words carefully. "It would be easier to make a new one than to try to salvage that."

"I assumed as much." Tikova kicked the raft. "Our resident fisher left for the other continent on a supply run and never returned. Our food supply is low as it is; we need this raft to fish."

"Couldn't you just call the fish to you with your crafting?" It wasn't an honorable thing to call creatures over for the slaughter, but she'd seen her mother do it on rare occasions when things got dire. She'd also heard her mother crying when she thought everyone had gone to sleep.

"They've gotten smart and don't come around. We have to fish for them out in the deeper waters."

Smart creatures indeed. "Do you have any more wood? If you can grab some of that, I can make a raft for you."

Tikova brightened. "I hoped you'd say that." He clapped and the water behind him swelled. Pebble's giant head broke from the churning foam, her jaw clamped around numerous planks of wood. The creature dropped the wood on the beach at Tikova's feet. "How long will this take?"

"As long as it needs," Adaris replied, keeping her gaze firmly locked on Tikova until Pebble disappeared once more. She pointed to a dry spot behind the hut. "Can you take the planks over there, please?"

Tikova pursed his lips but nodded. He picked up one plank and brought it over. Kye hauled the rest.

She looked around the broken fishing hut and gathered some necessary supplies—coils of thick rope, long nails, a hammer.

Even with her skilled hands, it took her the rest of the afternoon and well into the evening to create the raft. Doing this work reminded her of home, of her childhood, of long nights on the ocean with her parents and brother, looking at the stars and wondering what life would bring. A simpler time.

What if I never make it back? Adaris' hands stilled on the wooden planks. *What if I die here like the others? Or have my arms chopped off as an example—*

"Here." Kye lit a flickering lantern, and yellow light permeated the area. He misinterpreted her stillness for blindness, rather than the fear clawing within her.

Still, it was a nice gesture, and it shook her from her spiraling thoughts. "Thank you, Kye," she murmured, and got back to working on her raft. It wouldn't do to dwell on what might happen and get lost in fear. She had to focus on what she could do. What she had to do to survive. That meant making a raft, so she finished it. She stood and winced. It was getting harder and harder to ignore the spike of white-hot pain in her knee.

Tikova sat on the beach with Pebble. The massive suncreature slept, which was the only reason why Adaris felt comfortable walking closer. That, and Kye walking next to her.

Working with her hands to build the raft, doing something so familiar, had made her bold. She'd done the celebration like he asked, and she'd built this raft for his precious community. Adaris wanted that anklet. *Damn it all to the depths, I'm going to get it.*

"It's done," she said.

Tikova leaned to the side, looking around her toward the hut. The raft was shrouded in darkness, but Adaris knew he could still see. All Vagari could see in the dark. She'd always been jealous of her brother's ability.

"It looks quite sturdy," he finally said.

"It is," she replied. *Now or never.* Tikova seemed satisfied with the raft. She'd done more than her share in the bargain. She squared her shoulders. "I did more than participate in the sunlight celebration, by the way, I recorded it, too." The change of topic made a wrinkle appear between his eyes, but she ignored it. Opening to the start of the celebration, Adaris gave her book to Tikova and watched in silence as he read over her notes. "And I want to learn about bloodbinding."

He tilted his head back to look up at her, white hair flowing over his shoulders. His blue eyes shimmered in the rising moon. "Do you now?"

"Yes. Sroc mentioned the term when she showed off her glowing rings, and we offered blood in the celebration. I assume it's connected somehow."

Tikova chuckled. "Bloodbinding is one of our more interesting discoveries. You'll have to do more to earn your right to record that."

"Then you'd better believe I will." Adaris shocked herself when she realized what she'd said was true. She needed to figure out what this bloodbinding process was. It had caught her curiosity and hooked deep. She had to know more.

Tikova leaned back on his hands, gaze raking over her, through her. "I know you will," he said. He rummaged through his pocket for a moment, pulling out something that glinted orange and dark silver in the moonlight.

Adaris' eyes widened. *The anklet.*

He held it out for her. "And I think it would benefit us both if your leg didn't hurt as much while doing it." He offered her the anklet.

For a heartbeat, Adaris hesitated. This was a trap. It couldn't be this easy, even though she had faced a primal fear and given blood. It hadn't been easy.

This offer felt like another test, his grin more like a prowler's than anything else. If she took the anklet...what was she agreeing to? She leaned back on her heels. As if in reply, her bad leg throbbed. Even with that tiny a movement the dizzying pain was overwhelming.

Frustration seared through her, making her neck flush all the way to her ears. Her leg always held her back. She could do so much with that anklet, be so much with it. She could do more than record stories. She could have adventures all her own, ones scribes would talk about for ages after. Without her leg dragging her down, perhaps she could be the hero, instead of simply writing about them.

Adaris took the anklet from Tikova's palm and a thrill of excitement pulsed through her. Every part of her being wanted to wrap the jewelry around her ankle and activate it right away. Her crafting sang, answering the impossible joy coursing through her veins.

She didn't want to put it on in front of him. Didn't want to give him the satisfaction of seeing her so overjoyed by his offer. Forcing herself to contain her glee, she nodded. "Thank you."

He gave a dismissive flourish with his hand. "Make sure you put that in your book, scribe. Note how kind we've been."

Rhonwen's severed toes flashed through Adaris' mind. The bruises and cuts. The pain echoing in Rhonwen's frown, in the wrinkles around her eyes. Adaris blinked the memory away. "Of course."

"Now go enjoy it!" And with that, he waved her away.

She went gladly. Footsteps told her that Kye followed, as always, but she hardly noticed her surroundings or if anyone else was awake at this time of night.

"I haven't ever seen a scribe get a bound artifact before," Kye's quiet voice rumbled beside her.

"Really?" Adaris' lips tugged into a smile she couldn't contain anymore.

He nodded, a curt gesture. "You've done well."

"Thank you."

Clutched so tight in her shaking hand that the gemstones made impressions in her palm, Adaris had a piece of jewelry that would change her life forever. An anklet.

She could hardly wait to put it on.

Chapter Nineteen

AS SOON AS THE prison door locked behind her, Adaris searched the shadows for Rhonwen. Moonlight streamed inside, casting the shadows away in vivid slices of white light. The hut was empty. *Perfect.* She wanted to try the anklet before Rhonwen got back and didn't want to deal with her judgmental stare just yet. Adaris knew this simple piece of jewelry would literally change her life for the better, and that should be celebrated.

She all but melted into the stone chair by the desk, both excitement and fatigue making her wobbly. The anklet looked so neutral in her palm, the orange gemstones winking at her like stars in the dark, silvery metal. When she bent down to secure the artifact around her ankle, her knee protested even that simple motion. She dipped into her Blood crafting all the faster. She remembered, from her brief time with Sroc, that she had to activate her crafting to activate the anklet. A quiet warmth filled her core, spreading through her body like she had just sunk into a bath. White fog rolled over her vision, and a headache throbbed just behind her ear.

Adaris pushed past the pain, excitement pressing her onward. She directed her crafting to her ankle and activated the orange gemstones. Heat pulsed from the metal, wrapping like bands around her bad leg. She felt the crafting strengthen her bones and reinforce her knee, even twining around her hip. The shooting pain immediately vanished.

She stood and tested her weight on her bad leg. It held. She walked a few paces and quietly laughed when it didn't hurt. A few quick circles around the hut had Adaris beaming. Not even the slightest twinge. It was as if she had an entirely new leg. She wanted to see how far she could press this little piece of jewelry and the crafting locked within.

She clambered onto the desk chair and leapt off, landing on her bad leg in a way that would usually make her collapse in agony. She twisted, knelt, and rose. She even hopped on her bad leg. Not even a twinge of discomfort.

Adaris couldn't keep the grin off her face, the smile so wide it hurt. She didn't know when she'd last felt this happy—meeting her younger brother for the first time, landing her first big catch to help her parents, being handed her teal quill—none of that held a daygem to the joy she felt. She pressed her hands to her forehead, mind dizzy with possibilities, ideas unrolling before her like a scroll.

I can do anything.

Curiously, amazingly, astoundingly, the headache she always felt when calling up her crafting dulled. The white fog ebbed, clearing her vision. *What the depths is happening?* The price for her crafting never subsided, and the white fog never went away. Adaris lit a candle on the desk, then pulled out her book and quill, not even bothering to sit as she scribbled her findings. The prison door opened with a squeal, but Adaris didn't look up to see who had entered.

"Wouldn't it be easier to sit down when you write?" Rhonwen murmured in an annoyed tone. She set down some paint cans and brushes with a clatter and started to organize her paintbrushes.

Adaris chuckled. "It would, but not today."

Rhonwen must have heard the delight in Adaris' voice because she stopped. Her piercing, yellow gaze caught Adaris', questions clear in the wrinkle between her eyebrows. "Your smile is disconcerting. What's happened?"

"I got the anklet." Adaris pushed her bad leg forward and gestured to the anklet that glowed on her pale skin. It looked so simple, yet did so much. She was reeling from it all.

Rhonwen sank into the chair, staring. "Tikova...he gave it to you already?"

"Obviously, I couldn't do this without it." Adaris balanced on her bad leg and hopped a few times. It was silly, but she couldn't help being playful.

"It's active, like the others I've seen..." Rhonwen muttered. She didn't seem to notice Adaris' show, gaze riveted on the glowing jewelry. "Are you crafting right now?"

Adaris lowered her foot at the strange question. "Of course. I have to use my crafting to keep it active. I'm not sure how others are able to keep theirs active all the time, without using up all of their energy."

Rhonwen's eyes widened. She went to her bed and rummaged around the belongings she kept tucked against the wall. She retrieved a mirror no larger than her palm. "Are you sure?" Rhonwen lifted the mirror to eye-level with Adaris.

Adaris' own storm-gray eyes looked back at her. The milky glow from her crafting had vanished. *Depths!* That's why the fog had ebbed. The ember warmth was still there, her crafting still present, but the headache that came with it had dulled to nothing. Her energy didn't waver like it always would, like all Divus crafting demanded. Life energy for life energy.

She was crafting, without the price.

Crafting, without the sacrifice.

The world seemed to tilt with this revelation, and excitement made her pulse race. Perhaps it was how everyone could have a glowing piece of jewelry without their eyes brightening to match. They could use their craft without expending the usual price—life energy for Divus, strength for Vagari, elemental backlash for Nemora, scarring for Elu. Could the jewelry work indefinitely?

The experience stunned her. “Amazing.”

“Terrifying.” Rhonwen lowered the mirror.

“Why?”

Rhonwen looked at her as if she’d grown a second head. “What kind of crafting is this that doesn’t exact a price?”

“Maybe it’s part of the bloodbinding process,” Adaris said, recalling the conversation she’d had with Sroc.

Rhonwen blanched, backing up until she reached the desk and sat. “Which is what, exactly?”

“I’m not sure,” Adaris replied. When Rhonwen shook her head, eyes full of doubt, Adaris amended, “I’m not sure yet, but this is amazing, Rhonwen. Truly amazing.”

“I…understand how life-altering this is for you,” Rhonwen said in a quiet voice, “and a part of me is glad you have it, that you can use it to walk easier.”

Adaris heard the caveat tucked between her words. She noticed how sober Rhonwen looked and sighed. “But?” she prompted.

“I don’t want you to be manipulated by it.”

“In what way—

“Listen, it’s an astounding gift. The fact that everyone here has something like it says how powerful this community actually is, but these are terrible people and…and…”

“And what?” Adaris strode to the table and sat, her earlier worries crashing back into her mind and sticking like barbed hooks. She had wondered if it was a test. She’d hesitated before accepting Tikova’s offer of the anklet.

Rhonwen sighed and toyed with one of her paintbrushes, as if needing time to gather her thoughts. Orange paint stained her brown fingers. “Winter’s breath, it’s called bloodbinding. Bloodbinding, Adaris!

I've never heard of such a term before. I'm just worried that they're doing something awful to create such powerful artifacts."

Adaris let those words sink in, her excitement subsiding. Her shoulders slumped. She hadn't wanted to think the offer of the anklet was too easy. It probably was a manipulation on Tikova's part, but she could use it to gain what she wanted to know. She could discover what this bloodbinding was and bring the information back home.

Opening her book, she tapped a blank page. "Well, that's what I'm going to find out."

Rhonwen bit her lip and looked away, her body rigid. Adaris knew from the crease in the painter's forehead that she was still nervous. *Nervous for me.* Rhonwen's concern warmed Adaris' soul. She took a fortifying breath and reached for Rhonwen's hand. Rhonwen didn't flinch or move away, so Adaris took that as a good sign and twined their fingers together, just like Rhonwen had done for her when she faced the sunlight.

"If you ask the wrong question, Tikova might..." Rhonwen paused, squeezing Adaris' fingers tight. "I just don't want you to die like all the other scribes."

Adaris' fingers, palm, hand, depths, her whole arm tingled from Rhonwen's touch. The world seemed to dim, tighten, until it was just them, sitting alone, by candle and moonlight. "I don't want either of us to die," Adaris replied. "Did I tell you I made a raft tonight?"

"A raft?" Rhonwen tilted her head. "Why?"

"Most of their fishing stuff was destroyed in the battle, and Tikova wanted my assistance. I made a raft for them. A good one, too. They'll be quite happy with it. I think that's one of the reasons he gave me the anklet." She lowered her voice to a whisper. "The raft was actually my father's design. And now we have a way out, since Spectrum is too weak to fly. Once we get Spectrum and gather some supplies, I'm hoping you can call in a few favors with your Animal crafting to pull us far away from here."

Rhonwen leaned forward. Her stiff shoulders relaxed, yellow eyes full of what Adaris assumed was hope. "That's ingenious."

A burst of pride rushed through Adaris. "So, I'm not just a useless scribe anymore, eh?" She teased.

Rhonwen was staring at her as if she was seeing someone new. A curious expression lingered on her face. She gripped Adaris' hand tighter. "Thank you, Adaris. Truly. You've been like a lovely starlight in a place where all mine had vanished. I'm glad to call you my friend."

Adaris' heart tripped at the words, but she simply nodded. "Thank you for pushing me, for making me think about my actions."

Rhonwen nearly giggled, a light airy sound. "We shouldn't push ourselves much longer, I'm afraid. I'm quite tired. It's time to sleep."

Adaris agreed and they each went their separate ways. Rhonwen curled into her bed. Adaris blew out the candle and settled down on the floor. She didn't actually sleep. She couldn't. Her mind turned over their last moments of conversation. A grin settled on her lips.

Lovely starlight? Rhonwen's phrase felt like an embrace and made the emotions she was trying desperately to contain threaten to break loose. Rhonwen was clever, resourceful, loyal. Even the fact that she was an artist was terribly attractive. Adaris could feel herself falling for her more and more each night. Not in love, nothing as deep as that, but falling into emotions she wanted to explore. *She might not feel the same way,* a more logical voice whispered in her mind. *And here certainly isn't the place for a relationship. More than anything else, Rhonwen needs a friend.*

Once they escaped, perhaps Adaris could pursue something more. Perhaps more than friendship, if Rhonwen was interested, but not now. She shored up those emotions again, burying them deep.

She deactivated the anklet, and the bands of heat unwound from her bad leg, a small ache returning. The pain brought her back to reality like a fish slap to the face, to where she was and how much danger they were in...but nothing could erase the tingles she felt course through her each time her and Rhonwen touched, or the curious look in Rhonwen's eyes that evening. If nothing else, even if nothing happened in the future, the hope gave her another reason to get them both back home alive. She let her eyes close, still thinking of Rhonwen.

Adaris woke to the wisp of a paintbrush over canvas. Groaning, she rubbed the sleep out of her eyes and glanced through the barred windows. It was nearly as dark outside the hut as behind her eyelids. It must be well before dawn. A whispered curse floated to her. *Why the depths is Rhonwen painting?* Adaris rolled to her other side, facing the interior of the hut. Rhonwen sat by the desk, working on a painting by faint, flickering candlelight.

"What are you doing?"

Rhonwen looked over her shoulder, flourishing a brush that dripped crimson. "I didn't mean to wake you."

"That's okay," Adaris replied, even though she still wanted to sleep. Her body felt warm and heavy. Sleep still curled around her.

Rhonwen leaned down to grab another can of paint, and Adaris caught sight of what she was working on. Tikova, sword held high and dripping brown blood; the elderly Nemora standing before him, arms severed; Sroc nearby, raising the crimson goddess shard high in preparation. Like a splash of ocean water, the painting jarred Adaris awake. She propped herself on her elbow to look more closely.

Each figure was rendered in such clarity—Tikova's smirk, the pain in the Nemora's body, the confidence in Sroc's eyes—it was like Adaris was there again. Rhonwen emphasized the goddess shard in this rendition, the image stunning with shadows and highlights. The crimson color seemed aglow. Adaris knew that was meant to be the focal point, but she couldn't stop staring at the people. They looked...raw. There was no other word for it.

Tikova told Rhonwen that her work wasn't raw enough, so she went ahead and captured this.

"That's why you were out yesterday," Adaris said.

"I was in the community center. I actually went out to see Spectrum, but they wouldn't let me close to him." Rhonwen stiffened.

Adaris despaired for her friend. A Vagari not being able to see their companion animal was a soul wrenching experience, like half of themselves had gone missing. *That's why Rhonwen was in a sour mood when she came back last night.* "I'm sor—"

"It's what they do," Rhonwen cut her off. "So, I negotiated. I promised Tikova that I'd paint something truly spectacular. He said if I did, I could see Spectrum for a few moments."

"Your painting is stunning." It wasn't an overstatement. The painting, though gruesome, was striking. Adaris could see a wealthy merchant paying a good amount of coin for the likes of that back home—probably enough to pay for a small house.

"It'll be worth more than a few moments with Spectrum, but even that is more than I've had with him in over three hundred nights. I intend on showing this to Tikova in the morning." Rhonwen lifted her pink-tipped brush.

Adaris could tell by the straightness of her back that Rhonwen was trying to keep it together, but her shaking hand betrayed her. Some paint flicked to the desk. She quickly set it down again, probably before it splashed on her painting. "And I'm not certain I'll even get that with him," her voice broke.

A hot flicker of anger started inside Adaris at Rhonwen's words. Three hundred nights was ridiculous. Cruel, even for Tikova. Yes,

Spectrum was alive, but forcing a Vagari away from their companion for so long was just...unnecessarily harsh. Rhonwen had warned her about the sun goddess worshippers manipulating her by giving her the anklet. Rhonwen's anger made sense. They were doing the same by keeping her from her companion animal.

Adaris pushed herself to her feet, ignoring the sharp pain in her bad leg, and went to sit at the table. "Three hundred nights is too long."

"It is." Rhonwen shook her head and steeled herself. She tore her gaze away from the painting to look at Adaris instead. "I am sorry that I woke you."

"That's all right," Adaris replied, and that was the absolute truth. She couldn't go back to bed. Her tiredness fled the moment she saw the painting. Flipping open her book, Adaris lifted her quill. "I take it you won't mind my quill noises right now?"

Rhonwen laughed. "Not at all. Company would be nice."

They spent the rest of the darkness writing and painting in silence until twilight colors seeped into the hut—dark blues, deep purples, a hint of pink. It was nice, calm, and Adaris allowed herself the quiet moment of peace. She hoped Rhonwen felt the same.

They left the prison together before dawn. Rhonwen wanted to set up her painting reveal in the center of the community, by the Ponuriah statue, and Adaris was too curious not to follow. She activated the anklet before she left the hut, the thick bands of heat wrapping around her leg. The white fog rolled across her vision for only a moment before fading away more quickly than the last time.

It was still too dark for the worshippers' likings and there were no stirrings in the huts or flickering candlelight. They walked the pathway together in silence, Kye and Rhonwen's guard following close behind. Deep shadows tucked against the huts as they strolled past.
The only real lights were the stars dimming above them, the hint of pink at the horizon, and Adaris' anklet glowing a steady orange.

Rhonwen led them around the eastern curve. At first, Adaris wondered why. If they took the western curve, they could go past the enclosure and check on Spectrum, at least nonchalantly glance over.

Rhonwen had chosen the path that curved away from the enclosure, away from her companion, and seemed to lengthen her stride, too. Her steady gaze straight ahead and clenched jaw told Adaris exactly the reason. Just like Adaris had walked in the sunshine to prove she could, Rhonwen was walking away from her companion to prove the same thing. Only their guards were witness. Stubborn painter. It made Adaris respect her all the more.

As soon as they reached the Ponuriah statue, Rhonwen set up her easel and painting.

Just in time, for a few early risers were meandering out to the food hut or heading to the garden. Rhonwen immediately began engaging the sleepy community about her latest masterpiece.

Adaris could tell Rhonwen's excitement wasn't real.

She recognized the painter's stiff posture. The overly happy inflections in her voice were so unlike when she'd talked about her career, when it was just the two of them.

The people seemed thrilled by the painting, gawking and praising Rhonwen for her work. Adaris shuddered. They had all witnessed something gruesome together, and these people were thrilled about it. She was so focused on Rhonwen's act she barely took notice of the lighter pinks and yellows spreading across the sky, washing away the deep purple and black.

Wings rustled overhead. Suddenly realizing that dawn had arrived, Adaris tucked herself behind the head-high easel on instinct. She peered around the painting just in time to see a small thunderclap suncreature land on the ground near Rhonwen.

Adaris' entire body went cold like she had been doused with seawater, but then the more rational part of her brain clicked on. These people were sun goddess worshippers. Suncreatures defended this community, they were companions. The thunderclap wouldn't attack. *As long as I act compliant*.

Adaris looked again, forcing herself into the sunlight and into the sight of the suncreature. The bird immediately locked onto her. Celli's thunderclap. Adaris recognized it from how small it was. An odd sense of familiarity washed over her. She stood there for a heartbeat, watching it as it watched her, both of them bathed in sunlight. She slowly lifted her book and quill. The suncreature bobbed its head in return.

She quickly scribbled a description of the thunderclap, doused in sunlight, regal in all its tiny glory. Knowing it wouldn't attack her, she walked across the community center to the mines. There was another viewpoint she wanted to capture about the sunlight celebration, now that the community had fully awakened. Adaris meant to see one person in particular.

Berhn..

Chapter Twenty

ADARIS FOUND BERHN SITTING on the rocky ground just outside the mine opening. The darkness inside the mine called to Adaris, comforted her, but she didn't go into it. A shard of pale rock provided some shade that she tucked herself into. Kye stood next to the shard, eyes on the early morning passersby.

"Hi, Berhn," Adaris said quietly. Her gaze caught on a new earring glowing white on the Nemora's ear. *Where did that come from?*

He didn't offer a greeting. Tears wetted Berhn's eyes as he stared into the darkness and tucked his knees up to his chin.

Adaris tucked her knees up to her chin, mirroring him, to hopefully put him at ease.

"You got one, too?" Berhn's attention had shifted from the darkness of the mine to the anklet glowing on Adaris' ankle.

She nodded. "Yes. Mine helps me walk. What does your earring do?"

"I only just got it a few days ago." Berhn tugged on his earlobe. "I can heal scratches and the like with it. They gave it to me because I work in the mine."

"That's useful," Adaris replied, though she wondered if the earring was meant to appease him after they cut off his father's arms, but her words had rung true. A jewelry piece like that would be useful to a lot of people, including Berhn. "I bet you get cut on stones all the time, looking for those blue-green gemstones."

Berhn shrugged, glancing at the gravel beneath his feet.

"Are you doing okay?"

"No."

Of course he wasn't okay, but she was glad that he was open about it. "That must have been terrifying for you to watch your father go through what happened at the ceremony."

Swiping a hand across his eyes, Berhn nodded. "Tikova chooses randomly, but I never expected it to be my father." His voice cracked. "I didn't think he'd pick on the elderly."

The elderly. It was a curious turn of phrase for a young man to use, especially regarding their parents. *Berhn said Tikova picked on them, as if the demonstrations were a bad thing.* The idea was so unlike the joyous mood during the celebration itself. The crowd had cheered then. So had his parents. Adaris sat with that for a moment. "Are the celebrations always that brutal?"

Berhn winced, drawing back as if slapped. Adaris immediately regretted her word choice. After a beat of silence, he replied, "No. At the first celebration with a goddess shard, one of the Nemora built some extra living spaces for us. They created the entire north side of the community with one lift of their hand. Everyone cheered. It was...well, I wish this most recent demonstration was like that one."

Adaris nodded, staring into the mine. No sounds came from within, and Adaris wondered just how many people worked in there. "It would have been interesting to see that."

What the Nemora did would have been interesting, sure, but seeing a Blood crafter grow entire limbs back in the span of a heartbeat fascinated Adaris more. Unbidden, she saw it again—a flash of metal, severed arms hitting the ground, the rapid regrowth.

A terrible part of her wanted to see the demonstration again, and for the first time, her curiosity actually disgusted her.

It *wouldn't* be good to see that again. Not for the person who endured the pain of severing limbs or the forced regrowth. Or for their loved ones...the sane ones at least. How many times had they tried and failed? What if, the next time, it didn't work?

"I hope they never use the goddess shard to regrow limbs again."

"I hope that as well." Berhn sniffed. He finally lifted his gaze from the darkness and looked at her. "Can I tell you something, Adaris?"

He looked so serious, like this conversation meant something deep to him, the sort of secret only told to friends. A selfish part of her was thrilled at the connection, at what she might be able to learn from this sun goddess worshipper. A smaller part of her was just happy to have a semblance of another friend.

She shifted, facing him fully and giving him her full attention. "Yes, Berhn. Anything."

"I don't want to be here anymore," he said, his voice barely above a whisper.

The moment the words left his lips, his eyes darted around, as if checking to see if anyone was listening. None of the early morning passersby stopped, and it seemed like not even Kye had heard the boy's confession.

She sensed the weight behind the words, how hard it was for him to say them. She heard the slight tremble in his voice. Why was he worried someone might overhear? He was part of this community, a sun goddess worshipper like all the others. He should be able to come and go as he pleased. *Perhaps his parents are tied down here...* Yes, that had to be it; he didn't want to leave his parents. "And your parents want to stay?"

"They love it here," Berhn mumbled.

Adaris leaned back, taking in what he'd said. Love was such a strong word, especially when most of the other people she'd interviewed seemed to grumble about living on this broken and ruined continent. "Even after your father was..." She wanted to say tortured, but forced herself to finish with, "part of the celebration?"

"He said it was an honor to be chosen," Berhn replied. Tears filled his eyes again, and he rubbed at them with the back of his hand. "And now that Rhonwen's painted the moment, I know it will only fuel his belief."

Adaris glanced over her shoulder at the statue, where Rhonwen was still conversing with the community. She had Tikova's attention. Thankfully, he looked pleased. Turning back to Berhn, Adaris tried to gather her thoughts. Berhn didn't want to be at Slagrock, so why was he? Every Nemora's rite of passage meant visiting each of the seven Groves to honor them. Berhn had to have walked the path, had to have gone through his Choosing ritual. Even though he was painfully shy and soft-spoken, he was technically an adult. "Forgive my ignorance, but since you've walked the path and gone through your choosing, can't you simply leave? You're an adult now."

Berhn dipped his head. "I haven't done any of that yet."

Shock pulled Adaris upright. "But your markings are so angular. Younger Nemora usually have softer lines."

"I mean, I have chosen male." Berhn gestured to all of himself as if Adaris hadn't noticed. "So, my patterns are sharp, but I haven't walked the path or gone through the ritual. Officially, at least. When we came here, I had to choose so I could solidify my crafting."

Adaris' eyes widened at his implications. Before the choosing, a Nemora's crafting was erratic at best. Only after they chose their gender did their powers fully come to life. *They forced him to decide before his time.*

She had never heard of a Nemora choosing while still so young. The nox—the time between birth and choosing—was a time for exploration, for fluidity, for finding who they wanted to be, and for making the choice after they had enough life experiences. It was cruel to make a

Nemora do it early. There was no going back. "I'm...I'm sorry to hear that."

"I'm not," Berhn answered quickly. He leaned forward. "Even though I'm young, I'm glad I could connect with my crafting. I'm glad I could be of use to the community, too. They gave me and my family a place to stay, jobs, food. They were so kind to me."

"*Were* so kind," Adaris repeated, and Berhn's shoulders slumped. "It's okay to not want to be part of this community anymore. It's okay to want to move on. Perhaps you should talk to your parents again and—"

"Adaris!" Rhonwen rushed up beside the pair and grabbed Adaris' shoulder. "I get to see Spectrum. Come with me! Berhn, you can come, too."

Thrilled at the familiar touch, Adaris took Rhonwen's hand and squeezed it, looking up at the painter. "That's great, Rhonwen, but we're talking right now." She gestured to herself and Berhn, giving Rhonwen a meaningful look.

"It's all right." Berhn stood. His gaze drifted to the community center and Rhonwen's painting. "I want to see Spectrum."

Adaris sighed and allowed Rhonwen to pull her to her feet. She had wanted to help Berhn more, but obviously he was done talking. "Yes, let's go."

Rhonwen beamed, pulling Adaris to the animal enclosure. They stuck to the shadows on the way there, Rhonwen giving Adaris a wink as she chose a slightly longer path, and the simple act of kindness made Adaris smile.

It hadn't escaped her notice that Rhonwen hadn't let go of her hand. This handhold wasn't an anchor during a building storm or a desperate need for connection after a terrible sight. This was willing physical contact, and Adaris got all tingly thinking about it. *Don't make too much of it.*

Rhonwen certainly didn't. She seemed completely focused on seeing her companion animal. As soon as they reached sight distance of the stone cage, she broke into a run, nearly dragging Adaris behind her. Adaris followed willingly, marveling to only herself that her bad leg didn't buckle or ache. Berhn chased after them, too, and the guards followed.

Spectrum seemed to sense Rhonwen's presence, because the great winged, serpentine creature shifted in his enclosure, coiling again and again and again, until he looked like a knot of rainbow and black. High-pitched cawing noises came from him. Happy noises.

Rhonwen choked out a cry. She nearly crashed into the stone cage and immediately put her fingers through the tiny spaces between the rock bars, reaching to touch her companion animal. Spectrum shifted closer, so her fingers could skim his feathers and scales. Even as gaunt and weak as the creature looked, he immediately brightened when Rhonwen touched him.

"Spectrum," she said, her voice cracking.

As Rhonwen said hello, Adaris eyed the stone bars, taking in the thick, pale rock with no cracks or chips. Even the inside looked unbroken. Hoping to find some flaw, she walked around the entire structure, raking her gaze across the enclosure. Kye followed her the whole way round, but said nothing. It seemed he didn't mind her inspection, but when she circled to the front, Rhonwen's guard narrowed his eyes at her. He was Elu, judging by the scars on his bare arms.

Hoping to throw off any suspicion, she grinned. "I've never seen a slyther this big, just wanted to get the full image of him. He's a beautiful creature."

Rhonwen's guard scoffed, but Kye nodded. "He is."

Kye immediately pulled Rhonwen's guard into a conversation, hanging back a few paces to give them some space.

She had never seen the painter so happy. Rhonwen's eyes danced, her smile was as beautiful as a crescent moon. She actually vibrated with excitement. *This, right here, is true happiness.*

Rhonwen's yellow eyes glowed a bright orange. Her fingers, wrist, hand, and arm illuminated as well. Her hand and arm slipped through the bars up to her elbow, easily. The sight of the woman using her Animal crafting made Adaris' insides turn. It was like the painter no longer had bones! But Spectrum chirped in joy, dipping his crest of feathers to her hand, allowing her to scratch his forehead, rub his temples, and run her hand down his beak. His yellow eyes closed with obvious comfort.

Adaris' heart melted for the pair. She couldn't imagine what life was like for Rhonwen, so far away from everyone she loved and then deliberately cut off from her companion animal as well. Adaris' fingers itched to pull out her book and quill, to record this reunion in all its glory, a burst of joy in this terrible place, but Rhonwen had made Adaris promise not to record her story at all, and Adaris would honor that.

Berhn had already stuck his tiny fingers through the gaps in the stone bars, with eyes wide as two moons on the slyther's scales.

"Berhn, you should ask permission from the companion animal before you touch them," Adaris gently admonished him.

Berhn pulled his hand back like he'd touched a hot iron.

The Vagari culture had their own laws, and petting a companion animal without the animal's consent was one of them. They were, as far as Spectrum was concerned, strangers. She looked at the slyther, chirping and coiling in his cage. "Rhonwen, does he allow it?"

Rhonwen's grin softened into something that looked more private, something that would be just for the two of them, had they been a couple. "Thank you for asking."

"My mother taught me well," Adaris replied.

A curious look passed over Rhonwen's features—one that Adaris couldn't quite identify—before she turned to Spectrum. The slyther's yellow eyes illuminated to match Rhonwen's intense orange gaze, before locking his gaze with hers. He stilled.

Even though Adaris couldn't hear the conversation, she knew Rhonwen and her companion were talking.

A few moments passed, then Rhonwen grinned. "He says you can scratch by his eye if you'd like." She gave Adaris a sideways glance. "He also would very much like to know where you got that feather in your quill, says he likes the color."

Adaris chuckled, running a thumb across the white quill feather tucked into her belt. It made some semblance of sense that the lack of color in her quill would fascinate a creature with so many colors to spare. She didn't see a lick of white on his black feathers or rainbow scales. "Good question. Unfortunately, I don't know where the feather came from. I never asked. Though perhaps I should have."

Spectrum bowed his massive head and clicked his beak as if he understood—and perhaps he could. Sometimes, every once in a while, animals did listen to her. Adaris smiled to herself, then squeezed her finger between the stone to pet by his eye. "It's good to meet you, Spectrum."

The slyther cooed, pressing his head against her finger in an almost painful way. She kept petting him, anyway, for a few more moments, then pulled back and stepped aside to give Rhonwen room. She didn't want to take up the Vagari's precious time with her companion animal.

Rhonwen grinned at her and stuck her other glowing fingers, hand, and arm through a tiny space in the stone. She scratched both sides of Spectrum's face, locking eyes with her companion once more, and dove back into their conversation.

A few moments later, Rhonwen's guard stepped closer, ending the quiet conversation he and Kye had been having. Had Kye been intentionally stalling him? It seemed like it. "Okay, time's up."

Rhonwen's grin faded. "Already?"

"You've had more than enough," the guard replied.

"More than enough?" Rhonwen's voice lifted, disappointment stilting her words and drawing her brows together. "You haven't let me see Spectrum in three hundred nights."

Her guard stepped closer, lifting his metal spear. "Then perhaps you should have worked harder at Tikova's requests. Come. Now."

Rhonwen's expression hardened.

Before she could say anything more or do anything rash, Adaris stepped between them. She lifted her book and quill. "I don't believe we've spoken before. My name is Adaris, I'm a scribe."

"Yes, yes, I know who you are." The guard tried to wave her away. An armband that glowed a vibrant orange stood out against his dark skin.

"Good." Adaris stood firm, hoping Rhonwen could get at least a few more precious moments with Spectrum. "Then you know I'm here to record stories, and I'd like to write down yours. Have you always lived here?"

The guard stepped back a few paces to be an arm's length away. His black eyes narrowed. "I don't have time for this, scribe."

Don't push it. She thought her stalling had failed, but then Kye heaved a sigh that didn't have to be quite so loud. "Yim, we're supposed to answer her questions. Tikova's orders."

The guard—Yim—stared at him, then focused once more on Adaris. He frowned. "You asked where I was from?"

Adaris nodded, a rush of gratitude warmed her at Kye's aid, but she kept her attention on Yim. "Yes, it seems the people in this community come from all over the world."

"If you must know, I came from the islands."

"Oh? Which ones?"

Her quill scratched the parchment, recording everything he said. The guard scowled as he spoke, answering curtly and obviously trying to get through the conversation as quickly as possible. Being a dutiful scribe, Adaris had quite a few questions to ask. Her mood lifted with each word she scribbled as happy slyther chirps started again behind her. She knew happiness was fleeting for them, and would give Rhonwen as much time as she could.

Chapter Twenty-One

AFTER EVERYONE ELSE IN the community had gone to bed, Adaris and Rhonwen lingered outside under the glittering stars, settling on the edge of the tall columns of rock overlooking the ocean. The full moon painted the huts, the broken pathway, and the ocean in a silvery light, and stars glittered in the sky. The gentle whoosh of waves crashing against the beach calmed Adaris. Their guards didn't seem to mind the quiet evening, staying a couple of paces back. Kye commandeered Yim's attention in a whispered conversation.

Adaris and Rhonwen passed dried fish back and forth between them, enjoying the silence and each other's company. The happiness from earlier still lingered in Rhonwen's smile.

"Thank you for stalling my guard," she said, nudging Adaris with her shoulder.

"I was happy to." Adaris shrugged as nonchalantly as she could, though being this close to Rhonwen felt different tonight. More intense. She felt a spark between them but didn't want to make any moves. *Not here. Not in this community.*

Rhonwen's gaze softened. "Did you actually listen to his story? You kept looking back at us."

Depths, she noticed! Adaris hadn't been able to tear her eyes away from Rhonwen's joy, wanting to capture that moment not in writing but in memory.

The back of her neck heated, and she was, once again, grateful for the shadows. "Of course! His name was..." She pretended to need to consider. "Yen?"

Rhonwen leaned away slightly, eyes wide.

"I'm joking." Adaris laughed, pleased she'd gotten a reaction. "Everyone has a story to tell, and Yim's was just as important as anyone else's." She bit her lip, deciding on how honest she ought to be. "But you're right, I was preoccupied."

Rhonwen winked, making Adaris' heart flutter. "I'm glad I can be preoccupying."

"Bold of you to think I was looking at you," Adaris teased, and Rhonwen rolled her eyes. "Spectrum is quite the colorful slyther. I actually haven't seen one with a rainbow pattern like that."

"He's one of the reasons I decided to be a painter. When we became companions, he immediately became my muse. My early paintings are all of him."

"I'd like to see them sometime," Adaris replied. It would be nice to see something not inspired by the horror of being at Slagrock. She'd never really acknowledged the arts—painting, drawing, and the like—but after meeting Rhonwen, her appreciation grew with every passing night.

"They're not really meant for the public eye but..." Rhonwen's cheeks darkened, then she took Adaris' hand. "Yes, I'd...I'd like you to see them."

"Depths, I bet they're all stunning. Just like—" She wanted to say you, and for a heartbeat, the bolder side of her almost made her say it. *A friend. She wants a friend.* "Just like your slyther. I can't believe how colorful he is."

Dipping her chin, Rhonwen looked at their entwined fingers. She drew a spiral pattern on the back of Adaris' hand. "He likes you, by the way, in case you're wondering."

"Not just the color of my quill feather?" Adaris replied with forced lightness, heart quickening as she tried to ignore how lovely Rhonwen's casual caress was making her feel. The touch left a trail of burning tingles on her skin.

"Oh, that's the best part about you." Rhonwen's smile creased the sides of her eyes. "But he also says thank you for giving us more time together."

Adaris shook her head at the tease and her own conflicting emotions. Was Rhonwen flirting with her? It was hard for her to pin the painter down. "Well, next time you talk with him, tell him you're welcome from me."

"I will," Rhonwen whispered.

A particularly loud splash of waves on the shore far below drew their attention. A slimy, pure-white body heaved itself onto the sand. A shiver raced through Adaris, but she kept her wits. The suncreature was not only far away, it was nighttime, and the rock columns provided some protection.

Rhonwen ignored the creature. "The horizon looks stunning tonight."

"It does." The moon and stars above made the ocean gleam like metal. A breeze lifted a lock of Rhonwen's gray-white hair, and Adaris desperately wanted to tuck it behind her ear. She didn't, choosing instead to let the moment linger and enjoy this quiet time together.

It wasn't until they were both in the prison hut settling down to sleep that she realized what a personal thing asking to see Rhonwen's first paintings had been. Adaris had originally pictured the detailed renditions she'd seen already—glittering scales, stunning portraits, the rawness of it all—but Rhonwen's first paintings wouldn't be like that. They might be terrible. It probably took an artist a while to figure out her style. It was a mark of their friendship that Rhonwen had even agreed to show her something so personal. A smile tugged at Adaris' lips. Or perhaps a mark of something more.

She woke to a scream. Yellow and red light washed the stone walls of her prison, streaming in through the barred door, making the shadows flicker on the floor. *Fire.*

She pushed herself to her feet, hurrying to the prison door. A hastily made fire pit on the path outside contained a towering bonfire. The roil of flames obscured what sounded like cracking stone and screaming from the community beyond. Adaris shielded her eyes from the light, wincing at the waves of heat emanating from the bonfire. She squinted at the darkness beyond, trying to see what was happening.

It seemed as though Slagrock was being attacked. A few of the living huts on the eastern curve had been destroyed. The ground was littered with rocks and bloody limbs. Around the Ponuriah statue burned three more fires, while the statue itself was nothing but a column of white-hot flames.

Her heart pounded a frantic wardrum inside her chest. What the depths was happening? Between the fires, the white-clad figures of community members rushed for cover. One with a glowing circlet tried to yank a wounded man from the rubble. Another carried an injured woman into the food hut. More people hid by the gardens, tucked behind crates.

"Rhonwen, wake up!" Adaris shouted over her shoulder.

A thunderclap suncreature landed on the path just in front of the prison, sharp eyes darting to the side toward something Adaris couldn't see. Adaris stepped back with a gasp, knowing what the creature could do. She pressed her hands over her ears just in time as the creature opened its beak, gulped air, and expelled it in a thunderclap so loud it made the stone prison shudder.

More screams sliced the air. A few pebbles shook loose around Adaris. She stepped forward again and grabbed the bars of her prison door with both hands, trying to open it. The door didn't budge.

"Rhonwen!" Adaris shouted again, gaze locked on the suncreature standing outside. It had turned away to face something else in the darkness. "Get up!"

There could only be one explanation. The Moon Knights had finally reached the village. This could be their chance to go home.

Adaris spun. Pain brightened in her bad leg, white-hot inside her bones. She groaned and clutched her knee. *Depths!* The anklet must've stopped working while she slept. Taking a moment, Adaris sank into her crafting and reactivated the jewelry piece. The familiar roll of white fog crossed her vision, then immediately ebbed away. Heat burst from the anklet, wrapping around her leg. Adaris rushed over to Rhonwen's bed.

"Rhonwen." She grabbed the painter's shoulder and shook. How could Rhonwen sleep through this chaos? "Get up," Adaris bellowed.

Finally, Rhonwen stirred. Adaris recognized the cloudy film over her eyes. Aca nuts were dulling her senses. She must've eaten them before bed. "Winter's breath, Adaris, wha—"

"Slagrock is being attacked," Adaris said.

"Adaris!" Kye's voice cut through the hut.

Adaris turned to the prison door, open on its hinges, and saw Kye backlit by flames, trident clutched in one hand.

He gestured to her. "Come. Help us."

Help them? Adaris grew cold. *What the depths do they think I can do?* She couldn't fight, didn't have the skills necessary to defend against a trained Moon Knight. And she didn't want to fight the knights anyway. She idolized them.

Kye barreled inside. "We need your healing. Now!"

Adaris' eyes widened. *Healing?* Over Kye's shoulder, she watched a volley of arrows thud onto the pathway around the thunderclap suncreature. It squawked and flew off. A few community members surged past, spears and tridents held high, eyes glowing with their crafting. Another scream ripped the air. Her healing was dismal in the best of situations, and they wanted her to perform under this sort of stress? It felt like her legs had turned to stone.

Before she could protest, Kye herded her outside with the handle of his trident, Rhonwen stumbling after them. Yells erupted from their right, a flash of Moon crafting blue lighting the air. A handful of community members had erected Moon shields to ward off no less than twenty knights approaching from that direction. The knights' eyes glowed orange, their Vagari Animal crafting surging from them in orange claws and teeth, lightning, and flames. *But where are their companions?*

The vibrant cobalt shields held strong, repelling attack after attack.

But those members were not Elu, they were Nemora. Adaris stopped, trying to make sense of what she was seeing. It finally clicked. The glowing jewelry pieces. Sroc had discovered how to lash crafting to random jewelry—rings, circlets, armbands. Those Nemora must be using the ones with Moon crafting locked inside. That's how Nemora could create blue shields like that.

Rhonwen grabbed hold of Adaris' hand, mouth open in shock, as the battle around them finally seemed to sink in. She looked around, more fascinated than scared.

"Winter's breath," she murmured dreamily, glazed eyes on a frenzied clash of a Moon Knight's sword against a community member's trident. Orange blood dripped from the community member's forehead, painting her face in a grotesque mask that gleamed in the firelight.

Kye pushed them against the outside of the prison wall, as if hoping they might blend into the stone. "We need to reach the garden."

Amidst the rubble, a tall community member dropped to his knees, the Moon Knight attacker slashing until the blade was coated in brown. The Nemora with a gray splotch on his neck put both hands on the ground and a thick spike of rock burst upward before him, spearing the knight square in the chest. More blood sprayed the air, painting the rubble in flecks of orange.

Rhonwen murmured, "The colors are gorgeous."

"Gorgeous?" Adaris gaped at her.

The painter nodded, though her gaze had latched onto the broken pathway, as if the arrows embedded there were suddenly fascinating. How many aca nuts had she taken?

The Moon Knight brigade to their right gave a guttural yell, and Adaris swung her gaze to them just as their companions emerged in a wave from the darkness. Fangs, fur, scales, feathers. The beasts crawled up and over the cobalt shields in less than a heartbeat, but as they hit the ground on the other side, the Nemora raised their hands as one and pillars of rock rose, slamming the creatures backward.

Adaris' chest tightened at the sight. The Nature crafting was innate, natural to the Hallr Nemora, but the Moon crafting was channeled via jewelry pieces. Two powers channeled through one crafter, each of equal strength, simultaneously. Her people had no hope of combating such force once the sun goddess worshippers finally decided to attack the mainland.

A nudge against her ribs made her stumble, as Kye shoved her along the side of the wall toward the garden. They reached the low stone walls that surrounded the dusty dirt, and she spotted dozens of wounded lying among the crushed plants. The fires raging from the other side of the remaining huts made the sky burn orange and cast the leaves and dirt in dusky light, but couldn't disguise the blood soaking everyone's clothing.

Kye pointed to a young woman with light hair Adaris had only seen in passing. The woman sat propped against the dirt, her shirt sliced open on the side. Blood dripping from a wound just below her ribcage had formed a dark puddle on the parched dirt below. "Heal her," Kye ordered. "Quickly."

For a heartbeat, Adaris hesitated. Could she even craft while the anklet was activated? She hadn't tried, hadn't pulled from her reserves to heal another since obtaining the glowing jewelry. Not knowing what else to do, she knelt next to the terrified woman. The woman groaned in pain, eyeing Adaris with wide eyes.

"May I heal you?"

The question was foolish in a time like this, but Divus had a terrible reputation for using their crafting to kill—one that fueled people to keep them at arm's length—so the question was one of respect.

"Please," the woman gasped, her light hair washed yellow and red in the firelight.

Adaris sank into her crafting, the white fog pulling over her eyes, the familiar warmth filling her like a cup of tea. She pulled life from herself so she could pour it into this woman. The bands of heat wrapping her leg snapped away, and the agony of kneeling on her bad leg slammed into her. The anklet must've deactivated. She gasped but kept her focus.

White light traced the veins in Adaris' fingers as she put her hands on either side of the wound. Life energy ebbed from her, and her head started to pound. Her crafting wove in and out of the injured flesh, gradually pulling the cut closed. The wound wasn't as deep as she'd first thought. Even so, it seemed to take ages to heal. When she could take no more, she removed her hands, breathing heavy. The wound was closed. It would scar...but at least it no longer bled. The woman thanked her and promptly fainted.

A high-pitched shriek pulled Adaris' attention skyward.

Three dark creatures swooped into the firelight, curving up and around the community, before circling back toward the garden. Scales and leathery wings caught the light, a flash of sharp, curved teeth and long tails with spikes on the end of them.

Wyverns.

Adaris gaped at them in shock.

Hope lit up like fire within her. Maybe the Moon Knights would save her. Her and Rhonwen and Spectrum, too.

Except, as the creatures dove toward the garden, she realized something. She and Rhonwen looked exactly like sun goddess worshippers.

Chapter Twenty-Two

A FAMILIAR ELDERLY FIGURE with a cane shuffled into the path of the wyverns. A small thunderclap fluttered down, landing next to the woman. Celli raised her hand, fingers clutched around a familiar goddess shard. She tipped her face skyward. The shard glowed an impossible crimson—so bright it dulled even the firelight. A wave of heat ripped from it like a shockwave, making Adaris' skin itch even from this far away.

But nothing happened.

The wyverns sent a trio of lightning strikes from their maws, burning through the community center. The static jumped off rocks, broke through huts, scorched the ground black. Heading for the injured gathered in the gardens but destroying as much as possible before reaching them.

Rhonwen stepped forward, hand raised to the static as if she wanted to touch it.

Idiot! Adaris jerked Rhonwen behind her. "Stay with me!"

Rhonwen merely nodded, her attention floating to something else.

Celli continued holding the goddess shard, staring at the black sky above them beyond the crimson glow. As if waiting. As if calling to something.

Somewhere far above them, above Celli, the suncreatures answered. Balls of fire descended in blinding light almost as bright as the sun. From the brightness, impossibly large, twin pairs of white talons reached for the wyverns. Adaris gaped, making out white feathers tipped with flames and large, beady crimson eyes.

Rhonwen gasped, tapping Adaris incessantly on the shoulder. "Firebirds, suncreature versions."

The suncreature corruption had enlarged their standard form, making them as big as mansions instead of carts. The massive beasts grappled the wyverns midair, stopping their attack.

Suncreatures or no, Celli should be overcome with an intense headache from extending her powers so far, for calling creatures so massive to aid her. She should be curled into herself. The goddess shard had amplified her powers to a breathtaking, impossible scope.

Kye stepped in front of Adaris and Rhonwen, then lifted his trident toward the battle raging above them. The points of his weapon glowed blue—a new feature. When he muttered a word Adaris couldn't quite catch, a shield burst from the trident's points. Elu crafting, a Moon shield.

Adaris let out a small sigh. They were safe, for now.

Rhonwen kept tapping her shoulder, until Adaris rounded on her. "What?"

"We should run," Rhonwen said, leaning close to Adaris, her voice barely above a whisper even through the chaos. The aca nut film still glazed her eyes, but a new kind of furious determination steadied her gaze. "Leave right now. Everyone's distracted, and I haven't seen my guard at all."

"What? Now?" Adaris wrinkled her nose at the bitterness of the aca nuts on Rhonwen's breath. She was surprised the painter had noticed anything of merit in her drugged state, but when Adaris glanced around, she didn't see Yim either. Where had he gone? That man stuck to Rhonwen like wet sand. The realization tugged Adaris back a few paces, and she grabbed Rhonwen's hand to pull her along, eyes on Kye.

The guard was focusing on his shield and didn't notice. Didn't turn around. They could sneak past him, make it to the shore, grab the raft Adaris had built and leave this place behind.

They could do it.

They could run.

"What about Spectrum?" she murmured.

Rhonwen was grinning almost madly. "Perhaps the attack has broken his cage. Come on!"

She dragged her forward, sliding past Kye and his shield into the open and heading straight for the animal enclosure.

As they passed by a fire on the path, an arrow thudded into the rock a few paces away from Adaris. She swerved, her bad leg spiking with white-hot pain. Her anklet had deactivated when she healed the woman earlier, and Adaris hadn't reactivated it yet. Three more arrows crashed into the ground ahead, narrowly missing Rhonwen where she'd stopped. A fourth hit the fire, scattering embers. Adaris' bad leg almost buckled under her, so she activated the anklet once more, hot bands strengthening her bones.

Of course they're firing at us. They looked exactly like the community members. Clad in white outfits, they were running away like so many of the others. Adaris even had a glowing jewelry piece like them.

She turned to run as another volley of arrows sailed toward them. One grazed Adaris' shoulder, drawing blood in a flash of pain. She kept running. The animal enclosure was far enough away from the battle to cast it in shadows, and Adaris couldn't see if it was broken or damaged as they approached. She could hear the slyther thrashing around; its frantic cries were getting higher and higher pitched.

"Spectrum, I'm okay!" Rhonwen cried. She lifted a daygem and a burst of cool purple light sphered around them.

"Damn it all to the depths, Rhonwen, everyone will see! Where did you even get that?" Anger flashed hot in Adaris' voice as she shielded her eyes from the sudden illumination. She shoved Rhonwen around to the other side of the cage, hoping the stone would block some of the light. The woman had lost her mind to the drugs.

Rhonwen clutched the purple daygem like a lifeline, shoving it against the bars to light up the slyther inside.

Spectrum whipped his head around to see them. An arrow had lodged deep into Spectrum's feathered neck, and blood darkened the feathers around the shaft.

"Oh, he's bleeding." Rhonwen said, so casually that Adaris wanted to slap her. She knew Rhonwen wouldn't—didn't—want to be in this state. The painter needed to be here, be present, and heal her companion animal.

Adaris did the only thing she could think of.

Dipping into her Blood crafting, Adaris wrapped her fingers around the back of Rhonwen's neck and shoved her crafting into the painter. She couldn't clear the aca nut fog from Rhonwen's mind, but pain often put fog in sharp relief. It was the very thing her kind was feared for—hurting instead of healing—but the painter had to be alert to heal her companion.

Pooling her crafting into Rhonwen's mind, she envisioned bringing back the terror of this night like a wave to slap her awake. Using the small but piercing headache slowly building at the base of her own skull, she mirrored it in Rhonwen's. She carefully used her Blood crafting to cause pain instead of taking it away.

Rhonwen groaned and tore away from Adaris' grip. Betrayal creased her features, but the glaze was gone from her eyes. "What do you think you're doing, Adaris?"

"Spectrum needs you!" Adaris blinked her crafting away and pointed at Spectrum. "He's hurt."

The slyther writhed, the arrow still jutting from his neck, and blood creating a puddle on the stone floor.

Rhonwen shuddered, then squared her shoulders as if seeing her companion for the first time. Her eyes started to glow orange, and she slipped her hand into the cage. "It's okay, Spectrum. You're going to be all right. We're going to be all right."

At Rhonwen's touch, the arrow slowly backed out of the creature's skin and clattered to the ground. The wound filled with orange light as Animal crafting flowed between the pair.

Adaris took the opportunity to examine the cage, fighting to ignore the clanging of metal against metal and cries of pain and anger from the battle. Surely, in all the turmoil, the cage would be cracked somewhere.

The stone looked frustratingly whole, bars as smooth and strong as ever. Her hope of escape vanished. They couldn't leave without Spectrum.

She turned her attention back to the fighting. The suncreatures and wyverns had disappeared somewhere into the night sky, but another wave of Moon Knights had swarmed onto the burning paths. Celli, Kye, Yim, and a few other community members stood with their weapons readied.

A Vagari Moon Knight with thick black horns curling from her forehead charged ahead of the others, eyes glowing orange. Rhonwen's guard darted out to meet her, spear raised. The Vagari's legs flared with orange light as she lowered her head and rammed her horns straight into him, sending him flying backward twenty paces where he crashed into the stone and fell facedown. An attack worthy of any Vagari, pure crafting strength. Seeing the guard injured sent a thrill through Adaris. He had hurt Rhonwen more than once, and a cruel part of Adaris whispered that he wouldn't soon get up after that ramming.

Curiously, Celli handed off the goddess shard to a short, stocky Elu man.

Rhonwen grabbed her arm, face lined with rage. "We have to get Spectrum out, Adaris. This is our only chance to escape."

"The stone is too strong," Adaris muttered, gaze still on the Elu holding the shard. Despite the circumstances, her curiosity was burning a hole in her chest, and her hand instinctively went for her quill. What would the shard do with the Elu's crafting? She had to know.

The stocky Elu called up his Moon crafting and created a vibrant blue wall in front of him. The cobalt deepened, darkened into deep-sea blue instead of the usual azure and took on a crimson shimmer.

Like a bubble about to burst, the light swelled outward, passing Adaris, Rhonwen, Spectrum, and the other community members harmlessly.

The Moon Knights, however, were driven back like a wall.

A shimmering stronghold now protected the community, stretched high into the sky before curving completely overhead. The man had created a huge structure. A fortress. Four guardians—towering, armored women with spears—stood like compass points, protecting all of Slagrock.

Adaris' mouth dropped open. Her body went cold, frozen in shock. This was impossible crafting. Too much to take in. If an Elu could create a fortress and a Vagari could call so many massive suncreatures other than their own suncreature companions... *We can't escape, not from that.*

The thought jolted her into motion. "We have to blend in, Rhonwen, we have to do what Kye asked us."

"What?" Rhonwen blinked, gaping at the shimmering fortress surrounding them. Her eyes still glowed deep orange with her crafting. "He didn't ask me to do anything."

The Moon Knights and their companion animals crashed uselessly against the stronghold. A screech echoed in through the smoky night, the firebird suncreatures swooping again and again and again over the Moon Knights, picking them up and dropping them screaming to the ground. Adaris' gut flipped. Since the fortress held the knights back, Kye would be looking for them—for her.

Grabbing Rhonwen by the shoulders and spinning the painter to face her, Adaris said, "Help me then. Come with me to help the wounded. Right now."

Spectrum cawed, and Rhonwen ran her hand over his eyebrow one final time. "We'll be back, Spectrum. I promise."

The gaunt creature settled in his cage, huddling in the corner. Adaris' heart broke for him, but she pulled Rhonwen along anyway. They reached the wounded, but she didn't see Kye anywhere.

Throwing herself down next to a lanky Nemora with a deep gash on their forehead, Adaris sank into her Blood crafting.

She caught a glimpse of Kye racing toward them and bit her lip. Had he seen them come from the animal enclosure? Only time would tell. Shifting her gaze back to the wounded, she eyed their forehead. She didn't have much left, but she'd do her best to help. To hide. To conform, at least for now.

Chapter Twenty-Three

ADARIS KNELT NEXT TO a Vagari with a trio of claw marks across his torso. The center of the community had quieted, and most people were in the food hut resting. Sroc healed quite a lot of people, including Adaris' arrow wound. Adaris had healed a few, then did her best to mend the rest the non-crafting way. The first few wounded made her stomach turn, but after a while, she got used to the blood and torn flesh. The poultice her father used to make from seaweed came in handy.

She stitched the slashes up with twine and smeared briny green poultice onto the wound to help it heal. Rhonwen unrolled yet another measure of clean cloth, so they could wrap the wound. Kye stood next to them while they worked, his expression grim. The Moon Knight attack had ended during twilight. The cobalt stronghold and the suncreatures had turned the tide in the community's favor. The fires had been put out, but smoke still clouded the mottled pink-yellow sky. Scales and feathers and body parts and blood littered the ground.

"Rhonwen, can you help him sit up?" Adaris murmured.

Rhonwen gently eased the man to a sitting position.

Pain flashed across the Vagari's face. He groaned, sandy hair falling into his tired eyes.

"Sorry, sorry," Rhonwen whispered.

As Adaris wrapped the clean cloth across the man's wounds, handing the bandage back and forth to Rhonwen, she was careful to not touch her, not after hurting her with her crafting. Rhonwen seemed to appreciate the distance. Exhaustion and dismay at their rift crawled across Adaris' shoulders, making them slump.

Her bad leg throbbed something terrible. The once-glowing orange gemstones of her anklet were dull. It had deactivated when she used her crafting, which was odd. During the attack, the community members had used their inherent crafting and the bound artifact's crafting simultaneously. Two different crafting types at once. Why didn't her anklet work when she healed people? It was a mystery she intended to unravel—when she wasn't so tired.

Kye shifted beside her. Not for the first time, Adaris caught the hitch in his breath, the way his arm wrapped around his torso.

"Are you hurt?" Adaris asked.

Kye shook his head. An obvious lie, but a consistent one at least. Whenever she'd offered to help, he shooed her away to tend to the others. He barely said a word to her the entire night. The man was as stubborn as he was kind, and it did nothing to ease the worry churning in Adaris' gut. With the way he ran toward them after the cobalt stronghold appeared, he knew they'd left his side. Left his protection. His watch. But had he seen her and Rhonwen at Spectrum's cage? Did he assume they'd tried to run? A gleam in his tired brown eyes left her nervous.

The injured Vagari groaned and shifted, and Adaris gently secured the bandage.

"Can someone help?" Rhonwen called.

A young Elu with a limp shuffled out, hauled the man's arm over her shoulders, and helped him into the food hut. The shadows swallowed them both.

Sighing, Adaris leaned back. She rested on her palms, wishing she had some water and food and sleep. Sweat dripped down her temple, and she didn't even wipe it away. Soon they could get some rest.

A hand rested over her own.

Rhonwen.

Adaris stilled. She had betrayed Rhonwen's trust, had done the unspeakable, the thing the Divus were feared for. She'd hurt Rhonwen with Blood crafting, hurt when she should heal. Most would shy away from her after that; nearly everyone did. Yet Rhonwen tightened her grip. Nerves turned her words to ash. When she glanced at Rhonwen, the painter gave her a private smile that lifted only one corner of her mouth and crinkled the sides of her eyes. Her yellow gaze shimmered, and though she didn't say anything, she didn't need to. Her willing touch was all the reassurance Adaris needed. Her nerves broke and Adaris couldn't help but smile in relief.

Kye made a noise at the back of his throat, a cough or a growl.

Adaris couldn't be sure what she heard. When she looked at him, pain tightened his expression. It panged close to her heart, seeing him hurt.

Adaris squeezed Rhonwen's hand then let go and turned to him fully. "Will you let me heal you now?"

Kye nodded.

His white vest had been slashed down the side, and orange blood darkened the cloth. When he lowered himself to the ground, Adaris spotted the wound peeking past a hastily tied bandage. As gently as she could, she took off his vest. A hard, tan-and-white patterned shell covered his back, wrapping around his sides before meshing seamlessly with the skin of his torso. The slash carved a pale line along the shell before cracking through it and sinking deep into the flesh of his side. That same kind of shell crossed his forearm, neck, and shoulder. Surely this was a gift of his bloodline. She peeled the cloth from his light brown skin. The fabric snagged on dried bits of blood, ruined shell, and ragged flesh. Her heart seemed to stop. How could Kye stand with a wound that deep?

Rhonwen pressed a clean cloth against the wound, warm brown cheeks paling from the jagged gash.

Adaris' throat tightened. It would be so much better to heal this wound with crafting, to close the jagged edge from infection, but she could barely stand on her own, let alone dredge up enough energy for crafting. With that off the table, she could only do her best to stitch the wound by hand. Picking up the twine and needle, she swallowed her hesitation and went to work.

Kye remained silent throughout the entire procedure. From the moment the needle pierced his flesh to the breaking of the twine after the wound was shut, he didn't move. He didn't even seem to breathe. His eyes squeezed shut, sweat dripping down his brow. Her gaze found the other scars on the shell, pale lines crisscrossing, some deep, others not, before she focused once more on the current wound. She moved with precision, slow as she could and respectful. She smeared seaweed poultice onto the wound, then wrapped fresh cloth around his torso, passing the cloth back and forth to Rhonwen like they had been doing all night.

"It's done." Adaris glanced up at his face. This was the closest he'd been to Adaris since they'd met, and she spotted something glittering behind his left ear. Blood...sweat? No. She narrowed her eyes and leaned closer.

It was a design. A tattoo. Small and tucked behind the shell of his ear. Orange intertwined coils. Her eyes widened as she recognized the Silver Shade emblem. She'd seen that exact design on a band worn by a trader, Orenda Silverstone, who she'd met in the Athenaeum of the Ancients. The Silver Shade was an organization of assassins and undercover agents who believed in Aluriah, the moon goddess. Everything they did was aimed at unraveling the corruption of the Ponuriah worshippers.

Is Kye a Silver Shade? If so, what the depths is he doing here, acting as a guard for someone like Tikova?

"What made this wound?" Adaris pretended to adjust the bandage one last time, to cover her silence more than anything. She couldn't ask him about the Silver Shade, not while they were so out in the open. Not while Tikova could be watching. She hadn't seen the leader of Slagrock during or after the attack, but she didn't doubt that he was nearby.

"That." Kye tilted his head to the Ponuriah statue. A bloody dagger leaned against the statue, wicked looking edges running along the blade like dark flames. Pain crept into his voice. "The curlhorn Vagari carried it."

Curlhorn. That must've been the Vagari who rammed into the community members. "I saw her attack. I'm surprised she let you get that close."

Kye shook his head. "She didn't expect my kind of crafting."

His response prickled at the edges of her curiosity. She still didn't know anything about his bloodline, what kinds of gifts he and his companion animal shared, or even the form of his companion animal. If she couldn't ask about the Silver Shade, she could at least ask about his crafting. "What form does your crafting take?"

A rueful expression flickered across his face, and he puffed out his cheeks on an exhale. "My touch can paralyze people. Stop their hearts if I want to," he finally admitted.

Paralysis wasn't exactly rare in the animal world—insects, deep-sea dwellers, serpentine creatures, even some dragons had that ability. Kye didn't seem to want to expand on the topic. So even though she wanted to ask what kind of companion animal he had, Adaris didn't. "That's an amazing ability, Kye."

A shouted curse interrupted their conversation. They both looked over just in time to see Tikova charging over to them, vest flapping open behind him.

"Why are you out of your hut?" he shouted, gaze like daggers on Adaris and Rhonwen.

He nearly skidded to a halt an arm's length away, hands on his hips. Blood dripped down his face from a gash at his temple. His billowy pants were singed on the bottom, but he seemed mostly uninjured. Outwardly at least. Adaris knew, on the inside, the man was as cracked as they came.

Adaris rose to his challenge. "We're helping heal people."

"I didn't approve that." He scowled, eyes hard. "You should have stayed in your hut!"

Why was he so angry? They were helping. Tending to the wounded like he'd asked. Adaris grew cold. He…had asked, right? She searched her memories for the night before, waking up to fire and chaos and the battle raging around her. Kye had told her to help. Kye had told her, not Tikova.

If Tikova hadn't asked them to help, did that mean she disobeyed his orders somehow? The pile of dead bodies flashed into her mind. *Depths!*

Kye scoffed, getting to his feet. "She's a Divus, Tikova, and offered to help. She stayed by my side the whole time."

The lie spread between them so thick she could almost feel it. Surely Tikova could feel it, too. He blinked a few times, then his fury melted into a curious expression. "You…offered to help my community?"

She nodded, not trusting her voice.

His lips curled into a smile. His voice softened. "Then I apologize for shouting when I should be thanking you. I appreciate you healing my people."

My community. My people. Tikova was very specific when talking about Slagrock. If she wanted these people to trust her with their innermost secrets, like whatever the depths bloodbinding was, she had to be the same. *I have to convince him I actually want to be here.*

She swallowed her nerves and forced herself not to look at Rhonwen. "Our community, you mean. I'm always happy to help our people."

Tikova studied her. "So you've chosen to stay with us then. To live here."

"I've chosen to stay, yes. Slagrock is a fascinating community, and I want to record everything I can for you to celebrate your accomplishments." The lie slipped off her tongue easily, for truth rang through it as well. Slagrock was fascinating. She did want to record their lives, but not to celebrate their stories, rather to bring them back home and expose them. It was the best lie she'd ever told, and she hoped it would allow her more freedom to find a way out. "To tell history how it really is."

Mimicking his words back to him seemed to seal the deal. Tikova immediately brightened. "I'd like you to go back to Sroc, then, once everything is cleaned up. You asked about bloodbinding before. Sroc should be able to show you now. Perhaps even let you help."

The idea sent a thrill through Adaris. Bloodbinding. If she could record the ancient crafting technique and bring it back home for others, it might turn the tide of war. "I would like that. It seems like an important facet of our story here. And after the fight last night, I'd love to ask the other community members about their bloodbound artifacts. It was quite impressive how they turned the tide in our favor."

Her gut roiled with the sensation of Rhonwen's gaze at her back, full of accusations and fear, but if doors were opening for her, she had to move through them quickly. She had to know if any of those artifacts could break Spectrum's cage. There were so many people to talk to. If she had his blessing, they might open up more.

"Of course. Ask away." Tikova straightened. "But you'll have to continue to live in the prison hut with Rhonwen until we can make a better living space for you."

"That's fair," Adaris replied easily. She didn't yet have free rein, but there was hope for more freedom on the horizon. *Be more like them.* The rest had given some of her energy back and she dipped into her crafting for one final push to reactivate the anklet. The bands of energy reappeared, the pain vanished, and like always, the fog from her crafting ebbed away.

With a final grin at the gemstones glowing a bright orange on Adaris' ankle, Tikova swiveled toward the food hut, shouting something about a feast.

Adaris stood, brushing dust off her knees and glanced at Kye. Would he still accompany her everywhere she went? And if he did, would that really be a problem? He'd lied for her. He might be a Silver Shade.

Rhonwen rose more slowly, staring after Tikova's retreating back as it disappeared into the shadows of the food hut before turning her attention to Adaris.

Adaris winked at her, hoping she understood what had just happened, but the tears filming Rhonwen's eyes told a different story.

Chapter Twenty-Four

"GO BACK TO YOUR prison hut," Kye whispered over the growing murmur of voices emanating from the food hut. The community center was completely empty, save for the three of them. "Even though five of our people perished, there will be a feast to celebrate defeating the Vagari Moon Knights. There always is after a battle like this." He paused, his voice cracking. "And there's always quite the selection of meats."

At those words, Kye's eyes darkened, and Rhonwen grabbed Adaris' hand, squeezing until it hurt. It took Adaris a few heartbeats to understand why.

The companion animals? *They wouldn't.* She had to be sure. "The Moon Knight's companions?"

Kye nodded, but the despair in his eyes told the truth far more than the action did. He gave her a smile that was more of a grimace. "It's a feast."

Rhonwen choked back a sob, slapping a hand over her lips.

Bile rose thick in Adaris' throat. She had to get the painter away from there, away from the horror of what was about to happen. "Yes, let's go back to the prison hut."

Questions still swirled in her mind about Kye, about his companion animal. Could he possibly be part of the Silver Shade? Why had he lied for her, for them? "Could we talk to you as well?"

Kye shook his head. "It'll be expected for me to be at the feast. New members to the community, such as yourself, should attend as well. I'd advise you to hide in your prison hut while you still can. Perhaps no one will think of you."

Adaris nodded and tried to get Rhonwen to move. The painter held her ground, eyes riveted to the food hut and the cheers inside.

"Rhonwen, let's go," Adaris whispered. "We don't want any part of what's about to happen."

Rhonwen's lip trembled, but she let Adaris pull her back to the hut in silence, Kye trailing them like always. Dawn sliced blinding pink and orange rays onto the shattered rock pathway as the sun rose fully above the horizon.

As soon as the lock clicked into place behind them, Rhonwen engulfed her in a hug.

"Whoa." Surprise rippled through Adaris. For a heartbeat, she didn't know how to react, but then she wrapped her arms around Rhonwen. The painter shook, her breathing more pained gasps than anything else. Head tucked into the crook of Adaris' neck, she clutched Adaris' tunic as if she never wanted to let go.

"What if they eat Spectrum, too?" Rhonwen cried.

"They won't," Adaris whispered into her hair, rubbing small circles on Rhonwen's back. "They won't hurt him. Kye made it clear that it was the Moon Knight's companions."

Rhonwen let out a sob and, as if that cracked something loose inside her, she started to cry in earnest. Tears dampened Adaris' tunic and dripped down her neck.

Adaris had never seen this side of Rhonwen before. She knew Rhonwen to be angry in the face of danger, fierce and icy as a winter storm...not breaking apart. The pungent scent of blood and sweat clung to her, but Adaris didn't care. Nothing mattered except calming Rhonwen.

"The Moon Knight's companions," Adaris said again, a firm edge in her voice to try to slice through Rhonwen's tears. "Not yours. Not Spectrum."

Rhonwen sucked in a breath and drew away, drew back until her knees hit the chair and she crumpled onto it. She pushed her hand into her bag and drew out three aca nuts, palming them into her mouth and chewing. Adaris didn't move to stop her. Rhonwen needed to calm down and this was the way she did it, by dulling her senses. It wasn't the best way, but it worked.

Not even waiting for the drug to fill her system, Rhonwen took out two more and stared at them, gleaming white in her brown palm. Her hand trembled, vibrated so much the nuts rolled off. Then, as if that sharpened something in her mind and dug a point of pain even deeper, Rhonwen clutched her chest with both hands and squeezed her eyes shut. Tears rolled down her cheeks, over her lips, and dripped off her chin.

Adaris immediately went to her, kneeling on the stone floor and putting her hands on Rhonwen's knees. "Rhonwen, they're not going to eat Spectrum. Why would they, after keeping you captive so long?"

Rhonwen started shaking her head before the words even left Adaris' lips. "I know. I know. It's not that, Adaris."

"Then what?" Adaris squeezed Rhonwen's knees and leaned closer. Even kneeling, her tall frame let her bump Rhonwen's forehead with her own. "Tell me."

"Before. During the battle. I took too many aca nuts, and it dulled me too much, and I couldn't access my crafting, and—" She dipped her head.

Adaris palmed Rhonwen's cheek, lifting her face to catch Rhonwen's gaze. Pleading Rhonwen to tell her more, to let her in. Rhonwen's yellow eyes were bloodshot orange, like a sunrise. Even the thin film of the aca nut drug couldn't hide that. "You can tell me, Rhonwen."

"If you hadn't been there—if I hadn't healed—" She hiccuped, and her words dissolved into another round of tears. She reached out and found Adaris' other hand, clutching it with both of her own.

The Moon Knight battle. Adaris had snapped Rhonwen out of the stupor. It felt like that had happened ages ago, but it was actually just last night. From the way Rhonwen spoke, the memory weighed heavily on her. A companion animal was a Vagari's other half. The possibility that their companion wouldn't be alive the next dawn would ruin any Vagari, even one as fierce as Rhonwen. Adaris' breath left her. Every day, Rhonwen had to live knowing her companion animal might not be there when she woke up, knowing she couldn't help him or heal him. It was like living in perpetual torture. *"Oh, he's bleeding."* Rhonwen had said the words so nonchalantly in the midst of a battle. Spectrum cawed and coiled, clearly in pain. And all she had said was, *"Oh, he's bleeding."*

The aca nut drug must've dampened her ability to feel his pain and his desperation, it had dulled her senses too well at a moment she least expected. The drug removed that natural pull to aid her companion animal.

Adaris' heart broke down the middle for her friend.

"But I was there, and you did heal him," she replied in a quiet voice. She clutched Rhonwen's hands with her own. "Spectrum is okay, and so are we."

"But before you snapped me out of it, I didn't care," Rhonwen replied, averting her gaze once more. "I didn't care."

"But then you did." Adaris put a hand under Rhonwen's chin and tilted her head up so their eyes met. Rhonwen was the strongest Vagari Adaris had ever known. She wouldn't let her think anything less. "You were there when he needed you. That's all that matters."

Rhonwen's eyes shimmered with tears. "I can't stop eating the nuts. I knew I was addicted, but it almost cost Spectrum his life and I—" Her voice cracked. "I can't let that happen ever again. I need help."

Adaris sighed. The nuts were something they had joked about. Rhonwen had seemed so flippant about them.

Easing into the stone chair next to Rhonwen, Adaris twined their fingers together. This wasn't the conversation she thought they'd be having but it was something that obviously weighed heavily on Rhonwen's mind. *I have to think of something to help.* She knew Rhonwen had an issue with the nuts, knew Rhonwen depended on them quite a bit, but true addiction was another matter entirely. One Adaris had no experience dealing with.

And one they wouldn't be able to fix while they were still in Slagrock.

"Okay," she said slowly. "My crafting might be of some use. I can—"

"No!" Rhonwen tightened her hold, leaning forward. "No. Your crafting is already painful for you. I won't allow you to use it on me. Not for my mistakes. And you hanging around with me will look suspicious. I forbid you from healing me."

The rest of Adaris' reply crumbled like sand giving way to a wave. She rubbed her neck, trying to come up with a different plan. Spectrum's life could depend on it. Depths, if Rhonwen was as out of it as she was last night, all their lives could depend on it.

"Then you should cut back little by little."

Rhonwen looked at her like she had grown kark legs. "Too little is just as useless as none at all." She buried her face in her hands. "I don't know what to do."

Adaris looked around the hut, gaze skipping off the bed and over the desk, before landing on the easel in the corner. When she was stressed, Adaris often used her writing to calm herself, to get it all out on the page instead of it taking up space in her head. Her attention slid to the paintbrushes methodically placed on the nearby desk. "Have you tried painting?"

"I paint all the time."

"No, you paint what Tikova wants you to. The community. The rituals. Their history." When Rhonwen nodded, Adaris let out a woosh of air. "That wouldn't calm anyone down. Not with what they've done to you. Have you tried painting what makes you happy?"

Doubt filled Rhonwen's expression, pulling her lips down into a frown. "What would I paint?"

"Spectrum. Your mothers. Home. Something that brings you joy. Anything, just to give your hands and mind something to do." Rhonwen started shaking her head, but Adaris covered the painter's hands with her own. "I know it's not much of an idea, but it would just be something to try alongside slowly ebbing back from the nuts. And it's...well it's the only option we have while we're here," she confessed.

Chewing on her lip as if she was chewing on the idea, Rhonwen's gaze slipped from Adaris to the paint cans littering the floor. "I guess we could try."

"Good." Adaris gave her an encouraging smile. "When you feel the need to eat them, talk to me. I'll try to help."

"Without your crafting," Rhonwen replied.

Adaris sighed. "I can't promise that after what happened last night, but until that's absolutely necessary, I'll supply ideas of what to paint instead."

Rhonwen frowned. She scrubbed her palms over her face, then nodded.

Wanting to give Rhonwen some hope and a distraction, she continued, "I have some exciting news that might take your mind off what happened."

Rhonwen perked up. "Tell me."

She leaned forward, whispering into the painter's ear just in case someone nearby might be listening. "Kye might be a Silver Shade. I saw a tattoo just behind his ear. And the fight gave me a really good idea on how to break Spectrum free."

Rhonwen's whole face lit up at those words. "Free Spectrum. How?" Of course, Rhonwen would skip past the Silver Shade revelation; her companion animal was always a higher priority.

"The curlhorn Vagari," Adaris replied. "Her crafting attack—how her legs brightened orange and she rammed the worshippers—made me realize I don't need to ask every single community member about their artifacts."

Rhonwen's eyes widened. Always fast to catch on, she whispered, "If we find the right Vagari Animal crafting, we might find a way to break

Spectrum's cage. Or maybe even Nature crafting, like how the Hallr Nemora melt the stone. We could narrow our search to those artifacts."

"Yes, and I have Tikova's blessing now. If anyone gives me grief, I can use that as leverage." Adaris smirked.

Rhonwen straightened. "Your anklet. You have an Animal crafting artifact. Could you use that to help break Spectrum free?"

Adaris sat with that for a moment, turning the idea over in her mind. Could she use her anklet? It didn't seem to do anything other than strengthen her leg, but she didn't really try for anything else. The orange claws and lightning strikes from the Moon Knight attack came back to her. She focused on the anklet, willing it to do...anything else. The bands of heat circling her leg tightened, but that was it. No, the anklet didn't grant her any other crafting abilities. The revelation sparked through her mind. "I...I think each artifact only has one ability lashed to it. Mine can only strengthen my leg." The disappointment lingering in Rhonwen's eyes pushed Adaris to continue, "But if Kye really is with the Silver Shade, perhaps he can help us escape. I'll find a way to talk to him."

Rhonwen leaned back and rubbed her neck. Suspicion darkened her eyes. "Be careful with that. I don't know if we can trust him. Perhaps ask first why he lied for you."

Something inside Adaris did trust Kye. He'd been nothing but kind to her, and his gentleness had warmed her to him. She knew in her core that his lie had been to protect her. She had to know why he was so unlike most of the others in this community. "I will. You know I lied about wanting to join this community, right?"

Rhonwen nodded. "I know. Step carefully, though. Just because Tikova trusts you now doesn't mean he won't kill you anyway."

Terror curled up Adaris' spine at those words, as she remembered the callous way he'd hacked off Berhn's father's arms. "I'll be careful."

"Good." Rhonwen's gaze drifted to the prison door, the metal bars gleaming in the sunlight. "You're going to get a new living space soon." Tears welled in her eyes again. "How are we going to talk?"

"We'll find a way," Adaris assured her, squeezing her hand. That must've been why she looked so down after Adaris lied about wanting to stay in Slagrock—Tikova had promised her a new home, one away from the painter. She'd be alone, again. Adaris didn't exactly know how they'd talk yet, but she'd find a way. She scooped up the nuts on the floor. "Can you give me any nuts you have on you right now?"

Rhonwen's lips tightened, but she dug through the side pouch she kept over her shoulder. Ten small, white nuts dropped onto the table. "I don't have any others on me."

"Good." After handing two to Rhonwen, Adaris pushed the rest of the nuts into her own side bag. "Let's try painting for a little while to wind down."

"Only two?" Rhonwen asked, her eyes wide.

"For right now. If you need more after the painting's complete, you can have them." Adaris rose and went to the desk, desperately trying to ignore all the pains in her body and the tiredness pulling her eyelids closed. She lifted all the cans and set them on the table. "Paint your happiest memory."

Rhonwen popped the two into her mouth and chewed slowly. She stared at the blank page as if waiting. After a few moments, a shudder pulled a sigh from her lips. The film across her eyes thickened. "My happy place."

Grabbing a few paintbrushes, she began in earnest. Adaris settled back in her chair, fascinated by the way Rhonwen dripped small amounts of paint onto her own arm—mixing it on her skin then transferring it to the paper. Getting the right color, Adaris assumed. Strokes of thick green at the bottom dotted with multicolored specks, black-blue-orange swirls at the top speckled with white. Where they met, slashes of darker green vertical lines mingled in a gradual lift.

A grassland scattered with flowers.

The scent of paint filled the prison hut, thick and heavy as honey, but Adaris didn't mind. As Rhonwen continued to paint, Adaris went through Rhonwen's belongings and gathered every aca nut she could find, in Rhonwen's larger bag, under the crumpled blanket, inside a paint can Adaris thought was empty. It was like a wyvern's hoard, but Adaris was determined to find each one. She shoved all the nuts into her own bag so Rhonwen wouldn't have the temptation around.

Rhonwen's brush strokes slowed with each passing moment. Though her eyelids drooped, she stayed awake until the painting was complete. A smile lingered on her lips when she finished. She touched the corner of the sky. After a sharp intake of breath, Rhonwen lifted her gaze to Adaris. "I'm ready to lie down."

Rhonwen curled up on the bed, trailing one fingertip through the splotch of black-blue on her forearm. Within a few moments, she was snoring softly.

Adaris exhaled in relief. It had worked. She only hoped it would keep working until she had the answers she needed. Until they found the artifact to break Spectrum from his cage. Until she discovered what Kye was really up to at Slagrock. And until she'd recorded all Sroc's secrets about bloodbinding.

Chapter Twenty-Five

PINK AND ORANGE SUNLIGHT pooled in their prison hut, splashing blinding colors on the beige stone floor and walls. Adaris must've slept the day and night away. Dawn had clearly arrived again, and judging from the hum of conversation outside, the community had already awoken. She rose from the stone floor and activated her anklet. Rhonwen still snored, curled up on her bed, and Adaris was grateful for it. She left three nuts on the table with a note.

Use them sparingly, and paint joyful things. Come find me if it gets too much.

She knocked on the inside of the prison hut door. The lock clicked, and the door creaked open into a glare of sunlight. She walked outside, expecting to see Kye, but a woman with a gash sealing one eye shut stood guard. The woman glared at Adaris so forcefully with the good eye—a vibrant piercing purple—that it made Adaris shiver.

"Hello there," Adaris said.

The guard didn't answer. She closed the door with a slam and locked it once again, turning to face the sunshine. It was clear the guard didn't want anything to do with Adaris. After a quick glance at the woman's white armband, Adaris moved away from the prison hut.

White meant Blood crafting which meant healing, and healing wouldn't help them in breaking Spectrum out of his stone cage. Adaris needed to find an artifact that would help her and Rhonwen set Spectrum free. Nature crafting brown, like the ability to melt rock, or Animal crafting orange, like that thunderclap's ability to crack stone. Not healing. Not shields. Whatever creature's powers had created her anklet weren't the correct ability to break stone, but Adaris knew she could activate the right artifact just as she did her anklet.

Yim. Rhonwen's guard had a glowing orange band. She set out to find him.

Making a quick note in her book, she started the tally before heading toward the Ponuriah statue in the community center. Blood smeared numerous places on the ground, coloring the stone orange and blue and brown.

Curiously, Adaris didn't see Kye anywhere. Shock and disappointment warred inside her. To dismiss her guard so readily, Tikova must've truly believed her lie and Kye's, that she wanted to stay and help the community and that she'd stayed by Kye's side throughout the whole battle. Of course, the one time she wanted to talk to Kye, ask him about the Silver Shade tattoo behind his ear, he was no longer her shadow.

"Why are we gathered today?" she asked an older Elu with a cloth wrapping around her neck. She must've been wounded in the battle.

The Elu pointed. "We're watching."

Adaris followed the woman's outstretched hand to the space where most of the damage had been done. Most of the huts on one side had been flattened, reduced to nothing but shattered and blackened stone.

A trio of Hallr Nemora stood on the edge of the shattered path facing the rubble, hands in the air. Adaris noted the glowing blue rings on their fingers. Elu Moon crafting. She marked that down, adding three more to the tally, then lifted her gaze just in time to see the splotched markings on the men's gray skin glow bronze as each of them sank into their Nature crafting.

Smooth as water and just as fluid, one—two—three pillars of nearly white stone arched upward, spread like a blossom, then curved down and formed an unmistakable hut.

Adaris scribbled the whole thing down. Even though these people were the enemy, murderers who would kill her or Rhonwen for stepping out of line, she had to admire their talents. Begrudgingly so.

The trio of crafters moved to the next pile of rubble, and Adaris forced her gaze to the other people surrounding her, keeping a careful eye on their jewelry. Armbands, circlets, and rings glowed around her—but none the right color. Blue and white, not orange or brown. She did a quick mental headcount, determining there were twenty-three others to search.

No, less. Kye had told her five of their own had perished. Perhaps the five who died wore the artifacts she needed. Surely Tikova and Sroc would hand out those artifacts again. Until then, where would Sroc keep them? Maybe she took the spare artifacts back to her research area to keep with the others. Adaris checked her book. There were quite a few inert artifacts that had orange and brown gemstones set into them. It might be worth it to check those as well.

As she wandered toward the food hut, she made sure to walk in direct sunlight. If Tikova was watching, he would see someone unafraid of the daylight. Someone who had changed for him. He would see a scribe who'd joined his precious community. Her insides lurched with each step. She palmed an aca nut into her mouth and followed it with a slug of warm water. Addictive or no, one during the day wouldn't hurt. A few more people spilled from their homes, drawing her gaze, but a quick glance told Adaris they didn't have the right artifacts. The drug eventually found its way into her system, and the fear twining in her core unwound a little, enough to keep her in the sunshine.

Keep the ruse going, she told herself. Nothing more.

When she went into the food hut to try to find Yim, her heart sank. Four community members ate food together, and their jewelry glowed bright in the shadowed hut, as if mocking her. By her count, that left only two. Yim and Celli.

She sighed and turned away, wandered back outside. A scaled, six-legged suncreature lounged on the path, soft crimson belly turned up to the sun, so she skirted around it. Where had all the Vagari and Nemora artifacts gone? She had seen all the colors earlier; she was sure of it. A thought burned through her. The fight. Animal and Nature crafting would be key in battle. Strengthening the wearers like her anklet strengthened her leg. Being able to bend the rock to create rock spikes would turn the tide in the wearer's favor.

Adaris spent the rest of the morning and most of the afternoon trying to find Yim and Celli. Her skin burned in the harsh daylight, even with the cream Rhonwen had given her, and her eyes hurt from squinting so much. Her feet were sore from walking, even with the anklet. She scrubbed a hand across her face, her gaze roaming yet another empty hut. They weren't in Celli's animal research area, or any of the huts, or the gardens. Slagrock wasn't that large, so losing someone felt almost laughable. *Focus.* Only two community members had artifacts that might help them escape.

She had nearly given up on finding Celli. By chance, Adaris noticed the elderly woman sitting cross-legged on a particularly flat rock at the edge of the community.

"Hello, Celli." Adaris sat next to her.

"Good afternoon, scribe," the elderly woman responded.

A short conversation later, Adaris discovered Celli's circlet could allow her to grow a small bush the size of her palm. A cute tavern trick, but rather useless. It wouldn't help save Spectrum.

Only one active artifact left to find, save the five from the dead community members. The others in Sroc's research area are inert—just simple jewelry.

Her insides twisted. It had been foolish to hope that escape would be this easy. Her gaze drifted to the horizon, to the ocean, mind skipping ahead to her raft. At least they had a way off this continent once they freed Spectrum. The raft would easily carry her and Rhonwen. Spectrum could rest on it as well, settle his head, at least, and float the rest of his body behind. At least they had that.

A small figure sat alone on top of the rock columns that overlooked the ocean. Next to the figure, a blue-green gemstone glinted in a metal pan. Berhn.

Needing to rest her feet anyway, Adaris went to him. Berhn had started an interesting conversation before the fight, and she wanted to finish it. The young man wanted to leave Slagrock, leave the community, and that struck a chord in her. Perhaps they could leave together.

She settled down next to Berhn. He didn't say anything when she sat next to him, so Adaris waited.

Berhn stared at the gentle, cobalt waves, his small body rocking back and forth like he was on the deck of a boat. A dark, brown bruise spread across his chin. Scratches covered his bare arms. Why didn't he heal himself with the glowing artifact in his earlobe? The Blood crafting locked within should heal those wounds easily.

Adaris stared at the young Nemora. The crystal pattern glinted on his forehead, next to his eyes, and down his chin. "Why don't you heal yourself, Berhn?"

Tears gathered at the corners of his eyes. "I don't want to use anything given to me by them anymore."

"Because you feel like you don't belong?" Adaris pressed, their earlier conversation gentling her voice.

Berhn sniffed, gaze still locked on the ocean. "Because Tikova saw me helping my parents instead of helping the injured like I was supposed to."

His voice—usually so cheerful and full of hope—sounded hollow. Adaris nodded. "It's natural to go to your loved ones in times of fear. They could have been in trouble. You wanted to help."

"But it's not what he wanted. It's not what was best for the community," Berhn replied, an unchecked tone of bitterness in his voice. "I should've helped heal people. Other people."

"With your earring?"

He shook his head. "It only heals me, but I'm supposed to help stitch up wounds. That should have been my higher priority." It sounded like he was reciting a schoolbook, or the teachings of a madman.

"Don't be so hard on yourself. You were worried that your family was in danger."

"I just don't want to be here anymore." Berhn turned to her. "Last night wasn't the first attack, and ever since we got another shard, it feels like we're ramping up to something and I don't want any part of it."

Another shard. Her shard. The one she found by the cave so long ago. Had it unlocked a greater power somehow? If calling on the suncreatures to do their bidding or regrowing people's arms was any indication of their powers with the sun goddess shards thus far, she couldn't wait to know more about what a higher level could do. *And that shimmering Elu fortress?* Impenetrable.

"That's fair." Adaris tried to think of a way to broach the subject of leaving with her and Rhonwen without giving anything away. She didn't want Berhn to make any rash decisions or do something that would get him in trouble, but it also wasn't fair to make him stay when he was clearly so uncomfortable.

Berhn twisted his glowing earring. "Perhaps you should take this. You might make better use of it than I have."

Unease coiled in Adaris' gut. The way his voice sounded made her want to move, run away, bring him with them. "I don't think that's a good idea, Berhn. They wanted you to have it, giving it away might make Tikova doubt you. That could be dangerous, for you and your family."

"But I've already paid the price for it," he muttered. "And they already forced me to go through my choosing earlier than normal, shouldn't Tikova trust me after that?"

"He should," she replied gently, but something else caught Adaris' attention and she canted her head. "Sroc never mentioned a price."

"The blood price." He pointed to his ear. A tiny scar ran down his lobe where they cut the flesh to shove the piercing through. "So I can use the artifact's crafting and my Nature crafting at the same time."

Adaris shook her head. *They all paid some kind of blood price, and I haven't. That's why whenever I access my natural crafting, the anklet deactivates. Whenever I sleep, it turns off.* She made a mental note to add that to her book. "Sroc left that part out."

Berhn gave her a curious look. "Well, it just takes a drop. It hurts, but not that badly. And you don't need to pay it to use Sroc's weapons, since they don't need to be active all the time."

They spent a few more quiet moments together, watching the sun and the rolling waves. A suncreature burst from the waves, crimson eyes and scales flashing.

Berhn ended the silence with a confession. "I don't like their version of Ponuriah, Adaris. I'd rather be an envoy for what I believe in. For the gentler side of her. The warm fire." Berhn seemed to let go of any hesitation, as if he'd been wanting to say this for a long time. "I want to go to all the Groves and talk to the Nemora there and show them that Ponuriah worshippers don't have to be dangerous. That we're not all terrible people. That we can work together to make things better. Share resources instead of taking them by force."

Adaris leaned back on her hands, staring at the surprising Nemora man. The fire in his eyes was unmistakable, the passion clear in the way his voice steadied, but how could fire be gentle? She remembered his earlier explanation—how some things had to burn in order to sprout. "What do you think about Tikova and Sroc's plan to burn the Groves to the ground? It seems like the war is building to that, to kill the Nemora who cultivate the lands and begin anew."

"I would never do that," Berhn replied earnestly. "But I would like to create a new section of the Groves. One specifically designed to study what happens when you burn specific plants. To see what grows after you scorch the ground. It would be contained, though. I would like to use the Cinder Forest, maybe even see if the Nemora who worship the sun goddess could cultivate it. Using the sun goddess shards might even create new plant life, new rocks, new gemstones even! We don't really know."

His eyes shimmered with these ideas, and Adaris couldn't look away.

"I even have a symbol for her." Berhn pressed a fist into his palm, then opened his fist once more, spreading his fingers. "It's to symbolize her warmth, not her viciousness."

A simple symbol to denote such a unique statement. She opened her book and wrote his words down, noting the symbol he'd created as well. Words were powerful. An idea could ripple into many others, but Tikova and Sroc didn't want words. They wanted bloodshed and a new fiery beginning; they wanted to win. The Moon Knights and the rest of her homeland would respond in kind, in violence, because they had to defend themselves.

Berhn had a point, though. No one back home knew of the "gentler" side of Ponuriah. It wasn't taught in classes, and it certainly wasn't in any of the history books. Even though Adaris had a hard time believing in it herself, Berhn's faith in the kinder side settled something inside her. His was an untold story and she respected that.

"I feel like you'd be the right person to teach this side of Ponuriah," Adaris replied truthfully.

Berhn nodded, and though a smile curled his lips, he said nothing more.

"I have to go find Yim," Adaris said in a way of saying goodbye and pushed to her feet.

"He's over there." Berhn pointed behind him.

Adaris turned. Sure enough, Yim was headed their way across the community center, Rhonwen in tow. Adaris met them halfway.

"Scribe." He nodded hello, which Adaris returned. He shifted his gaze to Rhonwen, and a frown cut his dark features. Adaris had expected Yim to still be injured, getting thrown back by the curlhorn Vagari like he had during the battle. Sroc must have healed him. "I told you I'd find her for you."

"Thank you," Rhonwen replied quietly.

The dress Rhonwen wore wrapped around her like water, the color of the deepest ocean flecked with paler hues.

"I've already had two nuts," she said, voice tight, not bothering to keep her words low. Her eyes were bloodshot orange, like she'd been crying. She swiped a hand across her forehead, wiping away the sweat that beaded there, but leaving a smear of yellow paint behind. "Give me something to paint."

Adaris was about to respond, but Yim yanked Rhonwen around to face him. He gripped her arm so tight her skin paled around his fingers. "That's what we had to find her for? I told you what Tikova wanted you to paint."

Anger jumped in a muscle by Rhonwen's jaw. "And I told you that I'll paint those new huts for your precious records, but that I need a break first."

Yim scowled at her and tightened his grip. Rhonwen's lip trembled. She didn't back down.

Not wanting Rhonwen to draw more of Yim's ire, Adaris put a hand on Rhonwen's arm, pulling her attention. "What happened?"

"Nothing we need to discuss right now," Rhonwen replied, shaking her head. Tears shimmered in her eyes.

Adaris glanced at Yim, who rolled his eyes and tapped an erratic beat with his sandal. She turned back to her friend. "Rhonwen, tell me."

Rhonwen bit her lip. "Tikova joined me for my first meal. He was grateful for me painting the celebration for him and staying up to help the wounded."

That didn't sound so bad. Something else must've happened. Tikova rarely showed up at their prison for no reason. "But?"

"He brought the meal with him and—" Rhonwen's voice caught. She pressed a hand to her mouth.

"It was just meat," Yim interrupted again. "We can't stand around here for—"

"Wait," Adaris replied, putting a hand up to stop him. The man gave her a seething look but backed off. Apparently, she did have some respect now. Probably an increasingly smaller amount every moment she kept him waiting, but it was better than none. Adaris turned to Rhonwen once more. "And?"

Rhonwen's lip trembled. "It was a Moon Knight companion animal. Wyvern. Tikova told me—asked me to eat it with him."

A test. Adaris felt the world tilt. It made a sick sort of sense that they'd test Rhonwen. She was still their prisoner, still locked away after all this time, but to have her eat companion meat was just cruel. These people would stop at nothing to remind them of their viciousness.

"What did you do?" Whatever her decision, Adaris would support her.

Rhonwen dipped her head. "I...I couldn't do it, Adaris."

Adaris stilled, wondering what repercussions this failed test would bring.

"I tried," Rhonwen said quickly. "I honestly tried, but I couldn't bring myself to do it. Not a companion animal, never a—" Closing her eyes, Rhonwen clenched her jaw around a sob. Then, in an immense showing of will, her whole body stilled. When she opened her eyes, determination had solidified in her gaze. "So, give me something nice to paint or more nuts."

What would take Rhonwen's mind off what Tikova had tried to force her to do? Not Spectrum, it would hit too close to her heart. Not the grasslands, it would take too much time, and Yim was already restless. *Then what?* Adaris noticed the small orange and yellow paint cans dangling off Yim's belt. Orange and yellow, yellow and orange. She wiped some sweat off her brow, and a thought finally struck her. "Paint your favorite flower from the grasslands."

Rhonwen dropped her gaze to the pale rocky ground, as though seeing but not seeing. "All right."

With that, she sat down on the stone, put her spare paper on her lap, and gestured for Yim to give her the paint cans. He did, with a huff, and Rhonwen went to work.

Yim hadn't said anything since Adaris requested he wait, the scowl still firmly on his lips as if chiseled there.

Wanting to give Rhonwen the time she needed and wanting to talk to the man anyway, Adaris caught Yim's gaze. "Thank you for letting her take this break."

He grunted, obviously still not happy about it.

She lifted her book and quill, flipping to the page that held Yim's stories. "I realized that I never got to ask you about your armband."

"What of it?" Yim wrapped his thick fingers around the glowing orange band.

"What does it do?" Such a simple question, but her throat tightened as the more important one lingered in her mind. *Could it help us?*

He gave her a long stare, then lifted his spear. "It strengthens my arms, like the nigbaba that live in the jungle on the mainland."

Disappointment lowered her shoulders. She knew of the nigbaba. The furry creature would use its long, front arms to propel it forward and swing from the vines. Their strength was well suited to amplify Yim's already thick muscles, but it would do less for her or Rhonwen's frail frames. Surely not enough to break through the stone of Spectrum's cage. The armband wouldn't help.

"That suits you well," she replied, sketching a hulking, hairy creature as tall as her, with a chest as big as a wine barrel and arms like tree trunks. Flat face, long skinny tail, six limbs.

Rhonwen stood and stretched, then handed Adaris the painting she had completed. A vibrant orange flower with a yellow center and stem. She gave Adaris a tight smile. "Thank you. That helped...a little." She turned to Yim. "We should go back now."

Yim nodded, and after a final glance at Adaris, gestured for Rhonwen to move along.

Adaris watched them go. She knew painting alone wasn't what Rhonwen needed to break her addictive habit. That would take time and better healers and more support than Adaris could give. A safe place to sleep as well. *But the painting helped.*

Yim's armband glowed faintly, as if challenging the sunshine, and Adaris had to turn away. She couldn't believe their bad luck. So many people and not one of the artifacts they wore could break Spectrum free, aside from Sroc's brown ring.

That left the inert artifacts in Sroc's research lab. Perhaps Adaris could learn how to imbue one of them with power. Maybe Sroc would gift her one for her efforts.

She shook her head. It was a long shot, though she couldn't help the thread of excitement that wound around her. That long shot held something she hadn't felt in a long time. Hope.

Chapter Twenty-Six

ADARIS TWISTED A LOCK of her fiery red hair between her fingers, gaze skipping over the quiet community. *Why can I never find who I'm looking for?* She had searched high and low for Sroc, yet couldn't find the young researcher anywhere. Stars glimmered on a black sky, no moon in sight. Adaris' exposed skin stung from being so long in the sunshine. Tiredness pulled at her, its claws hooking into her limbs and eyelids, making them heavy. Most people had already gone to bed.

She covered a yawn with her hand, then paused, hand resting on her lips in thought. It was nighttime. She should be flourishing and wide awake, but all she wanted to do was sleep.

I'm becoming like one of them.

The longer she stayed in Slagrock, the more she got used to their cycle of things—sleep at night, awake during the day. It was odd that she hadn't realized it sooner. Fear wormed its way into her. She didn't want to be like one of them, but a part of her worried it was inevitable, especially since she had to act like one to survive.

She went back to the prison hut. Searching for Sroc at night would probably be useless, so researching Sroc's artifacts would be first on tomorrow's agenda. It would be the best place to find one that could set Spectrum free. The only place left, really.

It would be nice to speak to Rhonwen, too, get some of her own fears off her chest and alleviate some of Rhonwen's worries as well. Rhonwen had failed Tikova's test, and Adaris knew the midday painting had only helped so much.

And then, only after she found the correct artifact, perhaps Adaris could learn about Sroc's research into bloodbinding. An ancient ritual of her kin. That would be a story for the ages, she was sure of it, one maybe even worthy of a black quill. More than that, it was a story she herself was curious about.

She had nearly reached the prison hut when a Hallr Nemora stepped into her path. Despite Adaris' height, the Nemora towered over her. He gave her a gentle smile. "Anoc-suna, scribe Adaris."

He carried a sack of cloth and an unlit stone lantern, but Adaris' gaze snagged on the large, jagged gray splotch on his neck. The memory hit like a punch. This particular Nemora had speared a Moon Knight through the chest with a spike of stone. He'd killed the knight instantly with his Nature crafting. He could kill her just as easily if he wanted to. She swallowed her unease. "Anoc-suna," she replied. "Can I help you with something?"

The man chuckled, his dark-brown eyes crinkling. He set his bundle of cloth onto the stone path. "No, but I can help you. Tikova said you need better accommodations, and I'm the one he tasked that job to."

Better accommodations. Because she was now a member of the Slagrock community. She nodded numbly. A part of her didn't really believe Tikova would believe her lie that she wanted to stay with them. She realized she'd been staring in silence at the Nemora a beat too long.

Thankfully, he didn't comment. Instead, he motioned to the empty space next to him, a swath of flat stones on the outside edge of the curved pathway. "Your hut will be here."

Apparently, he's been tasked to create the hut right now. She watched in awe, as copper light filled his eyes, glowing in the darkness like coins catching firelight. He lifted his hands, the sleeves of his blue robe falling away to reveal more dark markings scattered across his pale arms. Those markings burned with copper light as well.

With a few deft hand movements, the Hallr Nemora melted the stone, expanded the molten rock into a bubble, and formed a hut that mirrored the other living quarters in this community. A large swath of molten stone melted away, forming an open archway, and a few smaller sections melted to create windows.

He moved the stone as easily as she breathed, the rock listening to his each and every whim. She got out her book and penned a quick description of the Nemora and his talents, just as he lowered his hands. The crafting light dimmed.

"That was impressive crafting," she said.

The Nemora simply nodded. He lifted a stone lantern from the bundle by his feet and handed it to her. Then, tucking his hands into his sleeves, he turned away.

"Wait." Adaris lifted her book. "Can I get your name?"

The Nemora looked back over his shoulder. "My name is Tiy."

"Tiy." Adaris wrote that down. "Thank you."

He didn't respond, and Adaris stared after him as he disappeared into another hut further down the curved path. Just like the trio from earlier, Tiy had moved that rock so easily, it was stunning. Beautiful even, a work of art created just for her.

Yet the image of him spearing a Moon Knight through the chest with equal ease made her squirm.

It didn't sail past her that Tikova had probably chosen this particular Nemora to build her home to show her that, while she was part of this community, she could be killed the instant she stepped out of line.

She rubbed her arms, a chill slipping under her loose clothing. Lighting the lantern, she went inside, and the soft yellow firelight spread inside the circular space. The single room was large enough for three people to spread their arms wide and still have space to spare. The windows gave her a view of the other living huts on one side and an expansive wall of darkness on the other, facing inland. A stone bed full of black sand sat in one curve of the room, a wide stone desk with a single stone chair on the other, and an empty bookshelf rested at the very back. It seemed as if they expected her to be the one to fill them with the stories of this community. She ran her hand over the smooth rock of the middle shelf. Just how long did they expect her to stay? How many books did they expect her to fill?

Tiy had left the bundle by the path, so she went to grab it, thinking perhaps some of her belongings would be inside. Not that she had a lot to begin with. She hefted the bundle into her arms. From her vantage point, she could see the path to the prison hut, a line of lanterns casting light on the bars on the door.

Guilt twisted inside her. She had a brand-new abode—and more freedom than ever—while Rhonwen was still stuck inside that prison. *How am I going to speak with Rhonwen now?*

"You don't have to grip me that hard." Rhonwen's voice floated toward her. "I'm going where you want me to, Yim."

Adaris turned to the voice. Her gaze instantly latched onto Rhonwen and Yim. They had reached the furthest curve of the path and stopped by a flickering lantern. Yim lifted a hand and a low slap ricocheted across the quiet community. The slap sent Rhonwen stumbling to the ground.

Adaris winced. She couldn't just stand by while Rhonwen got hurt. Dropping her bundle, Adaris started walking toward the pair.

"You're not walking fast enough," Yim's gruff voice rumbled.

Rhonwen scoffed. "Hitting me won't make me walk faster."

Yim leveled a glare at her, fury dripping from his expression.

Adaris' heart thudded in her chest like a frantic bird. Though she could hear the pain in Rhonwen's voice, the painter's ferocity amazed

Adaris. *Don't talk back. Just do what they say.* She started running toward them. "Yim, what are you doing?"

Yim lifted his eyes to her and waved her away. "Nothing you need to be concerned about, scribe."

As if she was part of this terrible community.

As if she condoned his actions.

As if.

Rage boiled inside her, making her skin hot. She skidded to a stop and put herself between him and Rhonwen, sparing the briefest of glances back at the painter. Blood dribbled out of a cut on Rhonwen's lip. Adaris turned a furious glare toward Yim. "I'm a scribe of this community, Yim, that means everything is my concern. Why are you hurting her?"

Silence pulled back like waters during the start of a tsunami. Adaris' palms sweated under her clenched fists. She was part of this community now, so she could ask questions like that. She could get answers. She should be able to help her friend, even though Rhonwen was a prisoner. And damned to the depths, she couldn't let Rhonwen be hurt anymore.

But Yim rose to the challenge in her stance. He stared down his nose at her, a good head and shoulders above her already tall frame. Cracking his knuckles, he gave her a menacing grin. "Because, scribe, it makes me feel better."

He looped around her with surprising speed, lifted one of his thick legs, and brought his foot down right onto Rhonwen's arm. The unmistakable crack of a broken bone shattered the night. Rhonwen's scream pierced the night and Adaris' heart.

Adaris gasped. Her Blood crafting welled within her, answering her fear. She reached for it. It filled her with warmth, willed her to kneel next to Rhonwen. To heal. A vibrating type of agony spread through her bad leg, her anklet deactivating. Ignoring that pain, she put a hand on Rhonwen's arm. The woman curled into herself, tears streaming down her face and arm broken at a terrible angle, the flesh puckering outward. At least no bones had broken through the skin. Rhonwen moaned, a low sound like a keening animal. Adaris' Blood crafting pooled under her palm. She almost poured her life force into Rhonwen to help heal her as much as she could...but Yim's hardened gaze stopped her.

The challenge she saw there stopped her.

Rhonwen was a prisoner.

It wasn't Adaris' right to heal her, to heal a prisoner. Tikova didn't give his permission to do so, and Tikova needed to give his permission for everything in his precious community.

She stilled her crafting.

Even while her hands trembled and pain clawed inside her at the sight of Rhonwen in anguish beside her, she rose to a stand and met Yim's gaze.

It was one of the hardest things she had ever had to do in her life.

If she stepped out of line, her newfound freedom would probably be the first thing Tikova would take away, and Rhonwen would only be injured more. Or worse. Adaris had to find a way to get them out of there safely. Staying outside, unguarded, would be the best way to do that. Seeing Sroc and obtaining a bloodbound artifact would help set them free. Adaris was sure of it.

She forced her voice to be even and calm. "Tell me the real reason why you injured her, *guard*." She spat out that last word. If he could call her scribe, she could do the same to him. After all, they were part of the same community. She took out her book and quill. "For the history books."

Yim started chuckling.

The sound sank into Adaris' soul. What a vile, vicious, cruel man. She itched to write that down, pen the truth of the matter, the truth of his being, but she knew Tikova would read every word, so she etched it into her mind instead. "Well? Tikova wants me to record everything in this community, so tell me."

Yim winked. The man actually winked. The audacity. "She just didn't listen to me, is all."

Adaris wished she was a fighter, wished she had a weapon to sink into this man's gut, wished her crafting was more powerful so that she could set his veins on fire with pain or drop him with a single touch.

"What's the matter here?" Kye asked.

They both turned toward his voice. The guard walked up next to them, a frown cutting his face. His brown gaze flitted from Adaris to Yim to Rhonwen and back again.

Adaris blinked a few times. She hadn't heard her old guard approach and didn't know where he even came from, but relief flooded her system. He would help her, help them. She knew it.

Yim shrugged. "I'm just teaching the painter a lesson in listening."

Kye took in Rhonwen's broken arm, and his expression hardened to stone. "I think you've taught her enough today. Take her back to her prison and leave her be."

Adaris darted her eyes to her old guard. Was that...a warning in Kye's voice? It sure sounded like it to her.

Yim rolled his eyes at the threat but didn't say anything.

Rhonwen still moaned and keened at their feet. Pain clearly washing over her features,

so Adaris reached down to help her stand.

Kye put a hand on her shoulder, stopping her. "Adaris, go back to your hut. You've done enough tonight as well."

Every part of her wanted to take Rhonwen's pain away, comfort her. Once she was in the prison hut, she would be in agony alone. Just like she had been for so many nights before Adaris' arrival.

But Adaris heeded Kye's advice and stepped back. Rhonwen turned her tear-stained face toward her, lip trembling, and the look in her yellow eyes nearly broke Adaris' heart. She wanted to help, wanted to ease some of Rhonwen's suffering, but she knew she had to listen to Kye. She had to do nothing to keep them both safe.

And she hated herself for it.

Kye helped Rhonwen stand and walked with her to the prison hut, Yim trailing behind. He shooed the painter inside and said a few more words to Yim before taking his usual post outside the prison door. Adaris hoped Yim would leave, but the taller guard stood by the door as well, on the opposite side of Kye.

Thoughts brimming with how much pain Rhonwen must be in and how much Adaris hated leaving her that way, she returned to her hut. Shaking out the bundle, she found some new clothes, her old clothes and ruined armor, and the jar of salve Rhonwen had gifted her to help with the sunshine. Dipping her fingers into the cream, she rubbed it onto her burning skin. The rawness faded to tingles. This cream eased her pain of being out in the sunshine, of appearing to belong. She only hoped she would be able to do the same for Rhonwen, soon.

Chapter Twenty-Seven

EARLY MORNING TWILIGHT BLED deep purple and blue light onto the stone walls of Adaris' new hut. She sighed and picked at her new set of clothing. The white sleeveless top showed off the peeling skin on her shoulders, and the billowy pants that cinched by her knees itched, but to play the part, she had to look it. Nerves grated her from last night, her dreams rife with breaking bones and Rhonwen's cries. Adaris calmed herself and activated her anklet, then headed straight for Sroc's research area.

As Adaris slipped through the small break in the stone pillars, the gentle twilight lit the cave, bouncing off the wet stone. A flickering light came from the open hatch. She knelt by it and called down the ladder. "Sroc, are you in there?"

"Where else would I be, scribe?" Adaris could practically hear the smirk in the young researcher's voice. "Has Tikova told you to work with me once again?"

"Yes." Not waiting for an invitation, Adaris lowered herself down the ladder.

As her sandal hit the smooth stone floor, her gut did a flip. The last time she was in this underground place, she had suffered through a test. Sroc had ground glass into her palm and forced Adaris to heal the wound. Adaris' fingers tightened on the rungs. *I found jars of blood here.* Blood. Since then, Adaris had offered blood to this community during a ritual. Was it for the bloodbinding ritual or for something else entirely? As much as she'd like to find out, she had to focus on one thing at a time. Her main concern was to find an artifact that would set Spectrum free, then get her and Rhonwen out of Slagrock. *Focus.* She turned to face the researcher and forced her expression into one of calmness.

Sroc waved at her using only her fingers. Her purple gaze raked Adaris' body, landing on the anklet that glowed on Adaris' ankle. "I see you're using Tikova's gift."

"Yes, and I have you to thank for creating it. I'd like to learn more about these bloodbound artifacts." Adaris walked to the stone bookshelf at the back of the room, the one lined with jewelry. The gemstones set into the jewelry's metal were dim, glinting in the lantern light but not with their own internal glow like the others the community members wore. Like the one she wore. "For example, you mentioned before that these don't have crafting locked within them, correct?"

"Correct." Sroc leaned against the podium in the center of the room, steepling her fingers together. She had taken her gloves off and each of her five rings glowed against her pale skin. One for each of the four crafting types, and the crimson one she'd said was just for show.

Adaris' gaze riveted to the golden-brown Nature gemstone, the ring Sroc had used to melt the stone and trap Adaris' foot during their first encounter. *If only I could steal it to melt Spectrum's bars.* But the young researcher never seemed to take the rings off, and why would she? If Adaris had all that raw power, literally at the tips of her fingers, she wouldn't take them off either. *Maybe I could ask to test it for research...*

The idea unrolled in Adaris' mind like a scroll. She'd get Sroc to give her the Nature ring and see if she could melt the stone as easily as Sroc demonstrated. Maybe go outside to test it more...then what? Run. Go straight to Spectrum's cage to melt the bars? Sroc would sound the alarm and the guards would kill her within moments. No, that wasn't a plan she could follow.

The jewelry pieces on the bookshelf were only pretty things until Sroc did her bloodbinding ritual on them. Among many other artifacts, her gaze locked on the orange and brown gemstones—the ones saved for Animal and Nemora crafting. An armband and a ring, each with brown gemstones, sat on one shelf. Two circlets inset with orange gemstones rested on another. Adaris longed to know how Sroc did her bloodbinding ritual but shook her head to chase the thought away. Her mission came first. The fastest way to get an artifact would be to use one that had already been created.

She turned her back on the inert jewelry. "I know we suffered some losses during the attack. Do those artifacts get passed along to someone else?"

Sroc's lips twisted into a grin. "Is the anklet not enough for you?"

"Who wouldn't want more power?" Adaris shrugged, trying to be nonchalant about it, though she felt as clear as glass beneath Sroc's unrelenting gaze. Sroc's grin widened, just like Adaris wanted. A quest for power was a longing this child would understand. Adaris had to be careful about being too obvious. Pretending to wave away her request, she said, "The anklet is enough, for now. I'm mostly just curious. For research, you see."

Sroc gave her an approving nod. "Four of them were too damaged to recover, and I'm studying the fifth to ensure it works properly."

Adaris flipped open her book and took down some notes, the scratching of the quill filling the quiet stone room. "And the fifth one was what kind of crafting, exactly?"

"Animal. A saltwater creature. Using it, the wearer could shock someone to death." Sroc's expression brightened as if she relished the thought.

Adaris' quill shook as she continued writing. This child was truly mad. The recovered artifact wouldn't help break Spectrum free, but Adaris' curiosity heightened all the same. "And how are you going to see if the crafting still works?" she pressed lightly.

"If the prisoners can't give us what we need, well..." Sroc shrugged. "They become the perfect test subjects."

Adaris suppressed a shudder. She'd assumed all the Moon Knights were dead, but knowing they were alive and test subjects made it all the worse. Not wanting to imagine what those people could be going through, she glanced around the room to distract herself. The jars of blood glinted in the lantern light. Blue. Orange. White. Brown. Her thoughts turned to the sunlight ritual, how Sroc had dipped her fingers into the bowl of mixed blood. "During the sunlight celebration, our blood mingled, yet here they're separated. Does your ancient book tell you how to do that?"

"No. The blood can't be separated. Those jars are merely for decoration." Sroc chuckled, and the sound sent a shiver down Adaris' spine. "We do the sunlight celebration as a way to find our community members again. If one strays."

Adaris felt like she'd been dipped into frozen water. "How?"

"My goddess shard allows me the ability." Sroc wiggled the finger with the crimson ring. The one she said was just for show. The one she apparently lied about. "It's an ancient kind of Blood crafting. My book calls it bloodstalking."

Blood...stalking? Adaris had never heard of it before and scribbled the phrase down. "You can track any member here?"

"Anyone who gave blood, yes."

Like me. Depths! She'd have to tell Rhonwen the moment they saw each other. Thankfully the painter hadn't participated in a sunlight ritual, yet. "Does anyone else know how to do this crafting?"

"Only me, as far as I know." Sroc winked. "Don't get ahead of yourself, looking for more power now."

Bloodstalking. Bloodbinding. What else could this young researcher do? Adaris shivered. She could learn a lot of terrible things from Sroc. Curiosity felt like a hook sinking deep into Adaris' mind and tugging her along. *Focus on an artifact that will free Spectrum.* It sounded like her only hope was to convince Sroc to activate the remaining inert jewelry. She picked up a circlet with the orange gemstones. "Can you show me how you do the bloodbinding process? On this circlet, perhaps?"

Sroc gazed at her and let the silence stretch, curling around Adaris like a thorny vine. Adaris kept steady. She had passed their tests, done their bidding, and Tikova had given her his blessing. She could ask questions like that, had every right to. Her best lie had given her that much. Still, she was sure the researcher could hear her heart's traitorous thumping.

Finally, Sroc turned away. "Of course, scribe." She made her way to the ladder and called up it. "Kye, help me bring a prisoner out."

Kye's here? Adaris' spirits lifted. He'd lied for her and protected Rhonwen last night, which strengthened her belief that he could be a Silver Shade after all, an undercover agent for their people back home.

Sure enough, the short, brown-skinned guard descended to the stone floor. He didn't look at Adaris as he moved to one of the longer bookshelves and heaved a shoulder against it. His sandals scraped against the stone. A grinding noise filled the space as the bookshelf slowly swung out and revealed a dark space behind that Adaris couldn't see through. Usually darkness was a welcomed sight, but a thick wave of rot and filth filtered out, assaulting her senses. Adaris gagged. Her stomach roiled.

"Move closer to the ladder. You'll have a better vantage point there." Sroc had grown serious as she flipped open the thick book on the podium.

While she walked past the young researcher, Adaris could see a page that was nearly black with ink. She put her back to the ladder and watched, her breath catching in her throat. Something twisted was about to happen, she could feel it. *Something twisted that I caused. Is a Moon Knight going to be tortured because of my request?* Guilt churned in her gut. Suddenly, Adaris didn't want to be part of this. Whatever it took to grant her request, she no longer wished it.

Kye went inside the dark hole and withdrew a snarling husk of a man with glowing white eyes. A Divus, like her. Like Sroc. With pale-skinned, sunken cheeks and heavy grooves around his eyes, the man looked like he hadn't slept or eaten in days. He bared his teeth, but the snarl was a weak gesture in his condition.

Kye threw the man toward the podium. He landed hard on his back. The white light in his eyes dimmed, and horror shimmered in its place. His chest heaved a low moan across his lips. He thrashed against Kye, but without armor, his thin skin ripped like paper under Kye's nails. White blood oozed from the wounds. Adaris' own skin itched.

What the depths are they going to do to him? She couldn't move, rooted to the spot by fear and a sickening kind of curiosity.

"Ah, our fellow Divus." Sroc reached over to exchange the orange circlet for an armband from the bookshelf, one that had a few white gemstones set into it like a constellation. White, not orange. Disappointment twisted Adaris' lips. This man, this Moon Knight, was going to suffer to create this artifact, and she wouldn't even gain something that could help her. She avoided meeting the gaze of the Divus man.

Sroc placed the armband in the center of the shallow depression on the floor in front of the podium that Adaris had tripped over on her first visit. Sroc motioned to Kye, who kicked the dazed prisoner into the depression next to the armband.

"Bloodbinding is something only Blood crafters can do. It's the shining achievement of this community." Digging into a pocket, Sroc pulled out a blue-green gemstone like Berhn's and stood over the man. With her other hand, she drew a small dagger from her belt. Her gaze flicked to Adaris. "Watch closely, scribe."

The man's moans turned into a pleading chant. "No, no, no," he murmured, shaking his head.

But Sroc had begun chanting as well, her voice louder than the man's. Adaris couldn't understand Sroc's words, but they sounded repetitive, like a ritual of some kind. Sroc's eyes glowed white, and her Blood crafting traced her veins from her forehead down her neck, shoulders, and arms into the tips of her fingers. When her crafting reached the blue-green gemstone in her hand, she leaned down. With one practiced motion, she sliced the man's neck.

White blood spurted out like a fountain. Adaris nearly retched.

The prisoner's eyes widened. He opened his mouth to speak, gurgling instead. His hands flew to his throat, trying in vain to stop his blood from gushing out. Thick streams of white soaked his fingers.

Sroc's chanting grew louder. Kye took hold of the man's ankles and pulled the bulk of his body out of the depression, so the blood poured freely into it.

When blood covered the armband completely, Sroc submerged both her hands into the liquid up to her elbows. Her chanting never ceased. Her eyes glowed brighter.

Adaris wanted to back away. To flee. The stench of blood filled the room, making her insides twist. Her pulse pounded in her ears, though her breath all but stopped as she took in the sight. It was horrible. What they were doing in this lab was ghastly.

She remained rooted in place, waiting while Kye held the dead prisoner and Sroc's voice grew hoarse.

After what seemed like an eternity, the blood stopped flowing.

Sroc's chanting reached a fever pitch. Sweat poured from her temples. Her veins brightened to the point of being painful for Adaris to look at.

Then, all at once, the pale-white blood rippled, boiled, and was sucked inward in a spiral like a tub emptied through a drain. Within two heartbeats, all that remained in the depression was the armband clutched in Sroc's shaking hands. The blue-green gemstone had vanished. Not a drop of blood could be seen, not even soaking Sroc's sleeves.

Between one blink and the next, Sroc's chanting stopped and her crafting dimmed. The room darkened to lantern light.

Kye lifted and heaved the body into the corner, where it landed with a heavy thump. The sound jarred Adaris out of her shocked state. The rock seemed to sway under Adaris' feet, a boat caught in a terrible storm with more clouds billowing. The room tilted, and she pressed herself against the ladder to keep from collapsing.

Damn it all to the depths. Her legs felt weak as she glanced at her glowing artifact. The glowing artifacts each community member wore had come at a great cost. The weaponry, the jewelry, who knew how many Sroc had already created and disseminated. Even the one on Adaris' ankle.

All dead people.

Someone died so I could be in less pain. Someone was sacrificed.

If Adaris wanted an artifact that would free Spectrum, someone else would have to die.

Sroc lifted the armband, showing off the glittering constellation that decorated the metal. The gemstones brightened, pulsed like a pure-white heartbeat, then dimmed. A triumphant look painted the crafter's young face. "That's bloodbinding, scribe. And if I were you, I'd start writing."

Chapter Twenty-Eight

ADARIS SHOVED OPEN THE hatch of the research lab, her stomach in knots. A briny gust of air blasted against her, and she clutched the rungs tighter. At least it was cooler than the stuffy air below. Pushing herself all the way out, she stumbled out onto the beach, walking down to the ocean. She desperately needed to feel the cleansing spray of the waves, the cool water lapping her skin. She couldn't handle being in the lab any longer, not with the stench of death already thickening the chamber. Death she'd inadvertently caused.

Next time wouldn't be inadvertent. Sroc would have to kill a Vagari or a Nemora to activate the artifact Adaris needed. *She'll have to kill again. For me.*

The ocean stretched far beyond her, the sun high in the sky. Adaris fell onto her knees and retched, dry heaving, clutching the damp sand between her fingers. She didn't care that her long hair grew wet with saltwater or that stones stabbed like knives into her knees.

Images of the Divus getting his throat sliced open wouldn't leave her mind. All she could see was the blood waterfalling from him as his life poured out in a pale, slick stain. *I caused that. With my question, my lust for knowledge.* Her guilt twisted deeper, bile rising to her throat once more. She slapped a sandy hand over her mouth and tried to breathe through her nose.

She'd seen terrible things over her seasons as scribe—a farmer with a broken bone jutting from his flesh after defending his home from suncreatures, knights impaled by trees during battle—but this? Adaris drew long, shaking breaths. Pure evil. *This was murder.*

Yet underneath her gripping guilt, one truth remained, one hooked so deep in her soul she could never untether herself from it.

She still had to know more about bloodbinding.

This was the keystone story for the ages, after all. A story any scribe would give anything to record. She needed to know more. She needed to read that ancient tome. She needed to hear Sroc's haunting chant again so she could record it clearly.

Adaris recalled Rhonwen warning her that the previous scribes never returned from seeing Sroc...how many of those artifacts were created from the lives of her fellow scrollkeepers? *Who gave their life for my artifact?* A sob broke from her chest. Drawing her injured leg in front of her, she unhooked the anklet. The gemstones dimmed. Bright white pain flared up her ankle, leg, knee, hip, a dagger slashing through her.

The sudden onslaught made her head spin. Depths, she'd gotten too accustomed to wearing the artifact. Too comfortable with it on.

"Drink and eat something, if you can." Kye's quiet, smooth voice startled her. "It helps."

Adaris blinked up at him.

The sunshine seemed to sink into Kye's warm brown skin. His eyes—so hard and unmoving in the research lab—had softened. His expression gentled as well. Patting the pouches along his belt, he produced a handful of dried fish then unhooked his flask from his belt and handed them over. "Here."

"Thank you." Feeling helpless to do otherwise, she took a nibble of the dried fish, choked it down, and followed it up with a glug of water. The liquid burned her throat, singed her nose like fire. Coughing, she sputtered. "What the depths is this?"

"Sugarsnap alcohol. Homemade." Kye smirked, taking the flask back and tipping it to his mouth. "I need it, living here."

At those words, Adaris' scribe mind snapped into place once more, connecting the threads. *Does that mean he can't stand it here either?* This was her chance to ask him about his Silver Shade tattoo.

Adaris rose. "Walk with me?"

Kye nodded, so Adaris led the way, a pulse of pain radiating with each footfall. She had gotten used to being pain free and found herself unsteady on the loose sand. Gritting her teeth, she led him away from Sroc's research lab. She walked away from the community, the stone columns towering over her on one side and the ocean horizon stretching out on the other. Once they reached a large rock jutting up from the sand some distance away, Adaris sat. Its shadow provided some comfort, cooler than the midday sun beating down on her. Her bad leg pulsed with pain, so she stretched her legs out in front of her to ease the pressure on her bad one. Even sitting hurt.

Kye followed her lead and settled easily on the sand, crossing his legs and placing his trident across his knees. He rested his dark-brown gaze on hers, still as the stone columns behind him, and waited.

"Are you a Silver Shade?" she blurted, all pretenses thrown to the wind like sand. "I saw the marking behind your ear."

He canted his face to the sky. "I was."

She couldn't believe it. Silver Shades were renowned undercover agents who could infiltrate any system, skilled assassins who could kill without ever leaving a trace, and keepers of all the sacred knowledge of Aluriah the moon goddess. Finding one here would've been the luckiest break she'd ever have in this place, but he'd said *was*. She felt like she'd dived too deep underwater, the pressure making her lungs burn and her ears pound. "You're not anymore?"

"No," Kye replied, his next words quick like he'd been wanting to say this for a while. "I came here as a Silver Shade to obtain information about what was happening on this continent. It was pure luck I stumbled into this community of Slagrock. When I realized what Sroc was doing—the ancient crafting she'd uncovered and was trying to master—I knew I had to stay. I've been here five seasons around the sun already."

Adaris' eyes widened. He looked to be in his early forties. She'd heard of longer jobs like this, where the Shade had to shadow the same group and get information back home when they could. "That long?"

"My bloodline is blessed with a longer lifespan. I'm actually sixty." He grinned at her, a flash of white teeth. "It's why I was originally chosen to come here. In case I discovered something that was worth staying for and took seasons to uncover."

She glanced at her book, some pages near black with all she'd written about the community. "Did you manage to funnel any of your discoveries back to the Silver Shade?"

"I made it back to the mainland by supply ship. They sent an aide behind me to funnel information back and forth, which was good, because by then, Sroc was already well into her research. I sent messages twice more through the aid, but he never returned." Kye shook his head. "I worry about what happened to him."

"What was the aide's name?" Adaris flipped to the back of her book where she listed the names of everyone she'd met and held her quill steady. Waiting. Wondering if she'd met the aide on her wanderings.

"Shadowhunt."

Adaris didn't see the name, chewing on her lip and his words. Despite the fact that he'd given up on returning to the Silver Shade, she respected Kye's dedication and drive to get every strand of information to weave together the best story. As a Vagari, Kye could talk to the beasts of the world—he could've sent a missive to the Silver Shade without an aide's help. "I know the vulnix messengers don't cross the ocean, but why don't you talk to the other animals? Have them message home somehow. Surely, after five seasons, you could find one that could make the trip."

Kye grew sober. "We're in suncreature territory, Adaris. There are no natural creatures for me to call upon here. It was a terrible flaw in the Shade's knowledge base, which I told them of during my first trip back. That's why they assigned Shadowhunt to me." He lifted one shoulder in a shrug. "Eventually, I didn't want to go back to the Shade anyway."

"Really?" Adaris' skin tingled. He really meant it when he said he didn't want to be part of the Silver Shade anymore. *Something about being here for that long must've made him turn against his original calling.* She had to know more. "Why not? What made you change your mind?"

Kye grinned. "Berhn. Little by little. His innocent faith in the sun goddess—a deity I'd spent my whole life and career knowing as cruel and malicious—was something I had never encountered before."

Of course. Adaris knew, since her first days in Slagrock, that Kye had a soft spot for Berhn. Every time he saw the Nemora, he stopped to chat with him. "I know you're friends."

"Yes." His smile was softer than she'd ever seen it. "I learned about the gentler fire from him, the opportunity for rebirth, the warmth of Ponuriah. How some things need to be burned in order to sprout. That creation could come through her fire just as easily as with the cool light of the moon."

Adaris nodded. She didn't believe in any of the deities, but she believed in people. And people had many sides. She believed in Berhn, enjoyed his nicer version of Ponuriah and of her followers. No matter what Adaris read in the history books, she'd come to acknowledge, and seen firsthand, that no one was completely good or evil. Nothing was night and day. There was always twilight and dusk, the middle ground. And in that middle, maybe everyone could find a common ground to stand on.

Kye ran his fingers through the sand beside him. "I had always believed in all the deities of the world, not just the goddess sisters, and Berhn's faith made sense to me," he admitted quietly. "Fire can be cleansing. I needed that."

"But if you believe in a gentler version of Ponuriah, surely you don't like what just happened in Sroc's lab," Adaris challenged. When Kye shook his head, she continued. "Then why did you help her murder that man?"

"I needed to make sure she didn't kill you," he replied gently, voice soft as a hiss of falling sand.

"Kill me?" A shiver of fear pricked Adaris' scalp. The waterfall of blood from the man's neck coursed through her mind's eye. "She couldn't have. Tikova gave me his blessing to go about the community."

Kye sighed. "That's of little meaning to Sroc. She's gone rogue before. Made up an excuse to appease Tikova. Those jars of blood she has scattered about her lab are the people she's killed without his express orders. She's obsessed with the ancients and wants to become like them, wants to harness all the best crafting abilities. She hasn't perfected her bloodbinding research yet, so sometimes she needs more sacrifices than Tikova can provide."

"That's horrible." Adaris cut her gaze away, remembering the multiple jars she had cataloged. Twenty in all. *Those jars are merely for decoration.* Sroc's words. "Why haven't you told Tikova?"

Kye leaned back on his hands. "Because if I told him, he might stop Sroc, and I need her to finish her bloodbinding research. If she stalls on that, everything I've done—everything I've been through in this wretched place—would be for nothing. Someone else would take up the mantle, and this whole nightmare would start anew. I'd have to earn that person's trust all over again."

The words twisted through Adaris. This callous streak in Kye shocked her. "But innocent people have died—are dying—for her research! And you're helping her!" They strayed off topic, but her curiosity had gotten the better of her once more. "I fear you might be becoming more like them than even you realize."

"Perhaps." His stare never wavered. "I did think I wanted to be part of this community when Berhn told me about the gentler fire...but not anymore. Not many people believe the way he does. Slagrock is focused on the fiery wrath that will burn the Groves to the ground." He shook his head, his words bitter. "I've done my part. If I didn't help Sroc when she needed me, it would've looked suspicious, and I can't have that. Sroc and I have done this unfortunate dance after every Moon Knight attack."

Adaris' interest spiked, but before she could ask how many attacks there had been, Kye barreled on.

"When the war happens, the people of the mainland deserve to know what they're up against. I've been waiting for the right scribe,

Adaris, one who Sroc would want to teach her bloodbinding ritual to. When there was talk that we'd found yet another scribe, I volunteered to be your guard. At the time, Sroc had no one to practice on, so she let me go. I lied to Tikova about you staying by my side during the Moon Knight attack because I wanted you to get closer to Sroc. Learn how she does her bloodbinding, understand it, and then escape. Bring that knowledge back to the libraries and to the Shade."

Relief washed through her at those words. He might not be a Silver Shade, but that didn't mean he was on Tikova's side. He wanted the mainland people to be able to defend themselves. It seemed as if she had an ally. "I want that, too."

A sigh rippled through him. "If you escape with those stories, I can finish up here and help Berhn get to the mainland. Finally leave these memories behind."

The memories he had with Sroc seemed bad enough, but Adaris couldn't shake the feeling that there was something more, something else. *Something personal?* When he shifted into the sunlight, the tan-and-white patterned shell on his arm caught the light, again piquing her curiosity about his companion animal. What could it be? There was a reason he never talked about his companion, a reason the creature wasn't always near him, a reason he warned Adaris to stick within Tikova's boundaries. She could only assume one thing.

"Your companion animal died here," she said softly.

He gripped the sand between his fingers, and his eyes went glassy with emotion. "Early on, Tikova gave the order to have my companion animal be part of the suncreature research." He looked down at the trident resting across his knees. "She didn't survive."

Her heart panged for him. A Vagari losing their companion animal was said to be the worst pain imaginable—a loss of their other half, a soul ripped in two. While Adaris couldn't ever know what that loss felt like, she had known deep loss.

Opening her book to a new page, she lifted her feathered pen. "Scrollkeepers record our losses as a way of honoring them, and so we don't forget anything about them. Will you tell me about her?"

He blinked at her. "Her name was Grit. She was a hollow conu, a smaller variety. About the size of my palm. Do you know what conus look like?"

Adaris did, but he needed to tell his own story. She shook her head. "Describe her to me."

He drew a spiral on the sand by his knee. "They're mollusks with large spiral shells on their back, which they live inside of. Their bodies are soft. Easily damaged. Their coloring varies—purple, brown, yellow, pink. Grit's spiral was stunning."

Adaris made a quick sketch of the creature, highlighting the pattern on Kye's shell, the one that would mirror his companion animal. "And I take it hers was brown and white."

Kye traced the pattern of his shell onto the sand. "Yes."

He launched into a story about when he first saw his companion animal, how he chose her from all the others for her unique coloring and her boldness to come close to him. Adaris wrote it down. She took note of the spiral he drew in the sand and the way Kye smiled when he talked about Grit. The terrible way in which she died. It was heartbreaking to record, but she had to. For Kye.

Kye's heartache burrowed deep within her. How many other people had Tikova hurt in order to build his precious community? In order for Sroc to complete her research? Too many.

She reached for her next words carefully. "You said you still need to finish something here...something more than just having me gain Sroc's knowledge and leave with it. Something else you have to do before you leave with Berhn."

Kye took a deep breath and met her gaze, unflinching. "Yes. Tikova ordered my companion's death. I will kill him for it. Then I'll leave."

Adaris glanced around at the quiet beach. "You want to kill Tikova? How will you manage that and still leave here alive?"

Kye lifted his hand, palm outward toward her. "Let me handle that. His death is my responsibility now."

My touch can paralyze people. Stop their hearts if I want to. Kye's words came back to her.

He cleared his throat and continued. "I've overheard your plans with Rhonwen. To use an artifact to free Spectrum and escape with the raft you've created. You're not as quiet as you would like to be, but I've always been the one to guard you, so I've kept the prying ears away."

"Wha—thank you." A rush of gratitude went through her. She couldn't believe how much he'd helped them all along. He was a good man. *A good sun goddess worshipper.* "And thank you for watching over Rhonwen last night. I know you didn't have to."

"I can only temper Yim for a little while. Rhonwen has failed too many tests, so he has Tikova's blessing to indulge his cruelty." His expression softened. "And be aware that community members aren't supposed to stand up for prisoners like you did last night. It's against Tikova's rules."

Anger flashed hot inside her. "But Yim broke her arm."

Kye nodded. "And as long as she can still paint, he has permission to break any other bone in her body, too."

"I can't just watch her get hurt."

"I've noticed." Kye frowned. "Which means others have, too. Be careful. If you step out of line, Tikova and Sroc and this whole community will use it against you."

The words sank into her like a dagger's edge.

"Have you found an artifact that will help you escape?" Kye asked.

Adaris shook her head, gut twisting at the thought of what she had to do to get one. "None of the active ones would work to break Spectrum free."

Kye sighed, then glanced down the beach, toward Slagrock. "I've had to do some terrible things to stay alive here, Adaris. What are you willing to do to survive?"

Her throat tightened. "Anything. I need to get us out of here."

"Truly?"

More people would die under Sroc's dagger, no matter what Adaris did, so she might as well take what little good might come out of it. Strengthening her resolve, she said, "Truly."

"Good, because I think Sroc will ask more of you than you've ever given." He leveled a gaze on her as sharp as glass. "And you have to be willing to give it without hesitation. To conform. For your own sake, and Rhonwen's."

Adaris nodded. Before rising, she lashed the glowing orange artifact around her ankle and activated it once more. Tikova had said from the very beginning that Sroc needed more Blood crafters and Sroc mentioned needing help with her research. Perhaps the flawed bloodbinding ritual was why. Adaris faced the community. "I'll do whatever it takes."

Chapter Twenty-Nine

AFTER DREAMS RIFE WITH waterfalling blood, haunted eyes, and twisted grins, Adaris rose with a headache and bleary eyes before the sun even touched the horizon. *What are you willing to do to survive?* Kye's question lodged in her chest as she slathered some cream to help her peeling skin. Her own answer worried her more than the question did. Steeling herself to visit Sroc's lab once more, Adaris shook her head and headed out. Kye would only move forward with helping them escape if she could learn about bloodbinding and bring that knowledge back home.

Yet she couldn't ignore how deeply rooted her own want for knowledge had become. She wanted to know more about the process—how and why the ritual worked. Where Sroc had found the book that told her how to do such ancient crafting. How the young researcher figured it out. It would be a story for the ages, a keystone story unlike anyone had ever seen, a story worth the black quill.

And Adaris would do anything to get it.

Kye met her at the food hut. After a quick meal, they headed toward the rock stairs that would lead them down to the ocean. The orange gemstones glowed on her ankle, the Animal crafting strengthening her bones. Guilt coiled inside her with each pain-free step, but she had to keep it active, to be like them, like she had claimed she wanted to be. *Someone gave their life for it.* Adaris' steps faltered. She swallowed hard and concentrated on taking steady steps.

Halfway to the stairs, Adaris' gaze caught on sword-straight, gray hair that lightened to white at the ends, pops of rainbow-colored feathers catching the early morning sunlight.

Rhonwen.

Adaris stopped. Kye stilled as well.

Rhowen stood by the edge of the stone columns overlooking the ocean, scowling at Yim, who stood next to her. A thick piece of cloth wrapped around her right arm secured two planks of wood into place. A splint. And a crude one at that. Yim was facing away from her, but Rhonwen caught Adaris' gaze.

"We should keep moving," Kye murmured out of the corner of his mouth.

She knew he was right, but she couldn't look away.

Yim grabbed Rhonwen's wounded arm and yanked her closer. She yelped and stumbled into his chest.

Adaris' heartbeat thundered in her ears. She jolted into movement, ignoring Kye's warning. She had to do something. Anything.

Kye was faster. He stepped in front of her, his short, stocky frame blocking her way.

"He's hurting her," Adaris said. "Get out of my way."

Putting a hand on her arm, he shook his head. "She's endured worse. She can hang on until we're ready."

Anger coursed through her, a flush crawling up her neck and cheeks. Her whole body tightened, her awareness sharpening onto the pressure of Kye's fingers on her arm. Her Blood crafting surged, the instinct to weaken him and push past strong as a rising tide.

Kye's gaze cut downward, and as if he sensed her thoughts. He lifted his palm from her arm. He lowered his voice, words quickly slipping past his lips. "I'll set up time for you to talk with her later, just not while the entire community is awake."

Beyond Kye, Yim dipped his head to Rhonwen's ear and whispered something. Rhonwen's expression twisted from pain to horror. She shook her head and tried to back away. Yim tightened his grip on her arm, and Rhonwen paled.

Waiting until later might lead to disaster. She had to help Rhonwen. Adaris stepped around Kye and started toward the pair. A streak of green skin and white fabric darted past, metal pan thudding. Berhn.

"Rhonwen!" Berhn skidded to a stop next to Rhonwen and Yim with a grace only a Nemora could manage, taking in huge lungfuls of air and pointing back at the gaping hole of the mine on the far edge of the open community. His young face held so much wonder as he stared up at Rhonwen, bouncing on his toes.

Adaris adjusted her course toward the stairs but listened intently as she neared. Kye followed close beside her.

"I found another one!" Berhn's chest heaved with the excitement. "Another gemstone. It's massive. You should paint it, Rhonwen, while it's still in the rock." He tugged on Rhonwen's blue tunic. "Come with me!"

Rhonwen shifted her gaze to Yim, who sighed and stepped back, motioning for Berhn to lead the way. A frown marred Yim's face, and a hardness settled into his step as the trio walked toward the mine.

Adaris breathed again. Before she descended out of sight of the trio, she glanced back to see Berhn watching them over her shoulder. He waved, and the sun glinted off his markings and teeth as he gave her a wide, wild smile.

Somehow, he'd known Rhonwen was in trouble. He'd protected her.

A rush of gratitude toward the Nemora filled Adaris. Someone else was keeping an eye on Rhonwen, and that thought freed her to move forward. She all but ran down the rock stairs to Sroc's research lab. Kye trailed behind, keeping in stride but also keeping silent. Smart of him, too; Adaris' anger hadn't subsided yet. She knew, deep down, that Kye was only trying to help her—help them—but seeing Rhonwen in pain and doing nothing? It wasn't right.

Then again, not many things in Slagrock were.

Adaris sighed as she lowered herself down Sroc's ladder, turning what happened over and over again in her mind. Kye said Rhonwen had endured worse, and Adaris had to believe she could endure a little more before Adaris could help them both escape.

The moment Adaris' sandals hit the ground of the research lab, Sroc called out. "Scribe! I'm glad you've returned."

"Not even a rogue wave could stop me," Adaris replied, keeping her voice light as she eyed the young researcher. *The murderer.* Worry gnawed her insides.

Kye followed her down, taking his place by the ladder. Waiting. Watching.

Sroc chuckled. "I thought as much. So, you came to learn about the bloodbinding ritual?"

"Yes," Adaris replied, her curiosity taking over once more, pushing her to learn as much as she could. *Even at the expense of someone's life?* A small voice whispered, nudging the lust for knowledge to the side, making room for rational thought. She didn't want to see another person killed in front of her, or a Moon Knight slaughtered for their blood. So she pivoted the conversation to a safer topic. "Could I take a look at the book you used?"

"Of course." Sroc went to the podium and gestured for Adaris to join her. Adaris silently swallowed a gasp. Her eyes raked over the thick binding. Despite everything, excitement shivered through her. She ran her fingertips over the cover. No letters were pressed into the bindings, no words at all embossed on the thick hide. "No title?"

"I call it the ancient's grimoire."

A thrill brightened inside Adaris. *A grimoire.* A book of the ancient workings of crafting. Most of them were lost to the erosion of time. She recalled their very first conversation, when Sroc had rambled about goddess sisters and firestorms and sunsick ideologies. "You said it survived the great firestorm, yes?"

Sroc nodded.

"Where did you find it?"

Almost lovingly, Sroc patted the thick binding. "Buried with a dead body on the eastern coast."

"In the volcanic region?"

Sroc gave her a smile. "You've done your research."

Of course it would be found in the hottest of all the climates, where only a slight few could survive the trek. She made a mental note to jot a small x on the map she'd drawn in her book, just in case the scribes back home wanted to know. "And did you find out who the body belonged to?"

"There were no markers, and their clothing had disintegrated." Sroc shrugged. "But the body was found among containers of dried blood and wore a pendant with the very first sun goddess shard we ever discovered."

Adaris reverently opened the ancient grimoire's cover. A dusty, sweet scent filled the air. She couldn't help but inhale deeply, the earthiness hugging her like an old friend. The yellowing paper crinkled under her fingers as she flipped through, skimming past musty pages and faded ink. Then her shoulders slumped. The handwriting was neat and precise, but Adaris couldn't read a single word of it.

"Is there...a key to reading this?" she asked, lifting her gaze to the young researcher.

Sroc smirked. "Of course." She patted the hand-sized bag that hung off her hip, made from a striking cobalt fabric. "I discovered it long ago, but rarely need it now."

"Would you allow me to see the key?"

"No," Sroc replied, sticking her chin out.

Adaris sighed, disappointment rippling through her. Sroc obviously took pride in reading this ancient's grimoire, and depths, who wouldn't? It would take ages to decipher it. Sroc obviously wanted to keep the knowledge to herself. *Smart.* Adaris had to give her that. She gave Sroc her best grin. "I had to ask."

Sroc scoffed.

A crazy thought sparked through Adaris' mind. *I'm going to steal this grimoire.* If a researcher as young as Sroc could figure it out, Adaris had all the confidence in the world that the scribes back home could, too. She just had to wait for the right moment.

She closed the book. "So, what else can you teach me?"

"Did you catch the words I said while performing the ritual?" Sroc asked.

The chanting. Adaris hadn't recognized the words enough to even try repeating them, much less write them down. She shook her head. "No. Much like the words in that ancient grimoire of yours, I didn't recognize the syllables enough to record your chanting."

Sroc's smirk twisted, her strange, purple eyes glinting. "Well, then I guess I'll have to show you again." Her gaze cut past Adaris to Kye. "Get another, would you?"

Kye shoved the prison door open, and enough light filtered in for Adaris to see three prisoners inside. One caught her eye, a woman with curled horns. The strong one who rammed Yim during the fight.

They're going to kill another Moon Knight. Her chest tightened. This conversation was bolting down a dangerous path, one Adaris didn't want any part of. She shook her head. "Oh, I didn't mean—"

"You wanted to learn about bloodbinding, correct?" Sroc snapped.

"Yes, but not—"

Sroc interrupted. "The best way to learn the words is to hear them, and the best way I communicate them is by doing the ritual."

"Why don't you just say them now?" Adaris suggested out of desperation. "If you say them slower, I can write them down."

It was a terrible suggestion, Adaris knew that the moment she said it. Of course the young researcher wouldn't go for an idea like that, not when she could use the blood to create more artifacts for her community. Not when Adaris was supposed to be a full part of the community, helping Sroc achieve her goals.

Surprisingly, Sroc pursed a lip out in thought. "Interesting idea. Would you be more confident repeating the words if I taught you like that?"

Repeating the words. Adaris' body grew cold. *Does Sroc want me to actually perform the bloodbinding ritual, not just help her?* She'd do anything to escape, but would she really murder?

She couldn't exactly say no, not when she'd already expressed interest. She had to blend in. She was part of this sunsick community;

doing anything less would be suspicious—or worse, get her and Rhonwen killed.

Plus, she couldn't deny the tingling in her fingers, the longing for this ancient kind of crafting to be written on the page. The twisted way her lust for knowledge leapt for the chance to record this keystone story.

"Yes," she found herself saying. "I learn better that way."

Sroc moved to a stone chair by a long, narrow desk butted up against one of the bookshelves. "Sit, then."

Kye slid the prison door shut once more, and Adaris felt safe again.

She'd spent the whole day with Sroc, saying the foreign words over and over and over again. The language seemed to be an ancient form of Divus, so thankfully the rough, sharp syllables flowed somewhat easily off Adaris' tongue. The words meant nothing to her spoken aloud, but according to Sroc's translation, they meant: *Blood is life, life is blood. Crafting is blood, blood is crafting. We give this blood, this life, to obtain a higher level of crafting.*

Adaris leaned back in her chair, her mind turning over the phrases she had said for the hundredth time. She had expected something different—an ancient invocation that unlocked the higher crafting maybe—but the words seemed to be rather mundane. Almost juvenile. The same simple, repeated phrase. An explanation of sorts. "Are the words a conduit of some kind?" she asked. "Do they channel your crafting?"

"No, but the grimoire says they're key to performing the bloodbinding."

Adaris wrote that in her notes. "Why? There are no verbal components in our crafting. Words are just for flair or a personal touch."

Sroc leaned forward, pressing both hands onto the stone desk, eyes wide with sudden intensity, as if Adaris had touched on something important. "I believe verbalization was necessary for the ancients. The humans, nymphs, elves, and venators had access to all four crafting abilities, and I believe they had to call specifically on each one to use it."

The profound insight rocked through Adaris, and she had to pause her scribbling. She hadn't thought much about the ancients. Her job was to record the here and now, the history of the people today, not the stories of old, but she knew the old races had harnessed all four crafting abilities. It made sense that they had to call up a specific crafting each time, and verbalizing might be the easiest way to do it. "That's probably why we need to say the word for the daygems to activate. Because the Elu who make them use ancient crafting as well."

Sroc nodded. "Exactly."

Kye shifted his position, sitting on the stone floor. "Is that why I have to say alahri in order to use my weapon?"

Adaris' eyes widened. Alahri meant activate. It was the word people back home used to light daygems, and it made sense that the same word would work on Kye's trident—they were both Moon crafting, both Elu.

Sroc slumped in her chair, looking much younger than her already young form. A frown cut her face. "Yes. Some of the bloodbound artifacts need a word or phrase to activate. Alahri, ziphri, phyrhi, wyhri. The more powerful ones I've created don't. It also depends on the type of crafter. Sometimes a bound artifact created from an Elu responds to a living Elu without them needing to utter the activation, whereas a Nemora might need the word. It's endlessly frustrating."

So Kye was right. Sroc's bloodbinding is flawed. The memory of Kye lifting his trident, a cobalt shield bubbling out to protect him and the others, burst into her mind's eye. His "flawed" trident needed a word to create a shield. She wrote all the curious words down in her book, noting alahri was for Elu crafting specifically.

"It's impressive crafting all the same," Adaris said honestly.

Sroc rolled her eyes to the ceiling and sighed. "I'm sure the system can be perfected. I just need to practice."

A shiver went down Adaris' spine. She never knew five words could hold so much evil. Desires warred inside her—a small part of her wanted to stay and watch and learn this ancient ritual so she could record it more clearly, while a larger part screamed at her to leave. Adaris pushed herself to her feet. "Do we have to practice right now?"

"Yes, it has been a long day already." Kye covered a yawn with his hand, whether it was fake or real, Adaris couldn't tell. "I suggest we leave that for tomorrow."

Sroc leaned back, eyes drifting to the bookshelf that concealed the prisoner's cell. A frown pulled at her lips. "Tikova did want to glean more information from them. Can't go killing them all off too quickly, I suppose, but my research is more important than any lies these prisoners tell us. I'll tell him to hurry it up."

Heart in her throat, Adaris left, climbing the rungs of the ladder slowly. Guilt rocked inside her, a wave crashing back and forth, making her head dizzy. Depths, she had wanted to stay. To stay! *Is my need for knowledge really that twisted? That painfully bright?* When she emerged into the sunlight, she held back the urge to run the rest of the way back to her hut. Perhaps she had spent too much time in Slagrock, surrounded by these people and their terrible morals. Perhaps they had rubbed off on her.

Perhaps she was getting sunsick, too.

Chapter Thirty

AS SOON AS THEY were out of the research lab and walking up the steps to the community proper, Adaris rounded on Kye. Stress from the meeting with Sroc rekindled Adaris' earlier anger. If not for Rhonwen's physical health, then for Adaris' own mental health, she needed to talk to Rhonwen.

She glared at Kye. "You said you could set up a meeting between Rhonwen and I. Can you do that tonight?"

Kye rubbed his neck and looked away toward the ocean. He didn't answer.

A cool, salt-laden breeze caressed Adaris as she continued to climb the stone steps, but it didn't calm her like the ocean usually would. The sun had already dipped well below the horizon and worry clawed within her—another day gone, another chance when Rhonwen could be injured by her guard. She hoped Berhn's gemstone discovery had claimed enough of Rhonwen's attention that Yim didn't get a chance to hurt her more.

Hope could only get Adaris so far. She had to know for sure.

Kye's silence cut her already frayed nerves. "Kye, tell me. Can you distract Yim long enough for Rhonwen and I to have a conversation?"

"Yes." Kye sighed. He stopped on the steps to light a lantern attached to his belt. The firelight bloomed, a pale, flickering yellow glow. His dark eyes met hers. "A short conversation."

A flush crept up her neck. Suddenly hot, Adaris pulled her long hair off her skin. "Look, I know it's suspicious, all right? I just...I need to talk to her."

Kye's gaze softened. He put a hand on her shoulder, thick fingers squeezing once before letting go. "I know. Let's go find her."

They climbed the rest of the stairs and went searching for Rhonwen and Yim. Lanterns lined the circular path, casting flickering light and shadows into the quiet community. Adaris hoped Rhonwen hadn't already gone to bed like so many others obviously had.

But luck smiled down at her this night. They spotted Rhonwen, Berhn, and Yim outside the shadowy entrance of the mine. Yim rested his spear on his shoulders, ignoring how Rhonwen struggled to lift a bulky set of four paint cans with her one good hand. Berhn hoisted a large, blue-green gemstone the size of Yim's head to the night sky, his young face split into a wide grin.

"That's the biggest gemstone you've found, Berhn," Kye called as they approached, smiling at the young Nemora.

They stopped by the trio, and Adaris tried to keep her focus fixed on Berhn and the two guards, not on how Rhonwen stood so close Adaris could feel the warmth of her skin. Not on how pain flashed across Rhonwen's face as she set her many cans on the ground, muttering how she was just going to leave them there for tomorrow. Not on how the air suddenly smelled of paint and sweat.

For her part, Rhonwen didn't initiate a conversation with Adaris. It seemed the painter knew to keep quiet.

Berhn lowered the gemstone, then stumbled as Kye clapped him on the shoulder. "Sroc will be so pleased."

Kye's smile wavered, but only a little. "She will, yes. You've done your job well here, Berhn."

Adaris' gut clenched. Sroc *would* be pleased to have another special gemstone like that so she could do more research. More murder. Berhn mentioned that he didn't know what Sroc did with the gemstones he discovered. Quite frankly, that was a blessing in disguise.

Kye turned his attention to Yim. "Can I speak to you for a moment?" At Yim's arched eyebrow, Kye cut his gaze to Rhonwen. "Away from prying ears?"

Adaris' heartbeat quickened. This was the moment Kye promised her—a moment alone with Rhonwen, a moment just for them—but from how Yim stuck to Rhonwen like wet sand, would the guard even allow it?

Yim thudded one end of his spear onto the ground with a solid crack. He let out a sigh. "She's been particularly grating today, so yes, I could use a little time away from her. Berhn, keep watch on her."

Berhn clutched his newly discovered gemstone and nodded, watching as Yim and Kye wandered out of earshot toward the Ponuriah statue.

Adaris leaned toward him. "Could you give us a moment alone? If you could do that without getting into trouble with Yim, I mean."

Berhn stepped back and gave her one of his wide, wild smiles. "Certainly."

He set his gemstone on the ground a few paces away, then pulled the smaller gemstone he always carried with him out of his bag and sat. He sank into his crafting, gaze burning to a bright copper in the darkness. With his back to Yim, it looked like he was watching them, but Adaris knew his whole attention was firmly on the gem. Using the gemstone as a key to look for more of the same.

She turned to Rhonwen. The lantern light barely reached where they were, casting dim light onto the painter's rigid form. "How are you?" Adaris asked.

"Never mind that. Did you find an artifact to free Spectrum?" Rhonwen hissed.

"Not yet, but I'm getting closer." Adaris' gut churned thinking about the cost to create said artifact. *Should I tell Rhonwen?* The painter was already alone and injured and worried for her companion animal. No, Adaris wouldn't tell her. It would add too much onto her weary shoulders.

"Well hurry it up. Yim's getting much worse, and I'm going to have to do something about it soon."

"Do something about it?" That didn't sound good. Adaris had a flash of memory of Rhonwen telling her how she'd poisoned one of her guards and tried to push Kye into a lava river. Adaris blinked away the image. They were in no position to be making waves. "Don't, Rhonwen. If you do something to another guard, Tikova might decide you're not worth keeping."

Rhonwen's eyes flashed with anger. "You have no idea what it's like being Yim's charge. You focus on freeing Spectrum, let me handle Yim. He's too busy spit-shining his weapon to actually pay attention to what I'm doing. Yesterday I stole some things right out from under his nose."

Adaris' eyes widened. "What? How?"

Rhonwen smirked. "They wanted me to paint the newly patched fishing hut, so I did, but I also grabbed a tight coil of rope from the crates when Yim was bragging to one of the fishers. I pocketed some nails a few dawns back, while I was in one of the supply huts, too."

The boldness of this woman never ceased to amaze Adaris, but Rhonwen could get caught, and Adaris knew Tikova's punishment for stealing would be harsh—especially for a prisoner. A thread of worry pulled inside her. "You can't put yourself at risk like that."

Rhonwen's gaze drifted to the ground. "You've been doing all this work to help us escape, and I feel like I should do something, too. I need to do something. So...do we need anything specific?"

Adaris understood and appreciated her friend's need to be helpful. Rhonwen didn't want to be a passive bystander in her own escape.

Adaris took a moment to think. What would they need on a raft out on the ocean that would also be easy to steal? "Flasks of clean water. Something for shade. Dried food. Oh!" She dug into her pocket and produced a handful of aca nuts. The white flesh glinted in the lantern light. "For the pain of your broken arm."

Rhonwen gave the nuts a hard look. "Thank you, but I could've gotten the nuts nights ago if I really wanted to." She shifted slightly so she blocked Yim's view, then folded Adaris' fingers over the nuts. "I don't want them," she whispered, not letting go of Adaris' hand.

Adaris' whole body tingled from the simple contact. The softness in Rhonwen's expression made Adaris' knees go weak. Talented, smart, brave, and now refusing a drug that would make this terrible experience a little easier. Was there nothing this painter couldn't do? Glowflies danced in Adaris' stomach. It took her a moment to gather her thoughts into a more coherent manner.

"And just so you know, Kye's on our side," she finally said. "He's a good guy."

Rhonwen's lips tugged into a smile, and she glanced at the Nemora still staring into the blue-green gemstone. "Berhn's a good one, too. He's been stopping Yim every chance he gets."

"It seems we're gathering allies here, Rhonwen," Adaris replied.

Rhonwen gave Adaris' hand a squeeze, then dropped it, gaze shifting toward the Ponuriah statue. Adaris took the hint and pretended to engage in conversation with Berhn, as Kye and Yim headed back toward them.

"Berhn, they're coming," Adaris hissed.

The Nemora blinked a few times, the crafting light dimming from his eyes. He pocketed his gemstone and stood, knocking the gravel off his pants. He lifted his newly discovered, massive gemstone once more and tilted it this way and that in the lantern light. "I just can't believe I found one so large!"

Rhonwen opened her mouth to respond, but Yim cut her off, grabbing onto her splint and pulling her toward him. "Time to go, painter."

Rhonwen yelped, twisting away from the taller guard and holding her arm close to her chest. Pain shimmered in her furious gaze.

"Take it easy, Yim," Adaris said.

Kye gave her a warning glance.

Adaris ignored it. She knew she had to be smarter, had to conform, for Rhonwen's sake. And she would, but she'd also protect the woman she cared about. "You've already broken her arm, guard. If you injure the painter so much that she can't do her job, how angry do you think Tikova would be?"

She forced herself to stay focused on Yim. If she met Rhonwen's gaze, her ruse would surely crack.

"You're right." Yim hooked an arm around Rhonwen's shoulder, pinning her to him. To Adaris' horror, he licked Rhonwen's cheek with his long, rubbery tongue. "There are other ways to make her behave."

Rhonwen shuddered, a visible ripple of disgust running through her.

Anger swept through Adaris hot and fast, and all ideas of conforming left her. Her hands balled into fists. *Conform.* The word repeated in her mind until she forced her body to respond. She hid her shaking hands behind her back, easing into a more relaxed posture on the balls of her feet. "Do what you wish, guard, but you don't want to be on Tikova's bad side."

With that she spun on her heel and stalked away, not even bothering to see if Kye followed. Which of course, he did. It took everything she had to not look back at Rhonwen. A pair of crimson eyes blinked open by the Ponuriah statue, but she ignored the suncreature keeping watch. Damned to the depths, all of them!

Adaris went straight to her hut. Worry pinched her lungs tight, heart drumming a frantic beat. She heard Kye's footsteps stalling in the doorway behind her and turned to face him. "Rhonwen won't take much more of Yim's abuse."

Kye moved deeper into her hut and set his trident on the sand mattress bed. "She's been through worse than him."

"She told me herself that she was going to do something about it. About Yim." Adaris spun to the window that faced the community, peering out. Yim and Rhonwen had reached the prison hut, and she watched Yim shove Rhonwen inside. Entire body trembling, she watched Yim take up his post outside. *Thank the depths.* Some of Adaris' anxiety uncoiled. She'd feared he'd go in with Rhonwen and force himself on her. *He still could.* "I worry that she'll do something reckless to get away from him."

Kye cleared his throat behind her. "Rhonwen is smart. She's been smart this whole time. She knows we're getting closer to freeing Spectrum, and she won't jeopardize that."

No, Rhonwen wouldn't jeopardize Spectrum. Adaris forced herself to breathe in and out slowly, trying to calm her rapid heartbeat. She turned to face Kye. "Then what do you suggest?"

Kye rubbed a hand over his bald head. "Do your job. Gather information. Force Sroc to kill a Moon Knight with the right crafting to set Spectrum free, and leave this place behind."

Kill another Moon Knight, like the three in the prison. Adaris stilled, an idea flashing bright through her mind like a lighthouse's blaze in the dark. *The curlhorn.* The curlhorn Vagari Moon Knight. The one who bashed Yim backward using her crafting prowess. Adaris had a sudden vision of the curlhorn using her impressive crafting powers to bash Spectrum free.

"The curlhorn Moon Knight might be able to help us." The plan was a shot in the dark, especially since Sroc was already using the Moon Knights as sacrifices, but freeing a Moon Knight was a much better plan than having Sroc murder one. It was a plan Adaris could get behind. The idea curled much more comfortably within her than the option she feared she might be forced to pursue. "What if we try to set the curlhorn Vagari free? Have her ram Spectrum's bars?"

He gave her a pinched look like he'd just eaten a sour root. "That's risky, Adaris."

"Well, it's a lot better than murdering someone!" Adaris stood her ground. "And it would be easier if you helped me. The faster we talk to the curlhorn, the less chance for Rhonwen to snap."

His gaze cut to the window, to the prison hut. "Fine. Sroc leaves the research lab for her meals. If we time it correctly, we might be able to get the curlhorn alone. Tomorrow morning, early, we'll talk to the knight."

Chapter Thirty-One

SUNLIGHT SPILLED DOWN THE ladder like molten lava, harshly bright in Sroc's cramped lab, but Adaris tried her best to ignore its heat on her shoulders. She paced, keeping her gaze on the young researcher as Sroc popped another hunk of cubed meat into her mouth, eating her morning meal while poring through her notes. This was the first time Adaris was down in the lab alone, without Kye behind her. Fear shivered through her every time she thought of it. She hadn't been able to find him, and between her worries about what Rhonwen might do to Yim and the possibility Sroc would murder the curlhorn before they could talk, Adaris didn't have time to wait. She hadn't expected Sroc to be in the lab, but the young researcher had apparently decided to do work first thing this dawn. A wrinkle, but not one Adaris couldn't smoothen out. A lie was already taking shape in her mind.

Sroc toyed with a hunk of seared flesh seeping orange blood. "Sit down, scribe, you seem anxious. Would you like some?"

Adaris sat but didn't take any of the meat. "No thank you, but may I ask what that is?"

"Curlhorn." She grinned, a dribble of blood running down her pale chin. "The companion animal, not the Vagari. Its meat is admittedly quite tough, but I like it."

Adaris didn't think these people would eat Vagari, but the fact Sroc had to clarify made her shudder. It was bad enough that the young researcher was eating a companion animal.

A guttural sob met Adaris' ears, coming from somewhere beside her, and fear rimmed her muscles. She glanced at the bookshelf where she knew the prisoners were being kept. The door was already open wide enough to pull a person through. Her insides twisted. Sroc was eating the companion animal while the Vagari was imprisoned mere paces away. It would be pure torture for the woman. Adaris' stomach dropped. Maybe Sroc had already done research on the prisoners. Maybe the curlhorn was already dead and the other Vagari knights sobbed for their friend. The back of her neck prickled. She should see the prisoners right away...at least see if the curlhorn was alive.

The pressure was too much. She had to act, Kye or no Kye. Adaris pulled out her book and quill and flipped open a blank page. "Speaking of, Tikova wants me to get some words from the prisoners about their crushing defeat," the lie slipped out easily. "Their point of view would help amplify how powerful Slagrock has become with the aid of the sun goddess shard research."

Sroc wiped her fingers on the tight strips of leather that wound about her thin legs, paying no mind to the smear of orange blood she left behind, then gestured toward the open bookcase. "If that's what Tikova wants, fine."

Adaris' heartbeat picked up its pace. That was easy. Almost too easy. No questions. No snappish retort. Sroc didn't even seem interested in tagging along for the questioning, just leaned back on her stone chair and ran her hand down a large glass jug next to her plate. The jug was empty, but it was just like the ones filled with blood that decorated the space. The gesture made Adaris' own blood go cold.

"Make it quick, though," Sroc said. "I got Tikova's blessing to practice again, and I want to see if you react to the gemstone."

The air seemed to thicken, and Adaris had to force herself to inhale. *Me? React to the gemstone?* She didn't like the sound of that. She nodded anyway, grateful for the opportunity to talk to the prisoners.

She rose and slipped into the bookshelf prison. Daylight seeped inside behind her to a bare stone room, no wider than her outstretched arms and twice that in length. Sweat and urine hit her nose at once.

Three Moon Knights huddled inside. She stopped. The knights weren't chained to the stone walls. There were no shackles of any kind. Madness. The knights could escape, could overpower Sroc and—it hit her like a lightning bolt. With Sroc, a Divus, a Blood crafter, the prisoners didn't need to be chained. They couldn't overpower her, as young as she may be. Sroc could kill them with just one touch.

One of the Vagari appeared to be unconscious. A second curled inward on himself, not meeting Adaris' gaze. Only the curlhorn sitting next to the wall glared at Adaris, a fierce edge to her jaw and posture. One dark horn had snapped off, leaving only a sharp edge, while the other spiraled out from the woman's brown forehead.

Breathing heavy, the curlhorn lifted her chin. "Are you here to break my arms now, worshipper?"

What? Adaris didn't understand until her gaze drifted from the curlhorn's intense glare to the woman's legs. Her dark pants had been ripped off at the thigh. Her legs bent at an unnatural angle, and jagged, white bones protruded from her skin in multiple places. It was a wonder the Vagari was still awake. Clearly, her bones had been shattered.

And with them, Adaris' plan of escape. Her crafting wasn't up to injuries like this, and the curlhorn wouldn't be able to smash Spectrum's bars if she couldn't walk, so what else could Adaris do? *Be a scribe.* "I'm here to get your story."

The curlhorn scoffed, averting her gaze to the wall.

The silence loomed like a creature waiting to pounce.

Adaris' voice seemed trapped in her throat. She'd dealt with stubborn people before, but this was an entirely different level of resistance. She couldn't blame the curlhorn for her anger. Heartbeats passed. Her book felt like ice in her palm.

"At least your name," Adaris tried again.

The Moon Knight regarded her with a wary gaze, her cracked horn glinting in the light. She huffed. "Corra." She bit off the word as if it were a curse she spat at Adaris. "That's my name, you sunsick fool, and you'll get nothing else from me. Go lick Ponuriah's ass, will you? That's where you so clearly belong."

Respect surged through Adaris at the resolve of this knight. She hoped, if she ever found herself in a similar position, she'd be as brave as this woman. "Thank you, Corra."

"Time's up!" Sroc moved around her. Her eyes glowed white with her Blood crafting, as she stalked toward the man huddled in the corner. The Vagari's face slackened in fear. When Sroc yanked him out of the rock room, he hardly struggled. It would be useless to struggle against a Divus. Not while her skin touched his. "Come on, scribe!" Sroc barked over her shoulder.

The curlhorn scowled at Adaris, as if daring her to do something else. Something more. Adaris wanted to. She had the fleeting thought that perhaps she could give this knight some aca nuts to help with the pain, but what if that act of kindness got her caught? Adaris couldn't allow that to happen. She wouldn't. Instead, she met the curlhorn's intense glare and left the cramped prison. Guilt followed her out.

When she reached the podium, the Vagari man already lay unconscious in the slump of rock that would collect his blood. Sroc had probably knocked him out with her crafting. Not wanting to think about what would happen to him, Adaris focused on Sroc.

"You asked about a conduit earlier. This is it." Sroc shoved a blue-green gemstone into Adaris' hands, her earlier easy going manner honed into an edge of interest. "It's called lazicon. During the bloodbinding ritual, the crafting will shatter the lazicon, the blood will be absorbed into those shattered fragments, and the fragments will be absorbed into whatever object I deem fit. The lazicon must be surrounded by blood in order to work, so yours will remain whole, while mine will be absorbed by the ritual." She plucked a circlet dotted with orange gemstones off her bookshelf.

Adaris hardly noticed. The lazicon gemstone fit perfectly into her cupped hand and felt eerily warm against her skin. Her mind was still reeling over her shattered plan to free the curlhorn, but it was slowly sinking in that she was about to help in another murder. *Conform.* There was nothing else to do. Adaris shook her head and focused wholly on Sroc.

Sroc pointed at the lazicon gemstone. "Clutch that as you chant. If you have the same power as I, you'll feel it activate, even if you don't murder the man yourself. That lazicon should grow cold."

Adaris swallowed. "And if I don't...feel it?"

"Then you'll just be a scribe with a weak skill for healing, and we'll have to kidnap another Divus." She grinned, her cavalier attitude making Adaris nauseous. "And since Kye isn't here, you get to be my primary helper. If we're lucky, we'll get the power to camouflage from this man."

So his death wouldn't even be helpful to Adaris' cause—her breath hitched. She didn't want to do this, didn't want to assist Sroc in the murder of this man. She didn't want to be a part of this. Not again.

But she also didn't move.

She couldn't. Her sandals seemed glued to the floor. Her gaze, once more, drifted to the Vagari.

She was doing this to protect Rhonwen and Spectrum. To conform. And so Kye would help them escape.

Nausea swept through her, making her skin feel hot and sweaty. Despite that, she stood behind the unconscious man and readied herself. Holding the lazicon gemstone in one hand, she put the other hand on the prisoner's back.

The young researcher flourished the blade and flashed a grin at Adaris. "Ready, scribe? Hold the gemstone, call up your crafting, and chant with me!"

Before Adaris could blink, Sroc began chanting and sliced the man's throat open. Orange blood gushed out, hot and thick along the stone floor. Adaris choked down a rise of bile and shoved the man onto the floor, facedown, so the blood ran freely out of him. Clutching the gemstone, she forced the words past the tightness in her throat again and again and again. *Blood is life, life is blood...* White fog rolled over her eyes as her crafting answered her call.

The gemstone cooled in her hands until the lazicon felt like ice.

To Adaris' horror, a tendril of white-hot power burned through her unlike anything she had ever felt before. Still chanting, she pushed through this new pain, her words becoming more guttural and rough. Her crafting was usually like sinking into a warm bath or putting a hot compress on her skin, an ember warmth, but this was nothing like that. Fire raced through her veins.

Sroc had said that if Adaris felt the lazicon grow cold, they would be similar. Her and Sroc would be similar. *I can't be like her. I won't.*

The dead man's blood swirled into a circlet dotted with orange gemstones, and as Sroc held the circlet up, the gems beat once—twice—like a heartbeat.

Silence fell, and Adaris realized she'd stopped chanting. Her veins still burned with power and pain. *What have I done?*

Sroc's wild gaze turned to her. "Did you feel the cold, scribe?"

Adaris nodded, throat tight, chest tighter. She could barely breathe.

A grin split Sroc's face.

Chapter Thirty-Two

THE FIRE COOLED FROM Adaris' veins, and with it, her crafting light dimmed. The scent of death thickened the air, making her nauseous. The dead man's empty eyes stared at her. Horror spread like a rising wave within her. *I can't be like her. Like Sroc.*

The young researcher came closer, clutching the circlet, a wild glint in her eyes. "You felt the heat in your veins?" When Adaris nodded numbly, Sroc smiled. "The true power of your crafting was unleashed!"

The rock room seemed to shrink around Adaris. Her gaze dropped to her shaking fingers clutching the lazicon gemstone. The true power? As in death? But Blood crafting was meant to heal.

The gemstone's rough edges glinted in the lantern light and jabbed into her skin. She'd always believed her crafting was next to nothing, but now it could be linked to something more powerful and twisted and sunsick than anything else she'd ever seen.

"We're cut from the same cloth, you and I." Sroc grabbed the lazicon from Adaris, then set both it and the circlet on the table next to her plate of meat. "I'm sure you have many questions."

Shock had frozen Adaris' usual stream of queries. Only one broke through the frost. *How can I be like Sroc?* She couldn't exactly ask it like that, in the disgusted, guilt-ridden tone hammering inside her mind.

A groan came from inside the bookshelf prison, and Sroc rolled her eyes before heading inside. After a few moments, the groaning stopped and the young researcher slipped back out again, blinking away the white light glowing from her eyes. "I healed some of the curlhorn's wounds," she explained with an exasperated sigh. "Tikova wanted at least one of them alive, and the other Vagari is too weak for questioning."

Sroc then plucked the large, empty glass jar from the table. "You'll have to ask your questions later. We have matters to attend to." She pointed her finger at the prison door. Her brown gemstone ring brightened to copper. The stone in front of the bookshelf door softened, then flowed inward, pulling the door closed with a heavy thud. "Come now."

Without another word, Sroc scurried up the ladder. The glass jar swayed in Sroc's grasp as the young researcher made it to the top of the ladder and pulled herself through. Adaris' gut flopped. Why was Sroc taking the glass jar, and whose blood would it be filled with? She had no choice but to find out. It would look suspicious if she stayed there alone. A ripple of pain shot up her leg, and she realized the anklet had deactivated during the ceremony…the murder. Bile rising in her throat, she reactivated the anklet. *I don't want to be like her.* The mantra was screaming in her mind, but she had to keep up appearances.

As soon as she reached the top of the ladder, she heard chanting. "Tikova, Tikova, Tikova," a crowd was yelling his name. She slipped out of the cave, watching as Sroc darted for the stone steps. Cheers rose above the chanting, and above that, an ear-splitting scream.

Rhonwen? A ripple of icy worry spread through Adaris. She ran, following Sroc and the noise to the community center. With each step, her worries grew. Had Rhonwen finally snapped and drawn the community's true ire?

The sounds of cheering were eerily similar to the sunlight celebration. The sun hadn't reached its apex, but the sounds of the chanting crowd drew back memories Adaris longed to forget of severed arms and dark-brown blood splattering on the ground.

She finally reached the community center, and it seemed like everyone had gathered by the Ponuriah statue. Shoving through the unhinged throng, she saw what had captured the community's attention.

Berhn! Adaris bit the inside of her cheek to keep from crying out. Tikova held Berhn's arm in a vice-like grip that made the young man's green skin pale to nearly white. Tears streamed down Berhn's cheeks as Tikova stared haughtily into the young Nemora's terrified face.

Adaris spotted Kye in the crowd and moved closer to him. "What's happening?" she hissed.

Kye's clothes were covered in a fine layer of dust, like he'd been handling stone, and his arms had scratches on them. A dash of crimson paint stained his white vest. He barely spared her a glance, eyes full of worry and lips pressed into a thin, bloodless line that told her everything she needed to know.

Was Tikova going to kill Berhn? No, of course not. He was part of Sroc's research team. He was the best at finding the lazicon gemstones, and he was so young. There was no way they'd kill him, but they could punish him.

"Berhn of the Ratnaa Nemora, you have done a disservice to the community of Slagrock." Tikova's voice lifted above the chanting.

The crowd booed.

Rhonwen's voice floated about the booing. "What disservice did he do?"

Adaris' gaze snapped to the opposite side of the ring of people, where Rhonwen clutched a small canvas in one hand and a paintbrush tipped in crimson in the other.

Tikova arched an eyebrow at Rhonwen, as if shocked she'd speak to him as a prisoner. "He tried to leave the community last night."

That drew jeers from the crowd. A Nemora—Tiy, if Adaris remembered his name correctly—threw a handful of stones at Berhn. The rocks struck Berhn in the face.

Berhn grunted, rubbing his face with his free hand. "Stop it! Put me down."

Tikova straightened his full, considerable height, lifting Berhn bodily off the ground by just his arm. Berhn gasped and cried out, feet kicking uselessly as he grappled Tikova's wrist.

The crowd cheered. Adaris noted the disgusting grin twitching Tikova's lips. *Clearly, he feeds off the power he holds over his community. He loves the attention from the crowd. The power-hungry sunsick fool.*

Rhonwen stepped closer. "That's it? You're going to hurt him because he took a walk?"

Tikova's eyes flashed, and a muscle in his jaw bulged. "He was carrying all his belongings."

The look on Tikova's face splintered Adaris' disgust into fear. This was already looking bad for Berhn, and now Rhonwen was putting herself at risk as well. The last thing Rhonwen needed to do was draw attention to herself.

Adaris pushed through the crowd to stand directly in front of Tikova. Her voice caught in the bubble of dread rising in her throat, but she forced the words out. "Yes, I thought community members could leave anytime they wanted?"

Just as she hoped, Tikova's gaze fell to her. Adaris lifted her book and quill, indicating she was waiting to document the answer. He gave her an approving nod. "I can understand why you think that, Adaris, but he's a deserter. He's the best at finding our gemstones, and he was leaving us without his skills. Abandoning his task. I even heard that he was spreading lies about who we worship. It's against the community's wishes and against our rules."

Spreading lies? Something clicked in Adaris' mind. This wasn't about Berhn leaving, not fully, it was about his gentle fire idea, the kinder version of Ponuriah that spoke of rebirth and regrowth in a positive manner. Berhn's idea of the sun goddess was very different from Tikova's, so of course Tikova would tell everyone it was a lie. He was threatened by Berhn's ideas.

Tikova lifted Berhn higher.

"Fire can be cleansing. It can produce beautiful things. Rare things grow after being burned," Berhn shouted. The Nemora's bare torso heaved with each ragged breath. Dust clung to his billowy white pants, drifting loose with each kick of his legs. "There's no need to murder people to get what we need. We could talk to the other side—show them Ponuriah's gentler fire. Ponuriah can be kind, not vicious, and so can we. There's no need to attack the Groves if we can cultivate lands to trade for our necessities!"

Standing solid as a stone pillar, Tikova's expression darkened. He turned to the crowd. "What do we do to those who break our rules?"

"Death!" they shouted back.

A shiver rose up Adaris' spine, the pile of dead bodies rising in her mind's eye with it. The threats that were constantly hanging over her if she stepped out of line. She realized Tikova was staring at her expectantly, and it took her a heartbeat to remember why. *You asked the question. Write the answer.* She wrote his words down, hand trembling, ink splattering like black blood on the page. She wanted to stop this, but she didn't know how. Perhaps, if she kept him talking... "But how do you know this? How do you know he wanted to leave?"

Tikova swatted his hand toward the crowd. "They told me."

The crowd parted, and Berhn's elderly parents stepped closer. Berhn's mother scowled, and Berhn's father wore a look of disgust.

Berhn openly sobbed. "Mother!" he cried, but she looked away.

His parents value their community over their son's life? The deep, shivering betrayal sent cracks through her soul. There had to be something—anything—she could do to help him. Save him.

Tikova's gaze swung back to her, and Adaris could only stand there, caught by the intensity in his eyes. The challenge. If she did anything contrary to what he wanted, he'd know she wasn't on his side. Know she'd lied about wanting to be part of his precious community.

He'd kill her, too. And probably Rhonwen and Spectrum for good measure.

She froze, pen dripping ink onto her page.

Tikova's grin widened. "His parents told us everything. Sroc!" He shouted her name over his shoulder.

Sroc hurried up to him from where she'd been waiting near the statue, still holding the glass jug. She drew a blade from her belt.

Berhn shrieked, eyes locked on the dagger. "No, no! I'll be good!" He looked to his parents, but they both glared at him like he was the evil one, not the community preparing to murder him.

Adaris' heart thundered in her ears, drowning the jeering and cheering crowd. Muscles trembling, her Blood crafting surged within her and propelled her forward.

A strong hand latched onto her arm and held her back. She twisted and found Kye imperceptivity shaking his head. His eyes held just as much fear and anger and sadness as she felt churning inside herself. Berhn was his friend, too.

Tears prickled the backs of her eyes as her gaze skipped from Kye to Berhn to Rhonwen across the way. Rhonwen gripped her paintbrush tight to her chest, a look of horror on her face.

There was nothing any of them could do to stop Tikova.

Face twisted and tears coating his cheeks, Berhn cried out for his parents, shouting their names again and again. Struggling uselessly in Tikova's grip, Berhn's gaze found Adaris, then beside her, his friend Kye. Adaris could barely see past the tears blurring her vision as she remained fixed in place. *I can't help. I can't doom the rest of us.*

Berhn fell limp as the final realization suddenly seemed to dawn on him. No one was going to save him. His community—and his family—had failed him. That would be the last thing he would know. The last thing he'd realize. The last thing he'd see.

Betrayal.

When Berhn twisted toward Kye and Adaris once more, Adaris caught his gaze. While Tikova was distracted and grinning at the crowd, Adaris made a hand motion. She curled one hand into a fist pressed into her palm, then opened her fist to spread her fingers outward. Kye, too, made the gesture Berhn had shown them to symbolize the gentler fire, his belief of a gentler Ponuriah. In that simple act, both Adaris and Kye let Berhn know they'd remember a kinder sun goddess, just like the kindness he'd shown them.

Berhn's gaze latched on like Adaris was an anchor in this terrifying storm. He kept his eyes on her the entire time. Even when Sroc drew back her blade. Even when the dagger sunk into his chest hilt deep, his own lifeblood pouring out. Even as more cheers rang out around them.

Adaris never looked away, even as his blood spilled into the jug clutched in Sroc's gleeful hands. Adaris willed, with every piece of her soul, for him to know that he was her friend, that he was valued, that he was seen for the good person he was among all the vitriol. She kept her focus on him right up until the light in his youthful, bright-green eyes dimmed. Until he slumped lifeless in death and Tikova dropped him with contempt to the blood-splattered stone.

Then, the cheering crowd and Tikova's sickening smile was too much weight to carry. Her knees buckled, and only Kye's hand under her arm upright.

Chapter Thirty-Three

NUMB WITH SHOCK, ADARIS hardly noticed Kye propelling her back toward the living huts or his rough voice in her ear. "Get inside," he said. "Rhonwen needs to tell you something. I'll distract them for as long as I can."

Rhonwen's arm looped around Adaris' waist and guided her over to the black sand mattress. Adaris dimly realized they were inside her living space. Sinking onto the sand, she rubbed her eyes with trembling hands. Waves of nausea rocked the room, tilting reality on its edge. The midday light pouring in from the open archway and windows made the space too hot, and the cheering from the crowd outside seemed to bounce off the walls.

The image of Berhn's dead body burned bright in her mind. He was so young. So determined and eager to make a difference. Forced to pick his gender early. Forced to come to his full powers early. All so this community—so Sroc—could use him to find lazicon gemstones for her precious bloodbinding ritual.

Rhonwen sat next to her and gently took one of Adaris' hands in her own. Twining their fingers together, Rhonwen held tight, not saying a word. When Adaris lifted her gaze, she saw quiet tears streaming down the painter's cheeks. Tears prickled the back of Adaris' eyes, too. There was no space in her throat for air.

He was her friend, and these people killed him.

He didn't deserve to die.

"I can't believe they did that," Rhonwen whispered, her voice cracking.

Adaris could only shake her head. There were no words for how she felt, the whirlpool of emotions inside her. Hurt, anger, fear, grief, each pushed aside the other, demanding to be felt.

It seemed like Rhonwen understood. She pulled Adaris close, her arm wrapping around Adaris' shoulders. They touched their foreheads together, breath and grief intermingling.

Rhonwen leaned away first, her yellow eyes darkening. She heaved out a sigh. "I have something to tell you. I killed Yim."

Adaris blinked. At first, the words didn't register. Didn't make any sense. Rhonwen knew how precarious their position was, and she knew how dangerous it was to step out of line.

"You...killed Yim," Adaris repeated, needing to hear herself say it to believe it. "How?"

"We left the hut before dawn and headed into the mines, because I wanted to see if there was anything else interesting to paint. Yim was being terrible, and the deeper we went into the mine, the worse he got. I can usually handle it—I've been handling it—but then he..." She paused and drew in a shaky breath. "Well, suffice it to say, he stepped over a line that I warned him not to cross."

Dread wormed through Adaris. "What...what line? What did he do?" A horrible image flashed through Adaris' mind of Yim forcing himself on Rhonwen. Adaris would've murdered Yim herself. "What did he do to you?"

"Oh, he did nothing to me. He showed me this." The painter's expression hardened. She dug into her side bag, which usually held painting supplies, and drew out a cloth bundle damp with orange blood. Unwrapping the bundle with trembling fingers, Rhonwen peeled back the cloth, revealing a handful of torn, black feathers, the tip of a tail covered in rainbow scales, and worst of all, a large yellow eye pulled from its socket.

"Depths," Adaris gasped, understanding dumped on her like a bucket of cold water. Yim hadn't raped Rhonwen. He'd done something terrible to Spectrum. Adaris couldn't tear her gaze off the slyther's flesh, ripped from him with barbaric force. "Oh, Rhonwen. I'm so sorry. Is Spectrum still alive?"

"He is. I would've felt it otherwise, but I did feel his pain. It startled me awake today before the sun rose." Rhonwen wrapped up the bundle and tucked it away in her side bag. Her gaze held nothing short of fury. Her entire being trembled with it.

"How did you do it?" Adaris asked. "And what did you do with Yim's body?"

"We stopped to talk to Celli while she was carrying some fresh vials of animal poison to the weapons hut. Yim started questioning her about her research, and while they were both distracted, I managed to pocket a vial without either of them noticing. I knew Spectrum was in pain and I had to do something, so I snuck it into Yim's drink this morning, and he collapsed in the mine." Rhonwen sighed. "I didn't know what to do with the body, but then Kye came in looking for Berhn. He found me and a dead Yim inside. After I told him what happened, Kye dragged the body away. A little while later, I heard chanting and went out to investigate."

That was why Kye hadn't been at Sroc's lab, and why his clothing was covered in dust. Why his arms had scratches. He'd been pulling a body through a mine. Covering up Rhonwen's murder.

"I had to," Rhonwen said in a quiet voice.

Adaris put a hand on the painter's shaking shoulder. "I understand."

But the tangle of fear gripped her insides. She understood Rhonwen's motivation. Her companion animal was like a second soul, but now it threw her into even more danger. Surely, someone would notice her guard was missing. And to top it off, Rhonwen had possibly jeopardized their whole plan.

Adaris had some bad news to share as well. "I talked to the curlhorn."

"You did?" Rhonwen gasped. "Will she help us?"

"She can't," Adaris confessed. "They broke her legs, and Sroc was eating the curlhorn's companion animal while I was there. She offered me some."

Rhonwen paled, reaching out to clasp Adaris' hand with her good one. "That's horrible."

"I didn't take it," Adaris assured her. "But the curlhorn can't help us if her legs are broken."

Rhonwen chewed on her lip. "Perhaps you could give her your anklet? Maybe she could use it for a little while, just to break Spectrum free."

Adaris looked down at her own trembling hands. "Sroc healed the curlhorn, somewhat, before we left the research lab, but her bones had been broken. Shattered! And Sroc wouldn't be so kind as to heal the knight completely. I doubt the anklet would strengthen her legs and dull the pain enough to walk."

"You could always just try," Rhonwen pleaded. "It's the only plan we have."

It was one plan, not the only one, but Adaris would rather try using the anklet on the curlhorn than the bloodbinding ritual. "I'll try."

Yelling erupted outside, startling them. It sounded like Kye's voice, but no one came inside Adaris' hut. No one came to look for them. Needles of anxiety pricked her skin. It felt like they didn't have much time left.

Rhonwen leaned closer, her words coming faster. It seemed she felt the shift in the air as well. "Will Sroc let you speak to the curlhorn again?"

"I doubt it, but she wants me to help with her research, so I might have access."

Research. The sensation of holding the prisoner while Sroc sliced his neck open came back to Adaris like a wave slamming into her, and she blinked the memory away. *I helped Sroc murder a man. A Moon Knight. A prisoner! I'm like her. Like Sroc.* Guilt cut through her like glass.

"That's good." Rhonwen nodded slowly. "If you get a moment alone, you could test the anklet."

"Rhonwen!" Kye at the door startled them both. "Come with me. Now."

Adaris and Rhonwen rose from the sand mattress. Adaris squeezed Rhonwen's hand and let go.

"What's happened?" Rhonwen darted to Kye's side.

Fear shadowed the man's face. "They found Yim."

"Already?" Rhonwen gasped.

"I didn't have much time with the body before Berhn...but I have a plan. You and I have to face Tikova and Sroc." His gaze latched onto Adaris. "Talk to the curlhorn while Sroc is distracted by us."

He didn't know Adaris had already spoken to the curlhorn Vagari. Their primary plan was most likely shattered, but Kye didn't wait for her to reply. He just pulled Rhonwen out of the hut.

Adaris wanted to follow them, wanted to help them somehow or at least be with them through Sroc and Tikova's questioning, but she knew the best help she could give was the anklet. She waited in her hut for a few heartbeats, letting Kye and Rhonwen disappear fully out of her line of sight before heading out. She wove around the community center and the lingering onlookers toward the steps leading down the cliffs.

Berhn's body caught her attention out of the corner of her eye. His sharp Ratnaa markings glimmered in the light like crushed gemstones, and resolve quickened her steps. A new strength burned inside her. She would do whatever it took to get her and Rhonwen out of Slagrock. If not for their own sakes, then for Berhn's memory. For his unique and beautiful take on the sun goddess. Using the anklet on the curlhorn was a long shot, and Adaris wasn't certain the Vagari would agree to help, but she'd rather try that than help Sroc murder someone again.

Chapter Thirty-Four

ADARIS STROLLED DOWN THE stone stairs, wishing she could run down them. Waving to a community member by the fishing hut, she slipped into the cave and lowered herself into Sroc's research area for the second time that day. As if she had every right to. As if she wasn't trespassing at all.

Once inside, she darted over to the bookshelf and pushed. It didn't move. She threw her whole weight against it, feet scrabbling uselessly against the rough stone floor. Still no movement. Depths! She didn't realize how heavy this rock door really was. Shoulder pinned against the stone, rocks jabbing into her skin, she propped her foot against the wall and pushed. The anklet cast an orange shimmer on the rocks. Her legs trembled but stayed strong. The door ground open a crack. Then a wedge. Finally enough space opened that she thought she could slip through.

She had to hurry. There was no telling how long Kye and Rhonwen could detain Sroc. If the researcher returned and saw the prison door open, there would be no lie compelling enough to explain Adaris' actions away. She'd already been warned that talking to the prisoners was against Tikova's wishes.

She couldn't help worrying about Rhonwen. Would she emerge from the conversation favorably? What if they realized right away that she had killed Yim? Adaris went still, picturing Tikova sentencing her friend to death.

No. Kye was there. He'd protect Rhonwen. She had to believe that and focus on her own task.

Adaris lit a candle from the bookshelf, then slipped into the crack. Her clothes caught on the stone, but she kept going. She wrinkled her nose against the sharp, rotten scent. In the pale, yellow light from her candle, she spotted an unconscious prisoner. On the other side of the small space, the curlhorn sat with her back against the wall, her legs still bent at awkward angles.

Adaris shuddered. She took the curlhorn in, hard stare and all. Sroc had healed her, but only just. The curlhorn's leg bones had been shoved back into her flesh, but only a crude amount of healing had been done—enough to knit the flesh back over them in dark orange bruises, not enough to knit the bones back together.

Knowing she only had a few precious moments alone, Adaris knelt before the curlhorn. "Corra, my name is Adaris. I am not a sun goddess worshipper. I'm a wandering scribe who got kidnapped by these people, and I'm trying to escape, but I need your help. If you help me, I'll help you escape as well, you'll come with us on our raft."

The flickering candle deepened Corra's scowl. "You're the one walking around free. Why should I believe you?"

"Because you have no other choice," Adaris replied, desperately hoping the curlhorn's antagonistic manner from earlier would fade. "It's either help me or die by Sroc's dagger."

The curlhorn's lips thinned, as she weighed her options.

The silence grew heavy, thick. A small part of Adaris wondered if the woman was going to be stubborn and not help, but why wouldn't she? If Adaris was in the curlhorn's position, she'd accept any help she could get. Depths, she *had* accepted any help she could scrape together, but it seemed like the curlhorn needed more proof.

"Look." Adaris dug her quill from her side bag, turning it so the black tip faced the curlhorn. Her quill would prove who she really was. In the flickering candlelight, the scrollkeeper's emblem glinted. "I'm a recognized scribe of the Athenium of the Ancients. I swear to you, on every book in that library, I am not one of these worshippers."

Corra flicked her gaze to the quill, then gestured toward her unconscious companion. "And what about him?"

Adaris bit her lip. As much as she admired the woman's need to help her companion, there wasn't time for negotiations. Sroc could return at any moment. "Right now, I'm focusing on you. If this works, I'll try to get him out, too."

It wasn't exactly a lie, but her current plan didn't include time to aid the unconscious Moon Knight. She couldn't exactly say that if she wanted the curlhorn's cooperation. So, guilt twisting within her, she let her words slide, let the curlhorn believe her. "I'm going to try to heal you a little first. With your permission."

At Corra's nod, Adaris gently set her hand on the curlhorn's arm and could feel the woman tremble beneath her touch. She sank into her Blood crafting and pushed as much life energy as she could into Corra. Slowly, ever so agonizingly slowly, her crafting mended the small bone fractures, but the line in the woman's femur remained crooked. There was nothing Adaris could do for a break that bad. A headache started behind Adaris' ear. Sroc's words about how Adaris' true powers had been unleashed lingered in her mind. Her crafting felt no different now than normal. She felt no more powerful, and her crafting was as warm as embers—not flames. Perhaps that feeling only came to her during the bloodbinding ritual? Shoving that thought aside, she blinked the crafting away and grimaced. "It's not much but it's the best I can do."

"Thank you," Corra whispered.

Adaris leaned back, removing her anklet. A pulse of pain shuddered through her, as if her leg was making up for all the agony she'd forgone. She held the anklet up at eye-level. "Try on this anklet to see if it'll help you walk."

The curlhorn forced out a laugh that sounded more like a cough. "You want me to walk?" Understanding dawned in the woman's eyes. "You need my ramming ability, don't you?"

"I do," Adaris replied.

The curlhorn shook her head. "That young Divus healed my flesh, but my leg is far from right..."

"My leg was badly injured when I was younger, and this anklet helps me." Adaris hooked it around the woman's ankle, trying desperately to ignore the agony thrumming in her bad leg. "Dip into your crafting. The anklet should activate. Please, we don't have much time."

The curlhorn closed her eyes. Orange Animal crafting glowed behind her eyelids, and almost immediately, the anklet brightened to match.

Adaris wedged a shoulder under the woman's arm. The overwhelming stench of sweat, dirt, and urine hit Adaris' nose as she pressed herself against the curlhorn.

The curlhorn braced herself, then tried to draw her feet under her. One leg bent at an unnatural angle, the flesh bulging and tearing as the bone moved freely under the skin. The curlhorn screamed and immediately straightened her leg once more, muscles twitching and flopping like a fish in a net.

Adaris' whole body went rigid. She looked toward the open prison door. Anyone close by would have heard that scream. She had to leave. Right now. Cover her tracks before Sroc discovered she was down in the lab and talking to the prisoners. If the curlhorn couldn't even put her legs under her, she definitely couldn't do her ramming attack. Their plan wouldn't work, even with the anklet. At all. Ever. How else would they free Spectrum? To make matters worse, she'd just put the woman through an immense amount of pain for nothing. She unhooked her anklet. "I'm sorry to have made you move."

Corra leaned heavily against the wall and gritted her teeth. "Do you have any other plans?"

Adaris only had one and it sank through her like a sword. Her lip trembled.

Before she could get the truth out, a string of curses broke somewhere above them, followed by a sharp slapping noise. Snatching the candle, she took one more look at Corra then slipped back out of the prison. The pain from her leg was nearly blinding, but she didn't care. Adaris shoved her whole weight against the bookshelf. It ground closed with a loud scraping sound.

"Get down the—" Sroc's voice stopped. "What was that? Who's down there?"

Adaris' pulse roared in her ears. There was no use hiding. How could she, with nowhere to go? Trying to come up with an excuse, she hurried to the podium. "It's Adaris. I wanted to look at the ancient's grimoire."

"Why? You can't even read it." Sroc sighed. "Stop stalling and get down there," the young researcher snapped. At first, Adaris thought Sroc was still talking to her, but it dawned on her that Sroc was ordering someone to come down into the research lab.

To her horror, Rhonwen responded. "Listen, give me one more chance. Tikova said I'd get one more chance!"

No, no, no. A wave of fear pulsed through Adaris. She hooked the anklet back on and activated it. The pain in her leg vanished and she straightened to her full height. She needed to conform, but she also needed to be able to move if she got the chance to save Rhonwen. *Oh, Rhonwen.* Adaris fought to breathe past her panic.

"Let me go down first so the painter doesn't try anything." Kye came down the ladder with a fluid grace Adaris had never seen before. He locked eyes with Adaris and shook his head, face pale and fingers tight around his trident. Adaris knew that the words he told Sroc were actually for her. *Don't try anything.*

She gripped the edges of the podium, trying to wipe the horror and worry from her expression before Sroc arrived.

"You've had enough chances, painter," Sroc said. "Now get down the ladder."

Rhonwen muttered a string of curses in the Vagari tongue, but Adaris saw her white sandals and bare legs come down through the hatch. Rhonwen reached the bottom and looked around, taking in her surroundings and shaking like a thunderfawn. An orange bruise formed under her eye.

Surprisingly, her hands weren't bound, but Adaris remembered that the woman could probably slip out of any knot these people could tie. Rhonwen's gaze latched onto Adaris, yellow eyes full of fear, and Adaris fought the overwhelming urge to rush to her side. Three other guards came down behind her, each holding a barbed weapon. None carried paint, which didn't bode well.

The moment Sroc's sandals hit the rock, Adaris could no longer restrain herself. "Why is the painter here?" She kept her voice light, even and steady, full of curiosity and not the fear rising in her throat.

Sroc brushed some sand off her leather outfit and turned to her almost lazily. "You wanted to learn more about the bloodbinding ritual."

Rhonwen's brown cheeks paled. She opened her mouth, but Adaris stepped past the podium, gaze pleading with Rhonwen to remain silent. "Is Rhonwen here to paint it then?"

Thankfully, Rhonwen snapped her jaw shut, the muscle twitching by her temple. Sweat beaded on her brow. She hugged herself with her good arm, the other still in a splint. Her gaze darted from her guards to the podium to the containers of blood.

Sroc leveled a look at Adaris that spoke more than words ever could. "You're smarter than that, scribe."

Adaris grew cold, as if her own blood had been drained. She forced her voice to be calm. "But you have two Moon Knights left. Why choose Rhonwen to be a sacrifice?"

The word nearly stuck in her throat. She couldn't let Rhonwen be the next sacrifice. She wouldn't.

"I didn't choose her." Sroc sniffed, tugging off her gloves and walking over to the desk Adaris stood by. She picked up a knife. "Tikova said she's outlived her purpose. Her guard was found dead, and we suspect she did it."

Sweat trickled down the back of Adaris' neck and fear clawed inside her. "She's just a painter, and she has a broken arm. Why would you think that?"

Shrugging, Sroc went over to the artifacts. Her hand brushed past rings, anklets, and armbands before finally settling on a circlet that had an orange gemstone set into the front. "She was Yim's charge. Who else would've done it?"

Kye had stayed by the ladder after he'd come down. He cleared his throat. "Respectfully, Tikova said he needed to gather more proof and assigned her these guards. We should throw her back into her prison hut and gather the proof for him." His voice lowered, grew more serious. He very deliberately glanced toward the jars of blood scattered around the room. "I've helped you do many things, Sroc, in the name of your research, but I don't think we should risk angering Tikova. Not without real proof."

Sroc merely smiled, her gaze still on the circlet clasped in her small hand. It was clear she had made her decision. "I don't need proof, Kye, I need practice. If you don't want any part in this, fine." She waved her knife at another guard. "You, guard, bring the painter to the podium."

The guard latched a firm hand around Rhonwen's arm and pulled her to the podium. Rhonwen yanked and kicked, but she wasn't strong enough to tear away from his grip. Suddenly her eyes flashed bright orange, her arm brightening to match. Her limb thinned, slipping from the guard's grasp, and she stumbled away.

The two other guards closed in. One grabbed her around the waist, the other poised a barbed spear against her cheek. The third wrapped a meaty hand around her throat.

Adaris stepped forward. "Stop!"

"Why?" Sroc asked. "Didn't you want to learn about bloodbinding? We can't let her get away with this."

"Of course, I want to learn, but I don't want to anger Tikova," Adaris replied, her words tripping from her lips. She had to stop this.

"I see." Sroc pressed her lips into a thin line. "I suppose, since this will be your first, I'll allow you to choose." Her lips twisted into a grin that read pure evil. She lifted the circlet and the knife. "Using the bloodbinding ritual, either I kill the painter, or you kill the Moon Knight."

"Me?" Adaris blanched. "But...I've never done the ritual by myself before."

She wasn't built for that, her crafting was meant to heal not harm. Not kill. Not murder.

"But your crafting sang with the lazicon gemstone, so it means you can. Kye, get another prisoner."

Kye's gaze cut sharply to her. She hadn't told him about the gemstone, hadn't had any time to do so. He recovered quickly and pushed open the prison door. He dragged out the male Vagari, who'd woken but was so starved and sleep deprived, he didn't even struggle against Kye.

A terrible wave of relief went through Adaris at the sight. Kye hadn't picked the curlhorn. There was no way Adaris could take Corra's life, not after trying to heal her, but Adaris wasn't ready to give in. "I'm not ready. If I fail, it's a wasted life," Adaris argued. "Wasted research."

With a shrug, Sroc motioned to the guards surrounding Rhonwen. "Then I kill her. We know it'll work if I do it."

"I—" Words stuck in Adaris' throat like a dagger's edge. There were no lies, no excuses, nothing to help her out of this.

"You're officially part of the community, which means you're willing to use your crafting for the community just like everyone else." Sroc pulled herself up to her full height. "Are you telling me you're not?"

Adaris blinked. Understanding struck her like a slap.

This was just another test.

Another challenge.

Kye caught her gaze. His words came rushing back to her. *What are you willing to do to survive?*

Anything.

Adaris wouldn't back down, not with Rhonwen's life on the line.

She swallowed hard. "Of course."

Sroc set the circlet, a lazicon gemstone, and the dagger down on the podium, gesturing toward them with a wicked gleam in her eye. "Then prove it."

Chapter Thirty-Five

AS ADARIS STARED AT the knife on the podium, Kye brought the male Vagari prisoner forward with practiced ease and pressed the man down to his knees. A vise clamped over her heart and squeezed tight. She didn't want to kill the man, didn't want to kill anyone, especially not a Moon Knight.

Her palms slickened as she closed her trembling hands into fists, trying to come up with a different plan. Any other plan that didn't involve murdering this Moon Knight, but how? She glanced at the three guards—two male Elu and one female Nemora, each clothed in layers of white and crimson. They had enough skin showing that if Adaris reached them she might be able to...her throat tightened. Well, she might weaken one of them. Each guard had a wicked looking barbed weapon, long enough to keep her at arm's distance. Then there was Sroc. The young researcher had four bloodbound rings and a sun goddess shard. Trying to attack her would be unthinkable with all that power in her fingertips.

And really, Adaris was a scribe, for depths sake, not a fighter! Rhonwen had a broken arm. Only Kye had some skill and strength, but four against one was terrible odds. Even if they did manage to escape this research lab...where would they go? They couldn't leave Slagrock yet. Rhonwen refused to leave without her companion animal. They had to free Spectrum first. They had to have a better plan.

The truth shivered through Adaris. There was no way out but one.

She had to get them out of Slagrock, had to save Rhonwen. Depths, she had to save herself.

I have to do this.

If she had to murder this man to save her friend, she'd at least record his story later on. The Vagari she was about to kill had a cut across his cheek, and his eyebrows had been singed away. The clump of dark hair that swept across his forehead probably looked nice before he'd become a prisoner of war. Up close, she could clearly see his bloodline traits. She noted the pattern on his neck, the light dusting of brown feathers down his chest. His companion had clearly been a bird of some type. She forced herself to memorize his face, his slight build, the ratty clothes barely covering his body.

"What's your name?" Adaris asked.

The man spit. A wet glob splattered on Adaris' cheek.

She had to get the knight's name, at the very least. She wiped the spit off her cheek with the back of her hand, forcing herself to keep the man's gaze.

She scowled. "Tell me your name."

Sroc's rhythmic tapping had started on the stone wall, a sure sign the young researcher was bored. She didn't care about the Moon Knight's name, only about the blood running through his veins and the crafting lashed to it, but Adaris was a scribe, first and foremost, and she was counting on Sroc to honor that. "I'm a scribe, and I'd like to record your sacrifice. If you don't tell me your name, I'll have to go on description alone."

The man cut his gaze away. "Mola."

Adaris' gut clenched. She was surrounded by a memory of white feathers and frost, sharp talons and even sharper screams. A mola suncreature had killed her parents and left her and her brother for dead. *Of course.*

It seemed fate had turned back on itself in a twisted way. She was going to kill a mola, not a suncreature or even a bird, but a Vagari. She was going to kill a mola Moon Knight to save her friend, to save herself. All of her senses darkened.

Sroc made a sound halfway between a scoff and a laugh. "Terrible name."

"It's not his name," Adaris said through gritted teeth. "Molas are great birds that live off the western coastline."

"Whatever. We need his sharp eyesight, not his life's story. Stop wasting time, scribe," Sroc muttered. "Unless you'd rather I use the painter for—"

"No!" Adaris replied, probably too harshly. Her gaze snapped to Rhonwen, who was still trapped against the large male guard, with the two others pointing weapons at her. Rhonwen's eyes were wide. Blood dripped from the cut on her cheek.

Adaris focused on the Moon Knight. Sharp eyesight would do nothing to break Spectrum free, but doing this—completing this ritual—would keep them safe for now. She reached for the dagger at the podium.

"Fine." The man's voice quaked, as if he was finally coming to terms with his fate. "My name is Qiath."

Adaris blinked and nodded. His yellow eyes pleaded with her to reconsider, but she couldn't back down. There were no other options. "I will record your death, Qiath."

Knife firmly in her grasp, she plucked the lazicon gemstone from the podium with her other hand. Muttering low, she began speaking the words of the bloodbinding ritual.

White fog pulled across her eyes as her crafting took hold, the gemstone like a shard of ice in her hand. The crafting fog didn't stop her from seeing the fear in the man's dark eyes, the way his lips trembled when she drew the dagger back. The vise around her heart clamped tighter still. Her anklet deactivated, and pain pulsed up her leg. *I can't do this, I can't.*

Adaris threw her arm forward, and the dagger sank into the man's neck. She yanked her arm to the side, slicing open his throat in a grim mockery of a grin. The knight stared in wide-eyed shock. Thick, orange blood gushed from the wound.

Kye pushed the man down, letting the blood flow into the stone basin.

In a daze, Adaris continued to mutter the ritual words while the man thrashed. *Blood is life, life is blood...* The ancient Divus language rolled off her tongue as if she had spoken it all her life. A headache started just behind her ears. The man grew limp as his blood pooled in the dip. The moment he died, a thick, heavy scent permeated the air. Her stomach turned, and shook Adaris to her senses. She wasn't done with the ritual yet; murder was just the first step.

Letting the dagger fall from her numb fingers, she grabbed the circlet from the podium and dropped to her knees. Pain jarred through her bad leg, nearly blinding in its intensity, but she shoved the circlet and the lazicon gemstone into the basin of blood.

The liquid warmed her up to her elbows. The sharp sting of blood filled her nose. It was as if the very air was biting back at what she had just done. What she was doing. *Blood is life, life is blood.* She shouted the words. Her crafting coursed through her veins like lava, like fire, like the sun itself.

The frozen gemstone shattered between her fingers. It was working. Whatever the depths this ritual was, it was working. Adaris kept shouting, though her voice grew hoarse.

Slowly, ever so slowly, the blood started to swirl around her arms. Her heart thudded against her chest like a war drum. The headache grew, and stars burst in her vision. She gasped for breath. A deep, steady thrum of agony in her leg pulled at her attention and threatened to topple her over. Her crafting ebbed, yearning to soothe her own pain, to end the anguish in her head. The swirling blood slowed.

No. Depths, no! She'd come too far. Done too much to let this end in failure.

She pushed more of herself into the ritual and her crafting responded. It burned brighter, yanking at her life energy and giving nothing in return. Her body shook. Her hand clutched the circlet so hard the metal bit into her skin. Sweat poured down her forehead. Her vision blurred and darkened near the edges.

Finally, the blood resumed its sickening swirl. The warm liquid grew cold around her arms. Then, like a stopper pulled from a tub, the swirling blood drew down, down, down, until every drop vanished completely, leaving only the circlet behind.

Gasping, Adaris snapped out of her crafting and blinked the white fog from her eyes. She knelt on all fours, both hands in the rock basin. The hand that had once held the lazicon was all that kept her from toppling over. Her other hand still held the circlet, cutting deep into her palm. The orange gemstone pulsed once, twice like a heartbeat.

The ritual was complete.

Relieved, she lifted the circlet for Sroc to see.

Sroc grinned at her, a wild sunsick look glittering in her eyes.

For one moment, a heartbeat, Adaris felt powerful. Her crafting had done something incredible. Something ancient. Even with her meager reserves, she'd bound crafting to an artifact. *I did that.*

Kye grunted, picking up the body and throwing it to the side of the room. The dead weight crumpled with a sickening crunch of breaking bones, head twisted at a terrible angle. The man's unseeing eyes were open, staring at Adaris. Judging her.

I murdered him. And I liked the feeling it gave me.

The thrill of power left her like a riptide.

Shaking her head, she drew back, crawling away from the dead body and the podium and Sroc and what she had just done. The burning power that once flowed within her had snuffed out, leaving her empty. A shiver pricked over her skin. She was too empty to even engage the anklet.

Kye moved with her, always her shadow, even now. He grabbed her arm and helped her rise. When he spoke, he kept his eyes on Adaris, but his words were for Sroc. "We're leaving." He pulled Adaris past Sroc and the dead body toward the ladder. He glared at the trio of guards. "Put Rhonwen back into her prison hut," he ordered.

The guards jerked into motion at his sharp command, one grabbing Rhonwen's arm, the other two raising their weapons.

Adaris caught Rhonwen's gaze as the painter moved toward the ladder. Horror shimmered in her yellow eyes.

"Fine, Kye, take you and your bleeding heart elsewhere," Sroc snapped, her excitement bleeding away. "But we still have a few more prisoners to utilize. I want Adaris to do that again. Soon."

Utilize. Not murder. Like they weren't people. Adaris bit back the bitterness rising in her throat. Would she ever find the end of this path she'd chosen?

Chapter Thirty-Six

ADARIS TRAILED BEHIND KYE up the rock stairs, pressing a shaking palm against the stone columns beside her to keep herself upright. Her gaze lingered on the blue-black bruise of sky as dusk settled in. It felt as if she was moving through deep water. Each step radiated a throbbing ache. Her leg burned, the knife twisting deeper with each step she took, but she didn't even have enough energy left to activate her anklet. *I killed someone, and I liked how powerful it made me feel.* The thought sliced through her as clean as a dagger's edge. She squeezed her trembling hand into a fist by her side.

Footsteps crunched behind her, the trio of guards from Sroc's research lab following Adaris, matching her slower pace. Keeping Rhonwen between them, they left a wide gap of empty air between her and them. When she glanced back, not one of them would meet her gaze. Something that looked like fear flickered through the shorter one's pale expression. *Good.* A twisted sense of pride rushed through her. *Let them be afraid.*

It might make what she had to do next easier. A plan was slowly taking shape in Adaris' mind. A terrible plan, perhaps, but in times like this, terrible might be the only thing they had left. The rush from the bloodbinding ritual was...intoxicating. Like a drug, it called for her to do more, be more, use it again to gain more powers. She could use her pitiful crafting to create powerful artifacts. *I can use this ritual to break Spectrum free.*

Finally cresting the rock stairs, Adaris found Kye waiting at the top.

Kye's deep brown eyes met hers, unflinching. And all at once, Adaris felt eternally grateful to have found him as an ally. He understood. He'd done unspeakable things to get by. He'd helped Sroc just like Adaris had been forced to. She knew she could count on him to help her in one last murder to help set them free. As they locked eyes, something passed over his features, like pride or excitement or maybe even triumph. Adaris couldn't quite be sure, then he looked past her to the trio of guards and Rhonwen cresting the stairs.

They clasped their weapons in shaking hands and gave Adaris a wary eye. One clamped his hand around Rhonwen's arm.

Rhonwen held herself tight, anxiety rippling from her in palpable waves. She kept her gaze firmly on the stony ground. A subtle shift of weight, a shrinking away, made Adaris' heart ache. *What does she think of me?*

"I'll take Rhonwen back to her prison hut and guard her tonight." Kye's voice held a hard edge. "You're dismissed."

The guards nodded and continued past them toward the living area until one by one, they ducked into their huts, leaving Rhonwen, Kye, and Adaris alone.

Adaris' gaze swept the quiet community, so different from how she had left it with people cheering loudly for Berhn's death, celebrating a murder. Dusk spread long shadows around the huts, but it was still light enough to see without fires and lanterns. The eerie silence crept across her skin.

"Where is everyone?" Adaris asked Kye.

"After a—" Kye's voice caught. He gritted his teeth and forced the words through. "A demonstration like Berhn's, Tikova usually gives out laru melon. It's a celebratory fruit that creates its own alcohol, which puts people to sleep."

Rhonwen snorted. "Works better than aca nuts."

They were the first words Rhonwen had said since the research lab, and they were directed at Kye, not Adaris. She hadn't acknowledged Adaris at all since that one glance in the lab. That fact pained Adaris even worse than her leg did. *I did what I had to do to save her life.* The thought gave Adaris little comfort.

They had just made it past the Ponuriah statue when Adaris noticed them.

One after another after another, glowing pairs of red eyes blinked open. On top of the garden. Inside the food hut. By the living area. Under some rocks by the pathway. Another set moved around her own living quarters.

Suncreatures keeping watch at night, as always.

An instinctual shiver passed through Adaris, but she boldly made eye contact with a large serpentine unceg with white, glinting scales and waved, feigning nonchalance even while her heart pounded against her ribs at the sight of them.

Kye opened the prison hut lock and shuffled them all inside. He closed the metal door but didn't lock it behind them, then turned to Adaris. "You've learned how to do the bloodbinding ritual." His whisper seemed to fill the prison. "You know the words and the necessary gemstone and how to use your crafting to do it. You know it by heart?" he pressed.

Adaris nodded, finding the answer too obvious for words. Of course, she knew! He'd just seen her complete it successfully. He was there. He saw her personally shove the dagger into the knight's throat. Bile rose up in her own.

A light bloomed in the far side of the prison, dim and flickering, drawing Adaris' attention. Rhonwen had lit a candle. She sank into the stone chair by her desk and stared at the pair of them, her yellow eyes dark and unreadable.

"Did you write it down?" Kye asked, forcing her gaze back to him. "All of it. How Sroc does it, where she learned it from, how she's using prisoners?"

Adaris had seen this intensity only once before in her usually stoic ex-guard—when he was talking about the death of his companion animal, Grit. His questions made sense. He was making sure she'd gleaned enough information for the scrollkeepers back home, making sure she'd completed his original task. He was making sure he could kill Tikova.

She put a hand on his arm and nodded, matching his low voice with a whisper of her own, "I've recorded enough to know I can do it again. I can show the scrollkeepers, and the Silver Shade."

A grin spread across his lips. "Perfect."

"So you can do what again?" Rhonwen asked, her frosty voice cutting through their conversation. "Murder someone?"

Adaris and Kye both turned to her. Kye stilled, but Adaris rocked back at Rhonwen's words. A spasm traveled through her—damn to the depths her bad leg! She went to the stone bed to sit down.

"I did it to save you," Adaris said quietly.

"You killed a Moon Knight," Rhonwen replied.

Adaris' throat tightened and the inside of her mouth turned to sand. Tears prickled the back of her eyes, but she blinked them away. Yes, she had killed someone, but there was no turning back, no righting that wrong. She'd made her choice, and he was dead, and that was that. Period. End of sentence. The ink had dried, and it was time to turn the page.

In the back of her mind, she knew it probably wouldn't be that easy, but she swallowed the guilt rising in her throat, forcing it down and away. "I had to."

"You could have tried something else," Rhonwen whispered, clutching her splinted arm close to her body, fingers digging into her skin until her brown knuckles turned white.

"Like...what?" Adaris asked. "You're injured, and I can't fight. The curlhorn can't walk, so she can't help. Only Kye has any real fighting skills, and with the three extra guards, that made it four against one down there. Not to mention Sroc has four bloodbound rings at her disposal. And her fifth ring is a sun goddess shard!"

Rhonwen didn't back down. "You could have tried something else. Anything else."

"Exactly what would you have had me do, Rhonwen?" Shock rippled through Adaris, and she leaned back, shaking her head. She'd expected more understanding from Rhonwen, and her friend's accusation hit her like a slap. Killing the Moon Knight had been the only choice she could make. "Tell me, how would you have escaped?"

"You had a weapon! I would've cut off Sroc's hand. Thrown the dagger at one of the guards while she was distracted. Asked the Moon Knight for help instead of murdering him. I would've done anything else rather than kill someone!" Rhonwen looked away, glaring at Kye. "You should've done something to stop this."

Kye didn't move, didn't even try to defend himself. His lips thinned into a line, and he flicked a glance toward Adaris. At once, she understood why he wasn't saying anything in retort. It had been a kind of test from him as well. Proof that she'd gained all the knowledge she could. The truth seeped into Adaris like ice water.

She shook her head at the realization and rounded on Rhonwen. "Your hands aren't exactly blood-free. You tried to kill your guards; you tried to push Kye into a lava river; depths, you actually killed Yim!"

Rhonwen's expression hardened. "That's different, and you know it. Yim did terrible things, to me and to Spectrum. The Moon Knight you murdered was innocent."

"You were the reason we were in that position in the first place, so don't judge me for my choices." They'd been trapped. There was nothing else for her to do. Why couldn't Rhonwen see that? Anger crashed through her like rocks crumbling to a wave. "Sroc was going to sacrifice you! It was either your life or his, and I chose you. How can you be angry at that?"

"I'm angry at everything, Adaris!" Rhonwen pressed a shaking hand to her forehead. "How can you not be? How can you not be furious? You're actually one of them now."

The words tore through Adaris, yanking her anger away. Now she understood why Rhonwen was so adamant, why she was so angry. Rhonwen had warned her of this since the very beginning—that Adaris would turn on her and become a true member of Slagrock. And Adaris had just confirmed Rhonwen's fear by giving in to murdering someone just like they'd told her to do.

Her heart cracked in half. To think that she might be turning into one of them–a member of Slagrock. A member of this horrible community that murdered Berhn. That used Kye's companion animal as research. That tortured Rhonwen. She even dressed like one of them and talked like one of them.

But it was all an act. To blend in. To protect herself and protect Rhonwen. She wasn't one of them, not really.

Yet she couldn't deny the pull of the ritual. The pure fire and power of the ancient crafting burning through her.

She leaned in close. "I am angry at them, Rhonwen. I'm furious at Tikova and Sroc and all of them for making me conform and forcing me to do horrible things. And perhaps I've gone too far, but I'll do whatever it takes to get us free. If that means becoming one of them, well..." She hesitated for a moment as her plan fully formed in her mind. "Now that I have the knowledge to bloodbind, I'm going to use that against them."

Rhonwen arched an eyebrow. "How?"

"I have a plan." She grabbed Rhonwen's hand and held tight. "We'll be gone before the rest of the community even wakes up. I'll need Kye's help. We'll need to meet in Sroc's research lab long before dawn."

Adaris looked toward Kye, who nodded.

Rhonwen didn't reply, the conflicting emotions on her face passing by too quickly to identify.

The silence stretched until Adaris couldn't take it any longer. "Can you think of any other way to get us out of here?"

With a sigh, Rhonwen shook her head.

Adaris squeezed Rhonwen's hand, then let go, pushing herself up to her feet. At once, her leg throbbed, but she still couldn't summon the energy to trigger her anklet. "I should get going. Get ready, Rhonwen. Tomorrow, before dawn, we're leaving."

Kye pushed open the prison door and stood to the side, waiting. Before Adaris could follow, Rhonwen stood and clasped Adaris' hand once more. "I was wrong. You're not like one of them. Far from it." Rhonwen's eyes burned, her voice steady with conviction. She ran her thumb down Adaris' knuckles in a slow circle then leaned close, close enough to share breath, close enough that Adaris could see the tiny freckles dotting her cheeks. Rhonwen touched her forehead to Adaris'. "Thank you for doing so much to save Spectrum. I really, truly appreciate it. Just...don't lose yourself."

The world tilted just a little. *Rhonwen cares for me.* Then something hit her like a rogue wave, sudden and all at once. *I care for her, too.*

She was falling in love with Rhonwen.

Heat swept through her at the realization, swooping inside like a bird, rushing from her head to the tips of her toes. Who knew what tomorrow might bring? Tragedy or success, but damn her to the depths if she wouldn't use every stolen moment she had with this brilliant woman.

Adaris palmed Rhonwen's cheek, nerves coiling tight in her stomach. "Can I kiss you?"

Leaning in, Rhonwen pressed into the touch. "I'd like that."

Adaris met her halfway, pressing her lips against Rhonwen's. Soft and gentle at first, then harder. More urgent. Rhonwen tasted like paint and salt, and Adaris loved it.

Rhonwen pushed the fingers of her good hand through Adaris' hair, then cupped the back of her neck. Sweet breath fanned Adaris' cheek, and Rhonwen's lips matched the fervent passion in Adaris' soul. Everywhere the painter touched warmed. Adaris tried to be gentle about Rhonwen's splint, but the painter pulled Adaris deeper into the kiss, crushing into her. Nothing else mattered but this moment, this easy breath of time.

But all things had to end. There were still things to do, and lingering in the prison risked discovery.

Adaris broke first, pulling back. They touched foreheads for a moment again, then Adaris turned and left. Kye locked the prison door and took his usual post by the side of it, gesturing for Adaris to move along.

The community was even more quiet and dark than before. Her sandals crunched over the cracked stone pathway, each step an agony, but she walked as confidently as she could without her anklet. She still had a ruse to keep up, and she needed every ounce of the ruse to make this plan work. The back of her neck prickled as the suncreatures' stares followed her the entire way.

Chapter Thirty-Seven

EARLY THE NEXT MORNING, Adaris activated her anklet, swept her bag over her shoulder, and crept outside, eyeing the pre-dawn sky. The sun hadn't even touched the horizon yet. The community was quiet. Everyone was still deep asleep, just like she'd known they would be. Being forced to live among them, getting to know the heartbeat of the community, made it almost easy to sneak around. The suncreatures had vanished, probably to hunt down their first meals. There were no guards trailing her now that she was a full member of the community. She met Kye's gaze across the community where he stood post at Rhonwen's prison and nodded, then she headed for Tiy's living hut, the one topped with a cresting wave.

Tiy. The tall Nemora had created an entire home out of stone and speared a Moon Knight with a stone spike. He'd thrown rocks at Berhn, then cheered when he died. An artifact with the Hallr Nemora's crafting would be able to free Spectrum.

She just had to convince him to come down to Sroc's research lab with her. Had she blended in with the community enough to request something like that of him? She took a deep, steadying breath and ran over the script she'd planned the night before, the lies she'd have to pour on him to coerce him to comply with her request.

"Tiy?" She leaned close to the cloth draped across his open archway door. A musty scent filled her nose from the old fabric. "Are you awake?"

A rustle came from within, and a few moments later Tiy emerged. The Nemora was pulling on a long, blue robe that fell past his calves. He cinched it with a wide cloth belt. His brown eyes held a question, no doubt wondering what Adaris was doing outside his home, especially before dawn.

She gave him her best smile. "Sorry to bother you so early, but if you have time, I need some help in Sroc's research lab. She's given me a task with the prisoners."

Tiy yawned and scratched the back of his neck, tangling his fingers in the messy knot of black hair at the nape. "Why not ask Kye? He always seems to be shadowing you."

"He is, isn't he." Adaris forced a laugh, her heart picking up its pace. Just as she'd been watching this community, they'd been watching her. Which is why it would be best not to lie. "Kye's going there as well, but it's easier if two people assist. Especially with your strength. Could you help?"

Tiy took in her white, sleeveless tunic and billowy pants cinched at the knees. He returned her smile. "Of course, Adaris. Give me one moment."

A wave of relief coursed through her. That was it, that was all it took to convince a member of the Slagrock community to come with her to Sroc's research lab. She asked for his help...and he simply gave it. All her prepared lies and excuses were left behind, unneeded. It was a stark difference between the first interactions she had with this community, when no one would even talk to her—and if they did, they did so rudely. Tiy's acceptance was an abrupt reminder that she was truly and completely part of this community. Her gut twisted a little at his willingness, knowing she was about to murder him.

They walked through the sleeping community and made their way to the ocean. Climbing down the ladder into Sroc's research area, Adaris came face-to-face with Kye. He had already lit the lanterns around the space, a courtesy for Adaris since he didn't need light as a Vagari. Before Tiy lowered himself down, Adaris gripped Kye's arm, leaned close, and whispered, "How's Rhonwen?"

"Awake and ready," Kye replied.

"Perfect. Keep Tiy distracted while I fill the curlhorn in on the plan." Adaris leaned away, laughing at nothing, appearing as if they'd shared a joke.

And Tiy, who finally got to the bottom of the ladder, actually grinned, as if he too was in on the joke. "What'd I miss?"

Adaris waved his question away. She went over to the bookshelf containing the inert jewelry pieces and plucked a ring with an orange gemstone set into it. Her heartbeat pounded with both dread and anticipation, but she kept herself as outwardly calm as she could. Setting the ring in the stone dip in front of the podium, she turned to the Nemora and pushed all the authority she could into her voice. "After we get the prisoner, I need you to hold her other arm, keep her pinned down by the podium. Sroc wants me to do the bloodbinding ritual on her."

"What's that?" Tiy asked, but he positioned himself by the podium all the same.

"You don't know?" Adaris parted her lips in mock surprise, as if everyone in the community knew of this practice. She shifted her expression to obvious glee, a transformation she'd seen one too many times on Sroc's face. "Well, then I guess it's time for you to find out." A look of curious excitement filled Tiy's expression, his grin widening. Adaris flicked her gaze to Kye. "Open the prison door for me and fill Tiy in on the finer details. I don't want him passing out on me."

Kye did as she commanded. The rock door opened with a loud grinding noise and Adaris slipped inside. The low hum of a conversation bubbled behind her—Kye speaking to Tiy.

"Back again, scribe?" The curlhorn's familiar voice hooked around her, barbed with anger and fear. "Here to slaughter me like my friend?"

The curlhorn Vagari sat in the far corner of the stone prison. Enough light spilled inside to show the jagged line of her legs and the bruises on her skin. Her glare could crumble mountains.

Adaris knelt before her, lowering her voice to a whisper. "No, I'm here to help you escape. All you have to do is be part of my ruse. I need to pretend to have to kill you—"

The Vagari's eyes widened. "Kill me?"

"Pretend," Adaris hissed. She didn't have enough time to explain the whole plan. "If the Nemora suspects something and uses his crafting, we're all dead. I won't harm you, I promise. Do you believe me?"

"No," Corra replied.

Adaris blinked at the stark response. The curlhorn was key to this plan working. Otherwise, how would Adaris get close enough to Tiy to kill him without suspicion?

"But it's the best shot I have at getting out of here," Corra said slowly, "so let's get this done."

"Thank you." A knot of worry untangled inside of Adaris. That was two parts of the plan falling into place. She looked over her shoulder and barked, "Kye! Forget Tiy, help me. This woman's heavy."

The conversation in the room outside ended abruptly, and Kye came in to help Adaris lift Corra out of the prison, hauling her over to the podium. Corra moaned, each step jarring her broken legs. Adaris' Blood crafting rose within her. Corra's moans could be an act, but they sounded real enough. Adaris wanted ever so badly to heal Corra, to help her even just a little.

But she knew she needed all of her crafting for the ritual. She had never felt as empty as she had after the last ritual, and she had none to spare.

Kye lowered Corra to the floor against the podium.

Adaris grabbed a lazicon gemstone from Sroc's desk. "Hold her for me, will you, Tiy?"

Tiy nodded and went to grab Corra's arm. He and Kye hauled her upright.

Corra groaned, but Tiy only smirked.

Adaris swallowed her mounting anxiety. They'd have only one chance to get this right, one chance to kill the Nemora. The man was much more powerful than any of them, crafting and otherwise. He'd folded the stone like it was paper when crafting her living hut, and she knew he'd fold stone right over her and Kye and Corra the moment he sensed something was off.

She had to play like everything was going as planned. And truly, it was.

Gripping the lazicon gemstone in one hand, she strolled to the podium and glanced at the ring she'd chosen. Her stomach filled with dread at what she was about to do, but she couldn't ignore the building anticipation she felt either. The ritual. A large part of her was excited to feel that rush of power again, that ancient fire in her veins so different from her usual crafting.

She grabbed the dagger that rested on the podium and stood in front of the curlhorn.

Fear played on Corra's features, making her lips tremble and her eyes widen. She played her part well, and Adaris made a mental note to thank her later.

Kye held Corra's arm on one side, his expression emotionless, the face of the stoic guard Adaris had known when she was first brought to Slagrock.

Only Tiy looked excited about what was going to happen. A lopsided smile curled his lips, as he held fast to Corra's other arm, but his hungry gaze was only for Adaris. The joy in the Nemora's eyes sent a tingle down her spine.

"I need her head to be over this stone dip." She crouched beside them and gestured to the floor with the blade.

Tiy and Kye held Corra between them, and her chest and head tilted toward the slump of stone.

Adaris deactivated the artifact on her ankle, and her leg immediately flared, calling for her attention. She ignored the pain. Nothing could distract her. The blade's metal glinted in the lantern light as Adaris lifted it high overhead.

Corra moaned. Her hands clawed at the men's arms, fingers digging into their skin. "No. Please, no!"

Tiy grunted, holding her in place with Kye.

Adaris began reciting the words in the ancient Divus tongue. Her hand clenched the lazicon gemstone so hard, the edges bit into her skin. The familiar white fog rolled over her eyes. Light traced her veins, power curling through her until it turned into fire inside her. Her body sang in response.

This time, the fire wasn't painful, wasn't frightening. It was just–power. Raw power. Adaris leaned into it, and the gem instantly cooled in response. Her gaze skipped from Corra's fearful eyes to the Nemora sun goddess worshipper crouching beside her. The one who laughed while Berhn was murdered. The one who killed a Moon Knight with a stone spear through the knight's chest.

Adaris plunged the knife deep into the Nemora's throat. Hot brown blood gushed over her hand. She twisted the knife and yanked it out, sending more blood gushing from the wound.

Tiy gasped, loosening his grip on Corra. A look of shock flashed across his features.

Kye dragged Corra away from the podium, then threw himself onto Tiy, pinning the Nemora's arms to his side. Now, it was Tiy's head over the stone dip.

Tiy gargled and kicked, but Corra fell onto his legs, pinning him with her meager weight. Copper light burned in Tiy's eyes in response, one last desperate flare of anger.

Adaris' heart missed a beat when she saw the flicker of Nature crafting from his eyes, but she kept muttering the ritualistic words. Her head started to pound, the familiar needling pain of knives twisting through her skull. Dropping the dagger, she grabbed the ring. The thick, rusty blood scent filled her nose.

Suddenly, chunks of the stone floor melted into shards. Tiy was calling on his Nature crafting, trying to stop the ritual, trying to save himself. One shard sliced Adaris' cheek, another slammed into her shoulder, burying deep.

She cried out, blinking back tears as pain pulsed through her. She heard Corra and Kye cry out as well but couldn't look to see what had happened. Her energy flagged.

Another rock sliced across her neck, a second embedding into her forearm, another into her calf, pummeling her, trying to get her to stop.

She didn't. The white-hot pain kept her alert.

She kept muttering the words, willing her crafting to push through, and shoved all of herself into the ritual. Tiy's dark-brown blood swirled around her arms. Power scorched through her as the ancient crafting drew from her own life force. The aching came with a familiar, welcomed thrill.

The copper light dimmed as Tiy's life force drained from him in waves, and the shards of rock fell from the air.

The gemstone shattered, its broken pieces glittering through the blood like blue-green stars, and the blood drew into the ring. A twin pulse of deep russet light emanated from the stone's surface, brown crafting illuminating the orange gem.

The ritual had worked.

Blinking her crafting away, Adaris toppled over, using her free hand to prop herself up. She drew in deep trembling breaths. Her eyes watered from the pain of her crafting and the agony of the rock shards embedded in her skin. The other rocks had melted away, but curiously, these remained.

"Are you two okay?" Adaris asked.

Kye had clamped a hand over his bicep. Blood seeped through his fingers, and the shell on his arm had a number of fresh scratches on it, but he nodded.

"Ponuriah's ass, scribe!" Corra groaned, shoving a hand on her bleeding forehead. She still lay toppled on top of Tiy, but other than her old injuries, she looked okay.

Thank the deepest ocean they'd survived.

Exhaustion dragged Adaris' eyes closed. She'd expected to feel guilt, to feel panicked, to feel scared that she'd just murdered a man in cold blood. She'd used her power in a twisted way.

But all she felt was a sense of justice, of righting the world, of ending a vile man's life. Of doing something to save herself, to save a Moon Knight, to save the woman she loved. What she just did was right, and no one could tell her otherwise. Peace spread through her like a balm as her crafting burned away to ashes within her. The lovely ache of the ancient crafting evaporated, too, and Adaris instantly missed it.

"We did it." Pushing herself upright, she slipped the bloodbound ring on her finger and grinned. She couldn't help it. Her own pathetic crafting had created this artifact, one she could use to break Spectrum free. Depths, they could finally, finally leave this sunsick place behind.

Chapter Thirty-Eight

ADARIS TOOK A FEW more deep breaths, trying to push through the exhaustion. Her shoulder, forearm, and leg spiked with pain from the jagged stone shards protruding from her flesh.

Despite their injuries, they'd been lucky. Really, really lucky. Adaris knew better than to assume their luck would hold. They had to get to Spectrum before the community woke for the day.

She dragged herself to her feet, conscious of her own sticky blood soaking her clothes. If any community members saw her like this, it would be obvious that something was wrong, but she didn't have any energy to heal herself; all her crafting had been used up by the ritual. She'd have to remove the shards and hide the wounds, then hide Kye's, too.

Her gaze strayed over Tiy's dead body, snagging on the armband wrapped around his upper bicep. She yanked it off and handed it to Kye.

"Thank you." He immediately tugged it on, wincing as it slid over the shredded flesh. Shrugging out of his long, sleeveless vest, he ripped it at the seams and gave the white strips of cloth to her.

Gritting her teeth to brace herself for the pain, she yanked the stone shards free from her shoulder, then her forearm, then her calf. Pain shivered through her, but she bit back a cry. Pale-white blood welled. Grimacing, she wrapped each wound with the strips of cloth from Kye's vest.

A wave of anxiety curled through her. They had to leave, immediately, before anyone woke up.

When she took a step to the ladder, the world canted to the side. She had to catch herself on to the podium to keep her footing. After a few moments, the world righted itself.

"We need to get Corra out of here, but I can't carry her," Adaris panted. "Do you think you can get her up the ladder?"

Kye glanced at the curlhorn, who was watching them both in silence. He looked at the ladder, judging his own strength. He nodded. "I believe so."

"Good. Let's go."

"Wait." A strange look passed over his face. "Sroc often said she needed energy after completing a ritual, and you still need to use the ring to melt Spectrum's bars." He held out his hand. "Take some of my strength."

"I—" Adaris drew back, impressed and quite frankly surprised that he'd offered. Not many people would offer their life energy for a Divus. It spoke volumes that he trusted her enough to even reach out his hand. "Thank you."

Taking his rough, calloused hand, she sought her crafting. It was difficult to nudge it awake just enough to draw energy from another person, but she managed to gather enough to begin the process. Her crafting connected, then pulled. Kye's warm life energy filled her palm, traveling up her arm, shoulder, and neck to her head. Kye grunted. Her veins lit up, dully at first then brighter, the familiar white fog finally filling her eyes. She felt stronger, better. So much that she wanted to draw more life from him.

Kye's eyelids drooped.

Adaris immediately let go of his hand, breaking their connection entirely. She blinked her crafting away. "Thank you," she said again.

Kye rubbed his forehead, panting slightly. If she'd taken too much, he didn't complain. Before she could ask, he grabbed the dagger off the floor and shoved it into his belt, hooked his trident to his back, and lifted Corra. Heaving her over his shoulder, he headed up the ladder as if the Moon Knight weighed nothing at all.

Adaris went to follow, but something stopped her. This was the last chance to grab anything of importance, any proof to bring back home. She grabbed a handful of small, blue-green lazicon gemstones and a palm-sized notebook of Sroc's research on the sun goddess shards, and stuffed these into the small pouch hanging from her belt.

The ancient's grimoire still sat on the podium. Adaris looked at it longingly. The scrollkeepers would give anything to have something like that in their library. She shoved the thick book into her shoulder bag. On the podium where the book had rested, a roughly hewn hole had been dug out, perfectly hidden by the book. Something glittered within. A blue-green lazicon gemstone the size of Adaris' fist. Familiar. *Berhn's.* The gem he'd used as a key to find others like it.

A sour taste filled Adaris' mouth. Sroc had poured Berhn's blood into one of her decorative jugs instead of lashing it to a gemstone—wasting his life and his crafting ability. Like the young man had been tainted by something and Sroc wanted none of it. Well, she'd use his gemstone then. For research. Adaris shoved that large gemstone into her shoulder bag, too.

Heading to the ladder, she hauled herself up the rungs. Her bad leg screamed in protest, the wounds on her shoulder, forearm, and calf spiking in reply, but she had to save all her crafting for her new ring. Finally, she reached the top. Adaris stumbled out the break in the stone that led to the beach where Kye had set Corra down. The edge of the sun had already crested the horizon, spreading bright pinks across the dark blue sky.

Dawn had officially arrived.

"What in Ponuriah's ass took you so long down there?" Corra's piercing green gaze met hers.

"Nothing you need to worry about," Adaris hissed back, hurrying over to them. She hefted her shoulder bag higher and winced at the sudden flash of pain. "Kye, can you carry her to the fishing hut so we're nearer to the raft?"

Kye looped his arms under the curlhorn once more, lifting her off the black sand. As they moved, they kept close to the curved stone walls of the hut. The shadows swallowed them as soon as they ducked inside the fishing hut. Kye set the curlhorn down gently, then stood just inside the open archway to keep watch.

A small sack of supplies waited for them by the archway—a coil of rope, nails, flasks of water, pouches that probably contained food, a long bundle of cloth. The supplies Rhonwen had stolen, already prepared. Adaris looked back at the raft bobbing gently in the ocean water. It seemed like everything was ready—now all they had to do was get Spectrum out.

"Stay here," she told Corra. "We'll be back soon." She turned to leave, but her shoulder bag shifted, rubbing against her wound. Pain shuddered through her. Depths, everything hurt. She needed every scrap of crafting she could get for her new ring. Not activating her anklet would be suspicious enough, she couldn't be wincing each time her bag shifted, too. She dropped the heavy bag next to Corra. "And don't lose that."

Without waiting for Corra to respond, Adaris walked out of the fishing hut. Kye's footfalls started up behind her.

She rounded the fishing hut toward the stairs and heard an audible gasp.

A small, slight Elu man draped in white stood a few paces ahead. He stared at her and Kye, lips parted in shock. "What are you doing with that prisoner this early in the morning?" he asked.

"What prisoner?" Adaris pulled up short, Kye stopping beside her.

"The one inside the fishing hut. I saw you carrying her while I was coming down the stairs," he said.

Not even twenty paces from the fishing hut and they'd been caught. A myriad of lies swirled through her mind, but Kye got there first.

"The prisoner needed to get some fresh air," Kye said.

Doubt shadowed the Elu's pale features. "But why leave her? Prisoners aren't supposed to be left alone. Tikova's orders."

Adaris' muscles tightened and her awareness sharpened. Directly next to her, a trident spear rested against the outside of the fishing hut. One like she'd used as a youth, catching fish alongside her brother. One she could probably use to kill this man, if it came to that.

Beside her Kye tensed, the lines of his jaw going tight. "Have you been tasked as a guard now? I get my orders directly from Tikova, so move along."

The Elu backed up a step, frowning. His hazel eyes narrowed. "What—"

Both Adaris and Kye lunged. Adaris grabbed the trident spear and hurled it at the man. This close, he was an easy mark. The sharp prongs of the trident sank into his neck right before Kye's palm hit the man's chest. Kye's eyes flashed orange for a moment, a heartbeat, maybe less, and the man dropped.

He hadn't even been able to scream.

Something like relief prickled through Adaris at the realization.

"I'll deal with the body. Get Spectrum," Kye muttered.

Adaris darted up the stone steps. The Elu had been a surprise out and about this early. How many community members were already stirring? She quickened her pace, gritting her teeth against the throbbing in her leg, and headed to the animal enclosure. Her gait rolled like it used to, but it didn't matter, because no one was awake to see—

Footfalls caught her attention to her right. She turned just in time to see Tikova jogging up to meet her. Adaris' heart tripped over itself. Of all people to be awake, it had to be him. She schooled her features, forcing herself to be calm. He thought she was one of them...so all she had to do was act like it. And hope he didn't notice her injuries.

Clad in only billowing light blue pants, the man stopped close to her. "You're up early, Adaris."

Cold spread over Adaris' body like she'd been dunked into the ocean. Soon he'd notice that she wasn't using her anklet. *Depths, he probably saw my terrible limp on the way over. There's no use hiding it now.* "Yes, I wanted to try walking without my anklet...see how different it was. So, I took a walk near the ocean." The lie came out shaky, as if she was out of breath, and she forced a thick laugh out behind it. "It's very painful. What a fool I was to think I should go without it."

Tikova clapped her on the shoulder, slapping the wound under the cloth. Adaris held her spine ramrod straight and grinned through the pain. "See?" he said. "Being part of the community has only made you stronger." His smile faltered, a flicker of what could only be suspicion darkening his features. "But...why is your arm bandaged? And your calf? Have you been injured somehow?"

Of course, he noticed that, too.

She kept her expression stoic, but worry tangled inside of her like a twisted net. Her heart thudded against her ribs in an incessant beat, demanding she move on. Move on. Move on. The longer she talked to Tikova the greater chance of him noticing even more things being off. She resisted the urge to feel her hair for rock flecks. *Why didn't I take the time to dust off?*

"It was difficult walking, as I said. I tripped on the beach." She gave him a sheepish grin.

Tikova removed his hand and stepped back. His voice took on a sharp edge. "What actually happened, Adaris?"

Adaris' throat tightened, and before she could stop it, a half-truth bubbled out. "The bloodbinding ritual didn't go as smoothly as we would have hoped."

"Yes," Tikova said slowly. "Sroc told me about it."

Depths! What had the researcher told him, exactly? She forced herself to meet his unwavering gaze. "The prisoner fought back."

A look of understanding dawned on him, the tension easing from his stance. "Ah, yes. Sroc did say that. Don't worry. She also says it gets easier each time."

Easier to murder people? Well, yes, Adaris had found that out already. Killing Tiy was significantly easier than murdering the mola Moon Knight, though she could feel the bite of guilt rising within her. She'd killed people in cold blood.

Pushing aside her nausea, she patted the pouch hanging off her belt, which contained her book and quill. "I should head back to my hut. I'd like to record what happened last night."

"Ah, speaking of!" Tikova dug into his pouch and pulled out a quill made of a white feather. At the base, the shaft turned a deep, dark crimson that met neatly with the dark, metal tip. The coloring looked familiar. He handed it to her. "I asked Celli to make you this, as a thank you for joining our community. It's from her companion animal after she healed him."

"This is..." Adaris clutched the quill, remembering white feathers and crimson eyes. A companion-turned-suncreature. The thunderclap had looked so ill, near death until the sun goddess shard and Celli's crafting had healed it and corrupted it in the same breath. The companion had been transformed, just as Adaris had been forced to conform to the service of this terrible community.

She worked her mounting fear down, flashing a smile instead. "Thank you."

Tikova chuckled and waved his hand as if swatting a bug. "It's a small token of our gratitude, really. I'm headed for my first meal, would you like to join me?"

"Thank you, but I've already eaten," she lied, this one slipping smoothly from her tongue. "I'll join you for a midday meal."

When he nodded, she stepped back from him then walked away, heading not for the animal enclosure as she'd intended, but for her living hut. She slipped the new quill behind her ear, her long crimson locks securing it in place.

When she looked back to wave, she saw Tikova meeting Celli at the food hut, then they both ducked inside. Taking one more quick glance around for observers, she limped as fast as she could back to the animal enclosure, ignoring the spike of pain with each footfall. The rest of the community would be moving soon. She heard rustling and the quiet hum of conversation from nearby living huts.

A suncreature—the same serpentine unceg she'd noticed the night before—uncurled itself from the shadows of the food hut and slithered inside after Tikova. Adaris found its actions strange. *It's not like the creature would eat anything in there...*

Then it hit her. The suncreatures were spying on her last night while they were watching over the community. They saw her and Kye go into Rhonwen's prison and now that serpentine beast saw her heading to the animal enclosure. Her gut twisted. The unceg would alert Celli of her strange comings and goings. It would give her away. And of course, Celli would tell Tikova.

Damned to the depths, she had no time to lose.

Chapter Thirty-Nine

ADARIS COULD ALMOST HEAR the unceg hissing to Celli in the food hut. A chill flashed over her skin. Spectrum swung his feathered head toward Adaris as soon as she reached the stone bars. She had to hold back a gag at the gaping hole where one of his eyes had been, the other a glaring, piercing yellow. His black neck feathers fluffed in agitation. When he recognized her, he blinked and the anger dissipated as quickly as it had come. A crest of rainbow feathers lifted from his head, as he bobbed his head hello.

"It's me, Spectrum, I'm going to get you out of here," she whispered.

The huge beast crowed in delight. She glanced around. "We need to stay quiet, okay? Stay back."

The slyther coiled back as far as he could in his cage, which wasn't very far, and watched with unnerving intensity. Adaris raised her hand and called up her limited Blood crafting. The familiar warmth of her crafting pooled in her finger with the ring, willing it to activate.

Nothing happened.

Depths, why was nothing happening? Panic crawled its way up her throat. She must've missed something. Her thoughts flipped one after the other, like pages in a book, as she tried to remember everything Sroc had told her.

Kye had said a word he used to make his trident glow blue. The word sometimes needed to make a bloodbound artifact activate. "Alahri," she whispered.

Nothing.

No, that was wrong. Alahri was for Elu crafting, like the daygems and Kye's trident...not for Nature crafting. The other words came to her in a flash. "Ziphri. Phyrhi. Wyhri!"

The gemstone finally glowed in reply. *Wyhri.* An odd color, almost an umber hue emerged, as the copper-brown Nature crafting brightened from within the orange gem. *Yes!* A thrill pierced through her. *It's working!*

She put her hand on one of the thick stone bars and focused, willing it to melt away. The harsh edges of stone smoothed under her hand but instead of melting, something sharp pushed against her skin. She yanked her hand back. A rock spike the size of her palm followed her hand movement, growing until it reached the length of her arm. *What's happening?* Shock tingled through her, skittering under her skin like bugs.

Sroc had said sometimes the ritual didn't work as intended. It seemed like Adaris got Tiy's rock spikes instead of his melting ability. Well, she'd just have to adapt. Hallr Nemora pushed and pulled natural rock—they didn't create it, they just manipulated it. She grabbed a nearby stone and knocked the rock spike away with a crunch. Sure enough, the stone was pitted underneath. Weakened.

Adaris looked around, nervous about the sounds she'd already made. The community was still so, so quiet, but she knew the silence wouldn't last. She saw Kye make his way over to the prison hut. Hairs prickled on the back of her neck. She had to move faster.

Creating spike after spike, she knocked them all off until the bars had actual holes through the stone. "Almost there, Spectrum."

The slyther blinked his good eye, then turned suddenly to the right, crest flaring.

Something crashed into Adaris and sent her sprawling to the ground. Rocks bit into her skin. Her wounds flared. White scales and crimson light filled her vision. Something wrapped around her, tight, pulling her upright again. She was suddenly face-to-face with a giant unceg head. A sand snake turned all white, the spaces between its scales bright crimson. Terror spiked through her, and her Blood crafting surged in response. Her innate crafting would be useless against the creature—only Vagari could absorb beast energy—but she could use the ring.

"Adaris?" Tikova's shout drifted from somewhere behind her. She couldn't see him, but she could hear the fury and disappointment in his voice.

The suncreature squeezed, crushing her and pushing breath out of her lungs. Its crimson gaze focused on Adaris as if to compel her to give in.

But Adaris focused, too. She focused everything she could on the stone around Spectrum's cage, ordering it to create the largest spike yet.

The unceg's warm scales cut into her skin. Her wounds burned. She couldn't breathe. Her world darkened around the edges.

The suncreature unhinged its jaws, ready to engulf her. Its long, black fangs dripped fiery saliva and a wash of burning breath singed Adaris' skin.

She struggled against the despair growing in her chest and concentrated on forming the spike. It couldn't end like this, not after all they'd been through. A heat greater than the serpent's raced through her hand as the ring answered her call, and a pale, stone spike the size of Adaris' forearm embedded itself into the creature's throat.

The unceg hissed, its coils loosening their hold and thumping to the ground. Adaris yanked the shard of stone from the unceg's throat. She watched death gurgle like a stream inside the open wound as the creature thrashed, spraying crimson blood onto the ground. The creature crumbled to blackened ash as it died. She threw the spike to the ground, kicking up some ash where it landed.

She turned away from the ash pile to the crumbling bars of Spectrum's cage. Her heart leapt. Her plan had worked. She'd stopped the suncreature and drawn enough rock away from the cage. Spectrum coiled to one side of his enclosure, his one eye staring with uncertainty at the ash pile.

"Spectrum, push!" she said to him, then turned to face Tikova.

"How could you, Adaris?" Tikova charged toward her, long legs rapidly shortening the distance between them. "Stop it!"

Adaris lifted her hand, calling on the ring's power again, fueled by pure desperation. A chest high wall of spikes jutted out from the ground between her and Tikova.

He skidded to a stop, fury in his eyes as he took in the glowing ring on her finger. "Where did you get that?"

"Sroc's knowledge finally paid off," she responded. "Tiy was glad to be part of my research."

Tikova looked at her in horror, as if he couldn't believe she'd dare to use their knowledge against him.

"What's happening, Tikova?" Celli cried. The elderly woman had stayed by the food hut, hand resting on the archway, white eyes blind to the world. Beyond her, Kye and Rhonwen rushed over.

Trembling with rage, Tikova turned toward Kye. "Leave the painter and get Adaris."

Adaris moved closer to Spectrum's cage, one eye on Tikova, Kye, and Rhonwen, the other on the giant slyther who could very well break free of his cage but didn't seem to know that just yet. "Spectrum, push," she said again out of the corner of her mouth.

Kye didn't move. He swept his gaze over the community. No one had come out of their huts yet. It was still and silent and only them awake, for now.

Something came over Kye's features.

"What are you waiting for?" Tikova barked. "Sroc—"

In a flash of motion, Kye pulled his arm back and hurled his trident. It sang through the air, cutting Tikova's voice short, as it sank deep into his chest.

Tikova grunted, gripping the trident in his hands.

Kye strode toward the leader of Slagrock, leaving Rhonwen and Celli in his wake. He grabbed the man by his throat and whispered something in his ear. Kye's eyes flashed orange, as his Animal crafting swelled within him. For a moment, Tikova stiffened. His whole body went rigid like a plank of wood, then he fell limp to the ground, dead.

Depths! Adaris froze by Spectrum's cage. She knew Kye's motivations for killing Tikova, knew Kye was trying to blend in before his revenge, but apparently, Kye had enough of the charade. Now only Celli was left alive to witness their rebellion.

Celli cursed and looked to the sky, Adaris' gaze swinging with her. A now-familiar thunderclap suncreature—Celli's companion animal—dove from the sky, streaking toward Rhonwen. Its talons sank into Rhonwen's arm, and it opened its beak to emit a bone-shattering cry. Orange blood welled.

Rhonwen screamed.

In Adaris' peripheral, Spectrum stiffened at the sound. The slyther cawed in fury and pushed against the weakened stone bars. The rock smashed outward in a hail of shattered stone.

Adaris lifted her arms to cover her face as some shards flew toward her.

He slithered past Adaris and used the stone spikes as a launching point. Flaring his six wings at the top and flapping once, twice, he snapped his beak at the unsuspecting thunderclap, ripping it off Rhonwen then eating the tiny creature whole. Spectrum landed on the ground next to his companion, then collapsed, muscles shaking and wings limp. His eye closed.

Gasping, Rhonwen dropped to her knees beside him, one hand pressing into his crest of feathers. "Spectrum!"

Spectrum was still breathing. Still alive. But during the time of his imprisonment he had thinned into a meager shell of an adult slyther. Adaris could clearly see the bones beneath his gaunt form, the hollowness around his eye. He'd been in the cage for so long. The confinement had atrophied his muscles. He'd pushed himself to get to Rhonwen, to save her.

And he was dying from the effort.

Rhonwen stroked her companion animal, looking into his good eye, tears brimming in her own. "No, no, no."

Adaris' heart clenched at the sight.

Kye watched over Celli, collapsed at the mouth of the food hut. The death of her companion animal must've hit her like a tsunami, and she was lost in her grief. She sobbed. Loudly. Kye shoved a rough hand over her mouth, muffling her cries, something that looked like glee curling his lips. He was enjoying her tears. "Now you know how it feels," he muttered.

They didn't have time for petty vengeance. Adaris narrowed her gaze on Celli and focused once more. A shard of stone emerged from the ground by her sandal. She sent it forward like a spear, embedding it deep within Celli's eye. The woman curled forward, dead.

Startled, Kye looked at Adaris and nodded once, then looked beyond her, behind her. He lifted his trident. "We have company."

Adaris spun. Three guards and Sroc rushed toward them. The community had finally awoken.

"Keep them away from me while I heal Spectrum," Rhonwen said, voice sharp and commanding. When Adaris glanced back, she saw how Rhonwen's yellow gaze brightened with the orange glow of her Animal crafting. She rested her good hand on Spectrum's beak, and a bright orange light illuminated beneath her palm. Rhonwen was healing him, like only a Vagari could. "Spectrum can help us once I'm done."

Adaris shifted her stance, placing herself protectively in front of Rhonwen. She focused on the ring, hoping it would answer her. If she could keep Rhonwen safe long enough to escape, all of this bloodshed would be worth it.

The three guards spotted Adaris and immediately slowed. *Cowards.* But it boded well for her. Sroc had stopped at the sight of

Tikova dead on the ground, at the pile of ashes that could only be a dead suncreature, at Celli's dead body. Her gaze fell onto the glowing ring on Adaris' finger and something like respect passed over her features.

And terribly, pride surged through Adaris in response.

A trio of shadows passed over them. As if called by Celli's death, two large, white thunderclaps and one white wyvern flew overhead. Suncreatures.

Sroc gestured upward. "Show me what you can do with that new ring, Adaris."

Even though she hated Sroc, she had to protect her friend. Determination straightened Adaris' spine, warmed her core. A calm washed over her, the last dregs of her Blood crafting easing her worry away. She needed to give Rhonwen time. Just time. She focused her energy on the ring once more, calling on the Nature crafting, willing it to do her bidding. Shards, she thought. Shards like arrows. Like spears.

She lifted her hand and the stone answered as if it was always meant to be. As if turning into rock shards was its true purpose. Thick heavy spears of rock splintered from the ground and shot toward the suncreatures like a volley of arrows, following her hand motions up and away.

Three of the shards punctured the wyvern's wing and sent it crashing into the living huts. Two shards embedded deep into a thunderclap's eyes, causing it to shriek in pain and pull up. The second thunderclap rolled out of the way of the volley midair, toward the ocean.

Adaris aimed another shard at Sroc, but Sroc activated her blue gemstone ring and a Moon shield appeared, deflecting the attack. The young researcher grinned, the expression stretching her face in an almost twisted way.

After that intense burst of power, the ring on Adaris' finger dimmed. The copper glow faded. Frantic, Adaris tried to activate it again, calling on her own Blood crafting and muttering the word once more. Nothing happened. Her own Blood crafting hummed through her, needling in her head, trying to heal her wounds. Heart pounding against her ribs like a wardrum, she snapped her crafting away.

The thunderclap suncreature dove toward her again at a terrifying speed.

Kye hurled his trident toward the diving bird, showing his true allegiance against the community. The weapon sank into the suncreature's chest.

The great bird shrieked and flared open its wings, brilliant white feathers tinged in crimson, stopping its descent and unhinging its jaw. A bubble of breath traveled up its throat.

Adaris slunk back. A thunderclap's caw could shatter stone. It could just as easily shatter bones.

With no other weapon, Adaris twisted and covered Rhonwen's hunched body with her own tall form.

Spectrum jerked away from Rhonwen, Adaris, and Kye, and with one powerful coil of his tail launched himself toward the suncreature.

In the same moment, Rhonwen let out a breath and slumped to the side. Her eyes closed. She trembled uncontrollably.

Adaris grabbed her by the shoulders, gaping as Spectrum caught the thunderclap suncreature by its throat, stopping its deadly cry.

Coiling his lower body around the thunderclap, Spectrum's rainbow scales were stark against the suncreature's white feathers. He dropped to the ground with his prey and snapped the suncreature's neck. The suncreature turned to ashes beneath him.

Adaris blinked a few times, not believing the sight she saw before her. Powerful muscles rippled under Spectrum's feathers and scales. Even though the tip of his tail was missing and his eye was gone, it seemed he had not only been healed of the atrophy but had gotten all of his strength back as well. A massive slyther now coiled between Rhonwen and the community. Swinging to face the community, Spectrum cawed, a deep shrieking battle cry.

But at what cost? Rhonwen lay limp in Adaris' arms, unconscious. She must've given up nearly all her life energy to bring him back from the brink. *Depths!* Worry and pride warred within her at Rhonwen's sacrifice.

The guards turned their attention to Spectrum, rushing to try to subdue him. More community members spilled from the huts, heading toward Spectrum, trying and failing to end his furious rampage with ropes and weapons. All were useless against Spectrum's fury. Even Kye seemed awed by Spectrum's rampage.

"Impressive," Sroc said. She'd used Spectrum's distraction to cover most of the distance between them. "And you did the ritual by yourself. But I'm still your better." She lifted her hand, her five rings catching the light.

Adaris stilled, holding Rhonwen close. *No ring, no crafting, Spectrum distracted, Rhonwen unconscious. How can I stop Sroc?* She had to do something before Sroc activated her rings.

Before she could form a plan, Kye launched himself at Sroc, his eyes already glowing orange. The ritual dagger glinted as he swung it down toward the young researcher.

Sroc shifted to the side, letting the dagger sink into her shoulder and smirking at Kye. She grabbed his empty hand, white light burning in her eyes. Kye went limp, and the orange glow faded from his eyes, his life going with it. Sroc tore the dagger from her shoulder and tossed it onto Kye's dead body. Her wound healed almost instantly in a flash of white light.

"No!" Adaris cried. Her throat tightened. He'd done so much—risked too much—to die now. She grabbed Kye's dagger and rose, facing off with Sroc. Anger rose with her, hardening her resolve.

Sroc smirked at her. "I don't want to kill you, Adaris. You're my—"

Adaris didn't let her finish, slashing at her with the dagger rather clumsily and hoping the young researcher would reach for her like she had with Kye.

Sroc grabbed Adaris with her ring encrusted hand, the glow in her eyes brightening like the edges of a white-hot flame.

Adaris was ready. She clamped her fingers around the researcher's hand and swung the dagger down, chopping Sroc's hand off at the wrist.

Sroc let out a blood-curdling scream. Clutching her stump, she moaned and sank to the ground. Pale-white blood gushed from her wound, splattering on the stone beneath her. She crawled away, bawling.

"Grow that back." Furious, Adaris yanked the five rings off Sroc's disembodied hand and threw the limb to the side, far away from Sroc's reach. No need to make it easy on the researcher. Shaking, Adaris turned away from the chaos, tucking the rings into her pouch.

Rhonwen still lay unconscious on the ground. Adaris' heart clenched.

She lifted Rhonwen from the ground, but her leg twisted at the wrong angle and pain sharpened inside her. Adaris cried out. *I can turn on the anklet.* Except the ring had stopped working, would the anklet respond? She dipped into her meager Blood crafting, pooled it in her anklet, and sighed as the familiar and welcomed bands of heat wrapped around her bones and muscles. The pain vanished.

She took one more look at Kye, dead in front of her, eyes unseeing, etching him into her memory. He'd given everything to help them escape, and she had to be sure his death was not for nothing.

Carrying Rhonwen, she darted for the stairs leading down to the ocean, hoping Spectrum would keep the community busy until she at least got Rhonwen onto the raft.

Adaris stumbled down the stairs. Her shoulder caught on the rough stone column beside her. Pushing toward the black sand beach, she stopped at the front of the fishing hut where she'd left Corra just inside.

The woman had vanished, along with their supplies. Along with the ancient's grimoire and Berhn's gemstone. Adaris didn't even see the raft on the watery horizon. Fury boiled inside her, making her skin flush all the way to her ears. "Damn her to the depths, she stole our supplies! Our raft!"

A loud cawing noise drew Adaris' gaze to the community. Spectrum curved above Slagrock, high in the sky, feathers like black ink and rainbow scales glittering. He cawed again, warning them. A man holding a trident had followed them down the rock stairs.

A stab of desperation jolted through Adaris. She set Rhonwen down and picked up one of the compact trident spears. Adaris aimed her spear at the man and hurled it. The rope attached to the spear slipped through Adaris' practiced fingers, long enough to reach the man without encumbering the flight. The trident sank into him with a meaty thud, and thick, brown blood oozed around the wound. The man fell with a groan. She yanked the trident spear back, catching it midair. More people spilled down the rock stairs, shouting and heading straight for them. The spear wouldn't work on all of them, and Adaris cast a terrified look over her shoulder at Rhonwen. The painter still lay unconscious on the black sand.

Dropping to her knees, Adaris called up her meager amount of crafting and shoved it into Rhonwen, urging her to wake up. The anklet deactivated once more. She ignored the spike of agony in her leg, willing with every fiber of her being that Rhonwen would wake up. *Please.* She pushed more of herself into her crafting, ignoring the needling in her mind, the convulsions running through her, the tiredness pulling at her bones. The world darkened at the edges of her vision. *Please, wake up.*

Rhonwen groaned, opening her eyes. She trembled from head to toe. "What's happening?"

"You pushed too much strength into Spectrum and passed out. Kye's dead," Adaris said in a rush, snapping her crafting away. When

Rhonwen gasped, Adaris barreled on. "The raft is gone and our supplies too, and now we have company that I won't be able to keep back."

Rhonwen blinked at her companion animal currently diving at the people rushing down the stairs. A small smile creased her tired face. "We don't need that raft anymore. Spectrum can take us home."

She whistled once—sharp and high—and Spectrum coiled midair to face her.

The slyther dove onto the empty beach. He landed in a spray of black sand, coiling his tail around Rhonwen and Adaris protectively, wings down so they could climb onto his back.

Adaris pushed Rhonwen onto Spectrum, not daring to look back as she yanked herself up the slippery feathers, hooking her knees behind a pair of wings.

As soon as they were both on, Spectrum coiled his lower half and sprung, hurtling into the sky. A slap of wind almost knocked Adaris off, but she tightened her knees and gripped onto the black feathers. Her stomach lurched into her throat and a dizzy sensation overtook her. The ground rapidly grew smaller beneath them, but the danger grew smaller as well.

Rhonwen twisted around in what Adaris considered a precarious position, though to the painter it seemed almost natural. She gave Adaris an exhausted grin and grabbed Adaris' hand over where Adaris clutched Spectrum's feathers. "We did it."

"We're free." Adaris returned the grin. They had escaped from Slagrock. They were going home. But when Rhonwen turned back to face the front and scratch her companion animal, a stone settled in Adaris' gut.

They were free, but Kye had given his life for them. And she hadn't killed Sroc. The young researcher could find Adaris with that blood stalking thing. Adaris had participated in the sunlight celebration, after all, and Sroc had no reason to lie about what she could do with the ancient rituals. Adaris had Sroc's rings, but Slagrock already had another goddess shard hanging off Celli's dead wrist.

Perhaps Sroc wouldn't be able to do the stalking, now that Adaris had stolen the ancient grimoire from her. Adaris looked down at the ocean below. Corra had it, at least. It was a small comfort that even if Sroc found her, the researcher wouldn't find her precious grimoire. It was a thin strand of hope Adaris desperately held on to.

She looked back again. The community of Slagrock was so small it seemed to blend in with the pale rock. She dug her hand into her pouch, feeling for her book and quill, the five rings, and the lazicon gemstones. Proof of what she'd been through.

How would she tell this story to the scrollkeepers? As Spectrum rocked beneath them flying away from that terrible place, Adaris sighed. The story of what happened turned over again and again in her mind like a sharp rock she couldn't quite smooth out. Where would she even begin?

Chapter Forty

ADARIS STARED UP AT the wide, double doors of the office of the guardian of knowledge. She and Rhonwen had reached the city of Juu—the closest coastal city—in four nights. With each passing dawn Adaris' lungs constricted tighter. She tapped her book in an uneasy rhythm. *Why the depths am I nervous?* Her heart rapped against her ribs, as she rapped on the door.

Every library had a guardian of knowledge, even the smallest, squattest, and grayest of them. The guardian was a step below master scrollkeeper and took over the role of being the main curator of that archive. Even though there were other scrollkeepers at this library, the guardian was the only scrollkeeper at a high enough rank that Adaris felt comfortable talking about what had happened at Slagrock.

Beside her, Rhonwen drew a finger across her eyebrow. She was nervous, as well. Somehow, that made Adaris less so.

"Yes?" A soft voice came from behind the doors.

The walls of the already tight hallway seemed to close in on Adaris even more. "Adaris Kavari, wandering scribe."

"Come in," the voice beckoned.

Steeling her nerves, Adaris pushed open the heavy wooden door. The circular room made her pause, remembering the stone huts of Slagrock, but there the similarities ended. Plush, multicolored couches spanned the far curve across the room, and a heavy, dark wooden table sat between Adaris and the couches. A steaming mug rested on the table, carefully set on a woven mat so as not to discolor the wood. Bookshelves lined the walls, and multiple daygems brightened the space. *Cozy.*

"What brings you to the library at Juu?" A short Elu stepped around the door, holding a book with thick, yellowing pages inside an even thicker hide cover.

Adaris smiled. Just like the libraries were the same, the guardians of knowledge tended to stay the same as well. The dark pants and rich purple tunic that fell to their knees could almost be a uniform of sorts. A monocle dangled on the androgynous guardian's chest by a thin, yellow chain.

"I've come to tell you a piece of history," Adaris replied. "A keystone story, in fact."

The guardian arched their white eyebrow. Normally, Adaris would've just handed over her book for the records, but a keystone story had to be retold from the gatherer's perspective to be classified as such. It was custom. The guardian eyed her and Rhonwen, then gestured to the couches and shut the door. Adaris and Rhonwen sat on one couch, the padding sinking comfortably around them like a hug. The guardian slipped the yellowing book back into its place on the shelf and settled on the second couch.

Opening their own notebook, the guardian looked at Adaris expectantly with kind, crinkly hazel eyes. "What color quill do you carry, Adaris?"

Adaris took out her scrollkeeper's quill, and the guardian nodded, jotting that down without judgment in their wrinkly expression. "And whose history are you going to tell me about today?"

"My own," Adaris replied, her breath catching in her throat.

And there it was, the reason why her nerves pulled her body straighter than a plank of wood, why her chest felt tight. She was used to recording other people's stories, telling other people's adventures, and now she had her own story to tell, her own journey to give to the history books. What if the guardian didn't believe her? Adaris' record had a mark on it from the awful lie she'd told about Mica Kia, and...well, it wasn't as though she had a lot of proof to back up her claims. She had some of Sroc's notes, the rings, and a few lazicon gemstones. The ancient's grimoire was lost somewhere on the ocean with Corra.

The guardian nodded, probably expecting a simple story and not one that would change what they knew about sun goddess worshippers.

"Go on," the guardian prompted.

Adaris leaned back into the couch, gaze dropping to the bloodbound artifact that glowed on her ankle. She had recorded everything in such detail at Slagrock, every conversation overheard, every crafting demonstration, every moment of the rituals, and had done unspeakable things to get those stories back home. She had...changed during her adventures, all to expose evil and possibly stop a war, to help the scrollkeepers round out history.

Her throat constricted like someone had grabbed her neck and squeezed. *Depths!*

Rhonwen placed a gentle hand on Adaris' knee, the pressure there comforting, the closeness of it sure. When Adaris lifted her gaze to

Rhonwen's she saw only love and respect and bravery shimmering in her yellow eyes. "Perhaps you should start at the beginning."

A nervous chuckle broke in Adaris' chest. Thank the depths for Rhonwen's calm presence. "I was out hunting for a sun goddess worshipper's hideout, trying to find a particular cave..."

Adaris told of her kidnapping. Of the community at Slagrock and their leader. How they forced her to participate in the sunlight celebration and record the community's story. When she spoke about meeting Kye, his name caught in her throat, but she told all of his story—him being part of the Silver Shade included.

"These are the gemstones I mentioned." When she put one of her precious few lazicon gemstones on the table, her hand trembled just a little, the memories of Berhn's smiling face coming back to her. *Honor him.* "A Ratnaa Nemora named Berhn found them for the community. They killed him. He had a rather unique view of Ponuriah."

She shared his message of the gentler fire of Ponuriah, a sun goddess who was not wrathful, but who embraced growth and renewal and change. She told how Berhn had wanted to start a trade, not a war.

With Rhonwen backing her up and telling part of her story as well, the guardian of knowledge believed her. Believed them. The guardian was so disgusted upon hearing about Sroc and the bloodbinding ritual she used to create artifacts that Adaris left her own involvement out of it. *What would the guardian say if they knew I did it, too?*

"The ancient's grimoire is currently lost at sea," Adaris winced, knowing that sounded like a lie, but Rhonwen nodded along. "A Moon Knight named Corra, who helped in our escape, took our raft and our supplies," Adaris said. "We didn't see her on the way back. Could you send a search party to look for her? The grimoire is rather important, and there's a large lazicon gemstone in my bag that I'd like to get back, if possible."

The guardian made a note and nodded.

"Here are notes and Sroc's rings." Setting Sroc's notes on the table, Adaris brought out the researcher's five rings as well, one by one, saving the goddess shard ring for last. A simple silver ring with a crimson gemstone set in it, the shard still glowed like an ember.

The guardian gasped. "Is that a...sun goddess shard?"

Adaris nodded. "A smaller version of the one I found by the cave hideout. Tikova mentioned they had discovered a few more as well."

The guardian stood. "Wait here a moment please, I need to gather some scribes."

The guardian left the room, closing the door securely behind them.

Adaris leaned back on the couch once more. Her throat felt parched from all the talking. She'd given enough to help the war and bend the tides in their favor, now that they knew the Groves were the target and why and when, but it wasn't the full story. Her actions in the rituals and during that final night turned to ashes in her mouth.

Her gaze rested on her own book. Her eyes glazed over, blurring black ink to the dark, dead eyes of Tiy, the Nemora she'd killed. She saw the deep-brown blood pouring from his neck and felt the ancient crafting ritual burning through her. She felt the accompanying thrill deep in her belly.

A warm hand wrapped around the back of her neck, pulling her attention. Adaris blinked the memory away.

"Where did you go, my starlight?" Rhonwen canted her head, thumb rubbing a small circle on the back of Adaris' neck.

Like so many times before, the truth fell from Adaris' lips in a whisper. "Sroc's ritual made me feel powerful. And...I don't know what to do with that knowledge."

Rhonwen leaned closer until their foreheads touched, so close they shared breath. "Tell the guardian about the rituals," she whispered back. "Help them understand what they're facing."

Heat rushed into Adaris' face and neck. "The price is awful, unthinkable, but the burn...the power...I want to feel it again," she confessed, her throat getting tighter with each word.

Each word felt like it came from Slagrock, like Sroc was speaking through her somehow. As much as Adaris wanted to deny it, she couldn't.

A myriad of emotions rippled through Rhonwen's expression: fear, anger, anguish. Finally the familiar fierceness so prevalent in her at Slagrock settled in her face. She palmed Adaris' cheek. "The time there at Slagrock changed you. The ancient crafting scares me, but you have to be better than them. You have to be better than the pull of power."

Something like disappointment flowed through Adaris, but she shook it away just as the door opened once more.

The guardian of knowledge and a flurry of new people swarmed into the small circular room. An actual sun goddess shard brought by a white quill scribe? It was unheard of. Unthinkable. No white quill should bring a legend home.

Even though the room was cramped, the scrollkeepers gave her a wide berth. She was still a Divus, after all. Only Rhonwen stayed next to her. They peppered her with even more questions about the rings and of Sroc. Adaris grew more and more nervous about telling them the rest of her story, of her involvement in the rituals and the final night. Of the burn she felt. So many people were in this room, so many scrollkeepers. Her stomach twisted at what they might say.

"Adaris Kavari, wandering scribe." The guardian's voice trembled with age or excitement, Adaris couldn't tell. "For this monumental tale and keystone story, I will recommend to the master scrollkeeper that you, Adaris, receive the black quill. Congratulations."

I'm going to get a black quill. A laugh broke in Adaris' chest. It all seemed too good. She'd survived Slagrock, earned the affection of a beautiful woman, discovered ancient knowledge, and now was getting the very thing she'd longed for since her brother became sick. The black quill and the coin that came with it. She could finally help him like she had always promised she would. "Thank you, guardian. It is truly an honor."

She clasped Rhonwen's hand, squeezing tight. A small part of her wanted to keep the knowledge about her part in the rituals a secret. She worried the guardian's reaction to her horrible deeds would be just like their reaction to Sroc's, but she couldn't hold it back anymore. She was a scribe, a newly donned, black-quill scribe. She had to tell the full story, her full story, no matter the consequences. "I do have more to tell you."

The whole truth fell from her in waves. She told them about learning from the grimoire and her part in Sroc's rituals. She confessed to murdering a Moon Knight and performing the bloodbinding ritual. She'd murdered Tiy that final night to gain his crafting that helped set them free.

Though Adaris saw horror reflected in the other scrollkeepers' eyes, the guardian's face grew stoic. "I see," the guardian said slowly. "There are other bloodbound artifacts here. Rings, pendants, stones, even special curved swords called ruk'shas. There was even a keystone story with a glowing pendant that could suck the life force like a Divus, not too long ago, on a woman named Misti."

Adaris swallowed. "Yes, I've read about that story, and I actually ran into Misti, once."

They looked at her thoughtfully. "And you can do this...this bloodbinding ritual? Create more of them."

She nodded.

"Fascinating. Most on this continent are bought from a criminal market or stolen from sun goddess worshippers, not made." The guardian glanced at the other scrollkeepers in the room, who suddenly started nodding. "Perhaps you can create more for us."

"More artifacts for the coming war you talked about," a scrollkeeper suggested. "But for our side, not theirs."

Rhonwen groaned beside her, palming her forehead. "You're not actually suggesting she becomes a murderer?"

"We're suggesting she use her abilities for good," the guardian replied softly.

Adaris shifted uncomfortably beside Rhonwen, knowing how vehemently the painter was against all of this, but Adaris *could* help the Moon Knights by creating artifacts to aid them in the coming war. Maybe she could even create artifacts that would protect innocent people who had nothing to do with the battle. All eyes turned to her, and Adaris' stomach clenched.

"I'll...think about it. For now, I'll show you what these rings can do." She called up her crafting. The anklet deactivated instantly, and the pulse of pain trembled up her leg. *Will the ring even activate?* She whispered the activation word, pooling her crafting in her hand where it rested on the stone floor. The ring listened, brightened. A spike of rock formed, melting upward into her hand.

Her onlookers gasped.

She picked up the four other rings. "The blue ring creates an Elu Moon shield. The brown ring melts rock as easily as a Hallr Nemora. The white ring bubbles out to pull life like my kind. The orange ring calls to animals as if a Vagari is calling them."

The guardian plucked the goddess shard ring from the table. "And this one?"

"That one..." Adaris hesitated, wondering if it could do many things depending on the wearer. "Well, when Sroc wore it, she said it let her bloodstalk. Remember how I told you that I was forced to give blood at the sunlight celebration? Sroc said she could find any of us—find me—by using that ring."

The guardian put the ring down, eyeing the door as if they thought Sroc would burst through it at any moment. "Are you saying she can't find you now?"

Adaris sighed. "There was another sun goddess shard in the community. I'm sure she could just use that one."

The guardian sighed. “So many things to ponder.” They shook their head as if shaking their thoughts away. A grin brightened their elderly face. “Tonight, celebrate your accomplishments. Tomorrow, you can think on what we’ve suggested.”

Rhonwen slipped her hand into Adaris’ and pulled her to the door, obviously eager to get away from this place. “Yes, we should celebrate your black quill.”

“Thank you,” Adaris murmured on the way out.

The guardian pressed a bag of coins into Adaris’ hand, a stipend until she received the real payment for being a black quill. The heavy wooden door shut behind her, but she still heard the hum of conversation that began immediately after the door locked.

Adaris leaned on the doorframe, pressing a palm onto her forehead. Her thoughts swirled like a rising tide around a stone. She’d gotten a black quill, but had also gotten a possible new path for her life, one she’d have to think hard about running down.

“Let’s get some fresh air,” Rhonwen suggested.

Adaris nodded and allowed the painter to pull her along, hoping the walk would clear her mind a little.

Chapter Forty-One

AS THEY LEFT THE library, they discovered that night had pulled a dark blanket of stars overhead. They'd spent a whole night and day in the library. Heading down the cobbled pathway leading deeper into Juu, Adaris looped her arm through Rhonwen's and sighed. "That was...a lot," she murmured.

Rhonwen chuckled. "Yes, it was. Can we go to the messenger center before finding a place to rest? I'd like to tell my mothers that I'm alive."

"Of course."

Juu opened itself up before them. For the first time in a long time, Adaris' heart felt light. Paved pathways connected stone and wooden shops, with colorful banners strewn about, and daygems hung above their heads in an artful manner. Music tinkled down the path from a market nearby, and vendors called their wares. People passed by this way and that, munching on handpies for their first meals of the night.

The scent of spiced meat made Adaris' stomach growl, but she guided Rhonwen past the stalls. Eventually, the colorfully painted stonework of the messenger center came into view. A carved wooden sign with the words *Vulnix Couriers at Your Service* swung above the archway.

They ducked inside the six-sided tower. Outcroppings of stonework jutted into the open center in a maze of stone above their heads. Bundles of grass and sticks sat on the ground and a sack of dark nuts spilled onto the floor. A few vulnix—small, colorful vulpine creatures with three tails and two wings—munched on the nuts.

Adaris was trying to coax a particularly glossy black vulnix down from its perch when two women entered the building. One of the women, an Elu, ignored Adaris completely. The second woman, a Vagari with short, brown hair and brown complexion, smiled politely before looking away. The dual-colored eyes—one orange, one blue—were unforgettable, as was the sunkissed vulnix lounging on the woman's shoulders, its orange and yellow wings and fur, all four paws dipped in red.

Trying to recall the woman's name, Adaris flipped through her book to the section when she was traveling with a musical group. The group had gotten attacked, and this woman had helped save them.

Misti Eildelmann, Vagari Moon Knight with a sunkissed vulnix companion and a curious pendant that radiates Blood crafting. That pendant took on a whole new meaning now that Adaris knew just how it was created. It was a bloodbound artifact. Misti hadn't been able to remove it. Did that have something to do with the item's power?

Adaris closed her book with a snap. "Still have that sunkissed creature, I see, Misti."

Misti started and turned, a little jumpier than Adaris remembered. "Of course, I—" she paused, blinked. "Do I know you?"

Adaris lifted her book. "Adaris Kavari—"

"Oh yes! Wandering scribe," Misti finished with a grin. She scratched her vulnix behind the ear. The beast cooed a little, wide eyes closing in relaxation. "How have you been? Gathered any good stories lately?"

"Quite a few," Adaris replied, letting her gaze drop to the front of the Vagari's tan tunic. "I see you got that Blood crafting necklace off."

Misti's hand flew to her throat and she pulled her collar higher. "I did." She bit her lip, suddenly awkward. "Orenda and I were just going to send a message."

"Orenda?" Adaris' attention slid to the Elu in dark, scaled armor, who'd accompanied Misti. *Depths, it can't be.* Adaris knew a trader with the same name. She was the only person Adaris had ever seen with the same Silver Shade marking as Kye. Could she be so lucky to have run into her here? "Would her last name happen to be Silverstone?"

Misti nodded and called over her shoulder, "Ren!"

The Elu stopped stroking a brilliant purple vulnix and came over, a question in her green eyes. Her bushy, black hair drifted around her head like a dark cloud. With her considerably darker skin, Orenda was like a shadow next to Misti. Her presence oozed confidence, from the steadiness of her walk to the firm set of her jaw.

She gave Rhonwen a sparing glance before her gaze locked on Adaris. "I...remember you."

"Yes, we met once in the Athenaeum of the Ancient," Adaris started, then she paused. The Silver Shade was supposed to be a secret organization. Did Misti even know Orenda was a part of it? "I recently met someone who has similar markings as your jewelry."

Orenda's eyes narrowed, and Misti laughed. The Vagari pushed the sleeve of her tunic up showing off a burnt-orange metal band on her wrist. "You mean like this?"

"Misti, you shouldn't just be showing that off to anyone," Orenda hissed. She glanced around, eyes falling on Rhonwen.

"It's okay," Adaris quickly said. "We both know."

Orenda turned her intense green stare back to Adaris. "You wanted to tell me something?"

Just like when they had first met in the Athenaeum, the trader had a no-nonsense attitude about her. Adaris appreciated the approach. She was ready to finish this last piece of her story.

"Kye, one of your former agents, died in Slagrock while saving me and Rhonwen," she spoke quietly and gestured to Rhonwen, who'd finished sending her message and was now standing beside her. The words felt tight in Adaris' throat, a flash of his death sliding into her mind.

Orenda blinked a few times. "Kye...Glass?"

"He never revealed his last name, but he was a Vagari. Short, stocky, warm brown skin with a patterned shell on his neck, back, and arm. Brown eyes, bald. His bloodline was that of a hollow conu."

Orenda sighed, sadness flickering through her expression. "That's Glass. He's like a legend to the Silver Shade. I can't believe he was still in that community."

Adaris nodded. "Kye died a hero. He wanted me to pass along the information he'd gathered. I gave the library all the information I had." Only a black quill could grant copying privileges, and a tingle of pride went through Adaris as she realized the authority now belonged to her. "Tell them you have my permission to make a copy for you to bring to the Silver Shade."

Misti gasped. "Your permission? Are you a black quill now?"

"Adaris is the best scribe the scrollkeepers have ever seen." Rhonwen twined her fingers through Adaris'. "Of course, she's a black quill."

Orenda arched an eyebrow at them both. "I have to let my people know." She spun on her heel and left.

Misti watched her go, then glanced at Adaris with a warm smile. "Always so abrupt, that one. Someday we'll have to chat about our adventures, you and I."

"Indeed," Adaris replied, and she meant it. She wanted to know how Misti got that Blood pendant off her neck. Not this night, though. She'd had enough storytelling for one day and wanted to turn her attention to Rhonwen. "Perhaps over a cup of tea on a different evening."

"I'd like that!" Misti's dual-colored eyes crinkled in the corners when she smiled.

They parted ways, Misti walking deeper into the city of Juu, Rhonwen and Adaris heading through the marketplace to finally get a decent meal. A few coins later, they had procured a small basket of bread, fruit, and honey. Adaris splurged on a small can of yellow paint. When Rhonwen gave her a questioning look, Adaris winked. As they wandered through the gates leading outside the city, she inhaled in the crisp, clean scent of the grasslands around them, loving how cool the air felt.

They walked a short distance from the walls. After so much time in the prison hut, so much time locked inside, Adaris knew Rhonwen would enjoy the open sky above her.

"So, what do we do from here?" Rhonwen asked.

"I don't know yet." Adaris gave her a sidelong look. They had been through so much together, Adaris couldn't bear the thought of not seeing Rhonwen every day. She put the basket down and pulled Rhonwen close. "But I do know you're beautiful, Rhonwen."

Rhonwen rolled her eyes, though an adorable orange blush darkened her brown cheeks. "You're not terrible to look at yourself," she quipped, then her smile softened. "My starlight."

Adaris laughed and pulled Rhonwen into a kiss. The kiss was hard at first, rough with need and want, then it softened. Quieted to serenity. Adaris touched their foreheads together. They didn't need to steal their affections in panicked moments anymore. No, they could take their time, stretch into it, and Adaris looked forward to every moment. She trailed kisses down Rhonwen's cheek, down her neck, into the dip of her shoulder and left the painter giggling.

Rhonwen gave a delightful sigh, her eyelids fluttering open, want clear in her vibrant yellow eyes. She caught one of Adaris' hands and lifted Adaris' knuckles to her lips. "I'd always assumed I'd look back on Slagrock with fear and disgust, but I don't. Because you were there, too, and those moments with you...well, if we hadn't endured what we did together, would we be here together now?"

"I never would've met you if I hadn't been kidnapped." Adaris ran her hands down Rhonwen's arms, careful around her injured one. "I could almost thank them."

"Don't." Rhonwen shook her head, then shoved her hand in her pouch and produced a small, yellow gemstone. "On a happier topic, I got this for you."

Adaris looked at the gem in surprise. About the size of her thumbpad, it was cut, polished, and worth more coin than they had between them. "Where? When?"

Rhonwen's grin grew mischievous.

"Did you steal it?" Adaris lowered her voice in a whisper.

"Yes," she admitted, "but the merchant had plenty. He won't notice it being gone."

Adaris should've felt bad for the merchant, but a giddiness rushed through her instead. A Vagari showed their affection by giving random trinkets. *She stole this gemstone for me.* Adaris clutched the small gem and grinned at Rhonwen. "Thank you."

"We have all the time in the world to make up for Slagrock."

Warmth infused Adaris' soul. "We do, do we?"

"Depths, Adaris, you're stuck with me," Rhonwen said with absolute certainty. She gently pushed a lock of hair behind Adaris' ear.

Tingles danced down Adaris' spine. It was more than she could've ever hoped. She pressed a quick kiss onto the tip of Rhonwen's nose. "Happily stuck, then. Shall we eat?"

Spectrum slithered out from the shadows nearby, and as Adaris and Rhonwen sat on the grass for their first real meal together, he coiled around them, creating a wall of rainbow scales and black feathers.

They spent the night there, tangled in each other's arms, Rhonwen using Adaris' skin as a canvas, and Adaris trying her hand at it as well. Soon, they were each decorated with painted flowers and vines and things too smeared to recognize.

While Rhonwen slept most of the next daylight away, Adaris didn't. She sat in full view of the sun, head tilted back to the sky, allowing the warmth to seep into her body. They were close enough to the city's wall and Spectrum was on guard. For the first time, Adaris didn't have to worry about suncreatures.

Her gaze drifted to Rhonwen, who slept peacefully in Spectrum's shadow. A curl of paint twisted around her injured arm—once a yellow flower, now a messy smear. The woman had never ceased to amaze her, the determination and the fierceness hiding within her. It was because of Rhonwen that Adaris found the courage to continue, to do something unimaginable to survive. Adaris would spend the rest of her life—or however long Rhonwen would have her—making sure Rhonwen knew just how important she was. Their stories were twined together, beautifully so, and Adaris couldn't be happier.

Even as happy as she was with Rhonwen, Adaris' thoughts turned. Her mind wandered back to the bloodbinding ritual, to the anklet glowing orange on her pale skin. She twirled the Nature ring on her finger. The brown gemstone glinted each time it turned up to the sun. *I murdered a Hallr Nemora for this ring.* She expected guilt to well up inside her...but it didn't. As far as she was concerned, the life of an evil man had been used for good.

She thought again about the guardian's request that she consider using her power to support their side of the war. Oh, how she wanted to use that ancient crafting again, to feel its fiery burn surge through her. If Corra was ever found and the ancient's grimoire ever recovered, Adaris longed to pore over its pages.

I do want to perform that ritual again. The thrill of the ancient ritual and the fiery power that came with it had hooked its claws into her. Adaris found that she didn't want to remove them. And that worried her more than anything else. She stopped twirling the Nature ring and tilted her head to look at the blue expanse of the sky.

I can use the ritual against the sun goddess worshippers. The guardian was right—the Moon Knights really could use such artifacts. She'd left four of Sroc's rings behind, but she took out the remaining fifth and slipped it onto her finger. The blue gemstone glimmered in the sunlight, Elu crafting locked deep within. A flicker of worry burned through Adaris at the thought of Sroc and her bloodstalking ability. The shield the Moon ring could produce could be useful if Sroc ever came hunting. *If I end evil lives for a good cause, my research could be helpful, not harmful.* Fingers running over the worn binding of her book, she flipped it open to a blank page.

About Kellie Doherty

Kellie Doherty is a queer science fiction and fantasy author who lives in Eagle River, Alaska. When she noticed that there wasn't much positive queer representation in the science fiction and fantasy realms, she decided to create her own! Kellie's work has been published in Image OutWrite 2019, Astral Waters Review, Life (as it) Happens, and Impact, among others. Her adult sci-fi debut novel—*Finding Hekate*—came out in April 2016 from Desert Palm Press and the sequel—*Losing Hold*—came out in April 2017. She's currently working on a five-book adult fantasy series. The first book *Sunkissed Feathers & Severed Ties* released in March 2019 from Desert Palm Press and won a 2019 Rainbow Award. The second book *Curling Vines & Crimson Trades* launched November 2020. An excerpt from *Curling Vines & Crimson Trades* won first place in an Alaska Writers Guild Fiction contest in 2020.

Contact Information

Website https://kelliedoherty.com/

Editing Site https://editreviseperfect.weebly.com/

Twitter https://twitter.com/kellie_doherty

Facebook https://www.facebook.com/KellieDoherty89

Email kellie.f.doherty@gmail.com

Cover Design By : Rachel George
www.rachelgeorgeillustration.com

Note to Readers:

Thank you for reading a book from Desert Palm Press. We appreciate you as a reader and want to ensure you enjoy the reading process. We would like you to consider posting a review on your preferred media sites and/or your blog or website.

For more information on upcoming releases, author interviews, contest, giveaways and more, please sign up for our newsletter and visit us as at Desert Palm Press: www.desertpalmpress.com and "Like" us on Facebook: Desert Palm Press.

Bright Blessings

Desert Palm Press

www.ingramcontent.com/pod-product-compliance
Lightning Source LLC
LaVergne TN
LVHW010052110826
845155LV00028B/311

* 9 7 8 1 9 5 4 2 1 3 5 1 7 *